BOOKS BY WAYNE THOMAS BATSON

THE DOOR WITHIN TRILOGY

The Door Within

The Rise of the Wyrm Lord

The Final Storm

PIRATE ADVENTURES

Isle of Swords

Isle of Fire

ISLE OF FIRE

BY
WAYNE THOMAS
BATSON

THOMAS NELSON
Since 1798

NASHVILLE   DALLAS   MEXICO CITY   RIO DE JANEIRO   BEIJING

© 2008 by Wayne Thomas Batson

Published in Nashville, Tennessee, by Thomas Nelson. Thomas Nelson is a registered trademark of Thomas Nelson, Inc.

Scripture references are from the King James Version of the Bible.

Thomas Nelson, Inc., titles may be purchased in bulk for educational, business, fund-raising, or sales promotional use. For information, please e-mail SpecialMarkets@ThomasNelson.com.

Interior art and layout by Casey Hooper.
Map by Peter Glöege.

Library of Congress Cataloging-in-Publication Data

Batson, Wayne Thomas, 1968–
     Isle of fire / Wayne Thomas Batson.
   p. cm.
   Summary: With eighteen-year-old Anne Ross at this side, Cat takes over as captain of the monks' fleet to find the legendary villain known as the Merchant, but they, the pirate hunters, monks, and Commodore Blake, have been betrayed by King George and a once-trusted advisor.
   ISBN 978-1-4003-1216-0 (hardback)
   [1. Stowaways—Fiction. 2. Pirates—Fiction. 3. Vikings—Fiction. 4. Buried treasure—Fiction.
5. Christian life—Fiction. 6. George I, King of Great Britain, 1660-1727—Fiction. 7. Spanish Main—Fiction.] I. Title.
PZ7.B3238Isf 2008
[Fic]—dc22

                                          2008010533

Printed in the United States of America
08 09 10 11 12 QW 5 4 3 2 1

My Captain, thank you for guiding me . . .
Even on dark and moonless nights
when the ship's bell strikes a lonely toll,
and the wind and wave buffets.
And may all who sail this lonely sea realize
You are the real treasure . . . and that
You are within reach of all.

Contents

Principal Cast

Anne

Declan Ross's adventurous daughter.
Anne has hazel eyes, red hair, and a fiery temper.
She longs to captain a ship of her own.

Bartholomew Thorne

The former captain of the *Raven* and an evil pirate; lost and
presumed dead after the New Providence tsunami.

Bjorn Ingalad

A champion Raukar warrior known for his deadly prowess in
battle. He wears a triple necklace of sharp bear teeth.

Cat

Griffin Lejon Thorne, the son of Bartholomew Thorne.
His memory is just beginning to return.
He goes by his nickname "Cat."

Commodore Brandon Blake

The leader of the British naval forces in the Caribbean;
commissioned to lead the pirate-hunting Wolf fleet.

Cutlass Jack Bonnet

A renowned pirate and captain of the *Banshee*.

Declan Ross

A Scottish pirate-hunter; captain of the *Robert Bruce*;
often called the Sea Wolf due to his notorious pirate past.

Dmitri

A dark-skinned Brethren monk. He is mischievous,
clever, and wields a weapon with lethal precision.

DOLPHIN BLAKE

The wife of Commodore Blake. She desperately wants to solve the mysteries surrounding her parents and her birth.

EDWARD TEACH

The young quartermaster aboard the *Raven's Revenge*; a beardless, tall, broad-shouldered man who longs for a command of his own.

EDMUND SCULLY

A spy formerly for Bartholomew Thorne and now for the Merchant.

EZEKIEL JORDAN

A friend of Commodore Blake and new quartermaster on the HMS *Oxford*.

FATHER BRUN

The abbot of the Brethren Order. He has built a fleet to go after the Merchant.

GUTHRUM

The door warden and right-hand man for Hrothgar, king of the Raukar.

HEATHER

Thorne's first wife who died in a fire but still haunts his mind.

HROTHGAR

The steward of the Raukar, who longs to resurrect Viking glory.

JACQUES ST. PIERRE

The chief gunner and blacksmith aboard the *Robert Bruce*; has a penchant for explosives, fire, and business.

JULES

The massive, barrel-chested security officer and deck hand aboard the *Robert Bruce*.

KING GEORGE

The German-speaking king of England who speaks
very little English. Later known as King George I,
one of the greediest kings ever to reign in Britain.

LADY FLEUR

The wife of Hrothgar and queen of the Raukar.

NATHANIEL HOPPER

Left orphaned by the New Providence tsunami,
he dreams of returning to England.

NUBBY

The cook and doctor on the *Robert Bruce*.

RED EYE

A powder monkey on the *Robert Bruce* who is blind in one eye.

SIR NIGEL WETHERBY

An English naval officer. He disappeared after the
tsunami at New Providence and is presumed dead.

STEDE

Ross's quartermaster on the *Robert Bruce*.
He is from the West Indies. Stede is Declan Ross's
closest friend and most loyal crewman.

THE MERCHANT

A legendary villain sought by the Brethren.

ULF

Lady Fleur's brother. After becoming a Christian, he left
the Raukar and moved to Västervik, Sweden, where he
and his family built a church. Soon many of the Raukar
followed him, and they established a Christian community.

Nautical Terms

Aft: the back of the ship.

Bow: front of the ship.

Bowsprit: long pole extending forward from the bow of the ship.

Crow's-nest: a small lookout platform usually high on the mainmast of a ship.

Forecastle: the front of the ship, often where the crew's quarters are located.

Halyard: rope used to pull a sail up.

Hull: the body of a boat or ship.

Jib-rigged: ship's sails that are triangular in shape.

Keel: the structural spine that runs along the bottom of the ship.

Mast: tall pole that supports all the ship's sails.

Poop Deck: rearmost deck of the ship.

Port: if standing on the deck and facing the front of the ship, port is left.

Quarterdeck: raised deck behind the mainmast where the ship's wheel is found.

Spar-collar: (sometimes known as a gooseneck) a moveable iron collar used to hold horizontal spars to the mast.

Spar: long horizontal pole that a sail is attached to.

Square-rigged: ship's sails that are square in shape.

Starboard: if standing on the deck and facing the front of the ship, starboard is right.

Stern: the back of the ship.

The watch: a four-hour period when a sailor is on duty.

Halyard

Square-rigged

Mast

Jib-rigged

Forecastle

Bow

Quarterdeck

Stern

Poop Deck

Keel

1

SHADOWS OF THE PAST

Dead leaves swirled across the cold stone as Cat approached the deepest corner of the empty cobblestone courtyard. He could feel the sentinels watching from hidden places within the surrounding walls and towers. His eyes darted about for any sign of a threat. Behind the ever-sleeping volcano, the sun struggled to midday height in the steel-gray sky.

Without warning, a fierce cry came from the parapets above. A shadow passed overhead, and Cat ducked. Instinctively his grip tightened on the quarterstaff as he prepared to defend himself against one of the most peculiar men he'd ever seen. His skin was very dark like the islanders, but his hair, eyebrows, and moustache were whiter than the sand on Aruba. He wore a silver ring in the lobe of his left ear and a small gray cross on a thin black cord around his neck. He held a quarterstaff of dark wood that was at least a foot longer than Cat's.

"I am Dmitri," said the man, removing his robe. He was shirtless beneath but wore an odd, baggy kind of breeches that bunched at his waist and ankles. His gaze was dark and seemed to smolder like volcanic rock. The warrior slapped his staff hard on the cobblestone and stepped forward menacingly.

Cat held up his own staff. He thought he was ready.

Dmitri's strike was swift and heavy. His dark staff crashed into Cat's staff with such force that Cat reeled sideways. Cat didn't see the second stroke, the one that swept his feet out from under him. He felt a sudden jolt on his backside as he hit the ground and found himself staring at the sky.

Cat swallowed, tightened his grip on his staff, and levered himself to his feet. He rolled his shoulders and his neck and then brought his staff up hard to his chest. *He's toying with me,* Cat thought. Determined not to let Dmitri strike first, Cat feinted with a sweeping right-handed attack to Dmitri's body. The moment Dmitri showed a vertical guard, Cat brought a furious left-handed stroke at Dmitri's right thigh. But Dmitri's initial guard was itself a feint. He turned in a blur, batted down Cat's attack, and shoved the left end of his staff into Cat's shoulder. Cat staggered backward, his weapon clattering to the ground.

The pain was sharp and throbbing. Cat tasted bile in his throat. He grunted indignantly and picked up his staff.

Dmitri swung at Cat's left shoulder and followed it with a swift poke at Cat's chest. Cat didn't block it but turned to let the blow glance off. Cat jabbed the end of his staff at Dmitri's legs, but Dmitri countered too quickly. Cat grunted. He grew fatigued and increasingly frustrated. It was like dueling Red Eye with a sword—Cat knew he was overmatched and hated it.

Cat grunted again, trying to clear his head and make himself think. He knew he needed to slow Dmitri's countermoves, needed to buy time. He had to think ahead—way ahead. Then he had it: a combination of attacks he felt sure he could pull off. It began with a high feint. Cat went at Dmitri's left ear with a strong, hacking stroke, but instead of bouncing off Dmitri's guard and spinning back inside, Cat stepped away and let his staff slide off. He spun quickly outside of Dmitri's sweeping reply, brought his staff under his arm, and stabbed it backward into Dmitri's midsection. As Cat expected, Dmitri parried away the jab. Cat used the momentum to spin a second time. This time, as Cat came around, he used both hands to deliver a crushing high-to-low chop at Dmitri's head. It was like splitting wood with an axe—just aim for the center. Cat knew Dmitri would have to block the blow with the center of his own staff, between his hands. When Dmitri did so, Cat kept the pressure on, momentarily pinning Dmitri. But in the span of a heartbeat, Cat jerked back with his left hand and wrenched a sudden upward thrust with his right. He meant to bring the right end of his staff under Dmitri's left shoulder, a devastating blow . . . if only he could connect. But he could not.

Dmitri ignored the coming attack. He simply let his own high block collapse down to shoulder level. Then he exploded both fists forward, burying them and the center of his staff into Cat's chest. Cat flew backward, his feet scrambling for ground but to no avail. He sprawled onto his back, and in a daze, he blinked at the sky. His ears rang, and he tasted blood.

Cat wiped a trickle of blood from the corner of his mouth, grabbed his staff, and tried to stand. He had been beaten soundly, and as he gained his feet, he found himself shaking. But it was not from fatigue. Rage boiled up inside of Cat such that every breath felt hot in his nostrils. Energy surged into his muscles, and his heart raced. He approached Dmitri with singular purpose.

Dmitri did not know Cat, did not recognize the intensity of

Cat's glare. Thinking the battle was over, Dmitri dropped his guard. Cat lunged and cracked his staff against Dmitri's left wrist. Dmitri dropped his weapon, clutched his hand, and began to backpedal.

"Cat, NO!" shouted Father Brun. But Cat heard nothing but the thunderous cadence of his own heart. Cat slammed Dmitri's right shoulder. Then he spun and drove the end of his staff into Dmitri's gut. Dmitri doubled over, and Cat went to finish him off. He raised his quarterstaff high and brought it crashing toward Dmitri's head. But a dark staff caught the blow and flung it away.

It was Father Brun. Quickly, he stepped between Dmitri and Cat. His eyes glinted as he stared at Cat. "What's the matter with you?" he shouted. He took a step toward Cat.

"No!" said Dmitri as he stood. He grabbed his own staff back from Father Brun and gestured for him to stand aside. "The lesson is not complete."

Father Brun reluctantly moved, but stood ready to intervene. Dmitri glared at Cat. Cat wanted to look away, but found he could not. "Is that the man you are?" Dmitri asked. He held up his staff and then cast it aside. "I am unarmed, you see? Would you like to strike me again?"

Cat's lips thinned. He swallowed, and all at once the rage drained away and he felt empty . . . and ashamed. He threw away his staff and sprinted back across the courtyard. He ran clumsily up a flight of steps, half stumbling as he reached the top. He raced back to his chamber and slammed the door shut behind him.

Cat turned and saw the mirror. He'd meant several times to ask one of the Brethren to remove it—to make his room as austere as their own, but the almost constant training had pushed the mirror from his mind. Until now. Now, it taunted him . . . drew him with the treacherous gravity one feels looking over the edge from some great height. Despondently, he drew near and gazed at himself in the glass.

Blue eyes, gleaming intensely beneath thickening brows, high angular cheekbones sliced by sideburns, a narrow tapering nose, and thin frowning lips—in all but the hair, the visage of his father.

"I . . . I am just like him," Cat whispered. Bartholomew Thorne's cruel image lingered like a scornful ghost. Cat wished he'd never remembered his father's face, his sickening voice, his heinous deeds. And worse yet were the newest memories to return, the ones concerning Cat himself. A horrifying image from the island of Roseau flickered in his mind. "NOOOOO!!" In a rage, Cat picked up a chair and flung it. The mirror shattered, scattering shards of glass all over the room.

Cat fell to his knees and grabbed a jagged knifelike piece of the mirror that lay nearby. He clutched it so hard the glass bit into the flesh of his palm. He dropped the shard and looked at the blood glistening on his hand. Cat wondered at the irony and felt the cold finger of fear on his spine. *Blood on my hands. If only I could remember.*

2
THE SEA WOLF GOES HUNTING

That's Cutlass Jack Bonnet, or I'm an eel," said Declan Ross, handing the spyglass to Stede.

"Uh-huh . . ." The quartermaster of the *Robert Bruce* nodded. "Him b' the only pirate this side of the Barbary Coast sailing a xebec. Him b' calling it the *Banshee*."

"Quicker than a sloop," said Anne, who stood at their side. "But not quicker than the *Bruce*, right, Da?"

"Yes," he said with a smile that conveyed a mixture of pride and affection for his daughter and her love of ships. Then he shouted, "Mister Hack, more sail!"

"Aye, sir!" called the musical voice of the ship's new master carpenter from some unseen nook on the main deck. A huge, square sail dropped down on the mainmast and filled with wind. The *Bruce*, a formidable Portuguese man-of-war with three masts loaded with square sails, lurched forward and gained on the smaller *Banshee*. Cutlass Jack's sleek xebec had three long shark-fin sails that allowed it to outrun or outmaneuver most vessels, but even with a gale wind it could not escape. The two ships raced along the northern coast of South America.

"That's more like it!" Ross bellowed. *This is going to be fun*, he thought. In the lean years, long before Ross and his crew found their fortune on the Isle of Swords, Cutlass Jack had beaten Ross to a plunder of silver and smoked meat—and this when Ross's crew hadn't eaten for a week. Ross still wasn't sure how Bonnet had gotten there first. But he couldn't wait to see the look on his one-time rival's face when he . . . Ross's smile disappeared. "He's making to lose us around that bend!" Ross pointed at a tall fist of rock that jutted out into the sea.

"No, Cap'n, him won't," said Stede. "We'll catch the rascal just after him b' making the turn."

Ross took back the spyglass. The *Banshee* still had a half mile to the bend. "Jacques, ready a few of the portside cannons!"

A wildly curly mop of dark hair appeared from a hatch on the main deck. "Oui, mon capitaine! They are ready to fire at your command!"

"To warn them first, and then—"

"I know," interrupted Jacques St. Pierre. "Warn them, but if they will not listen, shoot out their sails. Très bien. I am ready!"

"Well, would you look at that!" said Stede, his mouth agape. The *Banshee*, now only a few hundred yards ahead of the *Bruce*, started into its turn. To the crew's collective amazement, the slender xebec caught an unseen crosswind and darted around the corner in an instant.

Ross frowned. "How did he . . . never mind! Mister Hack, man the spar-collar! Let's show our agile friend what the *Bruce* can do."

"Aye, Cap'n!" called Ebenezer Hack, who raced around the mainmast and joined several men at the front of the ship. The long bowsprit of the *Bruce* was attached to an adjustable iron collar that allowed it to swing one hundred eighty degrees. A halyard hung overhead so, at a moment's notice, crewmen could hoist the vast triangular sail that attached to the bowsprit. If the wind was right, the *Bruce* could make incredibly sharp turns for such a large vessel.

"Steady, Mister Hack!" Ross yelled. "Steady . . . NOW! Full turn to port!"

Hack, whose forearms were bigger than most men's calves, yanked out a belaying pin in the iron collar, freeing the bowsprit to swing. Two other crewmen pushed the bowsprit hard to starboard. Then Hack dropped the pin back into the collar. He leaped for the halyard, and the massive sail rose—just as a powerful crosswind hit the *Bruce*.

Stede spun the ship's wheel, and the *Bruce* responded, grabbing the wind and banking around the corner.

"I love this ship!" yelled Ross, his fervor mounting. "Now, let's go catch this slippery rogue."

Cutlass Jack Bonnet's xebec had slipped out of a cove just a few hundred feet from the *Bruce*. "Give 'em a ten spot, Jacques!" Ross called out. Jacques led his gunnery team to train their cannons to fire overhead of the *Banshee*. After all, dead pirates did not make very good pirate hunters, and the survivors would likely hold a serious grudge. Thunderous booms sounded, all within seconds of each other, and the cannon shot surged above the masts. Each one splashed harmlessly in front of the xebec, but apparently Cutlass Jack had no intention of stopping.

The *Bruce* gained on its quarry once again. "He doesn't know who we are," said Ross. Then he slapped himself on the forehead. "Ah, thrice an idiot am I. Mister Hack, raise the standard!"

A huge black flag rose high on the *Bruce*'s mainmast. Emblazoned upon it was a wolf prowling above a horizontal Scottish claymore sword. Declan Ross's flag flapped wildly in the stiff wind.

"Ah! Him b' slowing down at last!" said Stede. The xebec did indeed slow, and the quartermaster brought the *Bruce* alongside. The ships anchored, and Jules—the *Bruce*'s towering security officer—lowered an enormous gangplank, spanning the gap.

Ross turned to Stede. "Bring your thunder gun. I don't know how this is going to go." Declan Ross led Stede, Jules, Anne, and a dozen crewmen down the steep gangplank. The *Banshee* sat much lower in the water, so they went slowly, careful of their footing. At the bottom a very tall man wearing a dark blue bandana stood, tapping his foot and wearing a very confident smile.

"Declan Ross," said the man, his twinkling eyes as dark a green as deep seawater under gray sky. "What you be doing chasing me down?"

Anne put her hands on her hips and glared. "If you hadn't run from us, Uncle Jack, we'd have had no need to chase after you."

"Little Anne!" cried Cutlass Jack. He drew her into a quick embrace and then stood her back a pace. Anne wore dark brown breeches, gathered at the knees with leather laces and at the waist with a dark green sash. Her leather waistcoat was new, and she wore it over a light green long-sleeved shirt. A piece of red coral carved in the shape of a lion glistened on the cord of her necklace. "Look at ye . . . ," Jack said, staring with pride. "Why a woman ye be now! And well dressed at that."

Anne blushed. It was nice to have someone notice her new clothes, but she thought it best not to mention the treasure at the moment. Jack was not really her uncle, just a close family friend. And with pirates, friendships didn't always last when treasure was at stake. "We've . . . uh, had a bit of good fortune," was all she said.

"So I see," Jack replied, gazing at the tall man-o-war behind her. "I wouldn't have run, ye know. But seems yer father has a new ship. What happened to the *Wallace*?"

"Bartholomew Thorne happened to it," said Ross.

A cloud seemed to pass overhead. "Grim news, Declan," he said, holding out a hand. "But from the look of things, you came out ahead." The two captains shook hands slowly.

"And Thorne's swimming with Davy Jones," said Jules with a snort of contempt for their former enemy. His deep voice dropped lower with each following word. "The wave took him out. Out . . . and down."

"We don't know that for sure," said Ross quickly. "In any case, I'm glad we've run across you. I'd like you to sail with us."

"Just like the old days, eh?" Cutlass Jack grinned. "What ye have in mind? A big merchant settlement? A couple galleons on the Spanish Main?"

"Something like that," answered Ross. "Care to join me in my quarters?"

"Ah, a private spot t' discuss the particulars, eh?" Jack looked over his shoulder to his crew. "My men be hungerin' something fierce. . . . While we talk could ye see yer way to givin' 'em some food and drink?"

"I'm quite sure we can arrange that," Ross replied. Then he yelled up to the deck of the *Bruce*. "Nubby!"

"Aye, sir?" The ruddy face of the ship's cook appeared at the rail.

"The crew of the *Banshee* could use a good tankard and a bite to eat."

Nubby's walruslike moustache flinched. "All of 'em?"

Ross nodded. Then the cook replied, "Aye, I can do it, Captain. A good stew would go down right. I'll get to cuttin' up the iguana fer the st—"

"NUBBY!!" Ross bellowed. "Give 'em the good stuff."

Muttering and grumbling, Nubby left the rail, and Ross led

Cutlass Jack on board the *Bruce*. Closely following the two captains were Stede, Jules, and Anne.

In Ross's cabin, Cutlass Jack tilted back a tall silver tankard until liquid dribbled down the corner of his mouth and onto his light brown beard. "Ah, that does good to me parched lips, it does. Now, tell me, Declan, what's this all about?"

"Pirates," said Ross, leaning forward in his chair. "I want you to help me hunt pirates."

Jack's face darkened, but only for a moment. Thinking it was a supreme jest of some sort, he threw back his head and laughed.

"I'm serious, Jack."

Cutlass Jack looked up at Stede, Jules, and Anne who stood behind Ross. No one smiled. Jack's brows lowered, and he tucked his chin like a bull about to charge. Anne tensed. Jules slid to the side of the desk and watched intently.

"Never thought I'd hear that comin' from yer mouth, Declan," he said. "Yer tellin' me ye want me and my crew t' betray our brothers in the sweet trade?"

"Yes, and if you do, the British will grant you and your men full pardon of ALL past . . . activities."

"The British?" Cutlass Jack's mouth dropped open for a silent moment. "Yer workin' for the Brits?" Ross nodded. Jack looked as if he'd just tasted something far fouler than Nubby's iguana stew. "Ye' can't trust 'em, Declan. Why, that's why I turned pirate in the first place!"

This is not going well, thought Ross and he said, "I understand your mistrust—the British have earned it in the past. But things are different. The British navy is led by a decent man now, Commodore

Brandon Blake. And as I've said, they are willing to issue letters of marque for all who renounce piracy and seek after those who won't."

"That's blasphemy, Declan Ross!" declared Cutlass Jack. He stood and turned to leave the cabin. "I will never betray my brothers."

"You'll be paid."

"How dare you ask—what? How much?"

Ross handed him a small brown satchel. "Jack, would this be enough?"

Jack opened the sack and gasped. "How come ye by such jewels?"

"Long story," said Ross. "But what's say we divide the satchel between you and your whole crew? That would make a proper first month's wage, wouldn't it?"

Cutlass Jack grinned and snatched the bag of treasure. "Tell ye what," he said tossing it into his pocket. "Me and my lads will mull these trinkets a bit and consider yer proposition." Then, before Jules could react, Jack drew a cutlass in each hand and said, "Course, we could settle it like the old days, Declan. I'll duel you fer it. If ye can disarm me, we'll join you."

"If you join the Wolf fleet, Jack"—Ross winked—"I personally guarantee all the swordplay you can handle." Ross motioned to a man who had suddenly appeared in the cabin doorway. This perilous-looking fellow had hard-looking, ropey muscles coiling on his arms and a slightly lopsided face. A ragged scar ran down the left side of his forehead, across his eye, and nearly down to his chin. The pupil of his left eye was blood red and floated in a sea of sickly pink. Ross said, "At the very least, Jack, old Red Eye here will give you a decent fight."

Red Eye bared his sharp teeth and gave a kind of crooked grin, all the while, fingering the blade of a long dagger. Cutlass Jack smiled back . . . nervously.

"Happy birthday, Nubs!" thundered Jules as he pushed through the crowd gathered on the main deck of the *Bruce*. He stopped to hand the ship's one-armed cook a small cylinder crudely wrapped in a swatch of gray cloth. Jules grinned so wide that the torchlight reflected off his new gold tooth. "Well, aren't you going to open it?"

Nubby's moustache twitched, and he sighed. "Yes, I'll open it," he said, trying to sound grateful but unable to hide the edge in his voice. Then he muttered to himself, "I'm just afraid I know what it is." He sat on a crate near the mainmast and was surrounded by dozens of small jars full of leaves, cloves, and powders—the gifts he had already opened. Nubby put Jule's gift in his lap and used his hand to untie it. He widened the opening with his fingertips and frowned at the contents.

"Awww, c'mon!" complained Red Eye. "Show us!" The crews from both ships had gathered there to watch, and they, too, demanded that Nubby reveal his latest present.

"Oh, all right!" Nubby shouted. He reached into the cloth and pulled out a tall cylinder of glass. "Well, would you look at that, a jar of spices. I'll just put it over here with my other forty jars of spices."

Jules frowned. The gold tooth went away. "Those aren't just any spices, Nubs," he said. "That's real tamarind from India. It'll add—"

"I know," interrupted the cook. "It'll add so much flavor to my stew. Enough presents!"

"Ah, mon ami," said Jacques St. Pierre as he burst through the group. "But there is one more present."

"It had better not be spices!"

"No, you see, we save the best for last, ha-ha!" St. Pierre cackled and handed Nubby a long, tube-shaped object.

Seeing that the size and shape were too large for seasonings, Nubby eyed the package greedily. Then, he frowned at the knots in the twine that sealed the gift, reached for his knife, and sliced through the twine.

The twine now loose, the wrapping fell away revealing a finely carved piece of wood—three pieces actually, joined by intricate hinges. At one end was a leather strap harness of some kind, and at the other end was a very realistic wooden hand.

"An arm?" Nubby muttered. "You got me an arm?"

Jacques smiled proudly. "It took some shrewd bargaining with a master carver in Barbados, and we had to part with a few jewels, but it is the finest craftsmanship, no?"

Nubby picked up the wooden arm and watched its forearm section sway on its hinge.

"Stede was in on it too," Jacques said.

Stede stepped into the circle. "Try it on, mon," he said.

Nubby stood, holding the wooden arm by its wrist. "Oh, I'll try it out, all right," he said. "I'll try it out on your blitherin' skulls!" Suddenly, Nubby swung the arm at Jacques, whacking him sharply on the shoulder. "What d' ya think I am, a blasted puppet? I'm plenty good with one arm, thank you!"

Then he whirled around toward Stede. The *Bruce*'s quartermaster was too quick, however, and he sped off across the deck. The crowd cheered every time Nubby connected with either Jacques or Stede. They raced around the deck until a clear female voice broke into song. They all turned, the crew of the *Bruce* especially stunned, to hear this beautiful voice coming from Anne.

> *Heave ho, to the sea we go,*
> *Where ships sail high and the soft winds blow.*
> *Where pirate hearts beat proud and true,*

We sing this birthday wish to you.
May the sweet trade winds always fill your sails,
And fat fish leap off the starboard rails.
May you spin the wheel 'til you grow old,
And find your pockets lined with jewels and gold.
May your black flag fly true and high,
And you never find your barrels dry.
Happy Birthday, Nubs!

The crowd cheered and then pleaded for Anne to sing again . . . which, of course, she did. And a couple of Cutlass Jack's men brought out fiddles and added a smart rhythm to Anne's melody. Many of the crew began to dance. Even Nubby, still clutching his wooden arm, danced a little jig.

Late that evening almost asleep at his desk, Declan Ross was startled by a sudden knock on his cabin door. "Come!" he said.

The door opened, and Cutlass Jack Bonnet entered. He closed the door with an air of secrecy and turned to Ross.

"You grow tired of singing and dancing up on deck?" Ross asked.

"Nay, Declan, I never tire of revelry. It's been a long time since my lads were this happy. It was a good thought to harbor here together and make merry. I missed seein' ye up there, though."

Ross gestured to his sea charts. "These charts have to be my dance partner tonight," Ross explained. "How's my Anne—none of your men giving her a hard time, are they? You know, she's signed the articles. She's family—and crew—now."

"I'm not surprised," said Jack. "Yer Anne is as spirited as they come. My quartermaster has taken a likin' t' her, ye know."

"I think her heart's spoken for," said Ross. "Though she'd keel-haul me for even speaking the suggestion."

"Who is he?"

"Ah, he goes by the name Cat," Ross replied. "A good lad. Captain material. He had a pressing errand at the Monasterio de Michael Arcángel on Saba, or he'd be here with us now."

"An errand with the monks? Who can tell what they'll do t' him." They both laughed.

"You know, you really have been like family to us," Ross said. "Anne still calls you Uncle Jack . . . she doesn't have any real uncles, real family, except me. It'd be good to have you around more."

Jack smiled proudly, but just for a moment. Then it became uncomfortably quiet. Ross looked on his guest, but Cutlass Jack stared at the floor.

"What is it, Jack?"

"Now it comes t' this," he muttered, shifting in place. "Seventeen years, Declan . . . that's how long I've been a' piratin'. I'd have never started if the Brits hadn't taught me t' sail, taught me t' fight at sea . . . taught me t' plunder the spoils of a defeated foe. And since the day they tossed me aside like so much flotsam, I've been puttin' my seafarin' skills t' good use. Declan, it's all I know. It's all I'm good at."

"You can still use those skills," Declan offered. "I'm counting on it! You're just using them for a different cause."

"But the British?" Cutlass Jack scratched under his bandana. "They cut us off once. They'll do it again."

"It's not just the British footing the bill, Jack," Ross paused, wondering how much he should say.

"Doesn't matter. The deal won't last, and we'll be left just like before." Jack turned to leave, but waited a moment. "Do ye truly

Father Brun tilted his head thoughtfully. "I see someone quite different. Your eyes, your mouth—none of those things make who you are. And I am quite certain that you are nothing like Bartholomew Thorne."

"You saw what I did!" Cat's face twisted with anguish. "You saw that rage. I would have killed Dmitri . . . if you hadn't stepped in."

"I doubt that," said Father Brun. "I've seen men stronger than you break a staff over Dmitri's head without doing him much harm."

Cat laughed in spite of himself but quickly looked away. "But, Father Brun," he said, "I've had memories come back. I've seen him go from perfect calm to a murderous rage in an instant—just like me."

"He's done unspeakable horrors," said Father Brun. "But you would never go that far."

"How do you know?" pleaded Cat. "There's still so much of my past missing. So much I don't remember. What if I really am just like him?"

Father Brun stood, and his voice had an edge to it when he spoke again. "Cat, do you really believe that this has already been decided for you?"

Cat looked at him and blinked. "I . . . I don't—"

"The way you are talking," Father Brun interrupted, "leads me to believe you think that who you are is a fixed thing, a doom that cannot be avoided."

Cat's mouth opened and closed, but he said nothing.

"See to it that you banish that thought from your mind," Father Brun continued, his voice sharpening as he spoke. "For it is a lie from the pit of hell! Now, I am very sorry for what you've been through, and you no doubt will bear scars from those unfortunate days in your mind as well as the scars on your back. But you, Cat,

YOU are responsible for what you do with the time that is to come. Do you understand? There is nothing in your past that guarantees who you will become. Have you forgotten the lives you saved on the Isle of Swords? Have you forgotten the miraculous path that led you here? If you must consider the past, then think on those things. I for one am convinced that the Almighty has great plans for you."

Father Brun walked to the chamber door. "You know . . . the Holy Scriptures say, 'Old things are passed away; behold, all things are become new!' Your past may indeed have a strong hold on your life, Cat, but the Almighty is stronger still. When dark thoughts come again, think on that instead." Father Brun paused to let his words sink in and then said, "I will return soon. It is time for you to learn why I have brought you to the Citadel."

Cat didn't know when Father Brun would be back, but he needed to get out of his chamber, breathe the fresh sea air, and clear his mind. He found himself wandering over the lush green hills outside of the Citadel. The entire island of Saba in the Caribbean was a long-dormant volcano, now green with trees and foliage and surrounded by smaller stony mounds and wavelike terrain. But through years of toil, the monks had flattened out several plateaus and converted them for their purposes. Cat followed a wide and winding path. Men in simple brown robes moved to and fro like worker bees in a hive. Some tended to mango or other fruit-bearing trees. Others tirelessly hoed long rows in the soil. But all who saw Cat stopped their work, smiled, and nodded slightly as he walked by.

Even after a week, it was still unnerving. The first day on Saba, Cat had asked Father Brun, "Why do they keep doing that?"

Father Brun had laughed quietly. "Word of your deeds has spread far and wide, even reaching little Saba. The monks show their gratitude to the one who delivered the Nails of Christ. All five hundred members of the Brethren who dwell here—and the hundreds more abroad—have been praying for you every day since your return."

Cat stopped on the crest of a green hill and looked back on the Citadel of the Brethren. Cat marveled at it still. For all its orchards bursting with flowering trees, its dizzying rows of lush crops, and its serene pastures, its other name—the Monasterio de Michael Arcángel—seemed to fit it best for it looked more like a fortress than an abode for monks. It was nestled in a mountainous crescent at the base of the volcano. The hills and rocks formed a natural defensive barrier, protecting the monastery on three sides. The structure's façade, which was all that was visible from Cat's vantage, stood tall with seven parapeted towers, implacable, curving, crenelated walls, and a high iron gate that looked to Cat as if it could withstand a dozen barrels of Jacques St. Pierre's black powder.

Cat wondered how these men of God could be so peaceful and, at the same time, be such formidable warriors. And he wondered what they could possibly want with him.

A bell tolled from the Citadel tower, snapping Cat back to awareness. Cat wondered how long he'd been standing there. The sun looked markedly lower in the sky. Cat rushed back to his chamber.

There he found Father Brun standing at the window. Cat began to apologize, but Father Brun turned and shook his head dismissively. In his hands, he held a large leather-bound book. He held it out for Cat.

"This"—Cat said, taking the volume from the monk—"this is the book I brought back from the Isle of Swords."

"Yes," replied Father Brun. "But what you did not know is that, aside from the Nails of Christ, no other treasure from that place is of more worth to the Brethren than this book. You see, this volume chronicles the pilgrimages of those blessed members of the Brethren who traveled to the Isle of Swords and looked upon the nails. There is great wisdom in such moments, and I think God speaks to us today through the writing within these pages. It is . . . precious to us."

Cat looked up questioningly.

Father Brun nodded. "You are wondering why I spirited you away from the crew of the *Robert Bruce* and brought you all the way to Saba only to see this book. How could I not? For in the final written pages of the volume you will find something that belongs to you, perhaps . . . something that will help you. Your memory has still not fully returned?"

Cat shook his head. "Only some visions, bits and pieces, but always as if I am watching the life of another."

Father Brun smiled sadly. "Read, Cat, . . . and may God deliver your memory or if not that, wisdom to live this life without pity for the missing years."

Cat stared at the book. With a combination of raw anticipation and fear, he opened it and began turning pages toward the end. So many amazing tales of men who had been transformed by an encounter with the nails that held their savior to a cruel Roman cross—in many ways it was inspiring to Cat. Of course, he couldn't read it all because most of it was in Latin or Spanish. He began to wonder what Father Brun had been talking about. There seemed to be nothing that concerned him directly.

Then Cat turned the page. He froze. Most of the entries in the journal had been written in large flowing script. What he saw written on this next page was actually quite ordinary and, well . . . sloppier than most. All the entries thus far had been addressed to members of the Brethren who would come after. The heading on this page said . . . *My son.*

Chills, like whitecaps on a windblown sea, surged across Cat's flesh. He began to read.

My son, you have come to the very place I prayed you'd come. I came here seeking gold and jewels. I found something else. And I suspect your father will not approve of the choices I now feel I must make. Whatever happens, my young lion, remember that I will always love you and be with you. Did you know that's what your middle name means? Lejon . . . it is an old Norse word for lion. With your mane of blond hair, and your courage, I always thought the name fit. If you are reading this, you truly have become the lionhearted man I knew you'd be. May you find here that which rescued me.

Hunt well.

Katarina Thorne

Cat stared at the signature at the bottom of the message. *Katarina Thorne. Mother.* He let himself fall backward onto the cot and lay with the book open on his chest. *She'd been on the Isle of Swords. Of course, that's how she got the map and the key to the chest that held the nails. And . . . she left them for me: a trail I could follow. The lock of red hair had been hers. The green diamond had been worth enough to hire Vesa Turinen to take them to Portugal. The cross had been the key. The pouch itself had the map etched inside it.* Cat closed his eyes and began to wonder how so many things had fallen into place so that he could journey to the Isle of Swords and rescue the nails. And how, in turn, the nails had rescued him. He also thought about his name—his full name—

Griffin Lejon Thorne. He had been named after a lion. *"Hunt well,"* she'd said.

"Extraordinary, isn't it?" Father Brun asked.

"My mother wrote this," Cat whispered. "She wrote it for me."

"Yes," Father Brun replied, but sensing Cat's need, he said nothing more.

"She died . . . she died not knowing if I would ever find it." Suddenly, he felt a pulsing in his head. His skin prickled. In his mind's eye he saw cold blue eyes flaring with venomous anger. A whip crackled. He saw a spray of blood on a stone wall. And then the vision was gone. He bowed his head quietly for a moment and then said, "My own father . . . tortured me. He left me for dead on that blasted island. If Anne had not come when she did I would have died. I would never have known."

"It goes far beyond coincidence," said Father Brun quietly.

Cat nodded. He had thought the same.

"Your coming to the Isle of Swords," Father Brun went on, "was a divine appointment. You were called by the Almighty."

"I don't know."

"Do you not? Remove one small event from the chain that led you to the Isle of Swords, and what happens? It all falls apart. No, Griffin Lejon Thorne, you were called to rescue the most sacred of relics. You were called to find your mother's final message to you. And, I think, for something more."

Cat's blue eyes flickered. "What do you mean?"

"I brought you here for you to read this book, but also to make you an offer. As you no doubt noted on the way into the Citadel, the Brethren . . . are not ordinary priests and monks. Not superior—

no, not by any measure that matters—only called for a different purpose. Some of the men here grew up in the church, but many others were grafted in. Some were members of the military. Others were pirates." Cat's mouth fell open.

"For many years, the Brethren order has remained hidden, involved only when our hand was forced and also to protect the holy relics of God. But the world has changed and not for the better. Evil roams abroad, preying unchecked on the innocent all around us. The Brethren has spent a season in prayer—seven years to be precise—beseeching our Lord for wisdom. What, if anything, should we do? And over this time, we have been brought to the conclusion that we cannot remain idle any longer. It seemed a great answer to prayer that Declan Ross and the British were willing to assemble a fleet to hunt down and redeem those who have made piracy their lives. But we are now convinced that their effectiveness may be undercut by powers beyond their control. They will need help to defeat the menace that yet stirs."

"My father," whispered Cat.

"Yes," said Father Brun. "He may yet live. Though, if that is the case, he is but one among many—and by far not the worst. The Brethren has been called to come forth as the Soldiers of God to stem the black tide that approaches. And we would like you, Cat, to join us."

"Me?" Cat was stunned. "But I don't even believe in God . . . not completely."

Father Brun looked at Cat knowingly. "We are content to leave that in the hands of the Lord."

"I don't know what I can do to help your order."

"You can captain a ship. The Brethren has purchased a trio of tall ships for a special mission. We have, through great research and prayer, selected captains for these vessels. And we want you to be one of them."

Cat closed the book and stared. After the training session with Brother Dmitri that morning, Cat figured the Brethren would want him off the island as soon as possible—and now they ask him to join them? "You mean . . . you mean, you still want me, after what I did?"

Father Brun frowned. "Of course, I still want you," he said as if Cat could not be any more absurd. "I want you now more than ever. You are a broken man, and a broken man in the hands of the Lord is a powerful weapon."

"But Captain Ross . . . the *Bruce*." He didn't mention Anne, but he could see her face in his mind. "I am one of his crew. They're my friends."

"And that is the decision you face. Declan Ross and the crew of the *Bruce* are fighting a threat to all who travel the sea. But there is an enemy beyond their means, an enemy the Brethren must face on its own terms."

Cat was silent, deep in thought, and then blurted out, "I need time to think about this. But . . . if I did decide to join the Brethren, do I have to wear a robe?"

Father Brun laughed aloud. "This is the simple and customary garb of the Brethren for most occasions," he said. "But there are times when we must conceal our identity. This may be such a time. Think on it. You have the whole week to consider. But when Declan Ross returns from the northern coast of South America, I will need your answer."

4

THE WHISPERING GALLERY

In the shadows of the great dome of St. Paul's in London stood a lone figure. Clad all in black, he faded in and out of sight as if tendrils of the night tried relentlessly to contain him but could not. He loathed being in a church. But the infamous pirate Edmund Bellamy had told him it was the only way to meet the Merchant. *The north side of the gallery,* he'd said. *Precisely six minutes after midnight—don't be late. The Merchant will speak to you then. If he trusts you, he'll tell you what to do next.*

"Very punctual," came a long whisper. It sounded as if spoken by someone right beside him, but the man in black looked left and right along the gallery's curling rail and saw no one.

A man of ordinary courage would have been startled by such a disembodied voice. But the man in black had seen too many horrors—caused most of them himself—to be affected in the least. He knew that his visitor, the Merchant, stood exactly opposite of him, 107 feet away, in the darkness on the southern side of the gallery. It was peculiar, if not frightening, that the acoustics of the great dome made it possible to hear even a whisper over such a great distance.

"Did Bellamy tell you what I want?" asked the man in black, his voice a raspy whisper.

"Your first request was easy enough," said the Merchant. "But the second . . . well, now, that required some digging."

"They exist, then?"

"Oh yes. That proud race will never die out. I have done business with them before. But they will not suffer anyone who is not of their blood to be among them for long. And . . . they demand much of a leader."

"And the other item . . . can you find it or not?" demanded the man in black. He hadn't climbed the 259 steps to play games.

Laughter drifted eerily across the gap. "I already have. Locating it was nothing for a man of my means. Wresting it from the hands of its current owner . . . that will demand time and my . . . unique methods."

"My errand cannot wait," said the man in black.

"No, I expect not," said the Merchant. "Nonetheless you will wait six days. Upon the sixth, you will find me in Whitechapel. Third alley west of Sullivan's Tavern. After nightfall, knock on the third door from the road. I will have the items you want. But . . . my price is high."

"I am quite sure I can cover it," said the man in black.

"Can you?" asked the Merchant, a note of contempt in his bodiless voice. "You and Edmund Bellamy are so alike. Arrogant." The word hung in the air. "In six days, I'll have what you ask for, and then we'll see what you are willing to part with in return."

The voice disappeared like a wisp of smoke. The man in black heard no footsteps, but he felt certain the Merchant was already gone.

His boots scraped on the cobblestone of the alley in spite of efforts to approach his destination in secrecy. Most Londoners had gone to bed long before. Still, the vacant passages between ever-crowding brick buildings amplified every sound.

He approached the third door from the road and raised his hand to knock. His gloved fist suspended in midair. The man in black had waited impatiently for six days for this, and yet he hesitated now. There was something foreboding about this door. It was tall and covered in dark filth as if blasted by fire. The doorknocker was a thick, tarnished ring clenched in the teeth of a hideous gargoyle of a face that seemed in the act of a scream. An icy chill pooled in the pit of his stomach. Fear was entirely foreign to the man in black, except that which he himself inspired. He drew back his hand and stroked a gray sideburn all the way to his jutting chin. Then he knocked. Before he could rap a second time, the top half of the door swung away. "Welcome . . . to my shop," a voice slithered out of the darkness.

The man in black saw nothing, just a gaping black hole where the top half of the door had been. "Were you successful?"

"Of course." The Merchant lingered on the "s" drawing it out to a hiss. "Given the time . . . and the motivation, I can get anything a mortal soul could desire." A long case of gray leather was placed on the ledge of the bottom section of the door. Then a thick, leather-bound book was slid next to it. "Mind the blood," said the Merchant. "It was . . . required."

The man in black put the pouch into a great pocket in his coat. Then he grasped the book. *Eiríkr Thorvaldsson* was the title carved into the leather flesh. "It's in there?" he asked. "Not just the saga, but the family tree?"

"Yes," the Merchant replied. "All that you need. But now to the matter of my compensation."

"This should be more than suitable payment," he said as he placed a new pouch on the ledge where the other had been.

A shadowy hand took the pouch. Suddenly, the pouch flew out of the darkness and smacked against the brick wall behind the man in black. Jewels, white and green, lay at his feet.

"This will not satisfy your debt to me," said the Merchant, his voice low and menacing.

"I assure you, the gems are real."

"I care not. They are baubles . . . trinkets. I know who you are. And I know your plan. None of it will come to pass without that book I recovered for you. But with it, you will succeed, and when you do, I want a contract."

"Contract?"

"A guarantee of sorts . . . compensation, favors, protection. This will be in writing and signed in blood. But for now, I simply need your word."

The man in black looked at the book and then into the void in the doorway. Who knew what the Merchant actually wanted? He seemed capable enough. Whatever he wanted . . . it would be worth it. "I accept your terms."

"The word of a pirate is hardly reliable," said the Merchant laughing quietly. The mirth in his voice disappeared, replaced with a deep, menacing whisper. "But mark me, you are now bound to your promise. And we will meet again . . . soon."

The top section of the door closed without a sound. The man in black held the book tightly to his chest. He picked up the discarded jewels. Then before leaving the dark door and the cold alley behind, he stood quietly for a few moments.

The *Saga of Erik the Red* lay open on the desk where the man in black furiously flipped its pages. The Merchant had assured him that the family tree was in this volume, but so far nothing but mythic stories of—*Wait!* And there it was at last. The script was faded in some places, smeared in others. The various hands that had updated it over the years were anything but examples of great penmanship. And it was all written in Norse, but the man in black had learned that tongue as a child and still remembered it well enough to read. The first name in the tree was, of course, Erik the Red. Dozens of generations later, another familiar name appeared, and the man in black grinned.

Gunnar Thorne. Dear Father, thought Bartholomew Thorne. *For once you didn't lie.* His throat constricted, and his breathing became rough and raspy.

There were two names beneath the old bloodfist. Thorne traced a finger across his own name and sneered at the other. He closed the *Saga of Erik the Red*. And from a long, leather case he withdrew a dark stave carved from a bough off a Jamaican ironwood tree. Thorne hefted it in his hand. It was heavier than his previous bleeding stick. But the weight felt good. How ironic that the natives called it the "wood of life" due to the curative properties of its resin.

Thorne reached into an open leather satchel, took out a handful of sharp metal spikes that curled like talons, and began to screw them into the top portion of the stave. He held his new weapon in the light of the oil lantern on the desk and watched with satisfaction as the dark red sap bled down the shaft. Thorne knew it was only a hint of what was to come.

5

THE NIGHTWALKER

Cat had been with the monks of the Monasterio de Michael Arcángel for more than a week, and Father Brun hadn't uttered another word about joining the Brethren order. And yet almost every waking moment, the decision had weighed upon Cat's heart like an anchor.

Day after day as he supped with the monks or as he took part in their physical activities, Cat became more and more confused. The monks of the Brethren were so kind and welcoming. They went about embracing each other as if they were all family.

And the Brethren prayed—a lot. In every corner of the Citadel, he found monks praying. Some prayed alone in small alcoves or closets. Others prayed in pairs upon stone benches, while others huddled in masses in the sanctuary or even out in the fields. As strange as the relentless prayer seemed to Cat, he also thought it intriguing. Tonight, for example, he found himself wondering what the monks said to God and whether God answered back.

A blackbird's harsh croak from outside the chamber window

startled Cat from his thoughts. He rose from the cot, went to the white basin on the table, and rinsed his face with the cold water. A knock at the door caused Cat to jump. When he turned, Father Brun stood in the doorway holding a flickering candle.

"I have just returned from prayer," Father Brun said. That was no surprise to Cat. The monk motioned for Cat to sit at the small table near the window. He took a seat across from Cat and placed the candle on the table between them. Cat watched the wavering flame and noted its movements were not unlike Father Brun's restless eyes. Those pale eyes did not dart to and fro out of nervous preoccupation but rather in continuous observation. But now, they stopped, and the effect was like sudden silence in the midst of a raging storm.

"The Brethren solemnly request your services, Griffin Lejon Thorne," said Father Brun. "But we would not have you decide out of a fleeting passion or in ignorance of the danger you will face." The room seemed to darken, and Cat glanced through the shutters as if some frightening thing might be approaching. The wind strengthened and the shutters rattled.

"We seek an ancient enemy—elusive and shrewd—malevolent on a level far beyond the darkest pirates of history. And history does not record this villain's true name. He is known only as the Merchant."

"I have never heard of him."

"And he would like nothing more than to keep it that way," said Father Brun. "For his effectiveness waxes in his anonymity. But tell me, Cat, have you ever wondered what has caused some of the great calamities of the world? Has it ever amazed you that throughout history, evil men have somehow had the means to carry out their infamous deeds? Black-hearted emperors and kings, despots and tyrants, and yes . . . even pirates—they have all risen to power on the might of a blood-soaked fist. But who provided the dagger for that fist? The sword . . . the cannon? Who first whispered malice into the eager ears of these violent souls? It was the Merchant."

Father Brun saw the question in Cat's expression and said, "No, history does not speak his deeds—nay, only the deeds of his customers. But the Brethren have collected traces of the Merchant's activity, and in our annals you will find his black thread weaving through the years like a serpent. The first mention of him comes from a letter dictated by Emperor Nero in AD 68, a month before he killed himself. In the letter, Nero claims that the gods sent him an advisor who helped him in times of great duress. It was this advisor who encouraged Nero to blame Christians for the burning of Rome . . . leading to the persecution and martyrdom of thousands.

"The Merchant turns up again in AD 334. Having failed in his attempts to worm his way into Emperor Constantine's council, he tried to poison him instead. The Brethren order was newly formed at that time, and Constantine was spared. But the Merchant escaped. And over the centuries, he returned, supplying and exhorting the most ruthless villains the world has ever known. Torquemada, Báthory, Chevillard, Bellamy—but always in the shadows, just out of reach . . . until now."

"How can that be possible?" Cat asked. "No man can live for centuries."

"True," Father Brun replied. "And yet a man's evil can live on long past his death. You see, the Merchant is not one man but many. In 1580, we captured the Merchant. He was ill and near to death, but from him we learned that he had trained an apprentice to assume his role upon his death. And so it has been for these many hundreds of years. One Merchant trains the next, and so, his malice lives on."

Cat leaned forward, his chin nearly over the candle's flame. "But you said, *until now*. Now we can get him?"

"You've made your decision," said Father Brun. "You said *we*."

Cat hesitated, realizing his mistake. "Well . . . no, what I meant was, *you* can get him now?" Father Brun smiled and studied Cat like a sea chart.

"We have a member of the Brethren secreted among Edmund Scully's crew," Father Brun explained. "Scully is sort of a go-between. He seems to have connections everywhere and exploits them for the highest bidder. He has provided information for many pirates, as well as foreign governments. The Brethren recently discovered that Scully once kept watch on the British for your father—"

"My father?" Cat echoed. He could not remember meeting anyone named Scully. "Would I know this Scully? Would I recognize him?"

"Only you can answer," said Father Brun. "You may have a chance. Scully now gathers information for the Merchant. Unfortunately, our spy inside Scully's crew became compromised, and he had to flee. But . . . not before learning a few of Scully's regular haunts. Saint Vincent, Inagua, Jamaica—we will scour those islands until we find Scully. And then we will force Scully to take us to the Merchant."

"But what if Scully won't?" Cat asked. "The Merchant doesn't sound very forgiving."

"I have been praying about this for some time," Father Brun admitted. "If greed motivates Edmund Scully as it seems to, the Brethren certainly possesses enough treasure to make his information worth the risk. But if not through riches . . . there are other ways. Cat, you must understand . . . it may be our best and only chance to stop the Merchant's dark influence on history. For the

Merchant is growing old, and he will soon choose his next apprentice. We must get him before he does." A gust of wind thrust open the shutters. Lightning flashed in the distance, bathing vaporous shreds of clouds in purple and blue.

"A storm is coming," said Father Brun.

Cat stared out onto the dark sea. "And that's not all," he said, pointing. "It's the *Robert Bruce*."

Father Brun watched for the next flash, saw the sails of a tall ship, and said, "Cat, the time for your decision has come."

Father Brun and the monks had prepared a special banquet in the Brethren's dining hall for Declan Ross and his senior crew members. Cat, seated between his captain and the leader of the Brethren, felt like a mooring line stretched between two drifting ships. Father Brun had agreed to give Cat one last night to make the decision, and the tension was relentless.

"Ha-ha!" Jacques St. Pierre cackled proudly from the end of the table. "The look on this man's face—the man we caught that day in Bristol—what was his name again?"

"Fremont," said Red Eye as if he'd heard the story a hundred times.

"Oui, Fremont, that was it. The look on his face when I lit the fuse, and he could not snuff it out—that was, how you say . . . priceless!"

"He stole the wrong barrel!" said Jules, his voice so deep the silverware rattled.

"Actually," said St. Pierre, "Fremont stole the right barrel. It was full of grain, not black powder. But Fremont did not know this. Ha-ha!"

Even Red Eye had not heard that part of the tale. "You put a fuse in a barrel full of grain?"

"I put fuses in everything, ha-ha!" To emphasize the point, St. Pierre held up his arm and showed all that a small length of hemp-fuse stuck out of his sleeve.

"You shouldn't be so careless with explosives," said Red Eye. The unfortunate accident with black powder that scarred the left side of his face also rendered his left eye blind, its pupil permanently colored dark red.

"You've never told me," said Ross, "how did you know Fremont had taken a grain barrel and not the black powder?"

"It is élémentaire, mon capitaine. I carve a letter 'B' on the side of every barrel that contains explosives."

"Ah," said Jules. "'B' for black powder."

"No, my gigantic friend, 'B' as in BOOM!!"

Cat absently shoved a little bean around his plate with a fork. *How can I abandon them?* Cat wondered. *They're my friends.* The bean skittered off the plate, so Cat went after a wedge of apple. *More than friends—they saved my life.* He recalled the day Anne had found him. He had been bloodied, wounded near to death, left alone on the island to die. At Anne's insistence, Jules had carried Cat to safety.

Anne. Cat stared across the table at her. Her long crimson hair swirled over her shoulder and across her neck as she playfully bickered with Red Eye and Jules. Her hazel eyes flashed with intensity even as she pretended to threaten Red Eye with a fork. The word *friend* didn't quite cover what Cat felt for Anne. He wasn't sure he knew of a word that would. But to leave the *Bruce* meant leaving her, and something about that thought twisted the pit of Cat's stomach. Anne looked up at him, but the instant their eyes met she turned demurely away. *Twist.* Cat's stomach continued to churn, as it would until late that evening.

"Ah!" Cat growled and thumped the mug on the table. The candle teetered. He caught it just before it fell and held it so that some melted wax would dribble into the holder. Then he reinserted the candle and . . . exhaled. He'd almost lost control again—AGAIN! Cat shook his head and looked up at the ceiling. *What's happening to me?* he wondered. He cleared his mind as best he could. He needed clarity of thought tonight of all nights.

If only there was some compromise, he thought . . . *some way to stay with the* Bruce *and help out the Brethren.* But he knew that Ross's plan was to coordinate the Wolf fleet with Commodore Blake. So there was no way to . . . Cat stood up so abruptly his chair fell over. He looked out the window. It was late, and Cat had no idea if Father Brun might still be up. *But what about Ross, would he agree to—? No, first things first.*

Cat grabbed the candle, slowly opened the chamber door, and quietly stole out into the hall. He passed by several doors, each leading to rooms occupied by his friends from the *Bruce,* but he could not stop there. Not yet. So Cat stealthily made his way through the corridors of the Citadel until he came at last to Father Brun's chamber. He was surprised to see light beneath his door. Cat knocked once lightly on the door, and Father Brun said, "Come in."

Cat opened the door and found Father Brun sitting at a small round table. He had several candles lit—one on the table, one on the windowsill, and several on various shelves. There was a second chair at the table. It was turned invitingly toward the door. Father

Brun had a book open in front of him and did not look up. He said, "I thought you might be along about now."

"I couldn't sleep," Cat said as he eased in and pulled the door shut.

"No," said Father Brun. "I expect not." He motioned for Cat to sit down.

They sat in silence for a few moments, Father Brun not looking up from the pages and Cat not knowing how to begin. At last, Father Brun said, "The Holy Scriptures tell of a young man named Samuel who heard a voice calling his name. He went to his master and said, 'I am here. What do you want?' But his master said he did not call. This happened twice more—a voice calling Samuel's name, but Samuel's master saying it was not him. But Samuel's master had an idea who might be calling . . ." Father Brun looked at Cat expectantly.

"God?"

The monk nodded. "People do not always recognize the call of God when they first hear it. He does not always choose to speak with a voice. For some, the call is a felt passion for service. Powerful— even tragic—events seem to conspire against some others until, at last, they stop running and surrender. That was how it was with me. I would turn to the left, but something occurred inexplicably and closed that road. I'd turn to the right and find hardship behind every door. It was only then, exhausted of my own stubborn will, that I said, 'Yes, Lord.' I wonder, Cat, is that what you've come to do?"

Cat hesitated. "I . . . I don't think I can join the Brethren."

If Father Brun was troubled by Cat's answer, he did not show it. "But?"

"But I will sail for you if . . ."

"If?"

Cat took a deep breath. "I will sail for the Brethren, captain one of your ships, and help you catch the Merchant if . . . if Anne can sail with me."

Father Brun finally showed some surprise. "Anne? Anne Ross, the captain's daughter?" Cat nodded. Father Brun's pale blue eyes narrowed, but then he smiled as if the solution to a complex sum had just become clear. "She is very fond of you also," he said. "But can she sail? We could face any type of sea, and the stormy season is not far off."

"Anne is a brilliant seaman," Cat said. "Uh, sea-woman . . . person. I mean, she can sail very well. She practically grew up with a ship's wheel in her hand."

"I do not need to tell you again how dangerous this journey will be."

"Anne can take care of herself. She's smart and good with a sword. I'd make her my quartermaster."

Father Brun drummed his fingers on the book. "You must first seek permission from her father," he said.

"You . . . you mean Anne may come? She may sail with me?"

"If Declan Ross permits it, I will accept it as God's will."

Cat had rapped softly on Captain Ross's door several times and had heard nothing. He felt foolish and somewhat suspicious standing in the darkness outside the door. What would other members of the Brethren think if they found him out slinking around so late? Cat tried again, knocking harder than he meant to.

"Stede," came Ross's sleepy grumble from inside. "This had better be blasted important!"

"It's Cat, sir."

The door opened and there stood Declan Ross, squinting and blinking. "Cat?" he said. "It's rather late."

Cat had never seen the captain of the *Robert Bruce* look so bedraggled. His coppery corona of hair stood in some places and bent wildly in others. His beard was nearly twisted in a knot, and his shirt and breeches looked like they'd been balled up before Ross put them on.

Cat resisted the urge to smile and said, "I'm sorry, Captain, but this couldn't wait anymore."

Ross opened the door wide for Cat. The captain wondered what could be so important that it had to be said in the middle of the night. It had to be something rather private, else Cat could have mentioned it at dinner. Whatever it was, it didn't feel like good news. Ross lit a candle and brought it over to a square table near the window. When he and his visitor were seated, he said, "What's this about, Cat?"

Cat squirmed a little in his chair. "Well, sir, I've really learned a great deal about sailing from you and the crew of the *Bruce*."

"You knew a great deal before you met us," said Ross, completely awake now and curious.

"True enough, Captain, but I really appreciate all you—you and the crew—have done for me. You . . . you've become like family to me."

This? Ross wondered. *This is what you woke me up in the middle of the night to tell me?* There had to be more, so Ross waited.

Cat sighed. This wasn't going to be easy. "All to say that, well . . . I've become quite fond of you all . . . Anne especially."

Anne? Ross thought urgently. *Wait just a moment. What does Anne*—

Cat continued. "I'm really not sure how to ask you this . . ."

Ask me what? Ross sat up much straighter.

"I mean, I wouldn't move forward without your permission."

Permission . . . Anne? Ross gasped. *Oh, dear Lord, no. He's not*—

"Captain, I'm not entirely sure how old I am, you understand," Cat stammered, "with my memory and all, but I must be seventeen, eighteen at the least. I'm a man now."

He is, Ross decided. *He's going to ask for my blessing for him to marry my daughter.* Ross stood up abruptly and paced around the room.

Cat watched the captain fearfully. "But, sir, if you'll just let—"

Ross scowled and held up a hand. His first thought was an emphatic *NO.* But then, as Cat fumbled for words, Ross looked him up and down. Cat was a natural sailor, a fine young man—much better than some Anne had taken a fancy to in the past. Of course, he was the son of a bloodthirsty—no, Ross decided, Cat was nothing like his father. He'd already saved Anne's life . . . he'd no doubt look after her well. Declan Ross closed his eyes and said the most difficult words he could ever remember saying. "Very well then, Cat, you have my permission."

Cat was stunned. "But you haven't even heard what I'm asking."

Ross raised a hand. "Oh, I think you've made your intentions perfectly clear. And I want you to know that I think it's right noble of you to ask me before you propose."

"Propose?" Cat nearly fell out of his chair. "Wait, Captain Ross, I . . . I don't want to marry Anne."

"What?" It was Captain Ross's turn to be dumbfounded. "Well, why not?" Then he turned angry. "I'll have you know my Anne is of the finest moral quality! She'd make a fine wife for any man—any man worthy of her, that is."

"Well, it's not that someday . . . I mean, she's smart and beautiful, and I guess I like her quite well, but I don't think we're quite ready for—"

Ross rubbed his temples, shook his head, and grasped Cat by the shoulders. "Well then, what were you asking me, Cat?"

"I want to take leave of the crew," Cat blurted out. "Father Brun has asked me to captain one of his ships."

Declan Ross released Cat's shoulders and sat down across from him with a thud. "When Father Brun asked you to come to Saba, did you know then?"

"No."

Ross nodded. "Cat, I . . . I'm not sure what to say. You want to leave the *Bruce*?"

"Not permanently," Cat replied. "At least I don't think it has to be permanent. Father Brun wants me for a specific mission. They're going after a dangerous man called the Merchant."

Ross shook his head. "I don't know that name," he said. "And the Brethren rarely goes on the offensive. What's this fellow done that's got the monks ready to sail after him?"

"Father Brun told me the Merchant is kind of a supplier—like his name sounds—but he's been involved with some of the worst men who ever lived, many of them pirates. Father Brun calls him the enemy of the Brethren."

Ross was thoughtful for a moment. "I can understand why Father Brun wants you to sail for him. Cat, the way you took command of the *Bruce* at the Isle of Swords—just a skeleton crew, the volcano blowing up all around, the *Raven* with a huge head start—and you didn't hesitate. You went after him and took him down. That's what I call a man, and that's what I call a real sailor. As I've told you before, I'll not be holding any of my crew against his or her will, but what I've got to know is, have you got your heart set on this?"

"I do, sir."

Ross nodded. "It's settled then," he said. "But you should talk to Anne. She'll be crushed to hear."

"Captain Ross," Cat said, "I want to take Anne with me. I want her to be my quartermaster on this journey."

"Is that right?" Ross asked, his voice trailing off and his expression thoughtful and distant. Anne had always wanted to command a ship—she had it in her blood. Ross knew she'd make an excellent quartermaster. But still, since his wife Abigail's death, Ross had not willingly parted with their daughter for more than a few days at a time. "Has Father Brun agreed to house a woman on board? A woman in a command position? He knows if you go down, Anne would become captain?"

"He told me to get your permission, but if granted, then Anne would be my second-in-command."

Ross wrung his hands in his lap. If he let her go, let her sail with Cat, there was always a chance that he would never see her again. Of course, keeping her aboard the *Bruce* as they sail about after pirates wasn't exactly safe. So far, they'd battled only weak, inexperienced pirates, but sooner or later they'd run into a Bellamy or . . . Bartholomew Thorne, if he yet lived. And what then? Thorne had almost killed Anne once. Ross knew the monks of the Brethren. He knew that, in spite of being men of the cloth, they were capable warriors. They would keep Anne safe. To let her go might just keep Anne out of harm's way and, at the same time, give her something she's always wanted.

"Before you decide, sir," said Cat. "I want you to know that I would give my own life to protect Anne. But this man we're after . . . he's a terrible fiend. A monster."

He's just a merchant, Ross thought. *Compared to some of the devils that sail under the black flag, how bad could he be?* Ross stroked his beard and made up his mind.

"This is not easy for me," Ross said. "Anne is my greatest treasure—my life's blood. But I trust you, Cat. Sailing aboard the *Bruce* or not, you are one of my crew . . . and you always will be. You take care of my daughter."

Cat's eyes brightened. "I will, sir." He stood up and extended his hand to Captain Declan Ross. They shook, and Cat said, "May I go to her chamber? May I go tell her?"

Ross nodded, and Cat ran to the door. He was halfway out when he stopped and turned back a moment. "Captain Ross?"

"Yes, lad?"

"What you said earlier . . . about me marrying Anne?"

Ross's eyebrows bristled. "Don't press your luck."

Anne answered the door, and Cat was struck by her sleepy beauty. Her crimson hair was all tussled, her eyes were crinkly and squinting, and her nightdress was creased and wrinkled.

"Cat, what are you doing here?" she asked, a lazy smile on her lips. She looked into the hallway both ways, feeling very suspicious.

"It's okay," Cat assured her. "I asked your father first if I could come see you." Cat smiled inwardly. He wouldn't dare tell her that her father had given him permission to ask her to marry him, but it was kind of funny. "May I come in?"

"Uh, yes . . . since my father said it was okay." She left the door open and walked across her chamber. She seemed like a ghost, all in white, moving so slowly until she glided to a seat on a chair. She lit a candle and looked up at Cat expectantly. "Well?"

Cat followed her in and sat down across from her. "How would you like to have command of a ship?"

"What?" Anne rubbed the sleep from her eyes and squinted.

"A command," he repeated. "Not just one of the crew, but a real command."

"My father commands the *Bruce*," she said.

"No, not the *Bruce*."

"Cat, what are you talking about?"

"Well, actually, you'd be second-in-command. You'd be my quartermaster. Would that suit you?"

Anne tilted her head and looked at him slyly. "Yes, of course, that would suit me." She laughed. "It's been my dream for longer than I can remember, but I'll never get the chance to—wait, what did you mean by saying I'd be your quartermaster? Cat?"

Cat had dragged it out long enough, so he told her. He told her about Father Brun's invitation to take command of one of the Brethren's three ships. He told her that he wanted Anne to be his quartermaster, and that her father had given his blessing. And he told her about their mission to find and capture the Merchant.

Anne was stunned. She sat very still except for her mouth opening and closing like a fish. "Are you sure, Cat?" she asked finally.

"Yes, of course, I'm sure," he said. "I spoke with Father Brun earlier tonight and then with your father. They agreed to—"

"No," Anne said, "I meant, are you sure you want me to be your quartermaster? You could probably have anyone from the *Bruce*, except Stede, of course. But my skills are—"

"Your skills are superior to most any man I know," said Cat, standing and taking her hand. "I trust you, Anne. I trust your judgment. I trust you to tell me the truth even when I don't want to hear it. I've made my decision. Will you sail with me, Anne?"

Merry tears spilled down her cheeks. "Thank you," she whispered. It was all the answer he needed.

Cat bent down and gently kissed her hand. "Then, quartermaster Anne, I bid you good night. Sleep well, for tomorrow . . . we sail!"

Cat left Anne and was so buoyed by the night's events he practically floated back to his own chamber. But as he extinguished the candle and lay on his cot in the darkness, he began to wonder if choosing to sail with the Brethren had been the right decision. And now, he'd drawn Anne in as well. Wind whistled through his shutters, and Cat turned on his side. Somewhere out there the Merchant lurked.

6
DIPLOMACY

Sir Nigel stared at the prowling red lions emblazoned on the tapestry that hung behind the tall throne and felt nothing but contempt for King George. *A German king on the throne of England—ah! It's a disgrace.* And on top of that, Nigel had been forced to wait days to gain an audience with the king—delaying Nigel's mission and infuriating Thorne. Now, feeling exasperated, Nigel looked up at the king waiting to see if His Majesty would respond to his proposition.

But the king did not move. He scarcely seemed to be breathing, although it was hard to tell with what looked like forty pounds of satin and silk draped upon his plump frame. The king simply stared out into the cavernous throne room. From Sir Nigel's position, the king's gigantic nose resembled a pig's snout. Sir Nigel imagined the lions from the tapestry chasing down and devouring the pig-king from Germany who dared sit on the English throne. But Sir Nigel kept his scorn concealed, thinking it best not to offend a man who, at the snap of his pudgy fingers, could have a person's head separated from his body.

A door somewhere behind a curtain quickly opened and shut, and a narrow man entered the room and knelt before the king. He had bulging eyes and a hawkish profile, and his powdered gray wig seemed to not quite fit. The king muttered something, and the other man arose and turned to Sir Nigel. "I am dreadfully sorry to delay," he said. "I am Jacob Vogler. Please tell me what you want the king to know, and I will translate it for you."

"Translate?" echoed Sir Nigel.

"Yes, of course," Vogler replied. "His Majesty speaks English haltingly and prefers not to at all."

It was only with great concentration that Sir Nigel managed to close his gaping mouth. *King of England . . . and he doesn't speak English?* If not so thoroughly disgusted, Sir Nigel might have laughed. But at least that explained the king's silence.

King George said something to Vogler. The translator said, "His Majesty wishes to know why you have come without Commodore Blake."

"Your Majesty," began Sir Nigel, "it is about Commodore Brandon Blake that I have come. I am sad to admit that I traveled here alone from New Providence because I question Commodore Blake's judgment." He waited for Vogler to translate before continuing.

"Certainly, we all commend Commodore Blake for his previous accomplishments—capturing the elusive Bartholomew Thorne—chief among them. But that obsessive chase has taken its toll. I believe that Commodore Blake has misrepresented the current threat of piracy in the Atlantic and the Spanish Main. And . . . his misjudgment is costing England a lot of money." Sir Nigel waited for the king's reaction. When King George raised an eyebrow, Sir Nigel smiled.

"As you know," Sir Nigel went on, "England is now financing Commodore Blake's pirate-hunting fleet—their task: seek out the scoundrels of the sea and convert them into privateers, making the seas safe for travel and trade—a noble idea. Noble, but . . . unnecessary. When we defeated Bartholomew Thorne and his pirate fleet and recovered that wonderful treasure, we eliminated most of the pirates who might pose any threat. The few pirates left out there— the very ones Commodore Blake has been enlisting in his Wolf fleet—are mostly harmless rogues and drunkards. England is pouring its treasuries into the pockets of worthless men to squander on rum and other worldly pleasures."

When the translator finished, King George raised both eyebrows and spoke rapidly in German to Vogler. Then he looked to Sir Nigel. "The king wonders about Bartholomew Thorne," said the translator. "Commodore Blake's last correspondence indicated that it is possible Thorne is still alive."

"Your Majesty," said Sir Nigel to the interpreter, "I am certain Bartholomew Thorne is dead. No one could have survived the wave that inundated New Providence. I saw the carnage in those cells. Thorne was dismembered by the current and washed out to sea with the others." Sir Nigel waited to let that image sink in. "Bartholomew Thorne and the pirates that served him represented the greatest threat to your kingdom, but now that threat has passed. There is no longer cause to waste a river of treasure on those reprobates masquerading as pirate hunters."

King George sat up in his throne so abruptly that it started a wave of silk and satin rippling from his shoulders all the way to his knobby knees. He pounded a hammy fist on the armrest and said something urgent to Vogler.

"His Majesty is dismayed and demands to know what you suggest."

Sir Nigel smiled subtly. "Bring Commodore Blake and the other ranking officers back to England. Dissolve the Wolf fleet. Turn off the wasteful flow of riches and use the assets in whatever way suits you best, my King."

King George grinned. He spoke again to Vogler, who translated, "What about the treasure provided by the monks? They delivered those vaults of gold and jewels in good faith that we would pay the privateers."

Sir Nigel had anticipated that question. "Your Majesty, not one gold coin, not even a single gleaming stone would have returned from the Isle of Swords—if it were not for the expertise of the British Royal Navy. Our forces waylaid Bartholomew Thorne and reduced his fleet to flotsam. If that treasure belongs to anyone, it belongs to England . . . to you, my King."

The king chuckled at that, and his nostrils flared. Then Sir Nigel added, "Besides, I doubt very much if the monks presented us with all their treasure. Not even the monks would have so much . . . faith."

King George scratched the tip of his nose. "And what of the disgruntled privateers? They will certainly turn back to piracy," Vogler said for the king.

"Nothing our royal navy cannot handle. Again, we're not talking about intelligent, organized villains like Bartholomew Thorne or his lieutenant, Thierry Chevillard. The few pirates who have become the so-called pirate hunters are a bungling crew of louts who can barely make it out of port, much less mount a formidable resistance."

His royal scepter now firmly in his right hand, King George stood and spoke in a heavy German accent, "You speak wisdom. England has no need of this pirate-hunting fleet. And we certainly have no need to dump treasures into the ocean. I will do as you suggest. I will dissolve this Wolf fleet . . . immediately." He looked to Vogler, who nodded as if to say, "Yes, Your Majesty, you spoke well."

"Thank you, my King," said Sir Nigel with a polite bow. He turned to leave and walked down the red carpet toward the doors. He wondered if the king would suspect—suddenly, Vogler spoke up.

"Ah, Sir Nigel? A moment. The king wonders why you would offer such news and give such advice. You sailed with Commodore Blake, and your actions do not seem to benefit you in the least."

Sir Nigel put on a grim face, turned, and spoke solemnly. "I seek only to serve the best interests of England. My reward must only be to see my king and my country prosper." He paused. "But, should Commodore Blake be unreasonable toward Your Majesty, should he contend with you and continue to show a lack of sound judgment, I would consider it an honor if you would see fit to grant me command of the *Oxford*."

Vogler translated immediately. The king smiled broadly and nodded to Sir Nigel.

Sir Nigel nodded back. As he turned to leave, he thought, *Ah, my pig-king, we understand each other at last.*

7
The Judgments of Commodore Blake

Lady Dolphin Blake slowly lowered an old, leather-bound book and frowned at her husband. "I still don't understand why the first mention of me in my father's journals is when I was already two years of age."

"I'm quite sure I don't know, Dolphin" Commodore Brandon Blake replied. He frowned back at his wife over a steaming cup of tea. Sitting across from her on a blue and white striped couch in the parlor of their New Providence home, he added, "Maybe he didn't take to journaling about family right off."

"Brand, darling, don't be absurd," she replied, a glint in her green eyes. "He mentions mother quite frequently. Mother . . . and ships—but that's all there is for years. And then, there I am, already two. I tell you, some of my father's journals are missing."

Blake, who had recently returned to New Providence after an eight-hundred-mile hunt ending in the capture of the Spanish pirate

Inigo de Avila, had been hoping to relax with his wife. But ever since the surprise delivery of her father's journals, Dolphin had been as anxious as Brand had ever seen her. "You could be right, of course," he said. "But there are several large gaps between entries. More than a year in some cases. Perhaps he was just too busy to write."

"Too busy to write about his only child?" Dolphin brushed a lock of dark red hair out of her eyes and looked at Brand. "I can't imagine." Brand sighed. He'd developed his own suspicions, but, for Dolphin's protection, he was hesitant to reveal them—especially since there was no way to know for sure. "Don't let it trouble you so, my dear," he said, sipping his tea and avoiding her stare. "But rather think of this as a blessing. If old Mrs. Kravits hadn't realized what those journals were, she might have left them to rot or thrown them out. Now you have a treasure in your hands. Let it—"

"I want to go back to England," Dolphin said suddenly.

"What?"

"I want to visit Mrs. Kravits. I want to search my old home in London. My father may have other documents—maybe even more journals hidden away."

"Darling," Brand said. "You know my commission. I have a fleet to command and a disorganized band of pirate hunters to coordinate. I couldn't possibly leave now."

"Then let me go without you," she pleaded. "There are ships coming and going nearly every day. Please, I need to do this."

There came a sharp rap at the door. Brand was thankful for the interruption. He patted Dolphin's hand and then left the parlor. Dolphin thought it was dreadfully quiet. She wondered what her husband would decide. Angry voices emanated from the main hall. A shout, and then a door slammed.

Brand returned. His cheeks were flushed, his brow was knotted, and his eyes looked small. In his right hand he held a large, rolled parchment. "It seems you shall have your wish," he said rapidly, his words clipped. "His Majesty, King George, has commanded that I bring the *Oxford* back home . . . immediately."

Nathaniel Hopper waited for nightfall to clamber down from his roost in the bell tower on the British fort at New Providence. His face and skin were grimy, his clothes soiled and dark. He was a shadow creeping along the roof of the British fort. For many months, none of the soldiers had noted Hopper's movements in the alleys, along the walls, or on the docks. One of the prisoners had seen him once, caught him scurrying past the cells with a bunch of bananas. "Some kind of giant, deformed monkey, it was," the prisoner had later explained to the guards. "It looks at me with eyes big as oranges and then climbs right up the wall!"

Hopper laughed at the memory. The guards had laughed too, but they didn't put any stock into the prisoner's claim. That is, until people began to notice things going missing. Hopper had mostly stolen food, usually in small quantities, just what he needed for the day. But the paring knife he couldn't resist. The hat too. A yard of cloth. A small spyglass. A few books to help pass the time. It had been relatively easy, and Hopper's nest in the tower became littered with all sorts of knickknacks.

The soldiers had become much more watchful since then. And that was okay. Hopper didn't need those other things. But food and fresh water were another matter. First, they tried moving the food storage two or three times, but Hopper always sniffed it out. When that didn't work, the Brits had begun posting guards around the food—day and night. Now Hopper had to scramble just for scraps.

He'd thought about going into town. There would be much easier pickings there, but no, he couldn't do that. He felt sure he'd die, if he did that. Of course he'd die, if he didn't eat. It had been three days since his last meal—an apple he'd fished out of the harbor. Hopper knew, risk or not, it was time.

Hopper saw the masts of the huge British ship of the line before he even got to the edge of the roof. Staying low and sliding his knapsack noiselessly along the roof tiles, Hopper crawled until he could see the ship. The HMS *Oxford* was as proud a ship as Hopper had ever seen—and perfect for his needs. *Shouldn't be too hard to stay hidden on a ship that big*, Hopper thought. His mouth watered as he considered the endless array of provisions he'd seen loaded aboard all afternoon and into the night. And, as far as Hopper was concerned, the most important thing about the *Oxford* was that the ship was bound for London that very night.

Hopper thought about London as he secured both ends of his knapsack, hoisted it on his shoulder, and began the long climb down to the docks. He hadn't been back to England in three years. He had no idea if he'd know how to get back to the row house where he had been born and raised prior to coming to the islands. He thought if he could just find the old house, maybe that nice lady next door, Miss Hamilton, would take him in and take care of him. It was a lot of ifs, but that was all he had.

Hopper slid down a drainpipe and crouched behind a rain barrel. He scurried over to a carriage and ducked under the bellies of a pair of horses that smelled almost as bad as he did. They didn't seem to mind their visitor. Hopper watched the guards, waiting for the right moment to sprint to the mooring lines. But he had to pause a moment to look at the ship. This close, the *Oxford* looked even more gigantic—like a small city floating in the harbor. Each of the masts were shrouded in rigging and crossed with huge spars and tightly furled sails. Lanterns glimmered like fireflies along the vast deck. And there were too many cannons to count.

Originally, Hopper had planned to clamber in through one of the cannon bays, but to do that he'd have to get wet. Hopper didn't like getting wet. So he'd decided to take his chances with the mooring lines.

Other than some painful splattered jellyfish smeared on the rope, the mooring line Hopper had selected was a good one. It led up to the top rail and ducked right under a web of rigging. Hopper found the deck on the back of the *Oxford* relatively quiet, but there were several sailors near the two hatches he could see from his vantage. There'd be no way to get past them. He needed to find another way down below. He looked up the rigging and saw that it stretched halfway up the mainmast and ended at a crow's-nest. Hopper figured he could get a better look at the deck from up there. He reached over to the rigging and pulled himself on. Then he wriggled all the way up to the crow's-nest.

From the small round platform halfway up the tall mast Hopper could see most of the deck. He gazed down and spotted at least a dozen hatches that looked promising—most within a few yards of a strand of rigging he could access from the crow's-nest. In fact, Hopper realized he could get to almost any part of the aft half of the *Oxford* from the crow's-nest. He decided he'd make for a little cargo hatch on the portside of the ship.

But as he turned, he looked out over the British fort. He saw the bell tower. It had been his home ever since the big wave. He'd celebrated his tenth birthday in that tower. Then, even though he knew he shouldn't, he looked past the fort to the sleeping town of New Providence. He could just make out the old gray road. He followed its curving line down into the valley, blinked, and saw a shadowy memory of his father walking with him back from fishing. They were laughing and telling stories, making plans for the next time. He saw them walk up to the first cottage on the left. There was warm yellow light. He knew his mother would be in there, busy with a pudding or some other sweet treat.

Hopper blinked again. He missed his parents. A tear trailed down his cheek.

He slumped down in the crow's-nest, exhausted from the climb and maybe more from the memory. Hopper closed his eyes and slept.

There came a quick rap at Commodore Blake's stateroom door, then a voice. "Sir?"

Blake recognized the voice of his new quartermaster, Ezekiel Jordan. "Come in, come in," said Commodore Blake.

The door opened and Blake's new quartermaster stepped partially in. He saw that Commodore Blake had company and said, "Beg your pardon, sir, I didn't know the missis was in here with you. I'll come back later."

"Oh, please do come in," said Lady Dolphin. "You're always welcome."

"I agree," said Commodore Blake. "Mister Jordan, what can I do for you?"

Mr. Jordan's face reddened. "Well, Commodore, we have a little problem . . . a very little problem."

Just then a high, heavily accented English voice said, "I ain't that little!"

Mr. Jordan opened the door the rest of the way, and at his elbow stood the strangest lad Commodore Blake had ever seen. He was completely bald and had no eyebrows to speak of either. His skin was so tan and caked with dark mud that his blue eyes sparkled like gems uncovered in a mine.

"We found him in the crow's-nest on the mizzenmast. He was fast asleep and right hard to wake."

"You mean to say, Mister Jordan, no one went to the crow's-nest until just now, four hours after leaving port?"

Jordan shifted uneasily. "Well, ol' Timmons was up on the main-mast, we didn't see no reason to—"

"Oh, the poor thing," said Dolphin. She went to the boy, knelt beside him, and patted him on the shoulder. "He's naught but skin and bones wrapped in dirty rags."

"Wiry skin and bones," said the quartermaster. "He near kicked me off the crow's-nest when I tried to grab him. Slick as an eel, he is."

"A stowaway?" asked Commodore Blake. Jordan nodded. The Commodore stood, walked around his desk, and stooped to look more closely at the lad. "Are you sick, boy?"

"No, Guv'nor, leastways not anyfin' you kin' catch."

"What happened to your hair, your eyebrows?"

The lad looked away and made a loud swallowing sound. "I don't rightly know," he said quietly. "It all fell out . . . after the wave."

"How terrible," said Dolphin. "You were on New Providence when it flooded?"

The boy nodded and blinked.

Commodore Blake asked, "Where are your—?" He realized suddenly, and said no more.

Tears left muddy streaks down the lad's face. Dolphin thought her heart would burst for this unfortunate lad. "What is your name?" she asked.

"Nathaniel."

"All right, Nathaniel, we'll just—"

"Nobody calls me Nathaniel."

"Oh, well, what should we call you?"

"Hopper," he said. "It's my surname, actually. It's what I go by."

"He had this knapsack with him," said Mr. Jordan. "I think we found the monkey that's been around the fort pinching everything that's left untended."

Commodore Blake looked at the lad. "You've been living alone at the fort?" Hopper nodded. "All this time?" Hopper nodded again. "Resourceful lad. We could use someone like you on this trip."

"Yes, Guv'nor," said Hopper. "I'm not afraid to work. I'll work hard, sir, I will."

"And through your hard work, you'll pay back what you owe?" Blake asked.

Hopper nodded so hard and so many times Dolphin thought he might harm himself. She gently stopped his chin.

"Right then," said the commodore. "Hopper, you are officially a deck hand on the HMS *Oxford*. Mister Jordan, see to it that he's washed and fitted with new clothing."

"That won't be necessary, my husband," said Dolphin. "I'll see to it myself."

"As you wish, my dear," he replied. A smile tugged at the corners of his mouth. He marveled at his wife's tender heart. She smiled sweetly back and then whisked young Hopper out of the room.

As soon as he felt Lady Dolphin and the lad were well out of range, Mr. Jordan said, "That's not what we usually do with stowaways, sir."

"True, Jordan," said the commodore. "But Hopper is not the usual stowaway. There is no malice or mischief in his face. Only need . . . and hurt. The sea took his parents, and yet he survived. We would do well to have a lad with such spirit among us. And I have a feeling about him."

"A feeling, sir?"

"I know, I am not usually prone to hunches. But I feel it now as strong as the sea breeze: young Hopper will make a difference in this world."

8

AMONG THE RAUKAR

After a three-day journey aboard the *Talon*, a forty-gun barque purchased in England, Bartholomew Thorne and a skeleton crew of twenty men neared Gotland Island. The vast island, just fifty miles from the Swedish mainland, had been a center of trade and commerce in the Baltic Sea for hundreds of years. Through the years it had hosted many peoples and occupying forces until finally falling back under the domain of the Swedish in 1645, less than one hundred years ago.

But on the south side of the island, far from the teeming markets of Visby, the island's largest city, dwelt a people who because of their ferocity and iron will had been left alone by those who came and went—and largely by time itself. The Raukar, or "stone ones" as they were sometimes called, were all direct descendants of Viking warriors. Bartholomew Thorne was counting on that for more than one reason.

The *Talon* was Thorne's newest ship since the British destroyed the *Raven*, anchored in Sigvard Bay a few hundred yards from the shore. Massive limestone rock formations stood out like eerie pale faces in the dark water as Thorne's cutter approached the shore of Gotland Island. "Reminds me of the shards," muttered Thorne.

"Shards, sir?" asked Edward Teach, Thorne's new quartermaster.

"Nothing." Thorne let his mind drift for a moment, replaying his failed attempt to plunder Constantine's Treasure from the Isle of Swords. His carefully sculpted plan had crumbled because of one man: Declan Ross. No, that wasn't quite right, he reminded himself. If it had not been for the efforts of his own son, Griffin, Thorne by now would most likely own the Atlantic and the Spanish Main. That day would come, he knew. Thorne fingered his new bleeding stick by his side. Ross and Griffin would feel its bite.

Thorne's landing party came ashore as the sun set. They kindled torches immediately and passed beneath a bone-white arch, the ruined remains of what must have once been a grand quay. Though Thorne had never been to the island before, it felt familiar to him . . . like a sort of homecoming. He led his men over a rubble-strewn hill and then down a winding path into a heavily forested valley. Carrying a belted leather satchel with as much care as he could, Teach hobbled along behind his captain. Teach was a big, broad-shouldered man, and strong, but even for him, the case was heavy.

"Sir?"

"Yes, Mister Teach," Thorne replied over his shoulder.

"I'm not complainin', sir, nothin' like that," he said, trying not to grunt from the strain. "But, well, what's in this here satchel?"

Thorne stopped but did not turn around. "That, Mister Teach, is the only thing that will get us off this island alive."

Thorne resumed his confident pace. Resolving to let his arms burst before he would drop the satchel, Teach hurried to catch up with his captain.

As the trees began to thin, Thorne and his band began to see flickers of orange through the trunks ahead. An unpleasant sweet smell drifted on the air, and small flies buzzed angrily by. Thorne led his men from beneath the canopy of a huge, sprawling tree. Standing before them suddenly, as if it had been dropped from the sky, was a massive gray fortress. Tall, octagonal towers—all crenelated and crowned with torches—stood between dense and winding expanses of wall. The walls wound back behind the tree line, but it was impossible to tell how far back they went. A relatively small gatehouse waited in the shadows between the two tallest towers, but, other than the torches, there was no sign that any living being remained in this castle.

Thorne hesitated only a moment at the tree line, then marched forward. The others, feeling vulnerable in the open, followed closely behind Captain Thorne. As a line of long arrows peppered the ground a few paces in front of them, all came to a sudden, heart-stopping halt. All but Thorne jumped when a similar line appeared behind them. So many were the shafts and so precise their spacing that it seemed a short fence had risen up from the ground in front and behind them.

"Stanna!" a deep voice commanded from somewhere high on one of the towers. The voice rang out in a language no one but Thorne understood, but the arrows made the meaning clear enough. Thorne and his men scanned the towers and walls and waited. Thorne was not so daunted, and he took one step forward.

"Stanna!" commanded the voice once more. "Om du ar inte av akta blodsforvant, maste ni vanda. Annars moter du samma odet som dom andra!"

Thorne glanced back over his shoulder and up into the massive tree behind them. He laughed quietly to himself and said, "*Humph . . . very nice.*"

"What?" asked Teach. "What did he say?"

Thorne looked at his new quartermaster. The Merchant had recommended Teach highly, but he was very young. Thorne wondered how he'd react. "The guard tells us to halt and return the way we came. If we are not of true blood, we will join the others." Thorne pointed up into the tree. Everyone turned. Having looked at the torches, the men found their night vision impaired. It was impossible to discern any detail. But soon, dark masses began to materialize, hanging from all but the smallest of boughs. Most took them to be some kind of hanging lichen or moss, but as their vision cleared even more, they began to recognize vacant, scowling faces. Most of Thorne's men gasped as they realized that the skeletal remains of dozens of men hung from the tree limbs like some morbid type of decoration.

Only Teach remained calm. He turned back to Thorne and said, "So that explains the smell."

Thorne smiled. "Perhaps, Mister Teach, you'll be worth keeping around after all." Edward Teach turned his head and glanced sideways at his captain.

Thorne took the satchel from his quartermaster. From it, he withdrew a thick, leather-bound book. He held the volume aloft and answered in a halting version of the same language. Then, to the horror of his men, Thorne kicked aside the arrows in front of him and marched forward. He held the book open and gazed up at the tower as if daring some unseen archer to loose a shaft. Thorne disappeared into the shadows of the gatehouse. He waited in the darkness for several moments until, at last, a great grinding came from within, and one of the huge arched doors began to open.

Teach and the others watched the shadows and waited for some sign. At last their captain emerged and motioned for them to approach. As they neared the walls, they saw silhouettes between the torches, tall men, motionless and silent. Thorne met them beneath the gatehouse and . . . he was not alone.

Standing behind Captain Thorne, and yet a head taller, was a warrior bearing a long spear and a stout round shield. Clad in a jerkin of chain mail with massive bare shoulders that shone in the torchlight, he seemed a storybook character come to life. His conical helmet stretched down in a kind of mask. And his eyes were like Thorne's, pale blue but merciless and cold.

"This is Guthrum," said Thorne. "He is the door warden of the Raukar. We will follow him in silence and make no sudden movements."

Some of Thorne's men began untying their baldrics and removing their swords. Thorne shook his head. "Keep your weapons," he chided them. "The Raukar have no fear of us."

Guthrum led Thorne and his men down a stone hall and out again under the night sky into a compound of houses. These were tall, built of dark timber, and unadorned except for gilded geometric patterns on the eaves of their high roofs. Each building was as long as a galleon and looked to be able to house hundreds of warriors. Thorne was impressed. *If these warriors sail as well as the Vikings of old*, Thorne mused, *then I shall command an unassailable fleet.*

They passed eight such houses until they came to one grander than the rest. Guards were posted, one on either side of a pair of massive wooden doors. Each guard inclined his head as Guthrum led Thorne and the others inside. The smell of rich smoke hit them first. More like the smoke of a cooking fire, it was not unpleasant, but it was pervasive.

They passed through a small anteroom and then into a vast, vaulted chamber lit with a golden light from dozens of mounted torches and a crackling fire that burned in the center of the room. Many warriors like Guthrum, as well as tall women adorned with colorful, multilayered dresses and glistening jewelry, dwelled in this place. Some stood in clusters, some sat at long tables, and others reclined on the stone floor. But all of them turned to see the new-comers, and in their collective gaze, welcome could not be found.

Guthrum brought them through the crowd of suspicious eyes, past the loud fire, and to the far end of the building. Tapestries bordered with more intertwining geometric patterns hung there, each one depicting a myriad of images: Viking ships full of warriors landing on anonymous shores; fierce, curling serpents doing battle with a hammer-wielding hero; and even a strange scene where a mace-wielding champion had his hand caught in the mouth of a gigantic snarling wolf. Thorne recognized the figure as Tyr, the Norse god of war. Beneath this massive image rested three magnificent chairs on a raised platform. They were thronelike, made of dark red wood and gilded intricately with crisscrossing strands of gold.

A broad warrior sat in the leftmost chair. This man wore a stud-ded silver helmet and had long black hair that draped over his shoulders. He was lordly and fierce and wore a triple necklace of sharp, curving white talons . . . or perhaps, teeth. Thorne took this monstrous man to be the chieftain of the Raukar.

Guthrum spoke to the man, and he glanced down at Thorne and laughed. Thorne understood the insult, but kept his tongue for the moment. The dark-haired man stroked his beard and then stood at last. He walked behind the tapestries and disappeared. A few moments later he reappeared with two others, a man and a woman. Thorne knew immediately that he had been mistaken about the chieftain, for surely this new man was he, and the lady his wife. The lord wore no helmet, but a golden circlet rested on his brow. He had large, deep-set green eyes and a mane of hair both blond and white. Upon his massive chest lay a dark corselet of mail whose rings were so small and intricate that none could see where one began or ended. His golden beard was forked and the two ends were braided. A silver pendant shaped like a hammer hung from his neck. He looked like he'd weathered many years, but his muscular build and the great axe he carried suggested that age had not diminished him in the least.

The woman at his side had the same ageless quality. Her face was smooth and serene. A silver circlet rested on her forehead above her deep blue eyes, and her hair was woven into a long braid that wound down her neck and over her shoulder. She seemed queenly and wise and placed her hand lightly on the forearm of her husband.

Once the lord and lady were seated, the dark-haired warrior with the tooth necklace took his place at their right hand. He turned to the lord and spoke gruffly. Thorne had had enough of his coarse humor, so he spoke in their language, "Ni skamtar pa egen risk—"

"I speak your tongue, outlander, . . . far better than you speak mine," said the chieftain. "Perhaps Bjorn's humor is lost on you, but it is a joy to me. And in the abode of the Raukar, I assure you, peril lies most heavily upon you." His stare burned like coals and lingered on Thorne for several moments. Thorne did not look away. "I am Hrothgar, steward of this people, and this is my wife, Fleur, who answers to no man but me. You are fortunate to gain audience here. Guthrum believes you have a claim. If that is so, then state your claim now, for my patience is fleeting."

Thorne had strangled the last man who spoke to him with such impudence, but greater diplomacy was called for here. "Lord Hrothgar," Thorne began, "it is indeed a rare honor to stand before you, but forgive me if I do not quake in fear or bow my head as one of lesser standing. I am Bartholomew Thorne, or the name your people might more readily understand: Bartholomew Gunnarson Thorne."

Hrothgar raised an eyebrow, out of amusement or interest, Thorne could not tell, so he continued. "I am descended in an unbroken line from Eiríkr Thorvaldsson, and I have come to the Raukar, not to beg, but to lead them." An angry murmur surrounded Thorne and his men. Apparently many of the Raukar could understand English.

Hrothgar was unmoved. He motioned to Guthrum, who took Thorne's book and laid it in his chieftain's lap. Hrothgar traced the border of the thick volume with his finger and then gently opened the book. He smiled as he slowly looked over the account of Erik the Red's many voyages. Then he found the diagram in the back, the family tree. Thorne watched Hrothgar's finger descend to the bottom, watched him pause, and watched his face grow taut. The chieftain whispered something to Bjorn, who practically leaped from his chair. He once again disappeared behind the tapestry and returned with another book, which he handed to his leader. Hrothgar opened the second volume to a well-worn page and began to look back and forth between the two books. He grunted something unintelligible and handed the second book back to Bjorn.

"Bartholomew Gunnarson is a name of pure lineage," Hrothgar said. "It is a high name and demands authority, but if you are indeed he, you must know that Hrothgar is the lord of the Raukar!" The room exploded with noise as swords smacked upon shields and the blunt ends of spears were bounced hard on the ground. Lady Fleur's heavy gaze roamed over Thorne thoughtfully.

"I don't wish to be called king or prince," shouted Thorne. "Only captain. I want to lead you by the seas to battle, lead you to the grandeur that harsh ice and the outlanders took away from you hundreds of years ago."

The crowd went silent, and Hrothgar's face reddened as he stood. "Our former kinsmen in the north have forsaken our gods, but the Raukar have endured. The Raukar serve the mighty Tyr!" Hrothgar slammed the flat of his axe against the tapestry behind him. The warriors bellowed their cheers.

"Yes!" Thorne exclaimed, his raspy voice rising above the din. "The god of war who alone of all the gods would place his hand in the jaws of Fenris—it is this courage that I seek. The courage to go to war against the enemy who surrounds you. You say the Raukar have not forsaken Tyr and yet," Thorne paused to choose his words carefully, "and yet, here you are hidden away. A proud race, yes, but strangely dormant as those who do not follow Tyr own the seas and grow stronger."

The tumult grew loud behind them again, but this time there was more confusion as not all were in agreement. Finally, Lady Fleur raised a hand. The crowd went silent. "I do not trust this man," said the Lady of the Raukar, ". . . whatever the books of lineage may say. His words ring true but appeal only to emotion, bringing dissent even into the hall of Hrothgar. I say he is a fraud. This book proves nothing."

"My lady is wise," said Hrothgar. "The Raukar have survived, nay flourished, these many years out of devotion to our beliefs. What did you think, Bartholomew Thorne . . . that we would blindly welcome you and give you a place of honor?"

Thorne stared evenly at the chieftain, but he was not worried. Teach was. The quartermaster admired his captain but began to think that it was a grand mistake intruding on these proud Vikings.

Teach scanned the room for a quick exit. He had several ceramic grenades in a pouch at his side and wondered if he'd have time to light one before one of the Raukar ran him through with a long spear.

"Look around you, Thorne," Hrothgar continued. "Each warrior in my hall has earned his honor, not with his mouth, but by his own sweat and blood. Eiríkr Thorvaldsson is a high lineage, but Lady Fleur is right to question your words, for any man may utter such. You must prove your worth."

"I am willing," said Thorne.

Hrothgar nodded. "We have a saying among the Raukar: True blood will be proved when it is spilled. If you are truly a descendant of Eiríkr Thorvaldsson, then you will prove it in the Bearpit." A roar of agreement went up from the Raukar crowd. Teach lowered his hand toward the grenades, but a look from Thorne froze the quartermaster in place.

Hrothgar silenced the room as he stood. "In the Bearpit, you will be tested in single combat by a warrior of my choosing." Again the crowds became frenzied, but this time it was warriors volunteering to do battle. Hrothgar said, "Nay, my valiant Raukar, if this test is to ring true, if we are to discover whether Eiríkr Thorvaldsson lives in this man's blood, he must face an ultimate challenge. For his opponent, I therefore choose: Bjorn Ingalad!"

The crowd became ominously quiet. Bjorn stood up from his chair by Hrothgar's side and glared at Thorne.

"As is our custom," said Hrothgar, reaching into a black pouch at his side, "the winner will receive this!" He held aloft a slim, curved spike. "This bear tooth belongs to the man who emerges from the Bearpit alive!"

Bartholomew Thorne noted once more the necklace worn by his

opponent. Three rows of bear teeth—that was how many men Bjorn had slain in the Bearpit. But rather than fear welling up inside of him, Thorne felt the lust for blood. He turned to Hrothgar and said, "Bjorn seems a useful man. Are you sure you want me to kill him?"

9
THE BEARPIT

With just a sharp sliver of the moon visible overhead, Hrothgar and Fleur led their champion, his opponent, and all the others from Hrothgar's hall. Horns sounded, and people began to stream out of their long houses and funnel into many paths. Like spokes attached to a hub, all paths led to a massive building at the center of their land. Unlike the other structures, this building was round and had a stone foundation. As the procession approached, two dark iron doors loomed before them. Hrothgar removed a long bronze key from his belt, turned it in the lock, and threw open the heavy doors. "May the courage of Tyr course in the veins of all who enter this place!" Hrothgar shouted.

Raukar warriors kindled torches all around the circumference of this vast round chamber. The ceiling was very high and vaulted, like the dome of a cathedral, but made entirely of wood. Except for a wide outer hall, sections of cunningly wrought grandstands filled the round building, rising up to within a dozen feet of its high ceiling. And as Hrothgar led Thorne and the others into the center, the Raukar poured into the stands and stood waiting.

In the middle of the grandstands, a great circle of the floor, at least forty feet in diameter, was cut away, revealing a vast black hollow. It yawned like the mouth of a gigantic beast and, in the dark, seemed bottomless. Hrothgar took a torch from one of his men and lit six fire pits that surrounded the great opening. Angry orange light flooded into the chamber below. Thorne and his men stepped to the edge and looked down. They saw walls made with layers of stone as if the chamber were a wide well. But between the stones, protruding from the mortar in irregular patterns, were dozens of long spikes, sharp as dagger blades and white as if made of ivory or bone.

"The Bearpit!" announced Hrothgar with his arms outstretched. He lowered his hands, and the hundreds of Raukar who stood in the stands took their seat. "Ever has this chamber purified our race. For two men may enter, but only one man, the strongest, most cunning man emerges." Hrothgar summoned Bartholomew Thorne and his opponent to approach. Then he said to them, "Bjorn Ingalad, you know well the rigors of the Bearpit." Bjorn fingered the bear teeth around his neck and grinned at his inexperienced opponent.

Hrothgar continued. "But for you, outlander, know this: Once you enter the Bearpit, you will not leave until one of you is dead. There is no surrender, no submission, no change of heart. So I offer you now this last mercy: Bartholomew Thorne, admit you are a liar or worse—a coward—and I will allow you and your men to depart with your lives. Should you fail, your men will die with you."

"I am neither a liar nor a coward," said Thorne. "I pronounce again my claim to lead the Raukar to their rightful place in the world. I accept the terms of the Bearpit—and my fate."

Teach and the other pirates shifted uneasily where they stood. Their lives now depended on Bartholomew Thorne.

"Very well," said Hrothgar grimly. Then he pointed past Thorne into the pit. "At the base of the walls you will find all manner of weapon: sword, axe, spear, bludgeon—these you may use at any time in the course of combat. But you may not use your firearms."

"I have the only weapon I need," said Thorne, opening his coat to reveal his bleeding stick. Bjorn examined Thorne's weapon curiously and shrugged. Thorne removed three pistols from his belt and handed them to Guthrum. He gave his outer jacket to Mr. Teach.

Hrothgar loosed a blast from his war horn, and six Raukar warriors wheeled in a strange device. It was mostly made of wood, but had a pulley system of some sort running along a lengthy arm that reached out from a locking hinge. Hrothgar stared into Bjorn's eyes and then to Thorne. "Die well," he said.

The six warriors maneuvered the pulley device to the edge of the Bearpit. A looped rope dangled high from its long, wooden arm. Bjorn approached, and once the others lowered the wooden arm, he put a foot into the loop and grasped the rope. Two men turned iron cranks and, in so doing, lifted Bjorn into the air. Then they swung him out over the hole in the ground and lowered their champion gently into the Bearpit.

The Raukar repeated the process for Thorne—though with much less care. Bartholomew Thorne stepped awkwardly out of the rope loop and watched as it was withdrawn. Thorne loosed his bleeding stick from its holster and looked at the spikes all around. They were longer than they had first appeared, each one more than a foot in length and sharpened to a fine point. Where each spike inserted into the mortar, there was a ring of dark red.

Excitement buzzed from the stands above, and Thorne looked

up to see the eager faces of this people. Men, women, and children, descended from the most efficient warriors the world had ever known, all looked down with great anticipation. Then Thorne looked up and saw a mural of a fearsome warrior-god on the domed ceiling above the pit. This being had greatly exaggerated musculature and swung his mighty ball and chain weapon, toppling a massive tower. But the most unusual feature of this deity was that he had but one hand. Thorne thought back to the tapestry of Tyr, the god of war, with his hand in the great wolf's mouth.

Chanting began overhead, and Hrothgar sounded his horn once more. Bjorn charged. He lashed out with the axe. Thorne ducked, and the axe whooshed above his head. Thorne knew the axe would return low, so he snapped a sharp kick into the side of Bjorn's knee. The huge warrior crumpled for a moment, one hand clutching his knee. The crowd above gasped. Thorne swung the bleeding stick at the side of Bjorn's head. But he only caught Bjorn's helmet, sending it clattering across the stone floor.

Bjorn stood tall and grinned. "Not so easily, outlander!" he barked. His axe came on again swiftly. One slash to Thorne's gut, and then back across near his chin. Thorne leaped one attack and batted away the other, but Bjorn threw a mighty punch with his free hand, connecting with Thorne's jaw and knocking him onto his back. The crowd roared.

Thorne rose quickly and checked his periphery to measure his distance from the wall of spikes. He had about six feet behind him, but that was all. Bjorn came on again, and his axe crashed down. Thorne blocked with his bleeding stick, making sure to catch the haft with his own. Again and again, Bjorn chopped, trying to strike Thorne's weapon with the blade and break it asunder. But each time, Thorne moved inside and forced the wood to strike wood.

Bjorn grew angry and unleashed a savage chop. When Thorne blocked it, the iron blade of the axe snapped off and whizzed by Thorne's ear. Thorne had a brief advantage. He swung his bleeding stick at Bjorn's midsection, but the warrior dodged backward. Thorne swung again at his enemy's stomach but followed it with a power- ful kick. The blow connected with the Viking's gut and sent Bjorn stumble-stepping backward to within a few feet of the spikes. He stopped easily in time, glanced over his shoulder at the spikes, and laughed.

The crowd grew restless, for they had not expected the battle to take so long. They cheered Bjorn on and yelled insults at his smaller enemy. Bjorn reached down and picked up a long spear. Thorne rec- ognized the trouble coming. With the spear, Bjorn had tremendous reach and would seek to drive Thorne into the spikes. But Thorne had his own attack that his opponent would never expect. He just needed the right opportunity.

As expected, Bjorn thrust the spear at Thorne. He dodged and parried, never backing up but moving left to right in a circle. Bjorn's skill with the spear was considerable, and he began to press in on Thorne without fear. He jabbed high as if he might ram the spear- head into Thorne's skull, but the moment he missed, he whirled the opposite end of the spear around and cracked it across Thorne's shoulder. Thorne rolled sideways, but not shallow enough. When he stood, one of the spikes tore through his clothing and ripped down his back.

The pain burned as if a branding iron had seared his back. Thorne growled. Moving quickly he pressed a sliding latch near the end of his bleeding stick and turned the spiked head counter- clockwise. As Bjorn was charging, the spiked head of Thorne's weapon came free. It dropped nearly to the ground, attached to the handle by a length of chain. Thorne began to whirl the mace-like weapon at his side.

The sharp tip of Bjorn's spearhead grazed Thorne's shoulder, but Thorne swung his weapon around and caught Bjorn solidly in the middle of his back. If it had not been for the chain mail, Thorne would have torn loose a chunk of his enemy's flesh. As it was, the blow was swift and hard. Bjorn groaned, arched his back, and turned to face Thorne. The crowd chanted in a frenzy above.

The temptation grew for the Raukar champion to bull-rush the enemy who had wounded him. But Bjorn was no amateur, and he was no fool. He knew that momentum in the Bearpit was a danger-ous—and perhaps, deadly—force. The plan crystallized in his mind, and Bjorn knew just what to do. Keeping the spearhead way out in front, Bjorn came after Thorne. He jabbed at Thorne high, then low, keeping Thorne moving backward and waiting for him to counter. At last, Thorne began to swing his flail weapon again. Bjorn dodged and ducked and was rewarded for his patience. Thorne swung his bleeding stick high overhead, and Bjorn blocked by holding his spear horizontally with both hands. The heavy head of Thorne's weapon wrapped itself around the shaft of the spear. Bjorn summoned all of his superior strength and jerked the spear backward, wrenching the bleeding stick from Thorne's hands. Only . . . Thorne did not let go.

Instead, Thorne leaped and let Bjorn's strength propel him up and over his enemy's head. Thorne released the handle of his weapon and dropped down behind the stunned Raukar warrior. Thorne drove a thunderous kick between Bjorn's shoulder blades, and Bjorn careened forward—into the spikes. The raucous Bearpit fell as silent as a mausoleum. Bartholomew Thorne untangled his bleeding stick from his enemy's spear and then stepped into the rope loop.

He was lifted out of the Bearpit, and the chamber around him filled with furtive whispers. Some wept for Bjorn and uttered curses at the outlander, but many more spoke fearfully. Some pointed to the mural on the dome. One warrior said, "See how he wields his mace. He is a messenger from Tyr!"

When Thorne stepped off the rope, he received his pistols from a thunderstruck Guthrum and his coat from a grinning Mr. Teach. He then turned to face Hrothgar and Lady Fleur. "Bjorn was a magnificent warrior," Thorne said. "We might have used such as he as we sail to conquer the Atlantic."

Tears ran angrily down Lady Fleur's blood red cheeks. She looked as if she might scream, but Hrothgar laid a hand on her shoulder. He stood, and his great chest heaved as he spoke. "Bjorn died valiantly," he said. "The Valkyries will bear him to Valhalla." His eyes seemed to gaze right through Thorne into a realm that no one else could see. But he blinked, and his back straightened. "The Raukar have hoped for such a day as this for six hundred years. Long have we prepared for the day when we might burst forth from seclusion and reclaim what has been stolen from us."

"Lord Hrothgar," said Thorne, letting the chain of his weapon fall a link at a time into the handle, "today is that day."

Hrothgar nodded, slowly at first, then with greater and greater conviction. The warriors in the chamber began to pound their fists to their chests and stamp their feet. They began to sing in their language, and even to Mr. Teach and the other sailors who knew nothing of that tongue, it sounded like an anthem or a call to arms.

Hrothgar raised his arms for silence and said to Thorne, "To do what you propose, we must wage the war of all wars. The British have become a force to be reckoned with."

Thorne screwed the spiked head back onto his bleeding stick and said, "I have a plan for the British."

10

CHASING GHOSTS

Thorne's gone back to Dominica?" said Ross.

Stede's only reply was a long, exasperated sigh. His hands never left the ship's wheel, and he stared straight ahead at the sparkling blue sea.

"If this wind keeps up, we could make it to Roseau by sundown." Ross wrung his beard between thumb and fingers and stared at his quartermaster. "Well, are you going to answer me?"

"Declan," said Stede, "what do ya want from me, mon? For the last six months, we b' sailing all over the Caribbean. Trinidad, Rogue's Cay, Death's Head Island—we been to them all and not a sign of that outrageous mon! We b' wasting time and provisions."

"It is not a waste," Ross argued. Sweat beaded on his forehead. "Thorne is still out there somewhere. And we have to—"

Stede interrupted. "Do ya want to know where we can b' finding Bartholomew Thorne? On New Providence, that b' where."

"But the British have rebuilt the fort," said Ross, puzzled. "Why would he—"

Stede shook his head. "Have ya no sense, mon? I said New Providence because that b' where Thorne's body lies—in the shallows or strung across a blasted reef. The wave took him, Declan. And we best b' looking after other concerns . . . rather than chasing ghosts."

Ross retied the green bandana around his forehead. "Stede, my friend," he began, his voice tight and words clipped. "We've sailed together a long time. Through storm and cannon fire . . . you've always trusted me. I need you to trust me now."

"I b' trusting the real Declan Ross," Stede said. "But ya have not been yerself, mon. And since we left Anne and Cat with the monks, ya b' warse."

"Blast it, Stede!" Ross smacked a fist into the palm of his hand. "The sea did not take Bartholomew Thorne. He's alive. I don't know how I know. I just do."

The two old friends gritted their teeth and looked away from each other. For several awkward moments neither said a thing. Mumbling something about not having enough herbs for the stew, Nubby climbed up the ladder to the quarterdeck. But when he saw the smoldering look on the captain's face, he quickly disappeared back down the ladder.

"Look," said Ross, "I know I've been hard on you and the crew. I know we're all worn down to the edge. But think of Abigail. Think of Midge and Cromwell. Their blood—and that of hundreds of others—is on Thorne's hands. If there's a chance he's still out there, we've got to find him."

Stede nodded, but said nothing.

"Just sail us to Dominica," Ross implored. "Then I'll give us all a nice long break."

Stede's dark brow lowered, and he turned to face his captain. "Not good enough," he said. "I'll sail us to Roseau, but then ya b' needin' to give up this mad chase once and for all. No more talking about Thorne, no more goin' to his old haunts—ya hear? No more of it. Oh, and we b' take that nice long break too. Antigua's nice this time of year. Them's my terms, Declan."

"I'll take them," Ross said, and the two shook on it. "But, Stede . . . if we do get word of Thorne . . . if we do find him . . ."

Stede sputtered out a laugh. "Then, mon, I b' sailing with ya through a hurricane to catch him . . . if that b' what it takes."

The wind hadn't stayed quite as strong, so the *Robert Bruce* was still several hours from Dominica as the sun began to set. "A sail!" called Kalik from the crow's-nest. "There be a sail southeast!" Kalik had many talents, but his sharp vision earned him the job of lookout.

"Captain?" Mr. Hack called from the deck.

Ross lowered his spyglass. "A galleon," he said. "It looks French. Let's go get him."

"Aye, sir!" Hack flexed his forearms and cracked his knuckles loud enough for Ross to hear it up on the quarterdeck. Then Hack was gone, barking orders for more sail and for men to get to the cannons.

Red Eye was running for the hatch when Ross called down, "Red Eye, tell Jacques I need him up here."

"Yes, sir," answered Red Eye.

"And you'll handle the cannon decks, won't you?"

Red Eye grinned and disappeared below deck. If it came to a fight, Ross hoped that Red Eye wouldn't get too carried away. The sixty-gun *Robert Bruce* was a potent weapon in the hands of a skilled artillery man. Red Eye was as skilled as they came—lethal more often than not—and Ross wanted to question the crew of the ship they were chasing, not watch them burn and sink below the surface. That was why, most times, Ross preferred Jacques St. Pierre to oversee the cannons. Of course, allowing Jacques to work with explosives was another kind of risk.

The *Bruce*'s sails filled, and the ship quickly ate up the distance between it and the galleon. "Him b' running," said Stede. "Him b' one foolish mon."

"Where is Saint Pierre?" Ross asked.

"Here!" A curly head of dark hair appeared at the ladder. St. Pierre, wearing a gentleman's frock coat and a tricorn hat, clambered the rest of the way up. He landed atop the quarterdeck and gave a slight bow. "Did you call, mon capitaine?"

"Quite awhile ago, as I recall," said Ross. "What took you so long?"

"I am sorry, but I had to convince Red Eye not to load thirty cannons."

"Thirty?" Ross exclaimed. "We're not storming Paris!"

"Of course, I know this," replied Jacques. "But Red Eye, he is—how you say—ridiculous! He wants to blow the ship out of the water. But I used my extraodinary negotiating skills and changed his mind."

"And what did you decide?"

"Twenty cannons."

Ross shook his head. The galleon continued to try to run, but it was heavy, loaded down with some merchandise, perhaps gold. Another time and Declan Ross would have been licking his lips at the prospect of looting this fat vessel. But not this time. "Raise the standard!" Ross yelled.

The wolf and claymore rose high up on the mast. Every time Ross saw it, pride swelled within. Stede, caught in the lust of the chase, grinned like a schoolboy. But the chase would not last much longer. No sooner had the *Bruce*'s flag gone up than the galleon lowered its sails and slowed to a crawl. Soon it had stopped altogether.

Stede brought the *Bruce* up alongside. "Red Eye!" Ross called. "Have the cannons ready if they try anything!"

"Aye, Captain!"

Ross went to the rail on the quarterdeck. He saw the name of the vessel. "*Le Vichy*," he said to himself. He turned to St. Pierre. "That sounds—"

"Oui, it is French."

"Hmmm," Ross muttered. "If they do not understand, I may need you to translate."

Then, using the most commanding voice he could muster, Ross called to the men on the other ship. "Captain and crew of the *Vichy*, you will turn your cannons and prepare to be boarded!" Ross watched with satisfaction as men on the other deck began to scurry about like ants.

Jules and Mr. Hack hauled the gangplanks over and bridged the gap between the two vessels. Declan left the ship in Stede's capable hands and led a boarding party including Jules, Jacques St. Pierre, and Hack. When Ross stepped onto the deck, he stopped short. In all his years as a pirate, he'd never seen anything quite like what he faced now.

The whole crew of the galleon was assembled on deck in four very neat rows. The first two rows of sailors were all kneeling with their arms behind them as if tied. Two rows of men stood behind those kneeling. Their hands were not bound, but each man held some kind of merchandise or treasure: gold and silver coins, candlestick holders, silverware, spices, jewelry—even sacks of grain or sugar.

Ross gawked at them and strode onto the deck, and any man he approached instantly shouted, "Je me rends, Je me rends!"

Ross looked at his explosives expert. "Jacques?"

"They are surrendering," Jacques replied.

A commotion broke out behind the back row. Two of the French sailors grappled fiercely and rolled on the deck. They shouted at each other and growled like dogs. Ross again looked to Jacques. "What is that all about?" Ross asked.

"They are fighting," St. Pierre said tersely.

"Thank you for that obvious information," Ross scowled. "I can see that much. What are they fighting about?"

"Sacre bleu!" Jacques spat and then muttered, "It seems they are fighting over who gets to surrender first."

"Oh, this is ridiculous," said Ross. "Jacques, tell them who I am. Convince them we have peaceful intentions. Tell them we just want information!"

Before Jacques could say a word, a tall man appeared from behind the rest. He had long greasy hair and a colorful variety of tattoos on his upper arms and chest. He strode over to the men still punching and struggling and kicked each one sharply in the rear end. Then, with his hands on his hips, he yelled at the two combatants. They instantly stopped fighting, stood, and slunk away to the back row.

Jacques took the opportunity to speak up. He spoke rapidly, telling all what Ross had commanded. Some of the sailors of the *Vichy* sighed and cracked relieved smiles. Others squinted and looked confused. The tattooed man approached Captain Ross and said something. Then, startling everyone, he drew his cutlass.

But before Hack could get to Ross's defense, the tattooed sailor bowed and placed his sword at Ross's feet. Jacques threw up his hands and said, "He is the captain. He says if anyone has the right to surrender first, it is he."

The captain of the *Vichy* said something rapidly, and his facial expression turned very serious, almost defiant. Ross looked again at St. Pierre. Jacques rolled his eyes and explained, "The captain says you can have anything you want from the ship, but you will have to kill him if you want the *Vichy*'s chef and their *boudain noir*."

"Boudain noir?"

St. Pierre licked his lips. "Boudain noir is a sausage made with boiled and congealed blood."

Ross made a horrid face. "Tell the captain he can keep his ship's cargo—especially the boudain noir. And please get him to understand we mean them no harm."

Through Jacques's translation, Ross at last convinced the sailors of the *Vichy* that he was not a pirate bent on plunder, death, and destruction. Ross handed the cutlass back to the *Vichy*'s captain whose name, he learned, was Lâchance. Captain Lâchance, more than a little embarrassed over the misunderstanding, explained that they had fled Martinique with a huge cargo of sugar and coffee.

"These have been very dangerous waters," Lâchance said as St. Pierre translated. "So many ships, many of them sailed by friends of mine, have never returned. Pirates have even become brazen enough to attack the settlements and plantations."

Ross had to ask, "Do you know which pirates? Was it Bartholomew Thorne?"

Captain Lâchance's eyes grew to the size of ostrich eggs. "Thorne?!" he exclaimed. "That devil is not still alive, is he?"

Ross sighed and shook his head. "Who then? What pirates still sail around Martinique?"

Lâchance explained, "There are many, most of them upstarts. They do not concern us, for we have adequate gunnery for such. But"—and here the French captain paused with such gravity that each man felt a chill—"we believe the Ghost has come to Martinique."

"The Ghost?" echoed St. Pierre. "Edmund Bellamy?"

Ross immediately understood the preemptive surrender of the *Vichy*. Edmund Bellamy was as brutal a killer as any pirate to ever sail. It was said that Bellamy liked to wound his prisoners and toss them into shark-infested waters just for sport. He would attack ships and settlements on land with equal ferocity and with no mercy . . . always leaving just one survivor behind to tell the tale. And worse, Bellamy was a brilliant sailor and tactician. He had a sixth sense for the sea and always found a way to maneuver his gray ship into superior—and often lethal—position. His attacks seemingly came from nowhere. And when his bloodthirsty missions were completed, he somehow always managed to slip away before he could be caught.

Ross asked, "How sure are you that Bellamy is in Martinique?"

Captain Lâchance's brows arched like a roof over his sad, dark gaze. "We are certain. He has already wiped out Dufour and d'Arlet on the southwestern coast. We have no doubt that Le Diamant is next. So . . . so we fled the island."

"You were right to flee Edmund Bellamy," Ross said, grasping the Frenchman's shoulder. "He is a wicked man."

"Mon capitaine," said Jacques, "Bellamy must be stopped." St. Pierre paused and studied his captain. "We are going after this man, aren't we?"

Ross had been staring to the south. He was so close to the island of Dominica and, perhaps, a trail leading to Thorne. But that would have to wait. "Of course, we're going after him," Ross said. But he thought, *The only problem is how does one capture a ghost?*

11
EDMUND BELLAMY

This b' peculiar fog," whispered Stede.

"Agreed," said Ross. "It's not the weather for such a patch as this."

The fogbank drifted like a gray shroud across the shallow waters approaching Martinique. It quickly enveloped the *Bruce* in its spectral arms, and all at once the crew knew that something was terribly wrong.

"This isn't fog," hissed Red Eye, sniffing the air. "It's smoke."

As the *Bruce* emerged from the vapors, the crew saw what they had feared: they were too late. The coastal French town of Le Diamant, once a bustling and prosperous port for trading smoked meats, sugar cane, and coffee, was nothing but a smoldering husk.

"Stede, take us in close," Ross said solemnly. "We'll take the cutters from there and search for—"

They all heard it. "Get down!" Jules yelled just as a cannonball tore through the main topsail, snapped a web of rigging near the foremast, and narrowly missed the bowsprit before it plunged into the dark water in front of the ship. The second and third shots came within heartbeats of the first. One blasted the quarterdeck railing, showering Ross and Stede with splintered wood. But the other was the most devastating blow. It careened off of the base of the mizzen-mast and slammed a deck hand named Perkins. Others on deck ran to the fallen man's aid, but there was nothing they could do.

"Who?" The question went up from ten men at once.

"Bellamy," Ross muttered. He couldn't see him, but it had to be. "Kalik?!"

"I don't see him, Captain!" Kalik cried out from the crow's-nest on the mainmast. "He's somewhere behind us in the mist!"

"Stede!"

"I b' getting us right out of here!" Stede said, spinning the *Bruce*'s massive wheel. The man-of-war responded and swung into the pre-vailing wind. The sails filled, and the ship lurched. But a sharp crack-ing sound came from just below the quarterdeck.

"Captain Ross!" shouted Mr. Hack. "That cannon shot cracked the base of the mizzenmast. The wind's going to finish it!"

"Blast him!" Ross grunted. "How did he get behind us like that?! *Argh*, lower every sail on the mizzenmast—RIGHT NOW!!"

"Declan, ya best b' getting the oars b'cause we're not outrun-ning him with a third of our sails gone." Again, they heard cannon fire from behind. Shots whizzed overhead. Several hit the water off the starboard rail.

"Well done, Stede!" Ross exclaimed.

"Ah, I guessed right," replied his quartermaster.

"Red Eye, Jacques, fire the chasers!" Ross commanded. Neither man answered. For a brief, horrible moment, Ross feared they had been hit in the first volley. But then, from the gun deck in the stern just below the captain's quarters, four cannons—the chasers—

opened up. Ross felt the jolt even up on the quarterdeck. "Chew on that!" he growled.

Hoping to keep their unseen pursuer from getting a good shot, Stede continued to maneuver the *Bruce*. Ross was desperate to know where his opponent was. "Kalik, anything?"

"No, sir!"

"Where is he . . . where is he?" Ross stood behind Stede and scanned the swirling mist behind them. "I don't like this, Stede."

"I b' thinking the same thing, mon."

Three more cannons fired, but the sounds came from the port-side of the ship. The first clipped the spar that supported the main topsail, and it began to topple. The next two cannonballs ripped through the sail, and to Ross's horror, the second largest sail of the *Bruce* was now rendered useless.

"He's crippling us!" Ross bellowed. "Jacques, Red Eye, port cannons!"

They were firing blind, but when all thirty cannons on the *Bruce*'s portside were unleashed it was a fearsome thing. A wall of fire and smoke erupted, and the ship actually seemed to roll slightly to starboard from the force of the cannons firing. Suddenly, Ross saw a flicker of angry red in the distant swirling darkness.

"There!" Ross yelled. "We've hit him! Reload the port cannons!"

"Declan . . ." Stede's voice was quiet, worried.

Ross looked at his quartermaster and then followed his line of sight to the stern just as a sharp gray shape materialized from the drifting smoke. Unique because of its low height, scooped-out fore-castle, and series of square sails, the bowsprit of Bellamy's frigate appeared first. Two lanterns burned red on the forecastle like demonic eyes, and the sleek hull—checkered with rows of cannon bays—slipped swiftly out of the mist and turned behind the *Bruce*.

"He's crossing the T, Stede!" Ross barked.

"Not if I can help it, mon," Stede replied. "Mister Hack b' need-ing to get on the bowsprit."

Before Ross could finish the command, Hack and three brawny deck hands manned the *Bruce*'s one-of-a-kind swinging bowsprit. "Hard to port?" Hack called, just to make sure. He'd already removed two of the pins on the spar-collar, allowing the bowsprit to swing forty-five degrees. Once Hack had Stede's confirmation, he removed the last two pins. The four men swung the bowsprit, locked it into place, and raised the huge, finlike sail. At the same time, Stede spun the wheel hard, and the *Bruce* made an incredibly sharp turn to port.

While the maneuver had probably saved them from being sunk, it did not take them out of the line of fire altogether. Bellamy, cut-ting broadside behind the *Bruce*, unleashed sixteen cannons at once. The barrage tore into the *Bruce*'s stern, blasting out the windows of the captain's quarters and killing more than a dozen men on first gun deck. The mizzenmast, having been struck once more, began to fall. Men fled the deck as the hundred-foot piece of timber crashed down onto the starboard rail. But it had not been a clean break. The fallen portion of the mast still clung stubbornly to the base.

"Cap'n!" Stede called. "I cannot b' steering with that blasted tree trunk dragging in the watah!"

Ross leaped down from the quarterdeck, grabbed a boarding axe, and joined Jules—who was already hacking away at the bottom of the mast.

"Captain, he be coming for another pass!" Kalik yelled from the crow's-nest.

"Merciful heavens!" Ross shouted. He saw the sharklike profile of Bellamy's ship as it began to slide behind the *Bruce* once more.

"With us stuck like this, he'll strafe us until we sink!" Ross and Jules alternately hacked at the mast, sending hunks and slivers of timber scattering over the deck. The boarding axes were very sharp but were not very heavy. Stroke after stroke fell, and yet they could not cut through. "Come o*nnn*!" Captain Ross demanded. He'd envisioned death many times, but never did he imagine being killed like fish in a barrel.

"Declan!!" Stede's voice was high and desperate. And then they heard the cannons once more.

12
THE PORT OF LONDON

Hopper!"

"Yes, Guv'nor?"

"Come up here and see this."

"Straight away, Guv'nor. I just need to finish stringin' up this cargo net."

Commodore Blake laughed loudly and then turned to his wife. "Dolphin, I don't think the lad ever stops working."

She squeezed her husband's arm affectionately. "I believe he's paid his debt to England thrice over on this trip."

"Yes, well, he's not going to miss this view. Hopper, get up here right now!"

There came a distressed squeak from the deck below, followed by a crash, and Hopper's hairless head appeared in the open hatch. "I'm here, Guv'nor, begging your pardon, but have I done somefin' wrong?"

"No, lad," Blake said. "You've done nothing more than work

twice as hard as anyone else on the *Oxford*. Now, come up here. There's a sight I believe you've been anxious to see." Commodore Blake gave Hopper a hand up onto the deck. Not that he needed it. Three weeks of hard work, regular sleep, and plenty to eat had put pounds of ropey muscle back on Hopper's frame. He was still skinny, but far from the emaciated youth they'd found in the crow's-nest just after leaving New Providence.

Hopper stood just about up to Commodore Blake's elbow, so he did not at first see what the man was pointing at . . . until he walked toward the port rail. "London!" he gasped. "It's really London!"

"Yes, my young sailor," said Lady Dolphin as she and her husband joined Hopper at the rail. Towering, puffy white clouds climbed in the bright blue morning sky behind the boxy customhouse on the north bank of the Thames. The great dome of St. Paul's Cathedral loomed in the distance. The Port of London itself was filled with sails, too many to count. There were the vast square sails of tall ships, many of them British naval vessels, as well as the slivered triangles of sloops and yachts. The many sails, teeming this way and that across the wide Thames River, were mostly white, but there were a few of every hue. And from the multitudes of their masts, one could see flags from many nations flying. Barges and merchant vessels lined both sides of the river, and the quays and wharves were bursting with ships. It was a breathtaking but busy scene. And, Blake noted, the entrance to the port was quite a narrow thing contrasted to the wide harbor within. The *Oxford* was the twelfth ship in line to pass through the congested bottleneck.

Seeing London again was, for Nathaniel Hopper, a bittersweet event. It was his first home and a glad sight after so long a time, but in spite of the hundreds of sailing ships and thousands of people on the docks and in the streets, Hopper's parents were not there. And so, the city would forever seem strangely empty. Hopper still held out hope that one friendly face might still live in London.

"Will we still go and look for Miss Hamilton?" Hopper asked, staring up at Commodore Blake. "Will we, Guv'nor?"

"Yes, of course," he replied. "A man's word is always a promise. First we need to announce our arrival at the palace. I doubt very much that His Majesty will see us right away—if he's even in England, that is. And if not, we will take a carriage all over London and find this Miss Hamilton." Hopper's beaming face looked up at Blake and Lady Dolphin. Then he turned back to the view and rested his chin on the rail.

"And let's not forget my little errand," said Dolphin.

"There is nothing *little* about that errand, my dear," he replied. "I will not rest until you have what you seek or are at least convinced that they do not exist."

Having left the *Oxford* in the capable hands of Mr. Jordan, Commodore Blake, Lady Dolphin, and Hopper made their way into London. Upon visiting the palace, they found that King George was indeed present but had business to attend to until five o'clock.

"Did you see them whispering?" Dolphin asked as their carriage pulled away from the palace.

"Yes," replied Commodore Blake, a finger sliding up and down his cheek. "The moment the guards recognized me, they seemed positively vexed about something. I don't like it."

"Nor I," she said. "But it seems we must wait until five o'clock for answers, so for now . . ."

"For now," Blake said, "we will explore the city of London with young Hopper as our guide." Hopper laughed.

"Now then," said Lady Dolphin, "where shall we begin our search?"

Hopper stared out the window of the carriage. The streets were filled with men in top hats and long coats and ladies in long dresses. "I don't think it was around here," Hopper said.

"All right, so not in the West End," said Blake.

"Well," Hopper hesitated. "I don't think it was the East End, really. My father said we weren't so bad off as that."

"Right then," said Commodore Brandon Blake with a sigh. "So you're not from the West End and not really from the East End. That narrows it down."

"Brand, darling, he's not been in London in years, so much has changed."

"Of course," said Blake. "Forgive my temper. I'm preoccupied, that's all." The commodore leaned out of the carriage door and shouted, "Driver, take us to the east West End!"

The driver answered with a muffled, "What, sir?"

Blake winked at Hopper and then yelled, "Just drive, sir. Just drive."

After several hours of searching, Hopper at last saw something he recognized. "That's my tree, it is! Stop!" He turned to Commodore Blake, who immediately signaled the driver to stop. The three of them stepped down from the carriage and found themselves staring at several sections of old row houses, each in varying degrees of disrepair. "Young Master Hopper, how can you tell?" asked Dolphin. "These look the same as so many others we've passed."

"This way," Hopper replied, and he scurried off.

Smiling affectionately, Dolphin noted that the boy ran with his shining head slightly bowed as if trying to avoid a low tree branch. It was a strange quirk Hopper had picked up on board the *Oxford*. Whenever he was below decks, he ducked his head, in spite of the fact that he was nowhere near tall enough to actually bump his noggin into anything on the ceiling.

When they caught up to Hopper, he said, "See!" He pointed up the trash-strewn narrow passage between two sections of houses. At the other end of the path stood a pale gray tree with darker patches of bark peeling off on its trunk and boughs. "That's my tree." Hopper had his hands on his hips and smiled with great pride. "See the string . . . up there in the top?"

Blake and Dolphin gazed into the leafless upper branches and did indeed see a blackened tangle of twine. "It's the only tree on the whole block," said Hopper. "And my kite's string always found!" Hopper laughed. "Come on, Miss Hamilton's place is right nearby."

They followed him up the shadowy path to the third house on the left-hand side. It once had been red, but now had faded to pinkish-gray. A window on the second story was broken, and the doorknocker was nothing but a clump of tarnish. Commodore Blake reached for it. "Shall I?" he asked.

Hopper nodded enthusiastically, so Blake rapped hard three times. Just a few seconds later, a man wearing a dark green robe over a pale green nightshirt answered the door. "Yes?"

Blake glanced down at Hopper, who was frowning and seemed confused. Then Blake said to the man, "We're looking for a Miss Hamilton. Apparently some years back this was her home."

"Hamilton?" the man replied, his eyes half-rolled back into his head. "You mean Miss Donna?" Hopper nodded eagerly.

"Ah, lad, sorry, but she's been gone these two years passed."

Commodore Blake's stomach knotted. This was all the boy needed to hear. Hopper stared at the ground sullenly.

Seeing their reaction, the man quickly added, "No, not *that* kind of passed on. Blimey, she weren't more than a year older than me. Flighty bird, she was, always had a thing for the theater. So she sold me the house, then up and joined some Shakespearean troop that travels all over doing plays. Last I heard, they were doing *Hamlet* in Scotland. But that was the better part of two years ago, if it was a day."

Commodore Blake thanked the man for his trouble, turned to Hopper, and said, "I'm sorry, my lad."

Hopper looked up and put on a brave smile. "Least she's not dead."

Still, the walk back to the carriage seemed long and difficult.

Mrs. Kravits had been more than a little startled to see the daughter of Emma and Richard Kinlan standing on her doorstep. But here was little Dolphin, all grown up no less—and married to a commodore. Mrs. Kravits regained her composure and insisted that Dolphin's father had left no more journals behind. She'd made sure of it before she sent them overseas to Dolphin in the first place. Dolphin, of course, insisted in searching her old family home personally. Mrs. Kravits grumbled, seeming a bit reluctant, but at last found the key to the estate. The carriage again sped off to London's West End.

They found Dolphin's family estate with no trouble at all. It was a tall building with one turret and three levels of sloping roofs. Built on a hill, it afforded them a distant view of St. Paul's and a bit of the port. The wrought-iron gate that surrounded the estate like a moat was ajar. The driver dismounted, opened the gate wide enough for the carriage, and then drove up the winding cobblestone path.

Dolphin's key fit snugly in the lock. The door opened with a high, whining complaint but little resistance. Light from the open door shone into the central corridor of the building, from which Dolphin saw a pair of other doors, a spiral stair, and the archway leading to the library.

"It looks so sad and colorless," she said.

"To be expected," Blake replied as they entered. "What with all the dust settled."

After kindling two oil lanterns, they decided to search the library first, which, due to the sheer numbers of books in the room, required all three of them. "I feel like a snowman," Hopper said when they finished the last of the library's contents. He sneezed. "Look at me. I'm covered in dust."

"We all are," Dolphin said with a laugh. "But you the most." She brushed off his head and cheeks with her sleeve. "Now I see why Mrs. Kravits didn't want us to come look at the house. She's not done much to keep it up these years. What did that woman do for the pay? Why, the furniture's not even covered. I'm afraid this is going to be a long and dirty ordeal."

"It is near three o'clock," Blake said, returning his watch to its pocket home. "We can search another hour and a half."

"I'm beginning to doubt that there ever were any other journals." Dolphin sighed. "I thought sure this would be the place to find them. My father would often write in this very room."

"Let's just stay here while we're in London," Blake replied. "We'll come back tonight and search, after our visit with His Majesty."

"Are you sure?" she asked. "It could be just a waste of time."

"You do own this house," he said with a wink. "And, as I said before, it is no waste to pursue that which is meaningful to you. Come now, while we search the other rooms, tell me about your family and what you remember of this place."

"Lady Dolphin," said Hopper timidly. He had in his hand a thick book with a dusty, dark blue cover. "Would it be all right with you if I stayed here a bit longer?"

"Can you . . . can you read?" she asked.

"I should say so," he replied. "Me mum taught me when I was just four."

"Well, then," said Blake, "I think you should stay here and read it."

Hopper grinned, ran over to the center of the room, and plopped down in a large padded chair. This sent a cloud of dust swirling into the air, and after Commodore Blake and Lady Dolphin left the library, they could hear Hopper sneezing even from far down the hall.

The chair Hopper had originally sat in was not comfortable at all. Neither were the other chairs in the center of the library nor the couch, for that matter . . . to say nothing of the explosive layers of dust. And then there were the paintings: at least one on every wall, all depicting dour, gray-haired people in a variety of stiff poses. *And they're all looking right at me*, Hopper thought. He'd moved several times to avoid them, but turning his back to one spooky face meant facing another. He'd tried to become engulfed by the story he was reading, but every time Hopper lowered the book, he'd see dark eyes staring down at him from the wall.

At last he found one spot where the ghouls couldn't get at him: a small slanted desk facing the wall in the corner of the room closest to the fireplace. Oh, the paintings could stare at his back all they wanted so long as Hopper didn't have to see their eyes. He spent several triumphant minutes enjoying his book, that is, until Hopper realized the wide desktop had hinges on the back of it. The tiny hairs on the back of his neck stood on end. Had they looked inside the desk? Had they even known it opened?

Hopper closed the book and placed it beside his chair. Then he carefully grasped the corners of the desktop and lifted. No, Commodore Blake and Lady Dolphin certainly had not looked inside the desk. The cobwebs stretching between the lifting desktop and the large storage compartment attested to this desk not being opened in a long time. Hopper saw a tarnished brass rod inside and thought it might be used to prop up the desktop. But no sooner had he reached for the rod than a large brownish spider ran across his hand, up his arm, and then off to skitter on the floor. Hopper jumped back with a yelp, and the desktop crashed down, sending more plumes of dust scattering.

Any minute he expected someone to rush into the room and scold him. But no one did. *Besides*, Hopper thought, *Commodore Blake and Lady Dolphin won't be mad when I show them the missing journals.* Hopper felt sure they were in the desk. They had to be. He just hoped there weren't any more spiders in there with them.

So again, he lifted the desktop. And this time, he was actually able to prop the desk open with the brass rod. Inside, besides more dust, Hopper found many things: quill pens, several inkwells, a few coins, a pair of slightly misshapen spectacles, and a couple of thin leather volumes. Hopper had high hopes for these until he opened them and realized they were filled with numbers, figures, and computations. Hopper knew that what Lady Dolphin was looking for was more like a diary or a memoir rather than ledger.

There was one other item of interest: a little black leather pouch. It made a clicking noise as he picked it up, and for a moment, Hopper was afraid the satchel held more spiders or something worse. He closed the desktop and then let the contents of the satchel spill out onto the desk. And spill they did. Nine marbles rolled down the desktop and then across the floor. Hopper loved marbles. His father had given him a similar set several years earlier, but those were made of polished stone. These appeared to be made of heavy glass.

Hopper immediately went to the floor, gathered up the marbles, and proceeded to set them up for a little game of King's Foil. Then Hopper crouched down to the floor. In King's Foil, he was the archer, and he prepared to knuckle the blue marble for his first shot. The red marble, the king, lay just a few feet away. But it was guarded by the seven other marbles—his knights—who were set up strategically in three rows between the king and the archer. The goal was to strike the king within seven shots without knocking one of the knights into the king or into other knights.

Hopper tried and failed several times—he was a bit rusty. But on the very next round, he had brilliantly cleared a path through the knights. He readied his marble and prepared to absolutely smack the king with his blue marble. He unleashed a potent shot that screamed through the baffled knights, sailed right by the king, and rolled under the footboard of the desk. Hopper crawled over to the desk and began to feel around under the footboard. His fingers hit the marble once, but caused it to roll away. He jammed his arm farther in and hit the wall behind the desk. But when he did this, he felt a draft of cold air on the top of his hand.

Hopper pulled out his hand, stood up, and stared at the desk. Where had the cold air come from? Then he glanced back over his shoulder at the entrance to the library. If he needed help, he could call out. Commodore Blake and Lady Dolphin were not far away. But neither were the paintings. He shook that thought away and went to the desk. He wanted to see what was behind it, so he grabbed two corners and began to push. It scraped the floor, but moved more easily than Hopper thought it would. Once the desk was far enough away from the wall, Hopper could see where the cool air had come from. A rectangular section of the wall had been pushed in. There was a dark cavity of some kind behind this strange panel.

Hopper retrieved the oil lantern, placed it on the floor by the open panel, and then lay down to look inside. He had a brief image of a spider as big as a cat crawling out and grabbing him and swallowed as he pushed the panel farther in. With the light of the lantern, Hopper saw webs aplenty, wafting in the steady invisible current of cool air, but fortunately there were no gargantuan spiders. About six feet in, past the billowing, gossamer webs, there was a square bundle. It was a stack of some kind, wrapped in dark material and tied up with a bow of thick string.

"Commodore Blake!" Hopper called. "Lady Dolphin, come quick! I've found something!"

13

A SLIPPERY CATCH

In a shadowy cantina on the southern coast of Inagua, Cat and Anne sat on one side of a wide table with Father Brun. Dutch Bennett, the captain of the Brethren ship called the *Dominguez*, and Brother Alejandro Cascade, captain of the *Celestine*, sat on the other side of the table along with Brother Gale Waverly, the Brethren's spy who had sailed with Scully for some time. Weary conversations passed between them.

"It's hopeless," Cat mumbled. He'd meant for only Anne to hear, but Father Brun stopped talking and turned to Cat. Now that it was out there, Cat figured he might as well say what was on his mind. "We've been after Scully for weeks, scouring Saint Vincent and now here. And what have we got?"

"No sign of him yet, true," said Brother Waverly. "But there is still Jamaica."

"Jamaica?" Cat shouted. "I still say we should go back to Saint

104

Vincent. There was a tavern on the west side of the island, a perfect place for a rat like Scully. Why won't you listen to me?"

The table was silent. Anne stared at Cat, concern etched on her face. Finally Father Brun spoke. "This group serves together. We—"

"But we always do what *you* want, Father Brun," Cat interrupted. "You told me I'd command the *Constantine*, but all I do—all any of us do—is what YOU want!"

"Cat!" Anne cautioned him.

If Father Brun had taken offense, he did not show it. "Cat, Scully rarely found refuge in Saint Vincent—especially the western side of the island where he has enemies. Brother Waverly informed us that Scully spent more time on Jamaica than anywhere else."

"That's an awful big island," said Cat with more spite than he intended.

"And so we will search every inch of it if we need to," answered Father Brun sternly. "Tell me, Cat . . . in the time we have spent searching, what have you lost?"

Cat felt his anger boil up, but he forced it down and spoke evenly. "Time is exactly what I've lost."

"I for one am eager to go where Father Brun commands," said Dutch Bennett. It was the first time anyone at the table had seen the jovial seaman from Aruba without a smile. "If it weren't for him, I'd still be sailing a smelly fishing schooner. But, Cat, I am curious about what you say. And I wonder what time you regret losing . . . time for what?"

Cat was silent for a moment. He did not speak the first thought that entered his mind. *Time to go back to the island where I was found. Time to go back to Dominica too. Time to find out who . . . I was.* But when Cat spoke, he said, "We could be out there like

Captain Ross, knocking out pirates all over the Caribbean and the Spanish Main. Then at least we could make a difference."

With his heavy Spanish accent, Brother Cascade was difficult to understand, but on this occasion, his message could not have been clearer. "We will do no thing that matters if we no listen to the Almighty."

"We will sail to Jamaica," said Father Brun. "And I believe we will find the man we are searching for."

"But what if we don't?" asked Cat.

Father Brun ignored the question. "We must return to our ships. It is clear that we all need rest."

There was a soft knock at Cat's cabin door. "Come in," Cat said, his voice thin and dry. "I'm awake."

Carrying an oil lantern, Anne came in and shut the door behind her. The *Constantine* had hit a patch of heavily rolling sea, and she steadied herself on the edge of Cat's desk. "Oh . . . uh, hello, Anne." Cat sat up in his hammock and swayed. "You couldn't sleep either?" he asked.

She shook her head. "I may have nodded off for a few minutes," she replied. "But no, not really."

It was quiet, dark, and awkward. Anne hung the oil lantern on a hook above the desk. She smiled at Cat. "You know what my father used to tell me if I couldn't fall asleep?"

Cat shrugged.

"He used to say . . ." Anne lowered her voice imitating her father's husky manner. "'Anne, my dear, if you can't sleep . . . you best stay awake.'"

They laughed, but Cat stopped first. Anne sat in the chair by the desk and fixed him with her penetrating hazel eyes. "What's wrong?" she asked abruptly.

Cat looked up, looked quickly away from her, and took a sudden interest in the stars outside the cabin window. "Nothing's wrong," he mumbled.

"Cat, I know you better than that," she said. "You've been snapping at people, you don't seem to be able to sleep, and you've been forgetting things."

"I have amnesia, Anne," Cat replied curtly.

"I'm not talking about that. But you seem to go blank on things I know you know."

"So why aren't you asleep?" Cat replied, trying to change the subject.

"Because I'm worried about you," she said. She got up and went toward him. She tried to take his hand, but he pulled it away. Anne tilted her head, and her brow knotted up with concern. "You . . . you haven't been yourself lately."

Cat looked up, his face a mask of disbelief and frustration. "I haven't been myself?" he echoed her. "Now that's a funny thing to say. What do you mean by 'I haven't been myself'?"

"I wasn't trying to . . . I didn't mean—"

"How do you know I haven't been myself? Do you know me that well, Anne? Do you really know me?" Cat dropped down from the hammock and stepped ominously close to her. Anne backed up a step, and Cat went on. "Bits and pieces of most of my life—that's all I know. How can you know any more than that?"

"I've known you almost two years," Anne countered. "And all you've done is save the lives of everyone I care about. You . . . you saved my life."

"But what about before? I was raised by not just a pirate—but a killer! What if I did unspeakable things . . . like my father? Anne, how do you know who I was before you found me on that island?"

Anne had heard enough. She poked Cat so hard in the chest that he fell backward and nearly flipped over the hammock. "You know what, Cat?" she asked. "I don't care who you were! Whatever happened in the past, leave it there." She softened her tone a bit. "I'm sorry for your memory loss. I can't imagine what it must be like to have to guess at the past, and I know it must be very hard. But from the moment you woke up and looked at me on the *William Wallace*, I knew you were a good man."

"But—"

"I'm not finished," she said. "You want to know what I think happened in your past? I think your father tried to raise you to be a monster like he was. I think he did everything he could to teach you that the lives of others meant nothing so long as you got what you wanted out of them. But I bet you wouldn't do it. I bet you wouldn't turn. I think he couldn't stand that his own son wouldn't follow in his footsteps. And in the end, I think he meant to kill you, Cat. You were a failure to him because you were good. That's what I think."

Cat blinked. He felt like he'd just been hit by a hurricane. But when he looked up at Anne again, she was crying. Tears washed down her face like channels on an inlet. Cat wanted to reach out to her, or at least part of him did. The other part was still thinking about what she'd said. "There's more to it," he whispered. "You know Brother Dmitri?"

She nodded and wiped her face on her sleeve. "He works mostly on the gun deck, but he's hard to miss."

"We sparred back on Saba, and . . . and I almost killed him."

"But you didn't."

"Father Brun stepped in. He stopped me."

"It was the heat of battle," Anne said. "You would have stopped yourself. Why, I've seen Red Eye get so mad he—"

"No," Cat interrupted. He grasped his temples as if trying to keep his head from exploding. "I would have done it. I was so angry . . . out of control. This murderous rage billowed up in me. It's happened again since. I get these ideas. I don't ask for them to come, but they're there. I . . . I'm afraid of what I might do."

Anne swallowed. "Look, Cat," she said, "you're talking to the queen of stupid ideas. I once thought being a pirate like my father would be fun—even though he tried desperately to tell me I was wrong. I didn't listen. For crying out loud, Cat, one of my brilliant schemes almost got us both hanged. Everyone has dumb ideas. Everyone gets angry."

"Not like this."

Anne exhaled loudly and turned to leave. "You're the captain of this ship," she said, opening the door. "And you need to get your head on straight because your crew needs you. I . . . need you." She was nearly out the door when she said, "And this Merchant, he's not going to care who you were."

The three ships of the Brethren docked in Montego Bay, and over the next several days, Father Brun, Cat, Anne, and the other senior crewmen vigilantly watched three of the four taverns that Scully liked to frequent in Jamaica. The last one was a small, twisting lump of stone at the top of a wooded hill on the edge of town. A very steep and very narrow path led up the hill to the establishment's arched double doors. Two men with tankards milled about outside. It was Dutch Bennett and Brother Cascade, who looked a little strange dressed like a pirate rather than in his brown robes. Inside, there was room for about fifteen people. Cat sat at a small table next to a window. He rested his arm near a tankard of water the tavern keeper had brought over. "Aren't you going to drink that?" Anne asked.

Cat looked ruefully into the mug. "If I die on this journey, it'll be at the edge of a sword—not from drinking some vermin-infested water."

Anne laughed but stopped short. "Here comes another group."

Cat brushed the hair out of his face, saw four men pass by the window, and then turned to watch Father Brun and Brother Waverly, who sat facing the entrance on the other side of the tavern. The four men entered, went straight to the tavern keeper, and began talking noisily. Cat didn't think Scully would draw so much attention to himself as these buffoons, but he glanced over to Waverly anyway. The monk slightly lifted two fingers from the table and waved them side to side. It wasn't Scully.

Cat turned back to the window, and suddenly a face was there. A man stood just outside the tavern and appeared content to stand outside looking in. He had long hair that fell in unruly curls over one side of his face. He had no moustache and only a little spider-shaped patch of whiskers under his bottom lip. The man scratched the side of his chin and glanced at Cat. Cat could feel the man's stare linger on him for longer than was comfortable. The group of loud men had clumped right in front of Father Brun and Brother Waverly, so Cat couldn't get a signal as to whether the man in the window was the man they were after.

Anne noticed Cat's tense expression, saw the man at the window, and wondered. The man began to walk away from the window, and Cat followed him with his eyes. The hair on Cat's forearm stood up. He blinked, and his mind filled with a vision of a cobble-

stone alley lit by a full moon's light. Two men stood talking. One
was Bartholomew Thorne. The other . . .

"It's him!" Cat whispered urgently, knocking over the putrid
water. Anne shot up out of her chair, but Father Brun and Brother
Waverly had not seen. Cat and Anne burst through the group of men,
sending tankards flying. "Dutch, Alejandro!" Cat called to the men
outside as he stumbled over a fallen stool. "That man, it's Scully!"

Scully was trapped by the two big men, but not for long. He
moved quick like a striking snake and slammed the bony ridge of his
hand into Alejandro's throat. Then, without a second of wasted
motion, he drew back his arm and plunged his elbow into Dutch
Bennett's gut. Both men fell to the ground. Scully did not take the
steep path but darted into the woods. Cat and Anne raced out of
the tavern. Father Brun and Brother Waverly emerged a second later
and went immediately to their wounded friends.

"Cat, are you sure?" Father Brun asked, looking up from Alejandro,
who was having a hard time breathing. "Brother Waverly did not
see him."

But Cat was already sprinting into the bush. "I'm sure!" he
called back.

"I'll go after him!" yelled Anne over her shoulder. But no sooner
was she in the woods than the ground seemed to drop away. The
incline was steeper here than on the narrow path they'd walked to
get to the tavern. Anne found herself painfully bounding down the
hill. Her vision became a green blur as branches whipped at her face
and sawed at her arms. She tripped once and gasped, almost going
over but somehow regaining her balance. Between the branches and
trunks she searched desperately. Where had they gone?

She finally slowed her descent just before she came to a ridge
of stone. *One more step*, she thought, shaking her head. The ridge

was a cliff of sorts, and the sudden fall could have been deadly. From this vantage, Anne spotted Cat—and Scully.

They were running though thick foliage, and Cat almost had him. He lunged for Scully, nearly grabbing his shirt, but a branch came whipping back and caught Cat full in the chest. Cat staggered, fell, and rolled several painful revolutions down the hill. He regained his footing and stood. Then, clutching his ribs with one hand and fending off branches with the other, Cat continued the pursuit.

Cat was falling behind. Suddenly, Scully veered left, doubling back toward the main path.

Anne darted back the way she had come, trying to follow just the right angle.

Little glimpses of black, that was all Cat saw of Scully as he darted ahead of him through the trees and foliage. *The man is as nimble as a rabbit,* Cat thought. The way he changed directions and made turns, all the while careening downhill—it seemed inhuman. Still, Cat managed to stay within sight of him.

Suddenly, a wall of the tallest ferns Cat had ever seen sprang up, and the whole world went green. The stalks were wide and feathery and spread in every direction. They grabbed at his ankles, which was not what Cat wanted as he plunged down the hill. Cat held his arms up to shield his eyes, but the plants were too thick. Cat could no longer see Scully at all. Cat slowed down. Then came to a stop. He listened for Scully's footfalls.

But there was nothing. Cat had lost him. *Think!* he told himself. *Where would Scully go? Back to his ship, of course, and then off the island. But where would he moor his ship?* Cat looked to the north.

Certainly not Montego Bay. Much too crowded for Scully's liking. No, he'd find a place where he could come and go without notice.

Cat tried to recall the map Father Brun had shown him. There wasn't really a proper inlet to the northeast, not without crossing over Montego Bay. There wasn't anywhere else to put a ship without being noticed, unless . . . *Scully doubled back on me! Mosquito Cove—it had to be.* It was the only inlet close enough to the main road. Cat made up his mind and tore off to the east. The more Cat thought, the better it sounded. The only question was, how far ahead had Scully gotten? And that depended on when Scully had doubled back on him.

But those concerns couldn't be helped. Cat sprinted diagonally down the hill. He found the footing awkward but still easier than going straight downhill. He picked up speed and raced on.

The wall of green ended just as abruptly as it had begun. Cat couldn't believe it. Scully was just ahead—thirty, maybe forty yards. Cat charged ahead, throwing his body recklessly forward and gaining speed. His heart pounded, and his thighs burned. Thin branches sliced his upper arms. Thick branches snapped, but left bruises behind.

Scully did not seem to be running at full speed, and Cat thought that perhaps Scully had not realized that Cat had come through the fern forest. Cat ate up the ground between them. Grabbing at the man's coat had not worked out so well the first time, so Cat decided to throw himself at the man's ankles. The distance between them shrank: twenty yards, fifteen, ten . . . he was right behind him now, near enough to—

Just before Cat leaped, Scully turned his head. He saw Cat and, like a ship catching a sudden gust of wind, Scully surged ahead. "It's no good, Scully!" Cat growled, but the man was fast. He started to pull away. And through the sweat and hair in his eyes, Cat saw that they were reaching the edge of the forest. There was some kind of clearing ahead. *No . . . not the road!* Cat thought with horror. If

Scully hit the open road, he would be gone. He could duck into a building, slither into an unknown crawlspace, or cut down a side street and disappear. Cat summoned all the strength he had left in his legs, sprinted a few more steps, and dove.

In midflight, Cat flung his arms out and then wrapped them around . . . nothing. He slammed into the mulchy ground and got a face full of dead leaves. Cat jumped to his feet and looked up only to see Scully run off. But then something incredible happened. Scully reached the forest's edge and suddenly flailed into the air with his feet flying up behind him. He crashed hard. Cat heard the scatter of gravel, several sharp curses, and then a low moan. He ran to the edge of the woods, and there was Anne with her leg stuck out in the path.

She shrugged. "Oops . . . he tripped."

The three ships of the Brethren had sailed out of Montego Bay and moored off the coast of a deserted cay. Father Brun and Brother Dmitri had taken a very defiant Edmund Scully into Father Brun's cabin. Cat and Anne waited just outside the cabin's door for an hour, but it seemed like an eternity. All their hopes of finding the Merchant depended on what Scully knew.

"What do you think they've done to him?" Cat asked.

"I can't imagine they've been smacking him with a club," said Anne. "We haven't heard a thing."

"He wouldn't, would he?" asked Cat.

"Wouldn't what?"

"Smack Scully with a club or whip him or anything like that?" Cat waited for Anne to answer. When she didn't, he said, "I mean, Father Brun and Brother Dmitri, they're monks, Christians . . . they can't just beat the information out of Scully, can they?"

Anne was silent a few moments, and her eyes became glassy as she remembered another member of the Brethren, Padre Dominguez, who had befriended her and protected her before Thorne tortured him to death. "I don't know, Cat," she said. "In some ways, the Brethren are at war. What the Merchant has done throughout history . . . what Edmund Scully has done . . . unspeakable things! If they have to hurt Scully in order to capture the Merchant . . . how many lives might be saved?"

Cat nodded slowly. He hadn't thought of that.

"Besides," Anne continued, "the monks, the members of the Brethren, they aren't your usual monks. I watched Padre Dominguez knock the starch out of a dozen pirates—all while I was reading the Bible to him. These Christians aren't afraid to fight, and you know what? I don't blame them. There are a lot of evil men in this world. Someone has to fight them."

Before Cat could comment, the cabin door swung open. "Cat, Anne, prepare the ship," said Father Brun as he emerged from the room. "We sail for Pine Island off the coast of Cuba."

Brother Dmitri appeared in the doorway. "The Merchant has built a stronghold on a unique tidal island. *La Isla Desvanecente*, it is called . . . the disappearing isle."

"But thanks to Scully," explained Father Brun, "we will be able to find it."

"Then," said Brother Dmitri, brushing between Cat and Anne and walking toward the stairs, "we will at last stem the Merchant's bloody tide."

When Scully didn't follow Father Brun and Brother Dmitri out of the cabin, Cat and Anne peered nervously into the room. They saw Scully seated on a small chair in the middle of the room. His wrists were bound and rested in his lap, but Cat and Anne could see that he was shaking. And his face was ghost white. Sweat dribbled down his forehead and poured down his cheeks. His eyes were as big as saucers, and his large dark pupils darted this way and that.

Cat leaned back into the hall and looked aghast at Father Brun. "What . . . what did you do, stab him?"

Father Brun laughed out loud. "We did no such thing," he said. "Neither of us laid a hand on Scully."

Anne looked again at their frightened captive. "Well, what did you do to him?"

Father Brun sighed. "Brother Dmitri has a terrible scar on his right forearm. Have you seen it?"

Cat and Anne nodded. It was hard to miss such a scar.

"Well," Father Brun went on, "Dmitri simply explained to Scully how he got the scar. You see, Dmitri was working for a blacksmith in Spain and caught his arm on a piece of metal that had fused itself to the roof of the forge. His arm literally roasted above the super-heated fires before he could tear it free. Tragic really, being caught in the flames for even a few seconds . . . unimaginable pain." Father Brun shook his head and began to walk away.

"That's all?" Cat exclaimed. "You got Scully to reveal the Merchant's secret location by showing him a scar?"

Father Brun stopped at the stairs but did not turn around. "Oh, there was one other thing."

"What?" Anne blurted out.

"Then we told Scully the truth about hell." Father Brun turned then, and his pale eyes seemed luminous in the torchlight. "After that, he was uniquely inclined to speak to us. In fact, I have a sus-picion that he may now desire to join the priesthood. Why don't the two of you bring Brother Scully up on deck?"

14

A Dead Man's Tale

Five, six . . . seven. Ross counted the cannon blasts even as he and Jules at last cut through the base of the fallen mast. The *Bruce* drifted to port, and the mast slid off the deck into the black water. Ross had already seen the precision of the Ghost's gunners, but he shut his eyes anyway, praying that Bellamy would somehow miss with every shot. Ross's thoughts turned to his daughter. He'd made the right decision to send Anne with Cat after all. Ross waited for the cannonballs to strike home. He waited and heard . . .

"Declan!" Stede shouted. Then more cannon shots in the distance. "Declan, get up here! Mon, ya got to b' seeing this."

Suddenly, Ross felt himself hoisted off the ground. He opened his eyes and saw the deck rushing by. Jules had picked up the captain and slung him over his massive shoulders. "Jules, what are you . . ." Ross groaned. "Jules, put me down!"

Jules did exactly that, placing Ross on the quarterdeck next to

Stede and the ship's wheel. Stede slapped his captain on the back. "Look, look!" he cried, pointing desperately to the stern.

Ross turned and saw not one but three ships. Bellamy's frigate was one of them, but . . . Ross squinted and saw that one of the new ships had three sharp finlike sails and a very low draft. It sailed behind Bellamy's ship and fired almost continuously. Ross exhaled a mighty sigh. The ship was a xebec . . . the *Banshee*. "Well, call me an eel!" he said. "Cutlass Jack, you rascal!"

"And Lâchance!" exulted Stede. "That other ship b' a galleon, *Le Vichy*! They come up on Bellamy like Bellamy come up on us," said Stede. "Now, they b' driving him to our portside."

Ross watched as the three ships exchanged fire. But Cutlass Jack had the best angle, and Bellamy couldn't get out of his pursuer's firing range . . . not without coming alongside . . .

"Stede, that's exactly what Jack's doing!" Ross's eyes glinted dangerously. "Don't let him slip by us! Stay on his starboard." Then Ross went to the quarterdeck rail and yelled, "Jacques! Red Eye!" He waited a few moments and heard no answer.

Ross leaped down from the quarterdeck and ran to the hatches yelling for his two master gunmen. Still there was no answer. At last, Red Eye's soot-streaked face popped up from a hatch near the foremast. "I heard you, Captain," he said, his voice agitated. "But it took some doing to get here. Jacques was down below . . . near the stern . . . when the second barrage hit. The first gun deck is sealed off."

St. Pierre had been in the worst possible place. "I'll get a team of men down there," Ross said hurriedly. He turned and barked out orders to anyone within shouting distance. Then he turned back to Red Eye. "What have you got portside?"

"Nine . . . maybe ten of the eighteen-pounders," he said. "More starboard. Captain, what's been happening? I thought we were done for."

"We have help," Ross said simply. "In a few moments, Bellamy will be driven along our portside. When I give you the signal, fire every ship killer you have!"

Red Eye wiped soot from his face, grinned, and turned to leave, but Captain Ross put a hand on his shoulder.

"And Red Eye . . . ," said the captain, his face as solemn as the grave.

"Captain?"

"Bellamy must not escape," Ross said. "If it comes to it . . . put him on the bottom."

"That I will, sir," Red Eye said, and he was gone.

Bellamy was indeed a brilliant seaman, and he'd mercilessly trained his crew until they could work the sails and master wind and wave in their sleep. But skill's treacherous companion was pride, and Bellamy had been so caught in the chase and so convinced of the kill that he never dreamed other ships could be stalking *him* through the mist. Cutlass Jack and Captain Lâchance had hit Bellamy hard and fast. There was some minor damage to the frigate's rudder, and with Jack cutting off every angle, Bellamy found it impossible to turn or escape. And by the time Bellamy realized where his attackers were pushing him, it was too late.

At a distance of about three hundred yards, Bellamy's frigate passed along the *Bruce*'s portside. Timing was crucial, so Cutlass Jack harnessed every bit of his xebec's shark-fin sails and raced up on Bellamy's portside. Cutlass Jack on one side, Declan Ross on the other, and Lâchance right behind, Bellamy found himself in no man's land with no choice left but to fight it out. The frigate opened fire from both port and starboard cannons, raking Jack's xebec and Ross's man-of-war from the inside. But Bellamy's attack could not last.

Cutlass Jack's xebec sat very low in the water, and Jack trained his cannons on the lowest sections of Bellamy's hull. Jack fired at will, and great wounds opened up on the frigate. Lâchance managed to cross behind and fired two deadly shots into Bellamy's stern. Soon, the enemy's ship began to take on water.

Captain Ross gave the command. Red Eye and his gunnery team lit the fuses on massive hulking cannons that, in the shadows, looked like giant grizzly bears growling out of the cannon ports. But while their growl was thunderous and fierce, it was nothing compared to their bite. These bears spat out eighteen-pound cannonballs. Some fell short or flew between Bellamy's masts, but those that hit the frigate did unimaginable damage. Bellamy's forecastle exploded from one strike, collapsing the deck beneath it and raining jagged wood and other debris on the crewmen below. Another heavy shot caved in a section of the hull on the frigate's middle gun deck, struck a cannon that was in the midst of reloading, and started a dreadful fire that kept a dozen men busy and unable to fire back.

The finishing blow came when an eighteen-pounder blasted the frigate's quarterdeck and helm, wounding Bellamy and killing his first mate. The crew saw their captain fall, and they began to panic. Several men took places on a launch and others lowered the cutters.

"We've got him!" Ross bellowed. "His crew—they're fleeing like rats in a flood!" Ross ordered a boarding party, and Stede brought the *Bruce* in close enough to lower a gangplank. Cutlass Jack had the same idea, and his men began to board Bellamy's ship from the other side.

Ross told his men, "Give them the choice: be arrested and face justice or die where they stand."

"Declan," Stede called from the quarterdeck. "Don't ya b' over-staying yer welcome over there. There b' no doubt more'n few fires burning down below."

"Point well taken," Ross replied, and he led Jules, Red Eye, Hack, and two dozen more crewmen across the gangplank.

The few pirates still left on Bellamy's main deck refused to be taken prisoner. They fought furiously but were quickly overwhelmed. Having disarmed his first foe and thrown him to the deck, Red Eye—against his better judgment—offered another man a second chance. This fellow looked all of twenty years of age. He had no beard, an apologetic moustache, and small eyes that looked timid and afraid. But he also had a dagger that he promptly put into Red Eye's foot. Red Eye howled and knocked the man unconscious with the heavy guard of his sword. *What's the matter with me?* Red Eye wondered as he yanked the dagger out of his foot. *It's like I'm becoming nice or something.*

The fighting all but over, Ross roamed the deck uncontested until he ran into Cutlass Jack Bonnet. "I reconsidered," Jack said.

Ross embraced him in a great bear hug. "How?" he asked. "How did you find us?"

Cutlass Jack pulled away and laughed. "Ye told me yerself you were goin' t' Saba . . . t' see the monks. We just missed you. The monks kindly told us where you'd gone, so we followed."

"You followed us all the way from Saba?"

"More or less," Jack replied. "We lost ye' for a good bit. It was providence that we ever found ye' again. We caught up t' this French galleon t' ask if they'd seen ye. After they up and surrendered to us a half-dozen times, they finally told us ye be headin' for Martinique. When they told us you were goin' after Bellamy, I figured you could use a little help. Their Captain Lâchance insisted on coming along as well."

"You saved us all," Ross said. "Bellamy had us dead to rights."

"That he did," said Jack, glancing over Ross's shoulder. "The *Bruce* isn't lookin' as fine as he might."

"We lost a mast," Ross said. "Maybe a lot more." His thoughts turned to St. Pierre and the others on the lower gun deck. He hoped that they'd survived.

"Captain!" came Jules's deep voice. "Captain, you need to come up here, right away."

Ross and Cutlass Jack climbed what was left of the ladder to the quarterdeck and found that the ship's wheel and the entire helm had been blasted to scrap. Jules knelt beside a body. There was no captain's hat, and his coat had been shredded. His sand-brown hair was matted with dark blood.

But Ross knew him. "Bellamy," he whispered.

And suddenly, their old enemy opened his eyes.

Bellamy drew in a deep, gurgling breath and did something no one expected: he began to laugh. It was a horrible, wet, hacking laugh that sounded to those gathered there like a man drowning. "Look at you," Bellamy said. "Old Declan Ross . . . and Jack Bonnet. Smug . . . arrogant—you think you've won." Bellamy's lids flickered, and his eyes started to roll backward.

"What do you mean?" Ross demanded. "Bellamy, what are you saying?"

Bellamy started to smile, but his body arched suddenly. He coughed once, so loud and so long that it seemed it would never stop. He lay still and glared up at Ross. "You really don't know, do you?" He hacked out a derisive laugh. "I wish you could see the looks on your faces . . . ah, you're in for such a time."

Jack drew his sword. "Enough of these riddles," he said, holding the point of the blade to Bellamy's chin. "Get you to perdition and say hello to the devil."

"Perdition?" Bellamy smiled, and his teeth were smeared with blood. "The devil's not in perdition anymore. He's in England, my friends. The devil's in England."

Bellamy's eyes rolled all the way back in his head, but Jack dropped to his knee and shook him. "Speak plainly!" Jack yelled. "Speak!"

Bellamy's last breath escaped his lungs as a kind of scraping whisper. "Thorne . . ."

Back on the *Bruce*, Declan Ross learned many things—some good, some bad. Jacques St. Pierre and several gunners on the first cannon deck had survived Bellamy's lethal attack. Nubby treated their wounds and broken limbs as best he could. But at least they were alive. The families of Le Diamant on Martinique had not fared nearly as well. Once he was sure St. Pierre and the others were taken care of, Stede had piloted the *Bruce*'s launch to shore. He and a handful of crewmen had found a massacre there. Everything had been destroyed . . . and then burned. In the carnage, they had found one survivor, but he had been so traumatized that he either would not or could not speak. An old fisherman sailing a small sloop arrived on the island and agreed to take the survivor to the next port.

Ross met one last time with Captain Lâchance of the *Vichy*. Lâchance invited Ross and his crew to sail to France to "sample the finest boudain noir in the known world." Ross declined but was so grateful for Lâchance's timely help that he offered to buy the Frenchman a year's supply of boudain noir.

Later that evening, Cutlass Jack anchored his xebec next to the *Bruce*, and Ross convened a meeting with Jack and the senior crewmen of both ships.

"We sail for England on the morrow," said Ross, standing in the middle of his captain's quarters to avoid the wreckage Bellamy's cannonballs had caused when one blasted out the gallery window and flattened his desk.

"Now I know you b' truly out of yer mind," said Stede. "Ya won't b' getting halfway across the Atlantic in the *Bruce*."

"He's right, Declan," said Cutlass Jack. "Your ship's full of holes. Mine too. We need to be gettin' someplace safe for repairs. That, ah, Commodore Blake you were tellin' me about . . . he be in New Providence, right? We could harbor there, eh?"

"That's backtracking!" Ross exclaimed. "If Thorne's in England, we've got to go now."

"And if we do," Stede replied, "we b' doing that black-hearted mon a grand favor."

"Pardonnez moi," came a voice from the doorway. "But I think I have an idea."

"Jacques!" Ross said. "What are you doing out of bed?"

"I pretend to be asleep," Jacques replied proudly. "When Nubby went chasing after a rat, I made my escape."

"Are you well?"

"It was just a little bump on the head," the Frenchman replied. "I have had worse. Now then, do I understand correctly? Bartholomew Thorne is still alive and in England? And yet we cannot chase him because neither ship is seaworthy?"

"That's about it," Ross said.

"Ha-ha!" said Jacques. "Then we do this: we sail just a bit farther north to Bellefontaine. I know a man there who can supply just what we need to repair the ships . . . for a reasonable price, of course."

"But how long?" asked Ross, gesturing toward his shattered window. "The stern is wrecked, our first cannon deck is ruined, and we've lost a mast!"

"This man I know, Spencer Montant is his name, but we call him Slash. If anyone can get this accomplished quickly, it is Slash. But for such speed, he will charge a fortune."

"I don't care what it costs," said Ross. "But even if our ships are finished in less than a fortnight, what then? Thorne is already in England. We could arrive too late to stop him."

"Ah, that is the second part of my plan," Jacques explained. "From Bellefontaine, we find outgoing ships, sloops or something fast, and we send messages to Commodore Blake—one to New Providence and one to England. That way we warn the British as fast as sailing there directly ourselves. Ha-ha!"

"Excellent," said Cutlass Jack. "The Brits handled Thorne once . . . they can do it again. What do you say, Declan?"

Ross was quiet a moment and then answered, "It galls me to wait. But in our current condition, I think it's the best we can manage. We sail for Bellefontaine."

Ross stood at the starboard rail and rubbed his eyes. A pink glow to the east suggested the sun would be up soon. Ross glanced back to the west where Jack's xebec kept pace with the *Bruce*. It had been a long, terrible night. The next day couldn't be any worse, but it wasn't likely to be much better. They had lost too many men in the battle with Bellamy. Nubby had said two of the injured didn't make it through the night, and that brought the total to an even forty to bury at sea.

Ross thought about burying his dead. He thought about the dead left behind in Le Diamant and the other small towns in Martinique. Bellamy had caused all of it in a matter of weeks. And Bartholomew Thorne was a man capable of far worse than Bellamy. *Thorne has been missing for more than a year. What has he been doing all this time?* Ross wondered. *And what does he have in store for England?*

15

ELDREGN

Thorne looked in a smudged mirror and scraped a sharp knife across his neck and chin. "Yes, Mister Teach?" Thorne answered his quartermaster.

"Shavin', Captain Thorne?" asked Teach, coming into the chamber and rubbing a hand on his own chin. "I'm thinkin' of lettin' me beard grow meself."

"What beard?" Thorne replied. "I doubt there'll ever be a beard on that boyish chin. Now, Mister Teach, I'm sure you didn't come to my chamber to entertain me. Have you news?"

Teach didn't much like being the butt of Thorne's joke, but he didn't want a taste of his captain's bleeding stick either. So he measured his tone before he spoke. "It's the Raukar, sir. Hundreds—I dunno—maybe thousands of them in full arms gone marching out of the main gate. You must have heard them."

"Yes," said Thorne, wiping his knife on a cloth and then putting the blade to his throat once more. "The walls of this longhouse shook for more than an hour. They are a formidable army. But this is not news, Teach."

"It's Hrothgar, sir. He's requested your presence at the gate."

Thorne raised an eyebrow. The knife hesitated a moment on his chin, and a thin line of blood appeared. "Are we traveling to Ostergarn?" Thorne asked, his voice thickening and eager.

"I think so, Captain," said Teach. "Hrothgar said his ships have all returned."

Thorne wiped his chin and neck and tossed the cloth on the chair. "Now we will see at last if Hrothgar's fleet is anything like what he promised."

Lord Hrothgar and Lady Fleur stood near the gray stone gatehouse at the front of the Raukar's fortress. Beside them waited a huge carriage drawn by six massive black warhorses. The ground was broken and pocked with muddy ruts where innumerable boots had trod.

"You have kept us waiting," said Lady Fleur, and as usual, her deep blue eyes blazed out at Thorne.

She never ceased to measure him . . . never ceased to provoke him with those eyes. Thorne wondered if something would have to be done about Lady Fleur, but that would need to wait. For now, he could do nothing to arouse the Raukar's suspicion. "Your pardon, my lady," he said with a subtle bow. "I came as quickly as I could."

"Gunnarson Thorne," said Lord Hrothgar, "today you will come to the coast of Ostergarn. Then, and only then, will you be fit to witness the twofold might of the Raukar."

"Twofold?" Thorne asked.

Lady Fleur's eyes narrowed but did not leave Thorne for a

moment. "Surely a descendant of Eiríkr Thorvaldsson would know," she said.

"Peace, woman," Lord Hrothgar said, and his voice was deep and commanding. "You speak to one of pureblood, even if his ways seem strange to you."

Lady Fleur said nothing more. She turned and marched rapidly away from the gatehouse. Hrothgar clapped Thorne on the back and ushered him into the carriage.

Thorne smelled the sea air even before the carriage came to a stop. It was much different from the Caribbean. There was a purity in the air. Thorne thought of his heritage. *I am a pureblood descendant of Erik the Red*. And for a moment he allowed himself to imagine victory over the British. He'd see their vaunted fleet crippled and sent to the bottom. With the seas under his control, the Brits would not trade anything without his consent. And Thorne would install the Merchant to oversee the whole new operation. Riches beyond reckoning would be Thorne's and then he would build his own altar . . . but not to some ridiculous one-handed god.

Heather. So many years had gone by since the fire had taken her life. He remembered tearing through the burning timber of the stateroom, trying desperately to reach her in time. But the roof had caved in, and the flames engulfed her.

Somehow she had come back to him . . . speaking velvety words in his mind that no one else could hear. But since his failure on the Isle of Swords and subsequent capture, Heather had not spoken to him. Thorne felt sure she'd come back. He'd already commissioned one of the Raukar, a painter of incredible skill, to paint her portrait for him. It was to be ready within the week.

When the carriage stopped at last and the door opened, Thorne thought there must be some mistake. He'd expected to be taken to the docks of Ostergarn, but they'd come to a huge outcropping of patchy gray and white rock. It was a massive knee of stone that seemed to have burst through the tall grass and trees. Thorne could not see over or around it. Hrothgar seemed to note nothing amiss and walked directly toward the tall stone face. Thorne followed cautiously. He started to call out to Hrothgar, for the Raukar chieftain increased his speed and looked as if he were about to walk right into the stone. Only he didn't. Hrothgar stepped past where he should have been able to step. He turned slightly and winked at Thorne and then disappeared.

Thorne looked to the warrior who drove the carriage, but he did not explain. Thorne thought he saw the slightest hint of a smile flickering in the man's eyes. Thorne looked back at the stone and noticed the path leading up to it was as rutted as the path near the gatehouse. The massive marching procession had come this way. Their footsteps went right up to the stone where Hrothgar had disappeared. But at the stone, the trail stopped.

"Come, Gunnarson," came Hrothgar's voice as if spoken from within the stone.

Thorne put a hand on the haft of his bleeding stick and walked toward the rock face. All of his senses warned him that he was about to smack straight into the mountain of stone, but after a few more steps, he hadn't struck a thing. He reached out his hand and found that the rock face was still out of his reach. The warrior near the carriage laughed aloud then. Thorne ignored him and walked forward. Then he noted a tall fin of rock to the left and behind it a cavelike opening. Thorne took a few steps back and stared. "Amazing," he said aloud. The rock face was a perfect illusion. It explained how

Hrothgar had seemed to disappear. In reality, he'd only stepped behind the rock fin and entered the cave.

Thorne laughed to himself and entered the cave. Hrothgar stood a few paces inside and gestured for Thorne. The cave was merely a passage, a forty-foot tunnel, and bright light gleamed up ahead. "Prepare yourself, Gunnarson," said Hrothgar, shaking with anticipation. "You will not likely see a sight so glorious this side of Valhalla."

Hrothgar stepped aside and let Thorne pass out of the tunnel and onto the pebbly shore of Ostergarn. After the darkness and narrow confines of the tunnel, the sudden, panoramic view of the coastline was dizzying.

There were more of the contorted rock formations in the shallows of the Baltic, but anchored in both directions as far as the eye could see were massive sailing ships. Thorne had seen etchings of the Viking ships of old, and these clearly borrowed from that tradition. Each one was a long, slender vessel with numerous round shields hung along its rails and a high, elegantly curving prow that ended in the fearsome visage of a dragon or some other fierce beast. But the ships of the Raukar were by no means antiquated like their predecessors. These vessels were much taller and boasted two, three, and even four masts, each one with two to three spars upon which vast sails could be flown.

The hulls of these amazing warcrafts were assembled from the darkest wood Thorne had ever seen—else they were painted black. The dark, overlapping planks from stem to stern gave each ship the appearance of being armored. Raukar warriors stood in precise rows on the main deck of each ship. The sun gleamed off their weapons, armor, and mail.

Thorne thought the Raukar ships sat amazingly high on the water for their size and the weight of so many soldiers, but he did note the absence of one essential ingredient for war at sea.

"Cannons?" Thorne whispered.

"RAUKAR!!" Hrothgar thundered as he held his battleaxe high.

"HRAH!!" came the reply from the ships, followed by the sound like a thousand waves crashing simultaneously. And on each Raukar vessel hidden cannon bays had slid open, and myriads of thick cannon muzzles protruded from them. And upon the main deck there were other devices. They appeared to be cannons of some kind, but the barrels were uniform—not tapered—and longer.

"The twofold might of the Raukar," said Hrothgar.

Thorne, still in awe of the fleet that would be his to command, whispered, "The sea and . . ."

"And fire!" Hrothgar exclaimed, gazing out proudly upon his kin. He clenched the haft of his axe so hard his knuckles whitened. Then he turned back to Thorne. "Would you care to sail with me?"

Hrothgar had led Thorne to a cutter at the water's edge, and a dozen bare-shouldered warriors quickly rowed them out into the deeper water beyond the first two rows of warships. There waited a craft so formidable and perilous that Thorne felt an electric chill skitter up his spine to the nape of his neck. Nearly black like the others, this vessel would be invisible at night. It was taller and longer than the others, and Thorne could actually see the outline of its cannon bays. He counted four gun decks, each with fifteen cannons. "One hundred twenty guns," Thorne muttered under his breath.

"More," said Hrothgar, "when you count the dragon necks on the main deck."

"Dragon necks?"

Hrothgar snorted a laugh. "You will see."

"But so many weapons . . . it must make the vessel exceedingly heavy . . . slow."

"Not so, Gunnarson," Hrothgar said as the cutter drew near to the great ship's keel. "Have you noted the masts and the spars? Four masts and one lanteen sail on the bowsprit. But the wood is treated and sealed with a special mixture of elements that hardens it without sacrificing flexibility. From those masts and spars we can fly sails much wider than even the English warships. We Raukar harness the wind like no other seafaring race."

Thorne exhaled sharply.

"I take it you like the ship," said Hrothgar.

"I have never seen its equal," Thorne replied.

"That is because there is none." Hrothgar looked upon the ship as a father might gaze with pride upon his offspring. "This ship is our command vessel. It is yours now."

A different sort of man would have lavished gratitude over the giver of such a gift, but not Bartholomew Thorne. The ship was indeed marvelous, but for Thorne, it was merely a tool. And he felt he deserved it. "I accept," was all he said.

"Come now, Gunnarson," said Hrothgar. "What name will you give this proud ship? The Raukar shipwrights who, by sweat and toil, built it have made some suggestions, but . . . I thought the ship's captain should have that honor."

"First, I will sail upon the ship," said Thorne, "and let the ship earn its name."

Hrothgar smiled a great toothy grin. Surely Erik the Red's blood flowed freely in Thorne's veins.

Unseen crew from the deck far above threw down long rope ladders, and the passengers on the cutter clambered aboard. Thorne had never seen a deck so vast, and it appeared nearly flat. The forecastle and the quarterdeck were very low, and a dark tarp stretched at an angle in front of each. Thorne guessed this design would cut down on the resistance to the wind. All along the side rails were more of the strange long-barreled cannons Thorne had observed before. Up close, he could see why they had been dubbed dragon necks. The barrel of each cannon was as black as ink, but some other silver metal had been skillfully wrought around it like reptilian scales right up to the muzzle. And there, a dreadful dragon's mouth opened. Thorne was anxious to see what sort of cannon shot would come forth from the jaws of each of these beasts.

Hrothgar began shouting orders, and Thorne heard a series of sudden snaps. He craned his neck up to follow the mainmast skyward and saw the last of three gigantic sails fill taut with wind. Thorne took an awkward step backward, for the ship lurched forward with incredible, sudden acceleration. The long hull stabbed effortlessly through the water, and the ship—with all its cannons and crew—moved faster than any ship Thorne had ever captained.

"We sail south," explained Hrothgar. "Near the inlet where you have moored your barque, the *Talon*, you called it?"

"Yes," answered Thorne. "Fast little ship, but not fit for battle."

"Not fast like this?"

"No," Thorne replied. "Not even close."

This pleased Hrothgar. "In a few minutes, we'll come to a rocky tidal island just a mile from shore. I will show you something then."

Hrothgar said nothing more to Thorne for quite some time. He stomped around the deck, checking hatches and rigging. Many words could be used to describe the Raukar, but careless was not one of them. Thorne went to the prow and was surprised to see how high above the water he stood. It was quite a view, and Thorne imagined hunting a British ship of the line from this vantage . . .

watching its masts crack and fall and smiling as its hull slipped below the wa—

"There it is," said Hrothgar, appearing behind Thorne. He pointed over Thorne's shoulder to a pyramid-shaped piece of stone several hundred yards off the starboard bow. A twisting gray tree was the only vegetation on the little cay, and waves crashed constantly against it.

"It is your custom," said Hrothgar with a wry grin, "a pirate custom . . . to fly a black flag, is it not?"

Thorne nodded. "The banner is used to paralyze the enemy, to frighten him into submission or a tactical error."

"Fear is a powerful tool," Hrothgar said. He studied Thorne for a few moments and then said, "I took the liberty of discussing this matter with your second . . . quartermaster, I believe you call him."

"Teach?"

"Yes," the Raukar chieftain replied. "He told me something of your previous ship, about the flag you once flew. But I did not choose to replicate the design. Correct me if I am wrong, but this ship was defeated by the British?"

Thorne did not answer, but sour hatred churned in his gut.

"Now that you have the might of the Raukar behind you, Gunnarson, you will fly a new banner on this ship, and no Christian will stand against us. RAUKAR!!"

The entire crew responded, "HRAH!!"

Hrothgar nodded to a giant by the mainmast who immediately hauled a length of rope. Thorne watched as a great black banner unfurled and flapped in the wind. Thorne looked once and looked again at the design. At first he thought it was the same as the *Raven*'s. The skull, the raven taking flight, and the hourglass were all there. But then Thorne saw the difference: instead of two cutlass swords crossed behind the skull, Hrothgar had a pair of crossed hammers.

"Do you approve?" Hrothgar asked.

Thorne felt his throat thickening. It was almost too good. "Yessss," he rasped.

One of the warriors on the starboard rail yelled something in Norse. It was spoken too fast for Thorne to translate.

"We are in range," Hrothgar said as he led Thorne over to a dragon neck cannon near the fore starboard rail. "We have assembled a formidable fleet, and the valor of the Raukar who will sail it is unmatched. But even so, the British so outnumber us that victory cannot be assured and would be costly beyond reckoning. Watch now and see the means by which our victory is assured."

Hrothgar motioned to the team of Raukar stationed there. He watched one man jam a black powder charge down the barrel until its fuse appeared in an eye-hole at the rear of the cannon. Thorne wondered again what sort of cannonball these dragon necks fired. He scanned the feet of the loading team but saw none. There was, however, a stack of odd-looking black canisters. One of the loaders grabbed one of these, and Thorne watched the man turn the canister carefully so that a wiry fuse stuck up. He unsheathed a dagger and cut off about ten inches of the fuse. Then, with the fuse on the canister sticking up, the man slid the canister into the barrel of the cannon. Another man took a ramrod and pushed the canister to the back of the cannon until the canister's fuse popped up next to the firing cartridge's fuse.

Then, two men went to work, each turning a crank handle so that the barrel of the cannon tilted upward. *Too high*, Thorne believed. *It'll sail right over that little island.*

A man approached with a torch and looked questioningly at

Hrothgar. The chieftain nodded, and the man put the torch to both fuses. The fuses began to burn, and the Raukar warrior looked up, grinned at Thorne, and said, "Eldregn!"

The charge went off. The cannon shuddered. And Thorne watched with some satisfaction as the shot went well over the rocky island. *Terrible aim*, he thought. *I expected bet*— Thorne never finished his thought. There was a painfully bright flash followed by a concussive blast. A harsh orange fireball kindled above the island, and it began to spread in the sky. Flaming streamers like tentacles stretched forth and descended upon the island. The lone palm tree was instantly consumed. But it continued to burn. Fire continued to pour down from the sky, and licks of flame sprang up all over the rocky formations of the island. To Thorne's utter amazement, fire burned even on the surface of the water.

"Greek fire," Thorne muttered. "You found the formula for Greek fire."

"Nay, Gunnarson," said Hrothgar. "It was a gift from Tyr. And the Raukar have made it even more . . . effective. It is eldregn!"

"Fire rain," Thorne whispered. Then, with his throat constricting, he grasped the armor on Hrothgar's shoulders and said, "The British . . . they will burn."

"Yes," Hrothgar replied.

Thorne looked up to the black flag once more and said, "I am ready to name this ship. I will call it . . . the *Raven's Revenge*."

"It is no coincidence," said Hrothgar, "that the servant of Tyr would distinguish himself under the sign of the raven. We Raukar call the raven the chooser of the slain."

"This eldregn, this fire rain . . . what would it do to a ship?"

"You will see . . . soon enough, Gunnarson. The British will see as well."

Thorne shook his head. "I need to know its range . . . the distance it spreads, and I need to see how quickly it consumes a ship."

"But we have no ships to waste," said Hrothgar. "There is a shipwreck on the western side of the island. Part of the hull is still visible above the waves. Perhaps that will serve—"

Thorne shook his head again. He had other ideas.

Edward Teach stood on the beach with a group of Thorne's crew. A long cutter rowboat rested half in the water, half on the pebbly shore. "So let me make sure I understand you," said Teach. "You want me to sail the *Talon* out into the harbor about two hundred yards and then anchor? But you want me to raise all the sails—even the lanteen?"

"That is correct," said Thorne.

"And then what?"

"Then," Thorne said, pulling the tarp off a skid and revealing a dragon neck cannon. "Then I suggest you and the lads explore the Baltic Sea."

"Awww, but, sir?"

"Quartermaster," said Thorne, loosening his bleeding stick, "this is not a request."

Teach lowered his eyebrows and glared at his commander, but only for a moment. Then he turned on the other lads and shoved them one by one into the cutter. *Teach will make a decent second-in-command after all*, thought Thorne. *If not the smartest man, he at least has some backbone.*

Several Raukar warriors dismounted their horses and went to work, unfastening the sled from the harness they'd used to drag the cannon to the shore. By the time Teach and his crew boarded the

Talon, the Raukar had the dragon neck cannon in position. Thorne watched eagerly as Teach sailed the *Talon* farther out into the harbor.

"What is the effective range?" asked Thorne.

"Eight hundred, maybe nine hundred feet for a direct hit," answered Brandir, the chief gunner. "But you must remember the inner barrel of the dragon neck is grooved in such a way as to impart spin on the eldregn canister. When it explodes, the eldregn spreads like a deadly cloud. Even a near miss will suffice."

"And the wind?" Thorne asked.

"None today," said Brandir. "But out at sea in a strong wind, the canisters will move off target . . . accuracy—and distance—are greatly diminished."

Thorne grunted. That was ill news. When was the Atlantic ever void of wind? Thorne raised his spyglass. Teach had at last anchored the *Talon*. Thorne watched with some amusement as Teach and the others tripped all over each other trying to get into the cutter and row away. They had some guess as to what was coming.

"Are they out of range?" asked Brandir.

Thorne watched through the glass and waited. "Yes," he said with a sigh. Normally, he would not have cared, but the Raukar might balk if he blasted his own crewmen out of the water. "Yes, they are clear of the ship, far enough, I think. So long as your shot is true."

"I will not miss," Brandir said abruptly. He growled something in Norse to his men, and they sprang up. They loaded the firing cartridge and ramrodded it deep into the barrel. Brandir stared at the *Talon* and cut the fuse on the canister before loading it into the barrel. Brandir and another man cranked up the barrel. "On your command," said Brandir.

Thorne looked upon the *Talon*. Its white sails were raised high but moved very little. Brandir was right: there was maybe a five-knot breeze, nothing more. The ship swayed gently on the dark water beneath a slate gray sky. "Fire."

Brandir lit the fuses, and the Raukar gunners stepped away. The cannon uttered a sudden, deep blast. Thorne watched through the spyglass. He watched the projectile arc high and sail out of sight. A heartbeat later, the sky flashed as if by lightning. The boom that came subsequently was thunderous, and a great fiery claw erupted over the *Talon*. Molten strands of flame fell upon the ship. The sails vanished first. Fire raced down both masts and in all directions across the spars. The main deck became a cauldron, and the ship was quickly enveloped in fire. Thorne lowered the spyglass and gasped. How long had it been? Fifteen . . . twenty seconds?

Suddenly, a great explosion rocked the harbor. The eldregn had reached the powder deck below the waterline. The *Talon* burst open spectacularly with whole sections of the hull and deck blasting outward. Flaming debris screamed into the sky and then rained down into the burning water below. The circle of destruction was enormous. Thorne imagined such an explosion in the midst of a different harbor . . . a harbor full of British warships, packed in tightly together.

Hrothgar, who had been watching from a nearby hilltop, descended and stood near to Thorne. "Now are you satisfied?" he asked.

"The British burned away my most precious treasure," said Thorne. "So I will turn their nation into an isle of fire."

16
TREASURE IN THE SPIDER'S DEN

Uhnngh! Commodore Blake strained, reaching his arm into the discovered passage behind the desk. He pulled out his arm and sat up. "I'm quite certain I cannot reach it."

"I could," said Hopper. "Back at the fort in New Providence . . . I, well, I did this sort of thing all the time."

"I'm sure you did, Hopper," said Lady Dolphin playfully, tickling him behind his ear. Hopper squeaked with laughter.

"It's awfully tight," said Blake. "Are you sure you want to try? The bundle's all the way in there."

"No problem, Guv'nor," he replied, dropping to the floor. "Just leave it to Hopper."

Hopper began to shimmy his way into the crawlspace. Blake held the oil lantern up to the opening in the wall. It didn't give Hopper much light, but he was glad to have it. After all, those spiderwebs wafting in the cool drafts had to have gotten there somehow.

The bundle was just a few feet ahead. Hopper inched along. He was now all the way into the passage. Commodore Blake and Lady Dolphin could just see the bottoms of his shoes slowly disappearing into the opening. But then his shoes stopped and became very still.

"Hopper, is everything all right?" Dolphin asked.

There was silence for a few heartbeats, and then Hopper tentatively responded, "Uh, yes . . . my lady . . . everyfin' is fine."

But everything wasn't fine. Hopper had stopped because the light of the lantern had illuminated the owner of one of the billowing webs—a large brown spider. Its long, fuzzy legs were drawn up close to its body so that it appeared as a jumble of rigid angles. At first, Hopper hoped it was dead, but as Hopper drew near, it scurried forward an inch. Hopper could feel its multiple dark eyes staring at him. *Come on, lad*, he told himself. *It's just a spider. You're a hundred times its size.* But Hopper knew, in this tight crawlspace, he could not easily retreat. And it was impossible to sit up or turn away. That spider could just skitter right up to Hopper's nose, and Hopper could do very little about it.

And yet . . . Hopper desperately did not want to let Commodore Blake and Lady Dolphin down. In spite of the fact that Hopper had routinely stolen from the British back in New Providence and then stowed away on the *Oxford*, Commodore Blake and his wife had welcomed him, given him meaningful work to do, and something more. Hopper looked the spider in its multiple eyes and said under his breath, "You'll stay put if you know what's good for you."

Then Hopper squirmed forward—inch by inch. He passed by the spider's lair and dared not turn his head to look back. He expected at any moment to feel hairy legs climbing up onto his elbow. But he didn't. He did, however, get coated in more dust.

The bundle was just ahead. "Almost there!" he called back over his shoulder. He stretched out his arm, grabbed the twine that bound the bundle, and drew it into his grasp. Then he began to wriggle himself backward. He passed the spider's lair, which, he noted, was now empty. At last, he pushed his feet out of the opening in the wall, and Commodore Blake carefully hauled the young lad the rest of the way out.

Hopper stood up and, with a slight bow, handed the bundle to the commodore. "Oh, Hopper," said Lady Dolphin. Hopper grinned, expecting to be showered with praise. But the next words from Lady Dolphin's lips were, "It seems you've brought back a stowaway of your own." She reached toward Hopper's shoulder, and when her hand drew back, the hairy brownish spider sat on top of it. The creature looked even more hideous in the brighter light, especially sitting there like a pet on Lady Dolphin's delicate white fingers. But it didn't seem to bother her in the least. "He's not dangerous . . . unless you're a roach or some such." She lowered her hand to the opening and shooed the creature back to its shadowy home.

Commodore Blake gave the bundle to his wife. "I believe you should be the one to open this . . . whatever the contents turn out to be."

Lady Dolphin carried the bundle over to the dusty couch and sat down. She untied the laces and opened the stiff cloth, revealing three very old journals. They were, in fact, exactly like the others Mrs. Kravits had sent over those many months ago. Her eyes glistening, Dolphin looked up to her husband and to Hopper. She opened the first journal and, in spite of the apparent water damage that had smeared the ink on several pages, she immediately recognized her father's flowing script. Dolphin smiled and her lip trembled as she spoke. "His writing is always so ornate. You'd think he was writing a treaty for the king, not a personal journal." Dolphin laughed, but her eyes remained locked onto the text.

"The king?" Commodore Blake mumbled. He retrieved his pocket watch and flipped open the brass face. "It is much later than I thought. My darling, I am caught between two needs. I must attend my meeting with King George, but I cannot bear the thought of leaving you at a time like this."

"It is never wise to keep a king waiting," Dolphin said. "And after your reception at the palace this morning, I want to be with you. I will read my father's journals in the carriage."

"What about me?" asked Hopper.

"What do you mean?" asked Blake.

"Can I go to see the king?" he asked.

"Well . . . no," Blake said, feeling odd. "I had planned to drop you back at the *Oxford* until after our meeting with His Majesty."

"I'll stay out of the way," Hopper pleaded. "I've never been inside the palace."

"I don't know if that's a very good idea," Blake said. "Dolphin, what do you think?"

"Once we clean off the dust, he'll be fine in his . . . vest and coat, crisp breeches, and shoes at a high shine. Why don't we let Hopper stay with me in the regent's box? We won't be in the midst of Parliament that way, but Hopper can still see the king."

"The Regent's box it is, then," Blake decided. "But, Hopper, I hope you won't be disappointed. These meetings are generally pretty boring. And . . . the king, well, he may be somewhat less impressive than you imagine."

As Commodore Blake expected, Dolphin quickly became absorbed in reading her father's journals in the carriage. She spoke for the first time as the carriage drew up to the palace's northside gatehouse.

"There's still no mention of my mother being pregnant," she said. "There should be . . . that is, of course, if I was born on the date my father told me." She was quiet for a few moments. "He mentions a trip to Barbados that he had planned. He was debating whether or not to take my mother. Ah, it will have to wait." She placed the journals on the seat.

"Bring them," said Commodore Blake. Then he leaned forward and whispered conspiratorially, "If His Majesty is as long-winded as they say, you might be glad of the diversion."

17
Commodore Blake Stands Accused

The driver opened the carriage doors to ripples of laughter. He looked at his three passengers curiously. Then he bowed and stepped aside so the three of them could depart.

Taking in the enormity and grandeur of St. James Palace, Hopper gasped. "Would you look at this place!" he exclaimed.

"Surely you've seen the palace before," said Dolphin.

"Yes, my lady, but never this close." Hopper's bright eyes seemed to triple in size as they danced over the intricate stonework and the sea of red brick of the gatehouse and its twin polygonal turrets. "It's huge."

"Actually, Saint James Palace is considered quite small," said Commodore Blake, earning a frown from the carriage driver, ". . . for the seat of a world power, that is. Did you know that it was constructed on the ruins of a leper hospital?"

"Brand," Dolphin said, playfully smacking his forearm.

ournals once more. Then Blake sat up very straight. She daubed at her face with a handkerchief. *Is she crying?*

Blake started to stand, but then heard the court herald announce, "And now the matter of His Majesty's Royal Navy against Commodore Brandon Blake."

AGAINST?? Blake sat down hard. He glanced at Dolphin, who ooked utterly miserable. "Commodore Blake"—came Vogler's nasally voice—"please come before His Majesty and His Court."

His stomach churning like a whirlpool and his mind reeling, Blake left his seat and walked across the court. He bowed briefly to the king before a guard led him to the boxed seat between the king's platform and the parliamentary section, a seat normally reserved for one accused.

The king stood. His many silks swirled around him as he gestured grandly and spoke to the Parliament. Blake couldn't understand a word of German, but even before Vogler translated, Blake knew he was in trouble.

"Commodore Blake," said Vogler, now the mouth of the king, "you stand here accused of squandering the resources of England, of allowing known and dangerous pirates to escape justice, and of cavorting with pirates."

"What is this?" Blake exclaimed.

"Commodore Blake," Vogler insisted, "these are the charges. How do you respond?"

"How do I—" Blake forced back the wrath that boiled within, letting out an exasperated laugh. "I respond by saying these charges are . . . well, they're absurd. Utter hogwash."

The court erupted in many frenzied conversations. Some thought Blake had just insulted the king, for it was well-known that His Majesty's large nose resembled that of a swine. When Vogler

"What's a leper?" Hopper asked.

"A leper—" Commodore Blake was about to explain i
less colorful detail, but Lady Dolphin intervened.

". . . is a person sick with a terrible illness. Now, let's
His Majesty waiting."

Upon entering the palace, they were guided to the parli
court by a quartet of guards, none of whom said even a sing
Court was already very much in session when they enter
Dolphin led Hopper over to the regent's box, a section of s
rounded by a half wall. It was unusually full, Dolphin thou
she passed in front of the others already seated, she thou
glimpsed a few very suspicious looks toward her. But it was
compared to the withering stares cast at her husband as he
to a seat among many other military commanders and quit
white-wigged politicians.

Commodore Blake felt his ire rise like bile in the back
throat. What on earth had he done to deserve such a receptic
was quite sure he had no idea. Even the king had glanced at
and made a face as if he had just eaten something sour. But fo
at least, Blake would have to wait to discover the reason, for
George was very much occupied at the moment. Several Sco
merchants were complaining rapidly about taxes levied against
imports. Vogler, the king's beak-faced translator, was having a ter
time keeping up with the Scots.

This back-and-forth went on for a terribly long time. Sev
politicians spoke on the necessity of the taxes—much to the Scot
merchants' dismay. On and on the discussion went—made infini
longer because of the delay time needed for translation.

This sort of thing was common, but nonetheless, Blake gr
tired of waiting. He looked to Dolphin, who had opened her fathe

translated Blake's words, the king glared down at Blake and issued several terse statements in German.

"You are advised," said Vogler, "to remember your station. You will please refrain from such contemptible outbursts."

"But who brings these charges against me?" Blake responded. "I am a decorated officer in the royal navy."

"Another decorated officer brings these charges," said Vogler. "The court calls his principal witness."

The doors at the back of the great chamber opened and in walked a man in the full naval uniform of a commodore, identical to Blake's own. The man was immediately familiar even though Blake could not at first see his face. He had a narrow, uneven walk as if he might lose his balance at any moment. But as he drew nearer, Blake felt the blood drain from his face. "Sir . . . Nigel?" Blake mouthed. "Nigel Wetherby?"

His beard was gone and his hair was much more neatly groomed than it had once been. But Blake was sure he was looking at his second-in-command. "Nigel, of all the unlooked-for blessings, I . . . I thought you were . . ."

"Dead?" Nigel raised an eyebrow. "Not hardly."

"But Carinne, she's devastated . . . she doesn't know."

Nigel waved away the mention of his wife as if it had been nothing. Blake's mouth snapped shut. *Why hasn't Nigel sent word . . . at least to his wife? Still, at least Nigel is here now. He will put down these ridiculous charges.*

Commodore Nigel Wetherby turned to those seated in the Parliament and proclaimed, "I served with Commodore Blake for nine years. And so it brings me very little pleasure to stand here before you today. But my allegiance is ever to England, and I cannot allow a friendship to intrude upon loyalty to my king." He stood dramatically waiting for Vogler to finish translating. "I first became concerned for Commodore Blake when he ordered most of our Western Caribbean fleet to abandon their normal shipping lanes to pursue the pirate Bartholomew Thorne."

There were rumblings in the courtroom at the mention of Thorne's name. Nigel went on. "Thorne was a horrible menace," he said, sounding like the voice of reason. "But I began to fear that Commodore Blake's actions were becoming an obsession. There were, after all, other threats in the Spanish Main. And to leave so many unprotected to pursue a single pirate seemed to me . . . unwise."

"We had a lead!" Blake stood. He couldn't believe what he'd been hearing from his friend. "You know that. We'd been given information about Thorne's stronghold."

"Information from a less-than-credible source," Wetherby said, showing his palms to the politicians. "It was another pirate who tipped you off, was it not?"

"Well . . . yes, but—"

"So at great risk to the Caribbean settlements, and"—here Wetherby spoke directly to the king—"at great expense to England, Commodore Blake drew most of our Caribbean fleet off on a wild chase across the Atlantic."

"A chase that ended in the capture of one of England's worst enemies!" Blake countered.

"Indeed . . . ," said Wetherby. "But at what cost?" He was silent, watching the crowds who had gathered. Even the disgruntled Scotsmen remained to watch. Then Commodore Wetherby went on. "Yes, it is true that Commodore Blake and our fleet captured the notorious Bartholomew Thorne. But in that same moment, Commodore Blake did knowingly let another well-known pirate and his crew escape. Tell me, Commodore Blake, did you or did you not have the pirate Declan Ross, the Sea Wolf himself, and his crew at your mercy, and yet you chose to let him get away?"

"Of course, I did," Blake thundered. "Without Ross, we'd have never caught Thorne. Besides, Declan Ross and his crew have all been issued letters of marque from King George. They are all free men, serving England now."

"Yes, now," said Commodore Wetherby. "But not . . . then. Declan Ross and his crew were wanted for innumerable counts of piracy on the high seas. And without consulting your king and country, you let him go. Is that true?"

Blake's face flamed to a deep, angry red. He literally shook with fury, but could not bring himself to speak.

"Your silence speaks volumes," said Commodore Wetherby with a momentary pause to let his venom sink in. "And now, ladies and gentlemen of this court, and Your Majesty, hear now the most damning evidence of all. You see, this same pirate Declan Ross, at whose request Commodore Brandon Blake put our Caribbean settlements at risk and was—with criminal negligence—allowed to escape, did then conspire to embezzle untold riches from the coffers of England—all with the aid of Commodore Brandon Blake!"

The chamber buzzed with indignant chatter. King George startled them all by slamming his royal scepter onto his armrest so hard that a small red jewel broke free from its setting and shot into the powdered wig of one of the politicians. The king pointed his finger, and his voice thundered out in heavily accented English, "You steal from your country? Answer me!"

The unexpected ire muddled Blake's senses. He found he could not think clearly. He looked to Dolphin, whose face was drawn in anguish, her eyes pleading with him, but . . . for what? Standing at her side, Hopper seemed so agitated that Blake thought the lad might jump over the half wall and come running. And all the while the weight of the king's glare fell upon him. *Think, think, think!* Blake told himself.

He took a deep breath and decided to be as plain and as concrete as he could. He was not without weapons of his own. "These bombastic claims levied against me," Blake said, "are nothing more than the speculations of an inferior officer and a conniving, greedy man." Blake threw a glare at Wetherby that would have withered a forest. "Wetherby thinks this. Wetherby thinks that. He thinks! But that is all. Here are the facts concerning Declan Ross. He was a pirate, and a particularly effective one. But his name cannot be mentioned in the same paragraph with a murderous fiend like Bartholomew Thorne.

"Thorne slew thousands, many of them our countrymen. He kills in battle or in cold blood—it makes no difference. Thorne is a conscienceless monster for whom life has no value. Completely different are Ross and his crew. They wanted nothing more than to leave piracy and return to legitimate work. So Ross, at great risk to himself and his family, gave me the information I needed to apprehend Thorne. Ross even assisted our royal fleet by flushing Thorne into the trap we had set. And in the capture of Thorne, England gained riches beyond the scope of my imagination to describe. So, yes, I let Ross and his crew go. In my eyes, they have done England a great service."

Blake scanned the room and saw many nodding heads and narrowed eyes. King George was still interested, but he had taken his seat. He was listening. Nigel Wetherby was about to say something, so Blake spoke up once more. "Ross did not return to piracy either. Nay, he and his crew came to me in New Providence with a plan to rid the seas of ALL criminals by using former pirates, thereby doubling our current fleet in the Caribbean. The noble monks of the Monasterio de Michael Acángel have put up great riches of their own to see this through. And this plan has been working. Dozens of pirates have turned from their ways. They want nothing more than to earn an honest living, raise families in homes of their own. Like all of us do. Why—"

Wetherby quickly seized the moment. "Perhaps, given the high and respected position of the people gathered in this room, you should speak only for yourself." Laughter rippled through the stands.

Blake felt like he had fired a dozen broadsides at close range . . . only to see them sail well over the target. And there was Hopper, practically bouncing in front of his seat. And now, he was pointing at Wetherby . . . or the king. It was impossible to tell.

"Nay, Commodore Blake," Wetherby continued, "these brigands, these derelicts are cut from an entirely different cloth than the nobility in this place. Do you even know what your redeemed pirates have been doing since they repented and became pirate hunters? Have you monitored their actions?"

Blake was silent longer than he meant to be. "The sea is quite vast," he found himself saying. Even to his own ears, it sounded lame. "But we rendezvous in New Providence every three months."

Commodore Wetherby let Blake's words hang in the air for a long moment and then said, "Would it surprise you to know that several of your reformed pirate crews have already gone back to the sweet trade?" Blake said nothing.

Commodore Wetherby smiled. "In point of fact, the crews of the *Buccaneer's Oath*, the *Black Cutlass*, and the *Raleigh* were found in Tortuga during a recent raid by the royal navy. They were too drunk to put up any fight at all. Some of them went so far as to thank King George for the ample donation to their drinking fund."

The chamber had been a hive, quietly buzzing with opinions and suspicions, but Commodore Wetherby had thrown a stone into the midst of it. The result was a whirling, angry swarm.

"Outrageous!" someone yelled.

"Scoundrels!" barked another.

Half of the military commanders and most of the politicians were on their feet shouting their ire or sending exasperating glares. A dozen soldiers appeared and hastily quieted the writhing throng. One red-faced man had to be dragged from the chamber. Blake's heart pounded in his chest. He felt as if the walls were pressing in against him, and he was helpless to push back.

Unlike the Parliament still shifting in their seats and breathing heavily, King George did not seem agitated in the least. He stood, adjusted his ever-swaying red robe, and motioned for Vogler to stand near. He spoke boldly and with more volume than he needed, especially since no one but Vogler understood him. In spite of the language barrier, it seemed to Blake that the speech the king now delivered had been practiced, rehearsed, and refined until the delivery was just so. Blake wondered what doom the king had pronounced, and he braced himself as Vogler began to speak.

"His Majesty declares a complete and immediate dissolution of the pirate-hunting fleet." Blake felt the bile rising again in his throat. "Not even a single additional ounce of England's gold will be paid to these doubtfully reformed pirates. England already has a pirate-hunting fleet. It is His Majesty's Royal Navy."

"You don't understand!" Blake leaped to his feet and roared, "You can't just cut them off again! They will live to curse England . . . you will create an enemy twice as large as it is, and ten times as fierce! You must—"

"YOU must take your seat!" commanded Vogler. "How dare you interrupt the king's word."

Vogler looked questioningly over his shoulder to the king. King George nodded and Vogler went on. "As for the matter of Commodore Blake . . . until such time as a thorough investigation of your actions can be completed, you will resign your commission as commodore in the royal navy and relinquish your command of the *Oxford*. Due to your distinguished service—in the past—you will be allowed your freedom. But do not leave England. This is the will of the king."

Cheers and shouts filled the chamber, but this time the soldiers did not restrain them. Clamoring, red-faced men left their seats and filled the aisles. Guards came and forcibly took Commodore Blake away from the throne, pushing him through the crowd toward the chamber doors. "Brand!" a thin woman's voice cut through the uproar.

"Dolphin!" Blake called, scanning over the heads of so many. There! He saw her red hair aflame in a bland sea. Bless her, she was knocking people aside to get to him. With Hopper right behind her, Dolphin drew near and stood in front of one of the guards.

"Stand aside, my lady," the soldier commanded. "Mister Blake must leave the king's chamber."

"I am not your lady!" growled Dolphin. "COMMODORE Blake is my husband. Now shoot me if you must or allow us the dignity of departing without an escort!" The guard's eyes widened, and he stepped back a pace to let Dolphin pass.

Blake embraced her, but Dolphin quickly drew back. He looked at her, his expression questioning. "Thorne lives," she said.

"What?" Blake could not believe he'd heard her correctly.

"Hopper saw him escape," Dolphin explained. And Blake noted for the first time that Hopper was right behind his wife. "It was Nigel, my darling, Nigel released Thorne, and they escaped New Providence just before the wave hit."

Blake's thoughts swam. "How . . . how can this . . . ?"

"It's true, sir," yelled Hopper, his voice shrill. "I was at the fort that night, I was. Well, I know I wasn't supposed to be there, but I wanted to see the pirate before he was hanged. First time I'd climbed the bell tower too. I was just on me way back down when I heard somefin'. I watched from above as this man came to the pirate Thorne's cell. And lo, he opens the door and lets Thorne out. I thought then he was takin' the pirate for a last meal or some such. But I never saw them come back."

"How can you be sure it was Wetherby?" Blake asked.

"I saw him full in the face, I did!" Hopper frowned.

"And did he look just like the man over there?" Blake pointed to Commodore Nigel Wetherby, who was talking with Vogler off to the side of the throne.

Hopper nodded repeatedly. "'Cept he had a dark beard and his hair was longer . . . a little more scraggly."

Blake felt a chill. It all made sense now. That's how he did it. Blake recalled the meeting with Ross and his senior crew that night in New Providence. He remembered Commodore Wetherby excusing himself just after dinner—not more than an hour before the wave hit. And now, Nigel was back in England manipulating the king's mind to think against the Wolf fleet.

Dolphin took her husband's hand. He looked down at her, saw her pained expression, and said, "There's more, isn't there?"

She did not answer him directly. "It must wait," she said. "Go, do what you need to do." Blake hesitated a moment more and then whisked Hopper off the floor and charged through the crowd toward the throne.

"Sir!" called one of the guards, trying to catch up to Blake. "Sir, you must leave!

"Your Majesty, Master Vogler!" Blake cried out. But at first, the crowd's clamor drowned out his voice. "Please, I must be heard!!"

The people nearest Blake began to quiet, and they turned to look. Blake yelled, "Your Majesty, grant me an audience one last time!" But the king had already turned and was walking away. Vogler and Wetherby were still deep in conversation.

Blake banged into several dignitaries. White wigs flew, and spitting mad faces turned to Blake. But the commodore paid them no mind. His rage, fueled by betrayal, gave him the volume he needed. "I MUST BE HEARD!!!"

Silence spiraled out from Blake, and the chamber became as still as a forest moments before a storm. Even the guards stood still, wondering what to do. The king turned around and walked slowly back to the step before the throne. He looked at Vogler. Vogler looked at Blake.

"What is the meaning of this?" Vogler asked, his eyes flitting between Blake and the peculiar bald child in his arms.

Blake placed Hopper by his side. Blake looked at the king and said, "What did Nigel tell you? Did he tell you that the pirate threat was diminished now . . . that Bartholomew Thorne was dead?"

Nigel started to speak, but Blake pointed at his former second-in-command and said, "Close your mouth, snake! You have loosed enough of your poison here." Nigel's face burned, his cheeks near burgundy, but he dared not speak.

"I have sure evidence that Bartholomew Thorne is alive!" Blake said. The words went off like a grenade. The crowds murmured. "This young man was there," Blake said, putting his arm around Hopper's shoulders. "He was at the fort on New Providence the night of the great wave. And he saw a man come to Bartholomew Thorne's cell and take him out just before the waters came. Hopper saw the man who set Thorne free. It was Nigel Wetherby."

The color in Nigel's face drained. Blake went on. "Why would Nigel do this? He is a traitor . . . that is why, a bitter, reprehensible man. And now he is in London to see the end of the Wolf fleet. I am sure this is none other than Bartholomew Thorne's scheme, a scheme to weaken England."

Nigel looked away from Blake and nodded ever so slightly to Vogler. Vogler hurriedly translated for the king. The chamber stirred, but all eyes were on the king, who listened intently to Vogler. In spite of the new evidence, the king seemed strangely unmoved. Without changing expression even once, the king replied to his translator.

Vogler spoke up. "The king is used to desperate pleas, Mister Blake. Desperate pleas from desperate men. Do not think for one moment that you can bring some—child—into this room and make such claims. How far you have fallen to resort to this. Guards, take Mister Blake from this chamber at once. And see to it that he does not enter into it again unbidden."

"You will regret this!" Blake yelled even as the guards took his arms and pulled him backward. "Thorne has no love for England! Mark my words!"

The carriage passed a gated cemetery. The dusky sun painted the white headstones lavender and red. Blake stared at the markers solemnly and wondered how many men had died because of Wetherby's treachery. He wondered, too, how he could have been fooled for so long. How long? How long had Wetherby been Thorne's spy?

So many times, Thorne had seemed within England's grasp only to slip away. Ross would want to know. But how? The *Oxford* was no longer Blake's to command. Blake shook his head and gazed at the graveyard. The ride back to Dolphin's family estate had been silent until this point. Even Hopper, who chattered like a squirrel most times, was quiet. But then Blake felt Dolphin shudder, and he remembered.

"My darling," he said, taking her hand, "I am terribly sorry. You have something to tell me. Is it about Wetherby, about Thorne . . ."

Dolphin shook her head. "No." She took her hand back from her husband and clutched one of her father's journals in her lap. She squeezed it so hard her knuckles whitened. "While those irate Scotsmen appeared before the king, I delved deeper into my father's writing."

He looked at her quizzically.

"I now understand why my father never wrote of me as a baby," she said, her body quaking. "I now know why he never wrote of my mother being pregnant with me."

Blake felt heat radiating from his wife, and his heart wrenched for her.

"My mother," she whispered, "was barren. She died of malaria having never given birth to a child of her own. I was an orphan."

"Like me," said Hopper quietly. Dolphin smiled sadly and put a hand on his knee.

"My father," she continued, "took part in an attack on a pirate stronghold here in England. He wrote about many dying in the battle, and the huge fire that ensued. And from the carnage, they pulled a woman who was with child. The mother perished, for her burns were severe. But the child survived unscathed." Tears came in greater torrents as she said, "I was that child."

"Miraculous," her husband whispered.

"Was it?" Dolphin asked. Her eyes glistening. "I am not so sure."

Blake pulled his wife close, embraced her with a gentle but firm touch. "You are a miracle to me," he said softly. "It doesn't matter how you got here."

"But it does," she said, pulling away. "Do you not see? This changes everything. I am not the daughter of an English naval officer. And I have never known my real parents. Why didn't he tell me?"

"I'm sure he planned to," Blake replied. "But you were too young when—"

"That never stopped him before. My father always told me things." She sighed. Sadness and exhaustion flooded out of her, and she collapsed to her husband's shoulder. "My real father . . . I don't even know who he is."

"Yes, you do," Blake assured her. "Your father was the man who adopted you and cared for you all the life you remember. He was real; his love for you was real. When you adopt a child, that child is sewn so deeply into your heart that he becomes your own. Your father loved you as his very own."

Dolphin's chin trembled, and a brave smile curled on her lips.

"S'cuse me, sir," said Hopper, tugging at Blake's cuff. "Is that the way it is . . . with all children who get adopted?"

"Yes, it is," Blake replied, and Dolphin drew Hopper close by her side.

Blake said nothing more, but his mind reeled over recent revelations. And something more troubled him. Dolphin's father had written of a horrible fire . . . of a woman with child pulled from the burned wreckage. Why did that sound familiar? He thought it might have been something Declan Ross had told him, but Blake couldn't remember for sure. *Ross.* Blake felt a chill race along his spine. *Ross needs to be warned, but how? A message by courier to New Providence, perhaps?* Blake sighed. The nightmare of nightmares had come true. Bartholomew Thorne lived, and the only ones who might be able to stop him had been rendered unaware . . . or powerless.

18

La Isla Desvanecente

Cat felt uneasy. He hadn't had any real rest the day before because of a wicked storm that had rocked the three Brethren ships as they sailed from Jamaican waters toward Pine Island. He knew he ought to be exhausted, but still he could not sleep. He covered his eyes with a hand and turned his head into the fabric of his hammock. Anne had the helm of the *Constantine*, and Cat knew she was as capable a sailor as anyone. And Father Brun was there if anything went wrong. So Cat couldn't blame this disquiet on fear for the ship. The sea at last was relatively calm, and if Scully's information was to be trusted, they had a long stretch of open water ahead of them. So it wasn't the sea that stirred his innards. Cat tried to convince himself that he was just too keyed up over the possibility of capturing the Merchant on La Isla Desvanecente.

No, he thought as he turned again in the hammock. *The ominous shadow of the Merchant inspired fear of another sort.* The dread that tingled in Cat's mind and grasped at his gut came from a different source. . . . The damp, heady scent and the warm, stagnant air of the cabin reminded him of another place, but Cat didn't want to recognize it for what it was. Even as he finally began to feel drowsy, he knew it was still there—faintly scratching at the back of his mind.

There was no sound at first. Only images. Cat was back on the island of Dominica, but it was night. Men carrying oil lanterns walked in front of him, and swaying light reflected off the wide swords at their sides. There was someone else there, leading their train. But he was a shadow, a dark blotch passing noiselessly up the alleyway. Gray buildings loomed up on either side of them. Black windows stared out like the sockets of skulls in a charnel house. Cat could feel the wind on his arms, on his forehead, on his chest—like tiny spiders creeping along his flesh. Even though he could feel this tingling breeze and watch it sway the palm leaves, he still could not hear it.

They passed around the back of one building and paused. Two of the men gave a mighty heave on a pair of heavy doors that protruded from the ground like a massive grave marker. Cat watched the doors open and saw a red light glowing from below. The two men started to descend, but a gnarled staff barred their way. The shadowy figure stepped before them, and Cat knew him. The man's cold blue eyes flickered with torchlight and found Cat. A snarl curled under the man's moustache, and he motioned for Cat to join him. Cat found himself hurrying forward. They walked together down a short but very steep set of steps. Cat felt his heart beating, pounding in his chest.

When he reached the basement floor, his vision slowly adjusted to the strange red light. Cat's stomach churned and tightened as he saw them at last. Five men and two women, straining at their chains, pulling as if they might break free and burrow into the earth at the back of the chamber. Then he watched as his father, Bartholomew Thorne, took up his walking stick and slowly unscrewed its spiked head. It fell away without a sound and hung by its chain at his side for a moment. Then, as Thorne walked toward the captives, the spiked head swung like a pendulum. Back and forth . . . back and forth. The prisoners were frenzied now, jerking and flailing, lunging so hard that their manacles cut the flesh of their ankles and wrists.

Bartholomew Thorne whirled his weapon around and struck. And at last, Cat heard everything: screams from the man Thorne had hit, shrieks and weeping from the others. There were other sounds too: the crackle of a great fire pit, from which the red light shone, the clanking of chains and manacles, and the horrible impact of the weapon.

Some part of Cat urged him to do something . . . to stop this. But he did not. He watched. Soon, Bartholomew Thorne turned away from the prisoner and carried the weapon over to Cat. "Your turn," he said, his voice raspy and cracking, ". . . son."

Cat clutched the hammock so hard his fingers tore the material and his own nails cut into his palms. He woke suddenly, disoriented and flailing, falling to the floor amidst the echo of screams. Cat hunched on his hands and knees, and sweat ran in hot rivulets down his cheeks and dripped on the deck. "What have I done?" His voice came in breathy heaves. The door to his cabin flew open, and some-one was there kneeling at his side.

"Cat?" Anne moved her hand lightly from his back to his shoul-der. She feared he might be hurt and wasn't sure if she should touch him. "Are you . . . are you all right?"

"What have I done?" he whispered.

"What?" There were other footsteps in the room. "Cat, what did you say?"

He lifted his head and saw her, but his eyes seemed to look through her and far away. He blinked several times and squinted. "Anne?" he said.

"Is he hurt?" Father Brun asked, standing in the doorway.

Cat shook his head and sat up. "No, I'm not injured . . ."

"Are you sure?" queried the monk. "I've never heard such a scream . . . like a demon pursued you. The whole crew heard."

"I am sorry," Cat said with a heavy breath. "Really, I'm fine now. It was just a dream."

Father Brun nodded thoughtfully. "Can I help—"

"No," Cat replied sharply, but realizing his tone, he softened and said, "No, thank you."

"After such a dream, you may not wish to sleep," Father Brun said. "But in truth you've only been below deck for a few hours. Rest if you can." Father Brun eyed Cat a moment more and then left.

Cat stood up and rubbed his forearms. He wandered slowly over to his hammock and saw the place where he'd clawed through. Anne saw too. "You did that?" she asked.

Cat didn't answer. "Cat, did you remember something?"

He couldn't lie to Anne, but he wasn't sure how to tell her what he now knew. "Yes," he whispered. "The island."

Anne thought she understood, thought Cat meant the day his own father had flogged him within an inch of his life. "Cat, I'm sorry," she said. Cat was grateful that she didn't ask anything more.

"Anne?" said a faint voice from the hallway. It was Father Brun.

"I've got to get back on deck," she said. "Will you be all right?"

Cat nodded. Anne smiled and left the room. Cat carefully got back into his hammock. He thought of Father Brun's words, *". . . sounded like a demon pursued you."* But, Cat wondered, *what if I am the demon?*

"I told you everything you need to know," said Scully. "Why must I remain on deck?"

Father Brun tightened his grip on the rogue's shoulder. "We are close now," he said. "I want to be sure."

"But I already told you, you must approach from the west. This time of day, the sun will make the island nearly impossible to see."

Cat shielded his eyes from the descending sun with his hand and looked out toward the horizon. He was perplexed by what he saw: a curling strip of land crisscrossed with wiry vegetation and an occasional palm. But this was just the bending finger of the island. Its knuckle was a looming mound of white sand. Its fist was a great angular shelf of rock, and a forest of dark pines crowded its slope. "But I can already see the island," said Cat.

"Do you think that massive island, mighty trees and all, disappears below the water?" Scully made a clucking noise. "No, that is Pine Island, still miles from our destination. What we seek you will not see until you are upon it and that only if you know where to look when the tide is right."

"I don't think he knows where it is," said Anne, glaring at Scully venomously. "Why would the Merchant trust the likes of him?"

Scully sneered at her. "The Merchant," he said, his eyes half-hooded and a sickly grin forming beneath his pointed nose, "has many connections, but even he has a need for information . . . the kind of information that only I can obtain."

Cat involuntarily shivered. There was something slippery and dangerous about this man. Cat examined the ropes that bound Scully's bonds as if, at any moment, he might slither out of his bindings and stab someone in the back. "I would not trust this man either," said Father Brun coolly. He released his grip on Scully's shoulder. "But there are some, ah . . . incentives for Mister Scully to be truthful here. Isn't that right, Mister Scully?"

Scully shifted uneasily and stepped a pace back from the monk. Cat realized at that moment that Scully was not the only dangerous man aboard the *Constantine*.

"So what does this disappearing island look like?" Anne asked. Father Brun took a step closer to Scully.

Scully flinched and began to speak. "La Isla Desvanecente is a . . . a freak incident of nature. A long time ago, molten lava spewed up from a fiery crack in the sea floor. As the rock cooled in the sudden cold of the sea, it formed a strange spiraling chamber not unlike the cavity of a conch shell. Again and again this vent opened, each time forming a new chamber until, at last, it rose up and breached the sea. Now, bone-white coral curls over its black surface and wraps around the column of volcanic rock like the skeleton of a great snake."

"It sounds charming," said Anne. She started to say something more, but stopped short. "What's that?" She pointed toward the glare of the sun and the silhouetted tail end of Pine Island. They all turned, squinting like Anne.

"I don't see anything," said Cat.

"Nor I," said Father Brun. "What did you see?"

"I . . . I thought I saw a sail out on the water," she said, doubt evident in her voice. Scully stiffened. "It was there for a moment," Anne continued, "but then gone."

Father Brun slid his fingers thoughtfully under his chin. "It is not uncommon for pirates to careen on desolate shores like Pine Island," he said. "But given our position, so close to the Merchant's lair, I am more concerned that he has ships in the area. Mister Scully, you have never said how your friend travels to and from his tidal hideout. He must have some . . . system, some way of alerting his ship."

Scully did not answer at first. Father Brun's eyes, normally restless and darting, fixed on Scully and burned with pale intensity. Scully stepped backward. "He's never told me how," said Scully. "And I do not ask him. From the beginning he told me never to ask questions of him. That was our arrangement. Now, keep away from me, priest!" Scully backed away even more, but Brother Javier, one of the *Constantine*'s gunners, stepped away from the mainmast and drew a bright cutlass. With that sharp blade behind him, a sullen Scully stopped immediately and glowered at Father Brun.

"Whatever the case," said the monk, "we must be wary. We need to alert Bennett and Cascade."

Cat gave the command, and several of the *Constantine*'s sails were immediately reigned in. He looked up to Brother Keegan at the ship's wheel. Cat still felt bad for the young monk. Father Brun had chosen Keegan to be the *Constantine*'s quartermaster before Cat had requested Anne. Keegan had accepted the news without a complaint—or even a frown. But since they left the Citadel, Cat had tried to give Keegan time at the helm.

They made eye contact, and Cat nodded. The young monk nodded back. The ship slowed until the *Dominguez* and the *Celestine* pulled even with them. Then all three of the Brethren's ships sailed west of Pine Island into the setting sun.

"I need a sextant," Scully said at last. "Otherwise, we may miss the island."

Cat went to the helm and brought back the navigational instrument. He held it up for Scully, but Scully did not take it. Nor could he; his hands were bound. "You tell me when to release the clamp," Cat said with a smirk.

"For mercy's sake, will you free my hands?" Scully sighed. "I cannot get a proper reading."

"Mister Scully, you don't believe me to be that gullible, do you?" asked Father Brun. "I may not know the sea like a tall ship captain, but even I know the sextant is accurate in the hands of anyone who knows how to use it. And I assure you, Cat—this ship's captain—is up to the task."

Scully glowered once more—it seemed to be his preferred facial expression of late. Cat sighted the horizon through the sextant's lens, released the clamp freeing the index bar, and brought the sun down in line with the horizon. He gave the reading to Scully, who nodded. The slightest hint of a smile played at the corner of his mouth. "We're almost there," he said. "Look off the port bow. If the tide is right—and I believe it is—you will see a round patch of black with here-and-there ripples of white. Not much different than the sea and its whitecaps . . . only this patch will not be moving."

Anne went to the rail first. "I see it!" she said.

Cat joined her. "That's amazing . . . it's black stone," he said. "We'd have never seen it—"

"If I hadn't directed you so accurately," Scully finished the sentence. "You see . . . I can be trusted." Scully grinned. He waited for Father Brun to go to the rail. Then he moved a step backward, a few inches closer to Brother Javier and his sharp sword. "Uh, Captain," Scully said to Cat, "you'll want the ship to come in from the leeward side."

"Right," said Cat, but he hesitated a moment. Then he called up to Brother Keegan and commanded him to steer the *Constantine* to the windward side of the island—opposite of Scully's recommendation. Scully glared at Cat but said nothing. The winds were steady, though not especially powerful. The *Dominguez* and the *Celestine* sluiced through the waves on either side.

Three warships, Cat thought. *Won't the Merchant be surprised when he realizes the might of the Brethren is about to descend upon him? It's a bit of overkill for one man.* The thought had barely traveled its course when several things happened in such quick succession that no one had time to react until it was too late.

There came a horrible, sharp cracking sound, and the *Celestine* was suddenly no longer sailing beside them on the right. Cat turned and looked aft. Their sister ship had come to a dead stop in the water, and a gaping black fissure had opened on its bow near the keel. The *Celestine* seemed stuck, perched at an odd angle, even as water poured into its hull. Someone yelled, "They've struck a reef, Captain! Trim the sail and come about!"

At that moment, Scully jammed his fists back toward Brother Javier. The cutlass blade slid across Scully's bonds right below the knot, and in a heart's beat, he was free.

"Scully, no!" Father Brun yelled, but Scully dove over the rail.

Cat, Anne, and Father Brun raced to the rail and scanned the waves. "Javier," Father Brun cried. "Look aft!"

Javier dropped his sword and sprinted toward up the stairs leading to the poop deck. He strained to see down into the dark water. He looked for a head to pop up amid the whitecaps, but none did. "There's no sign of him!" he called back.

"Look here," Cat said. He had picked up Javier's sword and held it up for all to see. Dark blood trickled down its blade.

"The fool," said Father Brun. "He paid for his freedom with his life." He was grim and silent for a moment. "Nonetheless, we cannot dwell on this. The *Celestine* is in need of aid." Brother Keegan had deftly turned the ship around. The *Dominguez* had followed suit. They could all see that the *Celestine* was lower in the water and listing to one side.

Cat looked from the ailing ship back to the circle of black known as La Isla Desvanecente. "But what about the Merchant?" he asked. "The tide's coming in. We could lose this chance."

"Believe me, Cat," said Father Brun, "no one would regret the loss of the Merchant more than I would . . . but my brothers are in need. Even now, the tide's pushing the *Celestine*'s hull onto that reef—the crew must be rescued."

"I understand," Cat said. "But with Scully gone . . . how will we ever find the island again?"

"We could just anchor and wait until tomorrow," said Anne.

Father Brun noted that the *Dominguez* had surged ahead and was already nearing the *Celestine*. Then he turned and looked toward the setting sun. "I wonder about that sail you might have seen," he said. "If the Merchant does indeed have ships near his disappearing island and they came upon us at night . . ." He didn't need to finish the sentence.

Cat couldn't believe it. How had everything gone so horribly wrong? How could they come all this way, get this close, and then just let him go? "So, that's it?"

"Either choice is grim," said Father Brun. "If we go after the Merchant, we neglect the *Celestine*. The *Dominguez* may not get the crew to safety in time. And yet, if we go to my brothers' aid, and we let the Merchant escape us, then how many will perish because of his black influence in the world?"

"What if . . . ," said Javier, still wiping blood from his sword, "what if we could do both?" They stared at Javier quizzically. "Ah,

I will explain. Some of you sail the *Constantine* and rescue the men on our wrecked ship. Some of you take a cutter to the little island and find the Merchant."

Father Brun's slow nods accelerated. "Yes . . . yes, that will work! Javier, you are a godsend. Cat?"

Cat grinned. "I'll give the order and get my sword."

The sun was setting as the cutter made for the black rock island. Father Brun, Cat, and Anne worked the oars in the front. Brothers Diego and Cyprian heaved the oars against the waves in the middle. And Brother Dmitri alone anchored the cutter in the rear. The *Constantine* was already a hundred yards behind them, joining the *Dominguez* to rescue sailors from the disabled *Celestine*.

"Does the Merchant have guards?" asked Brother Cyprian.

"Scully did not specify," said Father Brun. "But I have no doubt he will. You do not ask out of fear . . ."

"No, Father Brun," he replied, straining and arching his back. "But if the Merchant is not alone, how will we know which man is he?"

"I have seen him," Father Brun whispered.

"You've seen the Merchant?" Cat and Anne asked as one.

"Only once, and it was a long time ago . . . just after I joined the Brethren."

"Why haven't you told us before?" asked Cat.

"It is not something I like to remember." Father Brun winced. "But . . . you are right, you should know. I was studying under a great leader of the Brethren, Father Vincente, in Curaçao. One morning, I left the church on my usual visit to the marketplace. Halfway there, I realized I hadn't brought my money, so I returned to the church. I was on the steps when I heard Father Vincente groan.

I threw open the doors and found a man standing over Father Vincente's body."

"The Merchant?" Anne asked.

Father Brun nodded. "He fled, but I chased him into the rectory behind the church. I managed to trip him up on a narrow flight of stairs, and that's when I saw him."

"What did he look like?"

Father Brun replied quietly, ". . . Pale, diseased, cold."

There were no more questions.

The narrow cutter sliced between some waves, crested and slid down the backs of others, and blasted through the rest. It was growing dark, when the cutter reached the stony shore of La Isla Desvanecente. Brother Dmitri quickly found a curving hunk of coral and tied off the cutter. He gave the knot special attention. The last thing any of them needed was to have the cutter float away while they were inside.

Father Brun and Brother Cyprian each carried oil lanterns. "The island is much larger than it appeared," said Father Brun. "Much of it is already under the water. The tide concerns me."

"Ah, why the worry?" scoffed Brother Dmitri. "We're just going after one of the most diabolical madmen in history, chasing him into his own lair which at any moment could be completely submerged beneath the waves." No one laughed.

"Here!" Brother Cyprian called. "I found the bulkhead door." Cat and the others surrounded Brother Cyprian, and they all stared down at a circle of dark iron so crusted over with coral that it was hard to discern as having been a door at all.

"No sense wasting time," said Brother Dmitri, and he reached down and grasped an iron bar that protruded like a kind of handle. He gave a mighty pull, but it did not move. He shrugged his shoulders and adjusted his stance to get more leverage. He pulled again. "Ah!" Brother Dmitri jerked back his hand. In the lantern's light, all could see the blood surging from the gash on his palm. "That coral is razor sharp!" Without another word of complaint, Dmitri reached down and tore a strip of cloth from one leg of his breeches and bound his hand. "That door is shut tight."

"Maybe there's another hatch," said Anne.

"Scully mentioned only one," said Father Brun. "One way in. One way out, he told us."

"Scully lied." Anne called out, "Bring the lantern."

They joined her and discovered a dark iron door identical to the first. Cat reached for its handle. "Mind the coral," said Brother Dmitri.

Cat threaded his hands onto the metal and gave a tug. The hatch came immediately free, surprising Cat, who fell backward, barely keeping upright in a pool of ankle-deep water. Cat looked behind him and saw nothing but the dark sea. "That was close."

"Too close," said Brother Dmitri. "Be more careful. Now is no time for swimming."

Cat joined the others at the now-open hatch. "There's light," said Brother Diego. They stared into a five-foot-wide tunnel that plunged straight down into the rock. A seemingly never-ending ladder led down, vanishing and reappearing several times in the pale greenish light that emanated from unseen recesses in the glistening stone.

"Maybe he's expecting us," said Anne.

"I do not know how that could be," said Father Brun, and he abruptly closed his eyes in prayer. "Nonetheless we place our lives in the hands of the Almighty. Father, be for us a light in dark places, amen." Then Father Brun reached into a fold of his cloak and withdrew a short but wickedly sharp dagger. "I will go first."

"Are you certain?" the Merchant asked, his dark eyes glistening with interest.

"As certain as I live," said a sopping wet Edmund Scully. Blood still seeped from the wound on his forearm, and he clutched it to his chest. "He calls himself Cat, but he is the son of Bartholomew Thorne. There is no mistaking his features: eyes, angle of the brow, and the line of his chin. But to put it beyond all doubt, I overheard him speak of it."

"This is . . . an interesting development," said the Merchant. His tongue slithered like a serpent between his sparse teeth. "Of course, you should never have brought them here, Mister Scully. We had an arrangement."

"Yes, of course," Scully said, trembling from much more than the cold. "But given your new association with Bartholomew Thorne, I thought that you would want, that you could use, his son to—"

"Be silent." The Merchant barely whispered those words, but it may as well have been a voice as loud as a cannon blast. "Due to your weakness, I have lost much—the secrecy of my unique lair is forfeit."

Scully leaned backward. They sat in a wide oval chamber where many tunnels converged. Scully didn't know where each tunnel led, but he didn't like the cold look in the Merchant's depthless eyes. Scully's muscles tensed, and he prepared to dart for the nearest tunnel.

"Still," said the Merchant with a grotesque, canker-ridden smile, "in your ignorance you may have brought me a prize worth more than my loss." He rubbed at his pointed chin. "How many ships did the Brethren muster?"

"Only three," Scully replied nervously. "And one of them is impaled upon your reef."

"The *Perdition's Gate* is due to arrive within the hour," said the Merchant. "The Brethren vessels do not stand a chance."

"But two ships against one?"

"The Brethren are warriors, but their skill stretches very thin on the ocean. My men and my weapons are far superior." The Merchant stood. "Now, who will venture ashore? Will Thorne's son . . . Cat, will he—"

The Merchant became silent, but other voices filled the chamber. "Cat, there's a wrung missing. Watch your step."

"I see it," a voice answered. "Anne, be careful."

"That's Father Brun," whispered Scully. "And Cat is with him. But how—? They sound as if they are in the room."

"Nay," said the Merchant. "They descend the west tunnel."

"How . . . how do we hear them?"

"The acoustic nature of my abode," said the Merchant. "Tubes that formed long, long ago as this molten column cooled in the water of the sea. There is even a place in the center of my lair where I can monitor almost all of these upper chambers. Come, walk with me. I will show you. And, perhaps, you can be of some use yet."

Scully stood, pleased that he could repay his mistake. The Merchant led him along a winding corridor until they came to a doorway with a low arch. "You'll need to duck through here," said the Merchant, stepping aside.

"It's dark," said Scully. "I can't see—" It wasn't much of a push, just enough to cause Scully to lose his balance. Windmilling his arms and clawing at the air, Scully fell into endless dark. Scully's scream—a shrill, desperate wail—reverberated through the tunnels and then ended quite suddenly.

Father Brun and the others froze in their various places within the vertical tube. The anguished wail seemed to get farther away until they no longer heard it at all. "The Merchant," whispered Father Brun. "There can be no doubt that he is here."

"If that scream was his," said Brother Dmitri, "then he is none too pleased with our arrival." Cat didn't think the horrible wail came from the Merchant, but he felt certain that somehow the Merchant knew they were coming.

Slowly, they continued down the vertical passage. Cat had been counting the rungs. There were fifty-seven so far. Each one was barely enough metal to rest a foot on. And they were very slippery too. In fact, Cat noted, the walls of the tunnel were cool and smooth as if eroded by water over many long years.

Every ten feet or so, a small oil lantern burned in a pocket of stone. This provided intermittent pale light. Near one of the lanterns, Cat found odd markings and indentations—small spirals and segmented lines, as if small sea creatures had once been imbedded within this rock but had perished and rotted away leaving nothing but these marks. Cat had no desire to remain in these blasted tunnels and certainly no desire to perish. The sooner they finished this mission the better. A dozen more rungs and Cat began to feel uncomfortable pressure in his ears. They were deep beneath the surface, Cat felt sure. He held the rung in front of him with one hand, held his nose with his other, and gently blew to clear his ears of the pressure—a little trick he'd learned from the conch divers when the *Bruce* made port on Aruba. Then he continued down.

Father Brun dropped down out of the tunnel and found himself in a squat chamber lit by two lanterns recessed into the wall like the ones in the tunnel. Cat and the others arrived in turn, and each drew weapons upon landing. Cat had the cutlass Red Eye had given him long ago. Anne had a sword also, as well as a long dagger in her right boot. Father Brun and the others carried the black fighting rods that were the customary weapon of the Brethren warriors. With those simple weapons, they could disarm and disable most foes.

Anne looked left and right. Passages opened on either side. "Where did the scream come from?" she asked.

"Impossible to tell," said Father Brun. "But this passage"—he pointed to the right—"seems to go down. Cat?"

Cat nodded. Father Brun treated him with respect. As captain of the *Constantine*, Cat expected to command the ship, but feared that Father Brun would demand authority elsewhere. *No*, Cat realized, *he doesn't need to demand*. Men knew his wisdom. Men knew his faith. Men knew his strength. And yet he often deferred to others. Cat wondered at that. "Down we go," Cat said.

"Good," said the Merchant. He sat in an almost perfectly round room from which only one passage led. But there were dozens of small openings all over the chamber. Some were just big enough for a man's fist to fit through. Others were wide enough for a person's head. But all of these openings went deep into the rock, disappearing into shadow. The Merchant knew where each one of them led, and he listened intently. "They come closer and closer to my special den. But I am a patient spider . . . and cunning. I will divide them first and then devour."

He listened a moment more and finally heard voices from the leftmost hole in the ceiling. Then he sprang. The Merchant's right hand shot out of his cloak and grasped a dark iron lever, one of many that protruded from slots in the chamber floor. He pulled back on the lever and heard a deep metallic clang followed by the clicking of wheels turning.

19

Hack and Slash

Bellefontaine was an extremely busy port on the northwestern coast of Martinique. But all the sailing traffic in and out of the harbor gave the *Banshee* and the *Robert Bruce* a very wide berth. With Bellamy's attacks, Martinique had become more than a little sensitive to pirates—even those with a more noble reputation.

Jacques St. Pierre directed Stede away from the trade commerce and around a horn of land to the promised shipyard of Slash Montant. There were already a dozen ships in various states of repair anchored at the many docks. *This Slash is a busy man*, Ross thought.

No sooner had Jack and Ross moored the ships at the only open quay than a man came charging up the pier. He stomped right up to the bow of the *Bruce* and stood with his hands on his hips. He wore green breeches that stopped at the knee, a long sword on one hip, and a variety of tools on the other. He tapped his foot on the dock and scratched at his dark goatee. When no one hailed him from the ship, he began to yell. "Who are you?" he demanded. His voice was high, commanding, and distinctively English. "And who gave you permission to take up space in my shipyard?"

"Slash, you simpleminded Englishman," St. Pierre yelled back. "Do you mean to tell me you do not know a fortune when you see one?"

The man on the pier squinted in the sun. "Jacques?" His small-ish eyes opened wide. "Jacques Saint Pierre . . . you doltish French buffoon, you're still alive?"

Before Ross could stop him, Jacques drew his sword, grabbed a rope, and swung down to the pier. *Merciful heavens*, thought Ross. *St. Pierre's going to kill the man before he can fix our boat.*

Slash drew his sword as St. Pierre approached. The two exchanged a flurry of blows, but clearly Slash was the better swordsman. His rapier moved in a blur, and he quickly gained an advantage on Jacques. Red Eye joined Ross at the rail and lowered a long-barreled musket. He used his good eye and sighted it on St. Pierre's enemy.

"No," said Ross, putting a light hand on the musket. "Let them fight . . . for now."

Red Eye reluctantly lowered the rifle.

St. Pierre was sweating now. He did all he could to parry and block the advancing Slash, but the Englishman was too fast. He lunged, and St. Pierre's sword suddenly flew into the air. Slash caught it. Red Eye took aim.

Then Slash threw down both swords and grasped St. Pierre in a Herculean bear hug. "Ah, Jacques," he said. "So good to see you again!"

"Likewise, mon ami!" said St. Pierre. "You haven't lost your touch with the rapier, I see."

"Never," he replied. Then his demeanor became serious. "Now, what were you saying about a fortune to be had?"

Ross and the senior crew of the *Bruce* traveled down the gang-plank even as Cutlass Jack and his men did so from the *Banshee*. "Slash Montant," Jacques said, "allow me to introduce Captain Declan Ross."

As he shook hands with Ross, Slash said, "The Sea Wolf, eh? Your pirate reputation precedes you."

"I've left piracy behind me," said Ross. "But I've kept the name."

"As have I," said Cutlass Jack, holding out his own hand, which Slash shook in turn. "I am Cutlass Jack Bonnet."

"Cutlass Jack and Declan Ross . . . no longer pirates?" Slash smiled. "If only we could persuade Edmund Bellamy to do so, Martinique would be a much happier island."

"Then let Martinique rejoice!" said Jacques St. Pierre. "For Bellamy is dead."

"Dead?" echoed Slash. "Really?"

"Quite." St. Pierre laughed. "Thanks to these two ships and their crews. But during the battle that claimed Bellamy's life, each of these ships sustained considerable damage."

"Especially this one," Slash said, pointing at the *Bruce*. "Unless I am sorely mistaken, you are missing a mast."

"Yes," said Ross. "Jacques told us you had the supplies to repair our ships."

"Oh, I have what you need," said Slash. "And I can fix your ships."

"But we have urgent need of speed," said Ross. "We need to sail for England."

"They do not call me Slash for nothing," he replied. "But can you afford me?"

Ross started to speak, but Jacques stepped in front. "Pardonnez, mon capitaine . . . may I address this?"

Ross smiled and nodded. Jacques was not only the chief gunner, but he was also the chief negotiator.

St. Pierre took Slash Montant by the shoulder and said, "Slash, my friend . . . I see by your bustling docks, you are very busy, no?"

"All the business I can handle," Slash replied proudly.

"Oui, très bien," Jacques paused. "But, ah, this business is all local, ah? They pay you in what, chickens? Sugar cane?"

Slash frowned. "Look, mate, what are you getting at?"

"Nothing." Jacques held up his hand, pleading innocence. "I am sure you need these things, the *common* necessities of life. But, ah, my friends Ross and Cutlass Jack, they have spent years plundering the far reaches of the world. Do you not think they might have something to offer you . . . something quite a bit better than chickens?" St. Pierre watched Slash's expression change. He was hooked, and Jacques knew it.

"What sort of somethings might you gentlemen have to barter?" Slash asked. "Gold? Jewels?"

"Yes to both," said Ross. "How fast could you repair our ships if we were to part with some of these items?" Then, taking a page out of St. Pierre's book, he added, "Some of these *rare* items."

"Very fast indeed," said Slash. "A blink, and I will be done. But let us not discuss the fee any longer. I see that you are good to cover whatever I charge. Let me survey the damages, and then we can begin work."

After Slash assessed the damages to both ships, he assembled a crew of more than a hundred laborers—most pulled from work on other ships—and they went right to work on Jack's *Banshee* and the *Robert Bruce*. For three days, Slash and his men worked seamlessly with the crews of the two ships. But on the fourth day, things became suddenly difficult.

On the newly repaired quarterdeck, Captain Ross sipped at a mug while talking to Stede about potential routes to England and courses of action once there. "But Stede," Declan continued, "he has to hear us out. It's his country that's in danger."

"I tell ya about that king, Declan," said Stede. "Him b' stubborn as a mule and half as smart."

"Blake will listen," Ross said. "If he's even in Eng—"

The deck erupted in angry shouts, and men converged around the gap where the new mast would go. Ross and Stede leaped down to the deck and cut through the mass of people to see what had transpired. They found Ebenezer Hack and Slash Montant in the middle of it all.

"Ah, Captain Ross," said Hack. "I'm glad you've come. Tell this ridiculous corner cutter that I'm the ship's master carpenter, and in the big decisions I'm in charge."

"Corner cutter?" Slash objected. "You knuckle-dragging oaf, how dare you! I'm only providing the speed that Captain Ross here requested."

Ross raised both eyebrows and looked at Stede, but Stede had already begun retreating into the crowd. *Thanks a lot!* thought Ross. He turned to Hack and asked, "What is the real problem here?"

"It's like this, Captain," said Hack. "The new mast is sized and cut. I contend we careen the ship to put in the mast—the way it's always been done. But this tea-swilling crumpet head has the fool notion of hoisting the mast up with ropes and letting it drop in!"

"Tea-swilling?" Slash raged. "Crumpet head? That's it! I've had enough of this outrage from you, you no-necked gorilla." He pulled off a glove and smacked Hack across the face. "I challenge you to a duel."

"A duel?" Hack scoffed. "Gladly, but not with swords. You are a master, and I am no good with a blade. Let us battle with our bare fists, you bombastic blowhard!"

"Bombastic?" Slash thought for a moment. "Ooh, good word, but I must decline, for I am no match for someone of your immense girth. You would crush me in a brawl. Then we must settle this in the way of courtly gentlemen of old."

"You mean pistols at twenty paces?"

"Nay, we must play chess!"

"Chess?" Hack looked puzzled a moment, and then a sly look rippled across his brow. "Very well then, I accept."

To everyone's surprise and amusement, Ebenezer Hack went below deck for a few moments and then returned bearing a sack that contained a cloth chessboard and all the pieces. Hack and Slash then went at it on the chessboard: taunting each other with every move, exulting with every advantage, and miserably whining whenever a piece was taken by his opponent. But in the end, game one was a draw. The second game was a stalemate, so again, no one arose as victorious. By the third game, the entire crew of the *Bruce*, along with a great many from the *Banshee*, and more than fifty of Slash's carpenters and workers had gathered in a circle around the chess match. Still others climbed the rigging to watch and cried out possible moves.

As fascinated by the match as he was, Ross was impatient. "We've no time for this!" he said.

The two chess players ignored the comment, but Jacques took Ross's arm. "Ah, mon capitaine, it is Slash's way . . . the only way to avoid bloodshed." Ross rolled his eyes and crossed his arms to wait.

The match was incredibly close. Each move drew gasps from the crowds. Even Ross found himself suddenly spellbound. It was Hack's move, and he had been taking a very long time. Slash was beside himself waiting for the move. "Come on, you cross-eyed brute," he jeered. "Make your move."

Then Hack slid his bishop diagonally across the length of the board, slamming one of Slash's pawns and putting his king in check. Ross cringed, for giving up a powerful bishop for a lowly pawn was a terrible exchange. All Slash had to do was take Hack's bishop with his king. The crowd muttered. Slash scrutinized the board and was amazed that his opponent had at last made a foolish move. Then Slash said, "Hack, old boy, in these three hotly contested campaigns, you have gained my respect, but with that last move, I believe you have lost any hope of winning this game." Slash moved his king and took Hack's bishop. The crowd groaned. Hack looked as if he'd been trampled by a herd of buffalo.

But his expression changed. The dejected frown curled into the most mischievous grin, and Hack cracked his knuckles. "Slash, my good man, you also have my respect—and friendship, should you want it—for never have I faced such an adversary. But now, it is with greatest admiration that I say to you: you really fell for it this time! Huzzah!"

Hack slid his rook vertically until it toppled over Slash's queen. The crowd erupted with gasps of surprise and wonder. They all looked at the board, wondering how such a move could have been possible. It hadn't been there a moment before, they were all sure. Slash turned as white as a sail, for he alone understood what Hack had done. Slash shook his head a couple of times and muttered, "Brilliant . . . that was simply brilliant." He knocked over his own king, surrendering the game to Hack. He stood and offered Hack his hand. The two shook, and the crowd began to disperse.

Captain Declan Ross came up to them just afterward and said, "I watched the entire game, but I don't understand . . . how did Hack get your queen?"

"A magnificent ploy," Slash admitted. "Hack hid his rook behind his bishop, waiting for me to move my queen into position. Once I had, it was already too late. Hack moved the bishop, attacked, checking my king. By the rules of chess, I must get my king out of check, so I did the obvious thing and took his bishop. But when he'd moved that bishop, he opened up a lane of attack for his rook to surprise my queen. It was both a sacrifice and a forced play."

Ross understood. Hack had hidden his best move behind a first move that seemed foolish to his opponent. The result had been assured victory for Hack. "Well done, Hack!" Captain Ross said. "Looks as though we'll careen the *Bruce*, eh?"

It had turned out to be a good thing that they turned the *Bruce* on its side to put in the new mast, for it was then that they discovered some below-the-waterline damage that they had not seen before. Six boards had cracked near the keel, a wound that, had it worsened out at sea, could have led to the end of the *Robert Bruce* and its crew. Hack and Slash worked together to repair the hull. In fact, the two of them became the fastest of friends. In the days that followed, Slash taught Hack how to duel with a rapier sword, and Hack taught Slash how to fight barehanded, but this only during their spare time. The majority of the time was spent on the ships.

Between them, they organized the crew into several able groups of carpenters and laborers. And in less than two weeks, Declan Ross's man-of-war and Cutlass Jack's xebec were better than new.

The morning of their departure for England, Slash came aboard the *Bruce* and knocked on the door to the captain's quarters.

"Enter!" Declan yelled. When he saw that it was Slash, he said, "I suppose you've come for your payment."

"Yes, as a matter of fact." Slash scratched at his dark whiskers thoughtfully and then asked, "The work . . . I trust it is satisfactory?"

"Better than that, Slash. You are a gifted shipwright." Ross paused to think a moment. Then he reached into a drawer, withdrew a drawstring pouch, hefted it a moment, and dropped it into Slash's hand. "Will this be enough to cover your expenses?"

Slash opened the pouch and whistled. "It is quite . . . adequate," he said. Then he closed the bag and hesitated to say something he had been considering.

"But?"

"But there is one thing more I would request."

"I had a feeling there would be," said Ross.

Slash smiled. "You see, I grow weary of my current vocation. Always I get to build the boats, but I rarely get to sail. Always I hear the stories, but I never get to be in them. I want to join your crew and live an adventure. I want to sail to England and help you take down Bartholomew Thorne."

"You know of Thorne then?" Ross was surprised.

"He is only the talk of both crews! I must say I was surprised to hear that he is still alive."

"Slash," Ross cautioned, "we could certainly use someone of your skill—both with woodworking and with the rapier. But Thorne is a wicked and powerful man. If you come with us, you could forfeit your life."

"I laugh at death," Slash replied, puffing up his chest.

"The voyage itself is grueling, and the Atlantic can be tempestuous at this time of year."

"Ha, storms!" Slash scoffed. "I have made these two ships so strong that we could ride on a tidal wave!"

"Still, food could get scarce," Ross said. "You may end up having to eat rats . . . or worse."

"I will eat iguanas, if I must."

Ross laughed at that. "Nubby, my ship's cook, might just be able to arrange that."

"Please, Captain Ross," said Slash. "I want to sail with you. I want to join my new friend Hack in keeping this ship in good working order. I want to do something about the pirates that hurt so many. You see, many years ago, Edmund Bellamy raided a sugar plantation . . . owned by my favorite uncle. Bellamy slew him and burned out his home. I want to fight by the side of the man who stopped Bellamy's brutality forever. Will you have me?"

"What about your shipyard?" Ross asked, playing his last card.

"I will leave it in the hands of my apprentices," said Slash. "It is not a problem."

"Very well then," said Captain Ross. "Once we are out to sea, we will have you sign the articles of the *Robert Bruce*. In one hour, we depart for England. I suggest you go and pack whatever you'll need."

"It's already on board . . . , Captain," said Slash with a mischievous smile. He spun on his heels and was gone.

As Ross and Stede stood alone on the quarterdeck that evening, Ross asked, "Do you think we're too late?"

"What we b' finding in England, I do not know, mon," Stede replied. "But I b' having a bad feeling we not b' liking it."

20

MUTINY ON THE OXFORD

Where are you going?" Blake asked.

"For a ride in the carriage," answered Dolphin. "I will not be long."

"Darling, are you quite sure you are all right?" he asked. "This is so unlike you."

"Yes," Dolphin replied. "I am quite sure I am all right. In fact, I have a clarity of mind that I have been lacking for too long."

Blake didn't know what to make of that. "Will you not tell me what you are going to do?"

"Brand, my husband"—she said, taking his hands and fixing his eyes with her own—"have I ever betrayed your trust?"

"No," he replied. "No, of course not."

"Then trust me now." She kissed him and walked to the door. Even Hopper stared after her. But just before Dolphin closed the door, she said, "Rest while you may, my husband, and you too, young Hopper. For if my errand is fruitful, this could be a very long night."

Aboard the British frigate called the *Oxford*, quartermaster Jordan dipped a quill pen into a dark bottle of ink once more and completed his letter. He put the document in an envelope, tilted a candle, spilling wax on the flap, and then sealed it with Commodore Blake's official seal. Just then, there was a knock at his cabin door.

Jordan opened the door. "Mrs. Blake! What are you doing here?"

"I need your help," she said. "That is, the commodore and I need your help. I don't know where else to turn, and I fear that King George and the Parliament no longer have England's best interests in mind." Her lower lip trembled, and she looked over her shoulder before she continued. "But what I am going to ask you to do may put you and many of the *Oxford*'s crew in the stockade or worse."

Mr. Jordan ushered her in and closed the door. "Tell me what you have in mind," he said. "And hurry. Commodore Wetherby is due on board any moment."

After she told him her plan, he smiled at her and said, "Ma'am, if you only knew how providential your visit is." He held up the envelope. "In this envelope, I have my resignation from His Majesty's Royal Navy. But . . . I think I'll hold off on this for just a while."

"Brand?" Dolphin called as she unlatched the front door. Her family's old house was silent. She closed the door and stepped lightly down the hall. She found her husband asleep on a couch in the library. And Hopper lay nestled in the crook of his arm. The book of sea charts that Hopper had found so interesting lay open on her husband's chest.

"Wake up, sleepyheads," she said as she gently nudged them.

"You're back," Blake mumbled with a sleepy smile. Hopper opened his bright eyes and smiled as well.

"I'm sorry to rouse the two of you," Dolphin said, "but we have a long journey ahead of us."

Blake, still not quite awake, asked, "Where are we going?"

"The Port of Ipswich."

"Ipswich?" He was awake now. "Why on earth are we going there?"

"In time," Dolphin said, hoisting Hopper to his feet. Then she picked up a bulging gray satchel and said, "I took the liberty of gathering a few things we left on the *Oxford*."

"You . . . you went to the ship?" Blake sat bolt upright. "Dolphin, darling, what have you been up to?"

She smiled impishly and replied, "It is sixty miles from here to Ipswich, give or take. Plenty of time to tell you all things. But in the meantime, put this on." She tossed him a dark, triangular lump.

"My hat?" He ran a finger along the gold trip on the tricorn hat.

"Yes," Dolphin replied, her voice hard. "Yes, it is *your* hat."

The *Oxford* had left the Port of London near midnight. Commodore Nigel Wetherby had been instated as the captain of the ship, and he had ordered the ship ready to sail north to investigate pirate activity in the Baltic Sea. The *Oxford* had left the Thames River behind an hour later and now sailed into the Straight of Dover on its way to the North Sea. Commodore Wetherby stood next to Mr. Jordan at the helm of the ship. "It's quite sporting of you to stay on as quartermaster," said Wetherby. "You do understand, I do not hold you or any of the crew responsible for Blake's actions."

"Yes, sir," said Mr. Jordan. "I understand perfectly, sir."

The moon was barely visible behind the lumpy gray clouds. The wind was steady, and the ship slipped quietly through the water. Commodore Wetherby looked at the dark silhouette of England's coastline. There was a distant glow, and Wetherby took it to be Colchester. "It is a beautiful night for sailing," he said.

"Stunning, sir," said Mr. Jordan. He began to sing a cheery little tune until Wetherby gave him a look. "Say, Commodore?"

"What is it, Mister Jordan?"

"We're sailing for Sweden, then?" asked the quartermaster. "I've not heard of pirates operating out of those cold waters."

Wetherby hesitated. He wondered how much he should tell them. Of course, it wouldn't matter once they arrived and Thorne took over. "It's an island south of there. Gotland it is called . . . was deserted until the pirates came. We can't have them shutting down our shipping lanes."

They sailed in silence for some time after that.

Wetherby descended from the quarterdeck and strolled the deck. He passed a deck hand he remembered from the years he served on the *Oxford* under Blake. "Evening, Matthew," Wetherby said as the sailor passed.

"Evening, sir," Matthew replied, but the expression on his face was chilly. In fact, sailor after sailor, they all responded to their new commanding officer in similar fashion. Finally, Commodore Wetherby caught up to Mr. Tyler Dovel, a young officer who had just been assigned to the *Oxford*. "Why are the men so grim?" Wetherby asked him.

"Haven't the foggiest idea," answered Mr. Tyler.

"Well, I don't like it. Why don't you open up a cask of wine? Long trip ahead of us . . . might as well pass it merrily."

"It's not a good idea while we're on duty, sir." Tyler's face was virtually void of emotion.

The commodore pursed his lips. "Is that so?" he asked. "Interesting that everyone should be suddenly so by-the-book."

"If there's nothing else, sir?" Tyler looked at his commander expectantly.

"No, I suppose that will be all."

The carriage raced along the bumpy country road so fast that Blake feared the frame would snap. "What did you tell the driver?" Blake asked.

"Oh . . . nothing, really," replied Dolphin. "Just that the fate of England depends on us getting to Ipswich in time."

"This is fun!" said Hopper, bouncing six inches off his seat.

"In time for what?" Blake demanded.

Dolphin did not answer directly. "Did you know that Nigel Wetherby assumed command of the *Oxford*?"

"What?" Blake's face contorted. "Wetherby? That thieving—Ah! I should have known. The blighter's probably sailing it to his master right now."

Dolphin looked out of the carriage window. From the road she saw the dark expanse of the sea. "Not exactly," she said.

"Mister Jordan," said Commodore Nigel Wetherby as he looked through a spyglass at the English coastline.

"Yes, sir?" replied the quartermaster at the wheel.

"Is there some particular reason why we're hugging the coast?"

"Quite right, sir. That we are."

"But why?"

Mr. Jordan shook his head. "Aw, now, sir . . . you don't want to spoil the surprise, do you?"

"What on earth are you talking about, quartermaster? Everyone on this ship has been moping about like they've been baptized in vinegar and lost their last friend."

"It's all part of the scheme," Mr. Jordan confessed. "See, me and the lads have something real special planned for you. There's this bloke down in Ipswich who makes as fine a rum as—"

"Never mind," said Commodore Wetherby, happy to finally see some sparks of acceptance. "I will not ruin the surprise. But we cannot tarry in Ipswich."

"No, sir," said Mr. Jordan.

The *Oxford* slid quietly up the River Orwell on its way to Ipswich. Each time the ship approached a quay or dock, Commodore Wetherby found his hopes rising. But each time, Mr. Jordan sailed the ship by, and he looked forward without wavering.

"We're almost there, sir," said Mr. Jordan to the commodore's unspoken question.

And at last, up ahead to port, sticking out into the river like a dark finger, there was a long fishing pier. Mr. Jordan steered the ship expertly alongside. The crew of the *Oxford* tossed mooring lines overboard. Dockworkers tied off the lines, and the ship was secure. Mr. Tyler assisted several deck hands in lowering a gangplank.

Mr. Jordan and several of the *Oxford*'s crew escorted Commodore Wetherby down to the pier just as the deck hands rolled several barrels to a stop. The commodore eyed the barrels and smiled. "Is this the surprise you promised, Mister Jordan?"

"Yes, sir, it is," he replied. And then, nodding to the tallest of the dockworkers, Jordan said, "Evening, Captain."

The dockworker opened the barrel and removed something. He placed it snugly on his head and ran a finger lovingly along the gold trim. "Hello, Nigel."

"Blake!" Wetherby gasped, and his hand went to his waist. "What the devil—"

"Not a good idea, old friend," said Blake, lifting a pistol to Wetherby's eye level and cocking its hammer back. Wetherby looked around and saw that each of the men from the *Oxford* had also drawn guns. He'd be dead before he freed his own gun. He stared in disbelief as the other two dock workers looked up. It was Blake's wife and that meddling rat boy.

"Mister Jordan, if you please," said Commodore Blake, "take Mister Wetherby's weapons."

"Does that mean you wish me to cut out his lying tongue?"

"Don't tempt me."

Mr. Jordan removed Wetherby's pistol, his cutlass, and a booted dagger. "He was heading to the Baltic Sea, Captain," explained Mr. Jordan. "Said there's pirates on an island south of the Swedish mainland."

"Gotland Island?" Blake muttered. "That's where Thorne's holed up, is it?"

Wetherby did not answer. He stared back at Blake venomously. Mr. Jordan smacked the commodore's hat off Wetherby and growled, "Answer your commanding officer, you turncoat."

Wetherby's face reddened and his breathing quickened, but he didn't utter a word.

"Looks like someone's already cut out his tongue," said Blake. "No, I imagine you've already said too much, haven't you?" Then he turned to Mr. Jordan. "Take him below decks and lock him up. We have one brief stop to make in Edinburgh, but then . . . let's complete Wetherby's course. Bartholomew Thorne has been playing dead long enough."

"Yes, sir!" Mr. Jordan replied heartily.

But just as he jerked his captive around, the slightest hint of a smile appeared on Nigel Wetherby's face.

21
WHEN ALL BECOMES DARKNESS

"What was that?" asked Anne, who had followed right behind Cat. They'd heard a peculiar sound like a metallic wheel turning. Then there came a muffled boom from around the bend behind them.

"I don't know," said Cat, turning and pulling Anne back the way they had come. "Father Brun?"

No one answered. When Anne and Cat came around the bend, they found a dark iron door barring their way. "Father Brun!" Cat yelled.

"We're cut off," came the monk's muted voice. "There's no latch on this side."

"None on this either," said Anne.

"Cat, Anne, try to find a passage leading up if you can," said Father Brun. "We'll try to find you, but no matter what, try to find a way out."

"What about the Merchant?" asked Anne.

There was a moment of silence. Then Father Brun said, "In my zeal to capture him, in my fervor at nearly having him within my grasp, I . . . I've led us into his trap. Find a way out, Cat. Forget about the Merchant. He has the upper hand!"

"Yessss, yes, I do," said the Merchant. "Run little Cat, while you can. And good-bye, Father Brun." The Merchant reached down beside the levers and grasped an iron wheel valve. With great effort, he turned the wheel to the left, followed by a larger wheel next to it.

Father Brun led and, with Brother Dmitri at his heels, raced back along the corridor. He saw an opening on his right and, hoping to circle back and find some way to meet up with Cat and Anne, he took it.

"STOP!!" Brother Dmitri bellowed. "That sound!" Above their racing hearts there arose a breathy, whooshing sound like waves crashing one after another on a shore.

Father Brun closed his eyes a moment and clenched his teeth. When he opened his eyes, he said, "He's let in the sea."

"Run!" Cat yelled, racing down the tunnel away from the iron door.

"But which way?" Anne fired back. "We could be running to our deaths!"

"I don't see what choice we ha—" Cat went around the corner too fast. His boots lost traction on the slippery stone passage, and Cat sprawled to the floor. He cracked his chin smartly and tasted blood.

"Cat!" Anne ran to his side.

"Okay," Cat said, spitting at the wall. "Walking it is, then."

Anne laughed. "We'll walk fast," she said, helping Cat to his feet. As he stood, he noticed a fist-sized hole cut into the rock overhead. No, cut wasn't quite the right word. It looked as if some strange eel-like creature had bored deep into the stone. Cat eyed it curiously for just a moment more, and the two of them trod ahead. The tunnel soon branched off. One passage very clearly went down, spiraling into darkness. The other went on more or less level but was more narrow and wet.

"This way," Cat said. He opted for the lighted tunnel.

"No, not that way," the Merchant hissed. He looked down at his network of levers and valves and thought for a moment. Then he said, "More complicated, and I don't want you there for long, but still it could serve the same purpose." He pulled two levers at the same time and listened to the music of the metal wheels turning.

The water roared into the passage. Father Brun sprinted away. Brother Dmitri and the others bolted after him. They turned at the closed iron door and careened back into the main tunnel. A side passage leading downward opened suddenly on the left, but Father Brun saw another branch to the tunnel just up ahead. *Which one?* He had only three steps to decide.

"This way!" He took the first left, but no sooner was he through the opening, when a door swung slowly away from the wall and began to seal off the passage. Brother Dmitri tried to follow. His head and most of his body squeezed into the new passage, but the door caught his right shoulder. At that same moment, Brother Diego and Brother Cyprian tried to stop and help from the other side, but a torrent of seawater smacked into them. They scratched and clawed for a hold, but the flood took them screaming down the passage.

"Brun, leave me!!" bellowed Brother Dmitri, the water blasting through the gap between the door and the wall. "I am done!" The door continued to press on his shoulder. His eyes bulged, and he roared in anger.

Father Brun did not heed Dmitri's words. He fought through the spray and slammed his fighting rods into the narrow breach above Dmitri's shoulders. Then, using the rods as levers, he tried to pry back the door. Dmitri coughed, trying desperately to breathe, but the water pressure was so intense that every time he opened his mouth, it filled immediately. "GO!"

Father Brun lost hold of one of the rods for a moment but jammed it back into place. It was a better place, and the leverage started to work. Suddenly, one of the rods cracked and broke, and the door pressed even harder on Dmitri's shoulder. Dmitri made no sound, and Father Brun feared he was dead. He used both hands on the remaining rod and, uttering a silent prayer, pulled with all his might. The door moved just slightly, but it was enough. The water surged into the chamber, pushing Brother Dmitri through. He tumbled on top of Father Brun just as the door slammed shut.

"Dmitri . . . Dmitri!" Father Brun rolled him over and put his ear to Dmitri's lips. He wasn't sure if he heard or felt any breath at all. Even so, he hoisted his sodden friend up and began to drag him down the new passage. This was no easy task. Dmitri was a large man and, as dead weight, was extraordinarily heavy. Father Brun groaned with every step. His breaths came out in gasps, and he could feel his heart crashing against his ribs.

He stumbled around a bend into a small round chamber and found himself face-to-face with Edmund Scully.

Cat and Anne hastened along a narrow, curling passage when they heard a tremendous groaning from up ahead. They came around the bend just in time to see two large doors slam shut, sealing off two passages, leaving only the left-hand passage remaining. "Hurry, before he cuts us off!" Anne yelled, and she sped forward.

Cat ran after her and grabbed her arm just after they both entered the passage. He looked at the oblong door they had come through. It did not shut. "He's not cutting us off," Cat said, thinking aloud. "He's leading us this way."

"But how does he know where we are?"

"I . . . I don't know," Cat replied. *He can't be everywhere . . . can he?*

Cat and Anne crept up the passage, both fearing that like some vengeful spirit the Merchant would fly from an unseen crevice and drag them screaming into the sea. Each had drawn a cutlass, but somehow it didn't seem as though a sword would be effective against such an infamous rogue.

They walked in silence, following the curving and seemingly endless tunnel until Cat saw something ahead. "Look," he said. "The tunnel forks again."

They hurried forward just in time to see the door to the left branch shut in their faces. "This is impossible." Anne blew out an angry sigh. "It's like he's watching us, only he can't be."

Cat tightened his grip on his sword and wiped the sweat from his brow. Then he sighted another one of those strange bored-out holes in the roof of the tunnel. He grabbed Anne by the wrist and pointed his sword to the ceiling.

"What—" she started to say, but Cat covered her mouth. Then he held a finger to his lips and motioned for her to follow. He led her into the right-hand passage and found it coiling slightly downward.

After a few moments of walking and scanning the ceiling, Cat stopped and whispered, "He can hear us."

Anne's eyes roamed the passage walls, and Cat explained, "There are openings in the ceiling just prior to every junction or fork in the path. I don't know how exactly, but our voices must carry to some central place. The Merchant has this place rigged like a gigantic mousetrap."

"And we're the mice," Anne whispered. "What do we do?"

"Follow me," Cat said. "And don't make a sound until I do."

Being sure to place his boots softly as he walked, Cat crept along the passage until they came to the next junction of several corridors. He made sure there was a listening hole in the roof, but remained silent. He led Anne over to the opening of the leftmost passage and whispered in her ear, "Hold this door open with all your might." She looked at Cat curiously.

Then Cat stepped back into the main passage and stood directly beneath the listening hole. Then he practically yelled, "The path splits three ways. Which one do we take?" Then he raced through the door that Anne held open. Anne let go of the door, and in a matter of seconds, that door, as well as the middle door, slammed shut.

"How did you know which way?" Anne asked.

Cat smiled. "I didn't know for sure," he said, his voice barely audible. "I just remembered Scully describing this place like the coils of a conch shell. I figured it's better to be closer to the outside than the inside."

Anne tilted her head slightly and marveled at her friend. Buoyed by Anne's admiration, Cat said, "Now, let's go where the Merchant didn't want us to go."

Father Brun saw the motionless, glassy eyes and knew that Scully was dead. *How many deaths have my actions in some way caused?* Father Brun chastised himself. He laid Brother Dmitri against the cool wall and watched for the huge man's chest to rise. He could discern no movement, and the shoulder that had been caught in the door was bruised black. The leader of the Brethren had been in many difficult places but none like the Merchant's insidious under-sea stronghold. Here, death seemed to wait around every corner. He grimaced and, with two fingers, closed Scully's eyes.

It was then that he noted a strange round hatch on the other side of the chamber. Glancing back at Dmitri, he walked over to examine the opening. From the location of the hinge, it appeared that this hatch opened outward. And rather than a handle latch, it had a kind of pressured bond. Father Brun noted with apprehension that seawater dribbled in along the hatch's perimeter. "So this is it then," said Father Brun aloud as he walked past Scully back to Brother Dmitri. "There's no way out."

Even so, Father Brun determined to try. He slung Dmitri's arm up over his shoulder and hoisted the big man up once more. He thought maybe the water behind the door at the other end of the tunnel might subside at some point and maybe he could somehow pry open that door. It was a lot of maybes.

A great grinding noise shook Father Brun out of his thoughts.

But there was not time to react to it. A massive wall of water exploded up the passage, lifting Father Brun off his feet and launching him and Dmitri backward into the chamber. Father Brun felt himself smack into something that felt oddly like a sack of grain. As the water propelled him backward, Father Brun realized he'd crashed into Scully's body. But the irresistible force of the water blasted them straight back into that strange hatch. Father Brun heard a sickly crunching noise . . . then a crack. He felt his own body curl, and the water pushed him through the opening in the stone, jettisoning him out into the cold depths of the sea.

With one arm, he held Brother Dmitri. With the other, he flailed and pushed Scully's body away. His breath was already turning stale in his lungs. Nonetheless, Father Brun struggled to retain it. He could see nothing and dared not swim until he knew which way was up. He held his breath and let himself float. After what seemed like an eternity, Father Brun felt his momentum shift, felt himself rise. Then he kicked madly with his feet and clawed at the sea with his free hand. He had no idea how deep below the surface he was, but shoved thoughts of drowning away. His lungs burned deeply, intensifying to a searing sort of agony that sent showers of sparks into his mind. His thoughts became confused, and an odd numbing threatened to take over his limbs—just as he broke through the surface.

Father Brun gasped, sucking in a massive breath. Instantly his strength returned and he flailed to tread water. That was when he realized he'd heard someone else cough. He shook his head and blinked the water out of his eyes. And to his utter amazement, Brother Dmitri spluttered and spat. "You're alive! Oh-ho! You're alive!" Father Brun exclaimed.

"Am I?" came a hoarse reply. "I can't tell."

"Yes, you goat . . . yes, you are, praise the Almighty!"

"Where are we?"

Father Brun jerked his head back and forth, craning to see anything on the sea under the night sky. He saw nothing of the island and assumed that, by now, it was fully submerged. But there! Something floated not twenty yards from his position.

"I see the cutter!" he told Brother Dmitri. "Can you swim?"

"I've only got one good fin," he replied. "But . . . I'll try."

Smacked repeatedly by sudden whitecaps and moving slower than driftwood, they made their way to the small boat. Father Brun helped Dmitri clamber over the side and then hoisted himself in as well. They lay in the cutter and stared up at the stars for only a moment when Father Brun sat up. "Cat and Anne!" he exclaimed. "They . . . they're still down there." He reached frantically around the bow of the cutter and found the mooring line. He pulled it swiftly, hoping that it was somehow still attached to the now-submerged island. But when he drew the line in, it came back with a hunk of coral attached to it. "It's torn free," he said quietly. "We've lost them."

With a groan, Brother Dmitri sat up. He squinted at the rope and then over the monk's shoulders. "No, we haven't," he said. Then he pointed. "It's the *Constantine*."

Father Brun lifted himself higher and saw the huge shadow swaying gently on the water. There was a second ship with it, but not a third. Father Brun picked up an oar and began to paddle. "We'll wait this out," he said. "And when that island surfaces again, we'll take a larger force in, bring iron bars to pry open those doors, and get Cat and Anne back."

Brother Dmitri smiled. His spiritual mentor was also the fiercest warrior he'd ever met—a wonderful combination, Dmitri thought. Father Brun stroked the oar hard toward the shadows on the sea.

He never once looked back over his shoulder. He never saw the other shadow, carving the sea and moving swiftly toward them like a ghostly giant.

The Merchant grew restless. It had been utterly gratifying to hear Father Brun and the others scurrying through his network of tunnels like rats in a trap. And even more pleasing to hear their voices suddenly cease. But the silence from Cat and Anne was unexpected . . . disturbing. He scanned the openings all around his domelike chamber and wondered. Since the last junction, he had not heard a sound from them. Had he crushed one of them in the door? Had they split up? He doubted it. But still, the silence was troubling. "Where are you?" he hissed.

The light of several recessed lanterns led Cat and Anne to a sturdy door. It was very wide and had an iron wheel in place of a handle. Assuming it would be sealed tight, Cat grasped the wheel and turned. To his and Anne's surprise, the door opened. And to their everlasting relief, the door was well maintained. It moved soundlessly on its hinges. On the other side, bathed half in shadow, half in the peculiar green light from the oil lanterns, was a chamber full of metal cabinets and a very old desk made of half-rotted wood. The room itself was on a slight slant, and the books in the one open cabinet all leaned to the side like men pushing against a seawall to hold back the crushing tide.

Her eyes wide and curious, Anne turned to Cat and pointed. She started to enter, but Cat held her back and gestured toward the two openings that gaped like empty eye sockets in the ceiling. Anne nodded that she understood, and they went to the open cabinet. Cat carefully removed one of the old leather-bound books and opened it. The first few pages were inscribed with names—some in English, Spanish, or French—but many more in languages he did not recognize. After that, the book seemed to become a sort of ledger. There were columns of sums and figures, as well as names and dates. The dates showed this to be a very old volume; the first entry was 1596 for a shipment of cannon shot. The line beneath it indicated that twelve hundred pounds of black powder had been purchased and shipped to Romania. The next was an import sale of swords from Spain.

It went on like that for page after page—every weapon imaginable and every resource needed to make war—the Merchant had bought it from or sold it to the interested parties of the world. But, Cat noted, every so many years, the handwriting in the ledger changed. *That was when the new Merchant replaced the old*, Cat thought. It amazed him that for centuries the evil had passed from one hand to the next. He wondered how each generation could produce a young man so bent on destruction—so destined for evil— that he'd be willing to bear the mantle of the Merchant. Destined . . . was that right? Were some men just born with something broken inside, something that leads them to horrible, vicious ends? A sudden image bolt across Cat's mind. He saw his father's bleeding stick lying on the dark stone at his feet. And he saw his own hands glistening with blood. He shook the thought away and handed the book to Anne.

"This is incredible," she whispered. "He's sold enough cannons to start a war . . . and this is just one book." She flipped through a few pages and stopped toward the end. "This is different," she said. "Realgar, cinnabar, belladonna . . . what is this?"

"Those are poisons."

Anne looked at Cat curiously. "How . . . how do you know that?"

"I'm not sure," he replied, unconsciously wringing his hands. "But when you said belladonna, I just knew. They are deadly."

"I don't doubt it," Anne said, closing the book. "If the Merchant dealt with it, I'm sure it involved death."

There was no warning. From the crow's-nest of the *Dominguez*, Brother Perrin had scanned the calm black sea, but clouds had covered up the moon, and he'd seen nothing. He'd turned his back for just a few minutes. When he turned again, it was there, a wall of undulating shadow, the clear silhouette of a massive warship. Brother Perrin opened his mouth to yell a warning, but cannon fire drowned his voice in a sea of thunder.

Fifteen, maybe twenty cannon muzzles flashed at an absurdly close range. Heavy iron balls slammed into the forecastle and cabins of the *Dominguez*. Others gutted the ship's hull and touched off powder kegs on the lower decks. The *Dominguez* foundered and collapsed upon itself, killing most of the crew before they could respond to the attack. Even before the burning hull could slip beneath the surface, the enemy turned its guns on the *Constantine*.

Anne wished she'd never picked up the second book. It looked like most of the others on that shelf . . . perhaps a little older, that was all. *Just another ledger of the Merchant's deadly commerce*, she'd thought. But it had felt different. It was far heavier than the first book. And when she opened it, she noted that the pages were thicker, almost more like parchment than paper. And an odd, unpleasant odor drifted up from the pages. It wasn't the musty, mildewed smell of many old books. The smell of this volume was more offensive, more like something had died and then rotted within the pages. Cat frowned when he smelled it. But Anne turned the first few pages and found a text she couldn't read. She thought it might be Latin because the words sounded like the formal prayers she remembered the vicar reading in the church when she was little.

The next few pages were full of woodcut printed drawings of the human body: first the outside with Latin words and lines from them to the parts identified; and then the skin off, showing the muscle tissue and bone; and finally the vital anatomy. These pages were busy with footnotes at the top and bottom of each page—even some hastily scrawled in the margins.

"I think you should put that one back," Cat whispered. But he stared at the pictures nonetheless. Anne's stomach tightened, and if Cat's admonition had not been enough, there was a strange pressure on the top of her hand. It felt almost like a weight placed there to keep her from turning the page. But she did anyway.

Anne had seen many horrible things in her life aboard a pirate ship. But in all Anne's life she had never seen anything so detestable as the image in that book. She dropped the book and wretched.

"My study," the Merchant growled under his breath. "Very clever, young Thorne. I should not be surprised." He went to his network of levers, pulled several, and waited the few seconds it took for the right doors to open and close in his labyrinth of tunnels. Then he began turning the wheel valves, one after the other. The other valves would have to be triggered in person and at just the right time . . . otherwise his ledgers might be destroyed. He'd have to enter the tunnels, do it himself. There would be an incredible amount of water. A bit of overkill. But finality was what the Merchant wanted. The time for uncertain subtlety was over. Cat and Anne were still together.

The Merchant stood and drew his dagger.

Three of the doors began to close.

Anne screamed. "Go, now!" Cat yelled. But they were too late. Cat lunged for the nearest door and strained to keep it open. Anne was at his side, and together they held it for a few more moments. But that was all they could manage. Cat barely avoided being pinned by the door. He slipped back into the chamber and slammed a fist hard against it.

"I'm sorry," Anne whispered.

Cat spun toward her, and at first it seemed he wore a mask . . . a horrible combination of anguish, anger, and blame. But then his features softened, and he just looked tired. "It's not your fault," he said as he walked toward the lone open door. "The Merchant is our enemy, and this is all his design." Anne bit her bottom lip and nodded. She wanted to believe he meant it, but that look on Cat's face . . .

"He's forcing us to follow his path," Cat yelled over his shoulder. "We fooled him once . . . maybe we can do it again. But we must be silent at every junction."

"At least this path is going up," Anne said. And it was, just slightly at first, but the incline steepened as they proceeded, and climbing the tunnel became arduous. They were out of breath when they came to the first fork in this tunnel. They were also out of choices. The door to the right-hand path was shut. They took the only path open, daring not even to whisper.

The path leveled off as they came to a place where their tunnel

Cat saw no alternative. He lunged at the Merchant and delivered a devastating fusillade of slashes and jabs. Anne was sure he'd killed the Merchant. He struck so fast and with such deadly precision she felt no one could have survived. But the Merchant had survived. His dagger had moved like a snake's tongue, flickering and darting, and he intercepted all of Cat's attacks, until finally batting Cat's cutlass aside and whirling inside Cat's outstretched arm. Before Cat could react, he felt the tip of the Merchant's dagger at the base of his own throat.

"You see?" said the Merchant, and then he shoved Cat to the ground at Anne's feet. "Not so old . . ." The thin blade of the dagger intermittently disappeared in the folds of his black cloak as the Merchant came forward. But like a scorpion's sting, the dagger—even when out of sight—was a looming threat.

Cat clambered to his feet and then pulled Anne into the tunnel behind them. The Merchant, in no particular hurry, followed. This tunnel forked the first time fifty yards in. But the alternate path was sealed off by another iron door. Cat and Anne found several other passages shut to them, and still the central path went on.

"Why didn't he kill me?" Cat asked as they ran.

"What?!" Anne exclaimed. "Who cares why? Maybe he likes to hunt before he kills. You're alive . . . that's what matters."

Cat still wondered, but he hoped to use this second chance. They ran on, hearing the Merchant's taunts following them. "Run, run . . ." came his breathy hiss.

Cat and Anne raced on. The passage did not split again, but it did dead-end. Cat and Anne found themselves in a small round chamber with no doors and no other way out but the way they came.

"Running out of room . . . pity." The Merchant sounded very

and three others met. They wandered warily into the mid
crossroads. Sound holes punctured the ceiling in many pl
the openings to the other paths had no doors at all. Cat
exchanged glances, and each wondered which of the pa
lead to safety. The path on their right was as dark as pit
the path in front of them. The only path lit by the oil la
the path on their left. It seemed an obvious choice . . .
obvious.

"You are trespassers here," a voice slithered out of t
to their right.

Cutlasses drawn, Cat and Anne turned and watch
emerged from the gloom. His face came first: pale, su
a thin misshapen nose, and a gaping wound of a mo
dwelt in shadow beneath a mantlelike brow. Then his ha
and in one of them, he held a long, thin dagger. The r
line was difficult to discern because his black clothi
with the shadows.

Cat stepped in front of Anne and brandished hi
hoped to face the Merchant with Father Brun and t
the Brethren at his side. But it had come to this. "Y
take, showing yourself, old man."

"Old?" he replied. "Is that what you think of
made a strange grating sound like the lid of a ton
from its resting place. "Think rather that I am . . .

The Merchant stepped from the shadows. P
beneath his cloak were black belts and leather
crossed. Pistols dangled from some of these bel
other things, too, that neither Cat nor Anne cou

"Don't come any closer!" Cat demanded.

"No?" he replied. "But I want to come mucl

Cat and Anne turned all around, frantically looking for something they could use to their advantage. "Look!" Anne shrieked. Four feet above them was an opening to a vertical tunnel that looked identical to the one through which they entered the Merchant's lair.

"Here," Cat said, cupping his hands and holding them low. "I'll boost you up."

"The tide," Anne said.

"What?"

"Even if this is a way out, the tide's come over the island by now." Anne's eyebrows bunched. "If I open the hatch, the water will wash us back down the tube."

"The island can't be that far under," Cat said with little conviction. "We've got to try."

They stared at each other for a moment then, and it seemed to each that so many things were spoken in that glance: respect, fear, regret, and . . . farewell. Then Anne put a foot into Cat's hands and leaped up for the bottom wrung. She lithely pulled herself up and grabbed each consecutive handhold until she had made room for Cat to ascend beneath her. But then she heard something that chilled her blood. "He's here," Cat said.

"Yessss, I am here," came another voice.

Anne looked down and saw Cat staring forward. He was unarmed. "Cat!!"

The Merchant advanced on Cat and lifted his dagger. Cat had nowhere to go. Some part of his awareness heard Anne say, "Catch!" Suddenly, Anne's cutlass fell right into Cat's hand.

Cat lunged at the Merchant's chest and might have stabbed him through the heart, but the Merchant jerked sideways. Cat's sword sawed across the Merchant's dagger. Cat went swiftly back to the attack. He grew increasingly frustrated, for even though his cutlass was the superior weapon, he could not get to the Merchant. They fought back and forth beneath the opening.

Cat glanced upward just a moment and saw Anne descending. "No!" he yelled. "Don't you come down here, Anne! Don't you do it!" She took one more hesitant step down. "ANNE!!" Cat yelled in desperation. At last, she reversed course and began to climb up the tunnel.

"Drop your weapon, boy," hissed the Merchant.

Cat turned on the Merchant with a ferocity he'd not shown before. Now, the fear was gone, replaced by reckless rage. And Cat's first strike was a wheeling wide stroke made heavy by the lunge of his legs, the turn of his trunk, and the snap of his wrist. The Merchant caught the blow with the dagger at chest level, but he couldn't absorb the force and staggered backward toward the entrance to the chamber. Cat pressed his new advantage and drove his cutlass at the Merchant's throat. In so doing, Cat left himself off balance. The Merchant slipped away from Cat's killing thrust and lifted a solid kick into Cat's ribs. Cat stumbled backward, coughing, gasping for air.

"Cat!" Anne screamed, but her voice was distant.

Good, Cat thought. *Get out while you can.*

The Merchant took advantage of Cat's distraction and stepped backward out of the chamber. "You have made this very difficult," he said, and his voice trailed off. The iron chamber door began to shut. "Pity for your friend." Cat charged the door only to see it clamp shut in his face. He heard one more word through the door: "Pity . . ."

Suddenly, huge vents in the sides of the chamber burst open, and torrents of seawater gushed into the small room. The surge knocked Cat backward again and he fell into the water that was already boot deep and rising. By the time he struggled to his feet, it had risen to his waist. He slowly waded to the center of the room, directly beneath the tunnel. He tried to leap up to grab the wrung. Again and again he tried to no avail. "Anne!" he shouted, but only once. He did not want to risk Anne's life.

Anne was nearly to the top of the tunnel. She could see the hatch, a gray disk ten feet above. But she heard a grinding of metal from somewhere behind the tunnel walls and then a great roar. She looked down, but couldn't tell what was happening far below. Then she heard him call for her.

Anne had listened to Cat's desperate plea for her to go on. But now, even so close to the top, she had to go back for him. Her boots nearly slipping from the rungs, she descended. Then she saw that the chamber below was filling quickly with water. And there was Cat, standing chest deep in the water and looking up at her with eyes strangely dark and sad.

Anne uttered a muffled cry and tried to descend the last dozen rungs, but three valves in the side of the tunnel beneath her erupted. Pressurized water blasted out. She saw it pour like a greenish wave down onto Cat until she could see him no longer. Knowing it probably meant certain death, Anne let go of the rungs and let herself plunge downward.

Anne found herself submerged completely in water and darkness, but she wasn't sinking. Her momentum had reversed, and she felt her body being propelled upward in the narrow tunnel. Her speed increased. She stifled a scream, trying desperately to keep her breath. She realized suddenly that if she didn't slow her ascent, she would slam into the iron bulkhead door at the top. She began to flail, trying in vain to grasp one of the rungs and slow herself down. The back of her wrist struck one of the iron rungs, and the pain shot up her arm and into her shoulder. She struggled to lift her arms over her head and succeeded for a heartbeat before hitting the iron door.

This time, she did scream. The stale air blasted from her mouth until she somehow cut it off. Agony radiated from her elbows all the way to her heart. But the pain was fortunate. It kept her from blacking out. With precious little air left in her already burning lungs, Anne felt above her head for a latch or a catch. There was none. She pounded on the iron of the door and tried to push it open. It did not move. At last she was able to put her feet on the highest rungs, and using the strength of her legs, she tried once more to budge the door. She felt the tiniest give. It moved just slightly but fell immediately back into place.

Sharp pain lanced through her chest. She was suffocating and would soon lose consciousness and drown. She pushed lamely on the door for a few moments more and then gave up.

My knife! New energy surging in her veins, Anne reached down into her boot, found the handle, and withdrew the small blade. Feeling with one hand, she guided the tip into the small crack between the top of the tunnel and the door. She guessed that any latch would be on the side of the tunnel where the rungs were and began to poke and prod with the knife. She felt a small but definite resistance and pressed the blade hard against it. Something moved, and with one final urgent push, Anne threw open the door and surged out of the tunnel.

But her air was long gone and she was still underwater—how deep, she did not know. She kicked her legs and clawed wildly at the water. She broke through the surface and flailed frantically before she realized that her lungs were filling with new air. She found herself under a dark, star-studded sky. She waved her arms back and forth to keep herself afloat—like her father had shown her all those years ago.

Anne turned round and round and saw nothing but the dark sea. Father Brun was gone. The ships were gone. Then she remembered Cat's sad eyes, and she began to weep. Hard, gut-wrenching sobs followed, driven forth by a hollow ache that she felt would never cease.

Something bumped at the bottom of her boot, and she jerked her leg up. Anne's tears ceased, and her skin prickled. There was no place to go. She was alone . . . totally and completely alone.

22

ONSLAUGHT OF
THE BERSERKERS

I hoped you would come," said Hrothgar. He and Bartholomew Thorne sat in the Raukar's war room, a vast chamber full of weapons, armor, and tapestries depicting great battles. Thorne noticed that much of the room was coated in dust.

"You are the Lord of the Raukar," said Thorne. "And the tenor of your summons piqued my interest."

"I thought it might," said Hrothgar. "But I must confess this meeting was at Lady Fleur's request."

"Lady Fleur?" Thorne was immediately suspicious.

"Yes," Hrothgar replied. The long red curtains behind his chair rippled though the air was still. "Do not judge her harshly. She is overly wary of those who claim to be of pureblood, for others have failed her before. In fact, it is because of such betrayal that she brings this request."

"My brother," said Lady Fleur as she appeared from behind the curtains, "forsook the ways of the Raukar and mingled shame with the blood of conquerors."

Thorne stood as she entered, hoping to thaw the ice between them. "How does this concern me, Lady of the Raukar?"

"You are one of us now," she replied. "Our fight is your fight."

"His name was Ulf," said Hrothgar. "Once as true a warrior as Guthrum or myself. But on one of his trading ventures, Ulf befriended a Christian man. Ulf changed then . . . an inexplicable change. He came before the council one night and renounced our gods in favor of the Christian deity. Then he, his wife, and several of his best friends sailed to Västervik on the Swedish mainland."

"Even now," Lady Fleur added, "some of the Raukar forsake our ways and flee to my brother Ulf. We have lost several of our finest craftsmen . . . and even some brilliant warriors."

Thorne's eyes narrowed, and he stroked his knifelike silver sideburns. "You want to conquer Västervik," Thorne concluded.

"Not conquer it," said Lady Fleur. "I want to burn Västervik to the ground and wipe it from the face of the earth. And I want Hrothgar to plant a banner of Tyr in the ashes of their Christian church."

"We will test the eldregn on that city," said Hrothgar. "We will wear down their defenses with the fire rain. And then we will unleash the Berserkers."

"Berserkers?" This surprised even Thorne. "The practice of turning men into Berserkers was outlawed six hundred—"

"Outlawed by an outlander," said Lady Fleur. "We do not honor their paper decrees."

"We have one hundred such men . . . men more fearsome than Bjorn whom you defeated," said Hrothgar. "The Berserkers are the pride of Raukar, a special breed . . . brutally strong and utterly fearless."

Thorne was intrigued. In truth, he very much wanted a trial run with his new fleet and his new weapon. And . . . such an invasion offered a possible solution to a problem he'd been pondering for a long while. *Yes*, he thought. *In the chaos of battle, there will be opportunity enough.* But he must not seem too eager. "How long will this take?" Thorne asked. "For we must be mindful of our true objective."

"There will be time for the British," said Hrothgar. "Västervik will require no more than three days."

"When do you wish to sail?"

"Tomorrow at sundown," Hrothgar answered.

Less than a third of the Raukar fleet, twenty ships in all, left Gotland and sailed into the red setting sun before turning north for Västervik. The winds were steady, if not strong.

Bartholomew Thorne was not at the helm of the *Raven's Revenge*. Teach had the wheel, and he was more than capable. Thorne was alone in his quarters . . . and yet not alone. The time had come.

The painting had arrived two days earlier. Thorne had had an artisan mount it on the wall across from his desk and cover it, but Thorne had not yet removed the cloth to appraise its quality. Thorne felt sure it would be good. Noldi, the old Raukar artisan who had painted the portrait, had a reputation of being supremely talented. Thorne had spent hours with the man, describing every detail, and his original sketch had been quite breathtaking. Still, Thorne was nervous. Would the painting capture her beauty? Would it capture her fire? Would it . . . bring her back?

With a tremor in his hand, Thorne loosened the linen covering and let it drop away from the portrait. A blast of air rushed from his lips. His mouth remained open wide as he stepped away from the painting. "Heather," he gasped. It was no likeness. It was her. Pale, heart-shaped face, crimson hair that shone like fire in the hot Caribbean sun, and those fierce, deep-green eyes—Heather.

He backed slowly to his desk and sat down. "My wife," he whispered. "How I have longed to look upon your face again."

The cabin was silent. No sound from the wind. No sound from the ocean. Except for the slow roll of the ship, no one would have even known they were in motion. Thorne stared at the painting and waited.

A knock at the door. "Captain Thorne?" came Bill Tarber's tentative voice. He was one of the gunners from the *Talon*. "Teach sent me to get you," he said. "We're in sight of the mainland."

"Very well," Thorne growled. "I will be right there. In the meantime, alert Hrothgar's man Brandir. I want the broadsides and dragon necks loaded and ready."

"Yes, sir, right away, sir."

Thorne stood, glanced once more at the painting, and then went to the door.

Burn them all.

Thorne smiled. She'd come back after all. "I will," he replied. Then he left his captain's quarters and went to the deck.

"How far to Västervik?" Thorne asked. He put down the spyglass. It was so dark on deck with all the lanterns hooded and the clouds hiding the moon that it was hard to measure the distance to the mainland.

"No more than two hundred yards," Brandir replied.

Thorne smelled the mineral salt in the cool air. He looked down the deck at the crew, both the men he'd brought on the *Talon* and the broad Raukar warriors . . . they were a cold-hearted and menacing group. But Thorne knew there were a dozen men below, the Berserkers, who could, under the right conditions, slay everyone on the ship.

Twenty dragon necks lined each rail, and sixty broadside cannons on the four decks below. Thorne wondered if any ship's captain in history had ever sailed with so much firepower. *No, probably not.* Brandir nodded to his captain and descended to the main deck. It was time.

"Bring her about, Mister Teach," commanded Thorne, his voice thickening.

Teach turned the wheel and the ship glided, turning its cannons toward the Swedish mainland.

The Viking Raukar leader Hrothgar stood at the rail next to Thorne and lifted his head to the dark skies. "Long has this day been coming," he said. "And yet . . ."—he turned to Thorne—"I wonder if the Raukar would have awakened if you had not come."

Thorne smiled and said, "I believe it is foolish to dwell on the past. I have come, and the Raukar have awakened. Let us just be certain that we do not cause our own future regrets. We control our own destiny."

"You mean the gods."

"What?"

"The gods control our destiny."

"Yes," said Thorne, "of course." Thorne didn't believe any of this primitive god-speak, but he knew it was what Hrothgar wanted to hear. Then the captain of the *Raven's Revenge* removed the hood from the lantern on the quarterdeck rail. Crewmen on the main deck did likewise. And with mounting satisfaction, Thorne watched ghostly orange lights kindle one by one over the dark sea. The signal had been given. And like Brandir, the gunners on the other ships lit their fuses. *Whump, whump, whump!* The dragon necks disgorged their deadly breath. Each canister, as it rose and fell, left a thin, arcing trail of angry red in the sky. It looked as if some mythical giant-clawed beast had slashed the flesh of the night.

Then, all at once, over the sleeping city of Västervik, the sky exploded as canister after canister detonated, and liquid fire bloomed and streamed down upon the now-visible rooftops and steeples awakening the people. Ships in the Swedish port kindled, and tall masts went up like matchsticks. The city and the people in it were dying.

"Again!" Thorne commanded. He watched as the second volley careened through the sky, but these flew at a much higher trajectory—a height at which they would sail far deeper into the city. Flashes like lightning flickered behind the buildings near the water, and church bells began to toll. Cannon fire erupted on the coast as the men of Västervik sought vainly to defend themselves. But the shots were frantic and poorly aimed.

"Mister Teach, advance."

"Yes, sir," the quartermaster responded, and he brought the ship in closer to shore. That had been the plan: two volleys, then advance; two volleys, then advance. After six volleys it would be time to bring the ships in and let the foot soldiers go ashore.

The initial barrage lasted just two hours, and the northern horizon seemed aflame. The burning city of Västervik no longer even returned fire. Hrothgar, who had disappeared below, returned as the ships neared the shore. Behind him loomed the one hundred Berserkers. Thorne had seen these men before. He'd watched them train. He'd even eaten meals with them. But now, under the canopy of night, in the moments before battle, they took on a new visage. They wore menace like a cloak, and peril smoldered in their eyes. So grim and fell were these warriors that the other crewmen, the Raukar and Thorne's men alike, stopped what they were doing to stare. But none could look upon the menacing Berserkers for long without averting their gaze.

They were tall and broad as were most of the Raukar. But the Berserker warriors wore leather armor—sleeveless at that—so their bare shoulders and arms made them seem all the more immense and strong. Each man had a charging red bear emblazoned crudely upon his breastplate, and each man bore an array of weapons: spears, axes, swords, maces, daggers, and hammers. But none of these weapons gleamed as if polished, and none of them were smooth as if for display. These weapons were tarnished and gray, jagged and cruel.

Edward Teach watched the Berserkers line up on deck, and he found himself fascinated by the dread that these men projected. He watched curiously as Hrothgar uncorked a black bottle and passed it in turn to each of the Berserkers. Whatever was in that bottle must have had a bitter, biting taste, for each man grimaced as he drank it.

Hrothgar ushered his Berserkers into the waiting cutter ships. Bartholomew Thorne boarded a cutter with Teach and the rest of his men. Then came the Raukar warriors filling up six similar small craft that were lowered slowly to the surface. The slender cutters sliced swiftly through the water, the faces of the invaders lit eerily in orange from the raging fires. Thorne's cutter rode alongside Hrothgar and the Berserkers, and Teach found himself staring agape. "They . . . they burn," he whispered. And so it appeared to him at first. Thin, writhing tendrils of white smoke swirled around the faces of many of the Berserker warriors and then dissipated in the sea breeze. A Berserker suddenly turned. His eyes, huge and bulging, stared out from the ghostly wisps of smoke. Teach looked quickly away.

"Waxed hemp," Thorne explained. "The Berserkers weave strands of it into their hair and beards. It smolders very slowly, and the smoke gives them a most fearsome appearance."

"It does indeed," said Teach, thoughtfully rubbing the stubble on his chin. "And the drink . . . was that some kind of ritual they perform before battle?"

"Much more than that," said Thorne with an ominous, gravelly laugh. "That flask was filled with a potent mixture of the strongest rum and ground-up bog myrtle roots. It enflames their blood lust until it is nigh unquenchable and deadens the pain that they feel. When the Berserkers reach the field of battle, it will be with such blunt violence . . . such a bloody frenzy, that few—if any—who come in contact with them will withstand it. My advice to you, Mister Teach: stay out of their way."

The first cutters hit the stony Västervik shore and found it uncontested. Howling and shrieking, the Raukar Berserkers leaped from their boats and charged up the incline. Hrothgar and the other Raukar warriors sprinted after them. Thorne and his men followed.

The docks and boathouses had been abandoned to the flames, and the dwellings closest to the water were either engulfed in fire or already reduced to smoldering husks. Hrothgar's horn sounded from somewhere up ahead. Thorne and Teach led the others in pursuit. They found the heart of the city largely untouched by their eldregn barrage of fire rain. That had been a mistake—one Thorne did not intend to repeat against the British.

Only the tall steeple tower of a church and a few of the other buildings on the outskirts burned. But in the huge cobblestone square that divided the two sides of the town, a fierce battle raged. Västervik had a larger standing army than Hrothgar and Lady Fleur had anticipated. Their numbers were more than equal to the invaders' count. But this army was divided between fighting the invaders, fighting the fire, and escorting the women, the elderly, and the children to safety. And even had the Västervik army been four times its size, they still would have been at a disadvantage.

The Berserkers cut a bloody swath through the defenders. Screeching and growling like a pack of wolves, six Berserkers came upon a band of soldiers. These men looked at the red bear emblem, the dark, smoke-wreathed faces, and gleaming eyes of these wild men—but did not cower. The men of Västervik were skillful with their long swords and came at the Berserkers. One man, thinking his foe was dead, went to pull the sword out of his enemy's body. But the Berserker was not dead. He grabbed the man's wrist, pulled him close, and then butted his head with his own. The Västervik staggered backward. His enemy's sword still deep in his gut, the Berserker charged after him and hewed him with an axe. Then the Berserker yanked the sword from his stomach and howled to the sky. He ran off and looked for more prey until, finally, he had lost so much blood that he collapsed to the ground.

And that was the way it was with all the Berserkers. They did not feel pain, they did not tire, and they did not show mercy. Edward Teach watched as the Berserkers broke through the initial line of armed defenders and surged into the fleeing citizens of the town. And as he watched the carnage, Teach found he enjoyed it.

Hrothgar swept out a pair of fighting hammers and bludgeoned one foe after another until he stood on the edge of a fountain near the

burning church, blowing his war horn, and called out to the combatants for someone worthy to do battle with the Lord of the Raukar. At
first, no one answered and the battle in the courtyard became a rout.

Then Hrothgar began to watch one of the soldiers from Västervik.
This golden-haired man wore green armor and had a very long,
double-edged sword. His skill with the blade was considerable, and
he moved with great speed. Once he dodged one Raukar's axe
swipe and wickedly slashed the back of the man's knees. He rolled
to his feet just in time to plunge the blade into the chest of a second Raukar.

One of the Berserkers spied this man's exploits. He lowered a
bloodied pike-spear, howled, and charged across the courtyard at his
new prey. Hrothgar watched from his perch, wondering if the warrior
in green armor would turn in time. He did—at the last possible
moment. He spun and brought his long sword down on the
Berserker's spear, cleaving the shaft. The Berserker snarled at the man,
tossed away the useless weapon, and unsheathed a jagged sword. He
charged again, but the Västervik man did not quail at the onslaught
of this bestial warrior. He made a "C" out of his body to avoid a swipe
at his midsection, and then he slashed the Berserker's forearm.

It made a deep cut, and the Berserker dropped his blade. He
looked at his own arm, gashed and bleeding, and seemed to wonder why it wasn't working. By the time the Berserker looked up, his
enemy's sword was inches from his neck. Hrothgar's mouth fell
open. He'd never seen a man move like that. No one except . . .

Hrothgar leaped down from the fountain and closed the distance
between them in an instant. His hammers descended upon the
green-clad warrior, but found nothing but the cobblestone. The
target had rolled deftly away. He stood out of reach and looked up
in astonishment.

"Hrothgar?" Surprise contorted into pure fury. "YOU brought this bloodthirsty storm upon us?"

"A very long time overdue," said Hrothgar, "but a coward cannot cheat death forever."

The man was incredulous. "You attack Västervik . . . you attack my people while we sleep and call me a coward?"

"You abandoned your people, Ulf," Hrothgar replied. "You abandoned your family, and for what? This Christian myth?"

"It is no myth," Ulf declared. "Did you not ever wonder why the Raukar was the last remnant of the Vikings of old to cling to the ancient superstitions?"

"Superstitions, bah!" Hrothgar swung again with his hammers. The first missed but the second struck Ulf in the ribs. He sprawled backward on the stone. "You sicken me, Ulf. Now you will die . . . under my boot."

Suddenly, there came a crack from above. The church tower, still burning furiously, pulled away from its foundation. It began to fragment into fiery sections as it fell. Hrothgar took one step toward Ulf before the falling inferno slammed him to the ground. It crashed upon the stone, blasting out red and orange embers, burning planks, and a wave of searing heat.

Ulf stood up and swayed a moment, for he was still dazed. Pain from his ribs sharpened and called him to his senses. He stared at the collapsed structure, which, like a smoldering log poked into flames, began to burn all the brighter from the fall. Hrothgar was nowhere to be seen.

Still somewhat in shock, Ulf shook his head and started to turn away when something hit him so brutally hard in the shoulder that he spun. Ulf stumbled backward and crashed to the ground. Thorne advanced quickly on the fallen warrior but found him lying very still, not the slightest movement or sign of life. Ulf's long sword lay in a pile of charred debris by his motionless hand. Thorne took the sword and glanced sharply at Ulf. Had he stirred? *Better make sure*, Thorne thought. He was about to swing his bleeding stick when he heard a faint voice from behind.

Thorne turned and stared at the fallen church tower. It couldn't be. "Gunnarson . . . Thorne!" the voice called more urgently. Thorne searched the edges of the burning structure and found Hrothgar pinned under the wreckage . . . but still very much alive.

"Gunnarson," Hrothgar cried urgently. He struggled to move, but there was too much pressure on his chest and torso. Licks of flame crawled across the heavy lumber and threatened to leap down upon the fallen Raukar warrior. Hrothgar had one arm free and reached for Thorne. "P-pull me out! . . . Thorne! The fire . . . you must hurry!"

Thorne glanced over the wreckage out into the courtyard. There, the battle still raged. *No one will know.*

Thorne moved closer to Hrothgar. "Ulf . . . did you, is he—" Hrothgar's eagerness amused Thorne.

"Ulf is dead," Thorne said, raising Ulf's sword. "You see, I have his blade."

"Well done, Gunnarson. Well done. Now, release me." The helpless Raukar chieftain smiled and held out his hand. But Bartholomew Thorne did not pull the man free. Instead, he tightened his grip on Ulf's sword and slammed it down once. Thorne left Hrothgar there, the scream still frozen on his lips and fire inching closer.

The massacre ended before the sun rose. Fires had spread, devouring more than half of Västervik. Hrothgar's remains had been separated from the burning timber and borne with care back to the *Raven's Revenge*. Thorne told the story of Hrothgar's valiant battle with Ulf the traitor that ended tragically when the building collapsed upon Hrothgar. Thorne told of how he avenged the fallen leader of the Raukar by slaying Ulf. No one questioned Thorne. Nay, the Raukar celebrated, for Hrothgar had died in battle, and surely he had been taken to Valhalla to dwell with the gods. And while the loss of Hrothgar was great, the Raukar had not been left leaderless. Bartholomew Thorne, whom some of the Raukar now believed descended from the mighty Tyr, had thrown down the betrayer and led the Raukar to victory.

For the remainder of that day, Thorne and Guthrum led the invaders to scavenge what was left of the city. Their haul was considerable, for Västervik was a prosperous port city. Tons of gold bars and silver, rich, heavy fabrics and tapestries, spices and food stores—but the greatest wealth of Västervik was in its jewel trade. The Raukar found caches of diamonds, sapphires, emeralds, and rubies the size of a child's fist. When Thorne and the raiders had taken everything of value, the Raukar fleet sailed for Gotland.

Late that night in the captain's quarters, Thorne and his quartermaster discussed recent events. "Hrothgar's loss was . . . regrettable," said Thorne. "He was my most powerful ally among the Raukar."

"Hope this doesn't put a bad taste in their mouths," said Teach. "If they pull back, we have no chance against the British."

Thorne's upper lip curled in a sneer, and he glanced at Heather's portrait. "The Raukar will turn to Lady Fleur," he said. "I cannot imagine that she would shrink back—even with such a loss."

"But what will we do if she refuses to sail against the British?"

Teach ducked his head as if he expected to be smacked. "She didn't exactly take a shining to us right off."

Thorne fingered the prongs on his bleeding stick and thought. "If Lady Fleur is unfit to command her people, then . . . someone else will have to take her place."

23

AWAKENINGS

Anne heard voices. She whirled around frantically in the water, but saw only dark sky and dark sea. *Wait!* There was something there . . . a patch darker than the sky and moving across the water. It was a ship. Anne was sure, and it seemed to be coming closer. "Help!" she screamed, but even as she took a breath to call out again, she had an overwhelming feeling that she was in danger. *Of course, I'm in danger*, she thought humorously. *In danger of drowning! This ship could be my last chance.* But for some indefinable reason, she did not cry out again.

She heard the voices again as the ship advanced. They sounded English but not the polished, studied English like Commodore Blake. No, this was the heavy slurring talk of London's West-Enders. Anne thought the ship was a brigantine like her father's old *William Wallace*. But as it came closer, she saw the third mast and realized it was probably a barque or even a small frigate.

Anne watched as it passed within fifty years of her, feeling like she was watching her life sail away. But just a moment later, the ship's sails went down and stopped only a hundred yards away. Thinking maybe she'd been given a second chance, Anne swam as hard as she could for the dark shape on the water. She came up behind the ship and thought, *Definitely a barque.*

"Oi, watch it, ye ruddy fool!" came a voice from a small cutter being lowered from the main ship. "Yer gonna drop the lot of us in the water!"

"Bah, Henry, ye have to swim anyway," a voice answered from the deck. "What's it matter?"

"I'll tell ye how it matters," Henry fired back. "Mess around, Percy, and I'll tell the Merchant what you done."

Silence from the deck. *The Merchant!* Anne cringed.

"Yeah," Henry jeered. "Thought that would shut you right up. The Merchant would likely spend the whole trip to Gotland teachin' ye discipline at the edge of that dagger a' his. Ye know he likes t'teach real slow like."

Anne cringed back behind the stern of the ship and clung to an exposed piece of the rudder. Her heart slammed against her ribs. She thought about moments earlier when she had nearly revealed herself to the ship . . . the Merchant's ship.

Anne swam to the starboard edge of the barque and peered around. Her eyes had adjusted somewhat to the darkness, but still, she could see nothing more than silhouettes. Men rowed the little cutter out about forty feet. She heard three sudden splashes and thought that several men had gone overboard. She stared at the cutter and tried to make out shapes in the water. She counted two heads . . . three, but then they disappeared below the surface. *What are they doing?* she wondered. Several minutes went by and still they did not come back to the surface.

No one can stay under that long on one breath, Anne thought. Just then, she heard voices from the cutter. Heads popped up again at the surface. Dark figures clambered into the cutter. "Of course," Anne whispered. "That's how he does it." Anne reasoned that if the Merchant's tidal lair was submerged so much of the time, he'd need a way out.

Then she thought of Cat . . . drowned by the Merchant like Father Brun and the others. She wondered what the Merchant had done with all the bodies. Anne watched the cutter being hoisted up the side of the barque. The sails went up immediately after, and the three-masted ship cruised silently away. Anne swam to the spot where she thought the cutter might have been. If there was another way into the Merchant's lair, she meant to find it. Once in, she wasn't sure what she would do . . . maybe find some way to give her friends a decent burial. After that . . . look for something she could use to start a signal fire for the next time the tidal island surfaced.

Anne dove beneath the surface and swam using only her feet to propel herself down. She was blind in this night-blackened water, so she kept a hand out in front of her head at all times. She went down as deep as she could and stayed down until her lungs burned. But she found nothing . . . just endless water. The second and third dive produced the same. But on the fourth dive, her hand struck something solid. It was hard like stone, smooth in some places, barnacled and rough in others. She surfaced for air and then dove back down. It was cylindrical and went down ten or twelve feet. When Anne descended to its end, she felt around. Her fingers touched a ridge that traveled in a complete circle, but there was nothing that she could pull. The bottom of the cylinder was closed off. She slid her hand toward the center of the disk and hoped for a hatch of some kind. She found it— or something like it—just as she ran out of breath.

Up again she went and then down to what had to be a wheel latch of some kind. She grasped it with one hand and then the other. She tried rotating it to the left, but it didn't budge. She worked it as best she could in every direction, but, floating virtually weightless in the murky water, it was hard to get any leverage. She tried to grip the outside of the cylinder with her knees and found that she could put more of her strength into the wheel. But still, it would not move more than an inch in any direction. Again and again she tried to no avail. Anne broke the surface of the water after her last attempt, took in swift breath, and screamed. She'd used so much energy and come away no better than she was before.

She was back to treading water, and now it was a grueling effort. She knew her chances of survival were very slim, but she had to try. She found she could float on her back for short spans to conserve energy. But she never let herself float for long. She had to remain over the tidal island. So after floating, she'd dive back down to check for the cylinder. But her energy was nearly spent.

And the next time Anne let herself float on the surface, she found her mind too willing to wander. Anne thought it odd that an image of Padre Dominguez popped into her mind. He was leaning on the rail on the *Wallace*'s forecastle and reading the small leather Bible he always carried. Anne laughed to herself. *He made me read the Twenty-third Psalm to him as he protected me. "The Lord is my shepherd; I shall not want. He maketh me to lie down in green pastures. He leadeth me beside the still waters. He restoreth my soul."*

Anne stopped there. She'd never really thought hard about God until Padre Dominguez had come along. *What was it the monk had said? "You have the writing of God on your heart."* She let her eyes dance from star to star. *God has to be real . . . doesn't he? Something so beautiful couldn't be there without a creator. There'd be no painting without a painter. No song without a composer.* Anne decided then and there that God was real, and without thinking, she whispered, "God, if you're listening, I think . . . I think I'd like to meet you."

A shooting star streaked across the sky and disappeared.

Anne blinked. She had no idea how long she'd been floating there. The sky was still dark, though it looked somehow different. The reality of her situation became suddenly clear. Even if she could somehow last until the tidal island appeared, the Merchant had no doubt sealed it up tight. She'd have a few hours on the island until it dipped below the water again. But no, Anne knew she'd probably not last the night. She wondered when death would come. She wondered how it would happen. Would it be sudden? The little bumps she'd felt on her knee and heels—they could have been the exploratory nudges from sharks. Any second one of the silent undersea predators could clamp down on her thigh and pull her beneath the water. Even a nip from a small shark could finish her. A little blood in the water, and sharks would come from fifty miles. Or maybe she'd simply fall asleep and slide below the water.

Anne wriggled her fingers. They were pruned. She laughed. And then the tears began to flow. *I'll never see my father again. And Cat . . . Cat's gone.* But the despair was fleeting. Peace settled over her like a blanket. *The stars . . . how very beautiful they are.* And then she closed her eyes.

Cat opened his eyes to very unfamiliar surroundings. He lay on a firm but not uncomfortable cot in a small room lit by flickering candlelight. To his left were three long cabinets with glass windows and a dark counter resting on many drawers. On top of the counter and within the cabinets there was an endless array of jars, bottles, canisters, and boxes.

Cat turned his head and flinched. A man sat next to the cot. His legs were crossed. He had one hand resting on his knee, and in the other, he held a dark brown root that he chewed on absently. His head was nearly bald. A few wispy strands of white hair rested on his scalp, but that was all. His prominent brow was arched in concern, and his eyes were kindly but very dark. He removed the root from his mouth and smiled in a close-lipped sort of way. "Finally awake?" he said. "Good, good."

"Are you a doctor?" Cat asked.

"You might say that," he replied. "After a fashion, I suppose. You would have drowned if I hadn't saved you."

Cat rubbed his temples and whispered, "Thank you."

"Least I could do for you, lad," said the old man.

"This ship," Cat said, "I don't remember it."

"No, you wouldn't. You've never been aboard the *Perdition's Gate*."

Perdition's Gate? Cat thought. *What a horrible image to associate with your ship—No!* Fear shot up his veins like liquid fire. Cat started to sit up and found a dagger at his throat . . . the same dagger the Merchant had so expertly wielded in the tunnels.

"I had begun to wonder if you'd recognize me," said the *Merchant*. "It is not often that people forget one of my unique countenance."

"You tried to kill me!" Cat roared.

"Come now, my lad. All of that unpleasantness is over now."

"Where's Anne?"

"The girl?" he asked. "I really do not know. She got sucked out of one of my auxiliary hatches. My guess is she made it to the surface, treaded water for a while . . . and then drowned."

Cat tried again to sit up. "You black-hearted—"

The Merchant pressed the dagger firmly to Cat's throat. "Yes . . . you understand me now. But have you wondered why I spared your life?"

Cat gritted his teeth and shook his head.

"I know you," said the Merchant. "You are Griffin Lejon Thorne, son of Bartholomew Thorne, a pirate of some infamy. I didn't believe Scully when he told me, but now I see it—your eyes, your jaw. Oh, you are Thorne's boy, all right . . . and in more than appearance. I wonder what he'll say when he sees you."

"Bartholomew Thorne . . . he's here?" Cat's eyes widened.

"Nay," said the Merchant. "Not on board my ship. No, but we are sailing, making all possible speed to be witnesses of your . . . reunion."

"He'll kill me," said Cat. "He's already tried twice."

"Not getting along with your father, eh?" The Merchant laughed. "Well, if he will not take you . . . I will. You see, I've been searching for an apprentice. Searching for some time now."

Cat nearly gagged. "I know all about you," he said. "Remember? I read your logs. But even if I hadn't, I learned enough from Father Brun to know I would never serve a demon like you."

"That," said the Merchant, "would be an unconscionable waste of talent."

"I'm not like you!" Cat yelled.

"No," said the Merchant. "Someday you will be better than I am. But make no mistake: You were born a killer. I saw firsthand the blood lust in your eyes . . . down in the tunnels of my lair. I believe you meant to take my head."

"You're mad, if you think I'll follow you."

"Why delay the inevitable, Griffin Thorne? You cannot change the cloth from which you were cut."

"No." Cat's voice was just a whisper.

The Merchant jerked Cat up off the cot. Keeping the dagger in the small of Cat's back, the Merchant led Cat out of the room, down a narrow hall, and into an iron cell.

"In any case," said the Merchant, slamming the barred door shut, "you have a long voyage ahead of you to decide."

Anne closed her eyes and wriggled down beneath the blanket. It was so warm and comforting. She felt all her muscles relax as the blanket went up over her head. Down, down she went, her thoughts drifting . . . so tired . . . drifting . . .

Something bumped her hard on the leg. A shock of electricity. Her eyes opened to impenetrable murk and the sting of salty water. *Under water!* She opened her mouth to scream. Sea water poured in instead. Anne flailed, coughed, and spat. She climbed somehow to the surface. There, she hacked and gagged and struggled against the panic to stay afloat.

At last the mindless terror subsided and Anne realized just how close she'd come to drowning. Something had hit her leg again beneath the water—that had saved her, she realized. But still, she was anything but safe. The next bump could come with teeth.

It was still dark, and Anne treaded water, turning in slow circles. She found herself starting to fade again. Her muscles just couldn't keep going forever, and she was emotionally spent. BUMP. Something hit her in the rear end this time, and once more, Anne startled awake. She spun around in the water, looking frantically. Then she saw it: a triangular shadow protruding from the dark water . . . a dorsal fin. A huge dorsal fin. All those tentative bumps, the shark had been prodding her, testing her, and biding its time.

The fin sliced toward her. Anne readied her boots, intending to kick the shark, to try to drive it off. She had to. If the creature drew blood . . . it was over. It was just a few feet away, and Anne could see its familiar shape. It began to surface. It was going to attack. Anne kicked her feet out and flailed backward. And then she heard very strange sounds.

Whistles, clicks, and chirps. Anne stopped kicking and stared. The dark shark-shape suddenly broke the surface. It was not a shark at all. A large dolphin floated there. It turned its sleek head this way and that, spun around two or three times, and chirped loudly. Anne tentatively swam forward and patted the dolphin on the head. The creature whistled and spun around once more. Then it disappeared below the surface.

"No, come back," Anne called to the dark water.

Suddenly, the dolphin surfaced beneath Anne, and she clung to its back. The creature began to swim in lazy circles, clicking softly as if talking to itself.

Anne awakened to voices. "A fine catch, Captain!" bellowed one voice.

"Yes," a quiet voice replied. "But who would want such a wrinkled thing as this for dinner?"

"Maybe we should throw her back."

Anne saw a man with his right arm in a sling. He had very dark skin and yet very white hair—even his eyebrows and moustache. "Brother Dmitri?" Anne whispered. She turned her head and saw another man. He had pale skin, wispy light blond hair, and pale blue eyes. "Father Brun?" Anne blinked. "Are . . . are we in heaven?"

"Not yet!" said Dmitri.

"No, dear Anne," said Father Brun. "The Almighty has chosen to let us all elude death in the most extraordinary ways. A dolphin . . . who would have believed it?" The monk started to say something more, but closed his mouth. He seemed to be weighing some decision, and at last asked, "Where . . . where is Cat?"

Anne's lower lip trembled, and she shook her head. "He's gone," she said, urgency building in her voice. "The Merchant, he—"

"It is too soon for speech," Father Brun said quickly. "We will exchange such testimonies another time. For now, you must rest."

"No," said Anne, sitting up and throwing her legs over the edge of the bed. She winced and held her throbbing wrist. "No, I want to talk now." She was quiet a moment, trying to remember. Then she told the tale of running through the tunnels, the Merchant always seeming to know exactly where she and Cat were heading. She told how they realized the Merchant's lair had tubes delved through it, a network of tubes that carried sound. She told of discovering a potential way out only to be trapped there by the Merchant. And then, tearfully, she described how Cat had given his life so that she could escape. "I tried," she said, weeping quietly. "I tried to swim back down to him, but the water . . . it . . . it pulled me out."

Father Brun put an arm around her shoulder. "I am so sorry you had to endure such a tragedy," he said.

Anne quickly dabbed her tears with her sleeve. She cleared her throat and said, "We were cut off from you . . . down in those tunnels. How did you escape?"

With colorful interruptions from Brother Dmitri, Father Brun told their story. "The Merchant meant to drown us like rats in that chamber," said Father Brun. "But the Almighty, as he often does, transformed tragedy into triumph."

"By the time we surfaced, the *Celestine* had already gone below the waves," said Brother Dmitri. "The damage from the reef was too severe. We boarded the *Constantine* with scarcely enough time to catch our breaths. The Merchant's ship, it came from the darkness and sent the *Dominguez* to the bottom before we realized what was happening."

"We had no time to react," said Father Brun. "And we couldn't match its firepower. We did the only thing we could . . . we fled."

"The *Constantine* is lighter," said Brother Dmitri. "We harnessed the prevailing wind and sped away. The Merchant's ship gave up the chase and turned back."

"It was then that we took a chance," Father Brun explained. "We used our instruments and the stars to double back on them. We found that they had anchored near the Merchant's tidal lair."

"Dropped our sails and doused all our lanterns," said Brother Dmitri. "We let the darkness and distance hide us."

"We sent out a few men in a cutter to watch," explained Father Brun. "The Merchant's ship departed just before sunrise."

"We sailed in after," Brother Dmitri said, "hoping to dive and find some way into that accursed place. We found several hatches, but they were all sealed tight."

"We found you not long after," said Father Brun. "You were floating in the water. We thought you dead."

"Miraculous!" Brother Dmitri exclaimed.

"Where are we now?" Anne asked.

"We are north of Cuba, headed to New Providence," said Father Brun. "We hope to find your father there . . . or at least Commodore Blake." He was silent a moment and then added, "The Merchant

24
TRUTH AND CONSEQUENCE

Cutlass Jack's *Banshee* sailed alongside the *Robert Bruce*, keeping pace as they journeyed across the Atlantic. Aboard the *Bruce*, it was time for the evening meal. "I made 'his special for you, Mister Slash," said Nubby, placing a large bowl in front of their newest crewmen. "Cap'n Ross told me it was your favorite."

Rather than using his captain's quarters, Ross and his senior crewmen ate the evening meal with the rest of the crew. They sat around a hodgepodge of tables. Those who couldn't find room at an actual table used the tops of crates and barrels instead. All eyes turned to Slash to see what he would do with the "special" course that had been served.

Slash stared down at the bowl. He picked up his wooden spoon, dipped it into the creamy greenish stew, and nudged a chunk of something around the bowl. "What, what is this?" he asked, looking up with a rueful expression on his face.

St. Pierre covered his mouth with his hands. Jules pounded a fist

has eluded us once more . . . and now we don't even know
to begin to look."

"Gotland," said Anne.

"What?" the two monks asked.

"When I swam behind the Merchant's ship," Anne expl
overheard sailors talking. They said something about a lo
Gotland. But I've never heard of such a place."

"It is an island south and east of the Swedish mainlan
Brun explained. "I was born in Sweden, lived my chi
Stockholm. My grandfather used to tell me of the men o
men who still lived the old ways."

"What would the Merchant want with the Swedes?" as

Father Brun ran a hand through his hair and said, "I
no doubt some dark designs. What do you suggest we
Captain?"

Anne didn't answer at first. Then, with the two m
her, she said, "You mean . . . me?"

"Cat agreed to sail on this mission only if you cou
ond," explained Father Brun. "We will honor his wis

Anne swiped at her watering eyes. She missed
than ever. She wished he was there by her side, the
mand. She never wanted it to happen this way. "I
continue for New Providence," she said. "We'll nee
to fight the Merchant and that fortress of a ship h
sail for Gotland and get this man once and for all.

"For the Almighty," said Father Brun.

"Amen," said Brother Dmitri. "And . . . for C

on his barrel-table. But Ebenezer Hack couldn't contain himself any longer. He let out a deep, chesty guffaw and had to lean on Red Eye to keep from falling out of his chair.

"It's . . . it's iguana stew!" Captain Ross exclaimed. "You said if I let you join the crew, you'd eat iguanas!"

"This"—Slash held up a glop on his spoon—"is iguana?"

"Go on!" Hack bellowed. "Take a bite."

"Just shove it on in there," said Jules. "It's really quite good."

Slash figured he didn't have much choice, so he pinched the bridge of his nose and put the spoon in his mouth. He tasted garlic right off, a little onion, a lot of pepper. Then he chewed a hunk of meat and experienced a flavor that took him by surprise. It was spicy and hearty, full of savor and salt. "Hey," he said, plunging the spoon into the bowl for another bite. "This is good!"

"Ha!" Nubby exulted. "That'll teach the lot of you to doubt my cooking!"

Ross and everyone except Jules, who generally enjoyed Nubby's iguana stew, sat in stunned silence for a few moments before the entire deck erupted in laughter.

Later that night, Ross, Stede, Cutlass Jack, St. Pierre, and Red Eye met in the captain's quarters aboard the *Robert Bruce*. Ross had a sea chart spread wide upon his desk. He pointed emphatically at England. "What's Thorne going to do?" he asked.

"Shoot King George?" St. Pierre suggested.

"Jacques!" Red Eye slapped him on the shoulder.

"Well . . . that is what I would do," said St. Pierre. "What better way to exact vengeance upon an enemy nation."

Ross shook his head. "No, half of London would line up to

shake Thorne's hand if he got rid of King George. The English have little love for their imported king."

"Maybe Thorne will blow up the palace?" said St. Pierre. "Or some other English landmark."

"I think that is likely closer to the truth," said Ross. "Thorne's hate of the British is an obsession. In his mind, they murdered his first wife and took away his chance to become the dominant naval power in the Atlantic."

"But can we believe Bellamy?" asked Cutlass Jack. "Thorne could be intendin' an attack in the Caribbean fer all we know."

"In life, I b' not believing a single word from that bedeviled mon," said Stede. "But with him dying I think him b' trying to hit us with the only thing him b' having left . . . the truth."

"I am convinced that Bellamy told us the truth about Thorne," Ross said. "It makes sense. He has it in for the Brits—that's clear. But what can he do? He's lost his ship, his fleet, his stronghold in the Cape Verde Islands. More than a year, we hear nothing from him."

A comical smile appeared on Stede's face. "I don't suppose him b' rowing a little cutter up the Thames . . . just to say hello."

"Not likely," said Ross. "A man with Thorne's contacts could do a lot in the time he's had. And yet we've scoured the Caribbean and Thorne's usual haunts. None of his previous suppliers have done business with him. More than anything else . . . it's the not knowing that worries me."

Half an ocean away, the *Raven's Revenge* sailed into Sigvard Bay and found a familiar British ship of the line anchored among the limestone rock formations. "That's the *Oxford*," said Bartholomew Thorne.

"Commodore Brandon Blake's ship . . . in Gotland." His breathing deepened to a throaty rasp.

Teach had the wheel but wished someone else did. Thorne looked like he was ready to skin half the crew. Nonetheless, Teach managed to guide the ship to port without getting a taste of his captain's bleeding stick.

Thorne suddenly felt like everything was falling apart. Intending to take command of the Raukar, he'd secretly slain Hrothgar. The Raukar did not suspect, but what if, as Teach suggested, they decided to pull out? And now, Blake appears? Thorne thought perhaps Wetherby had completed his mission and simply brought back the *Oxford* as a trophy. But seeing that ship, a symbol of British might, anchored here led Thorne to believe that something had gone terribly wrong.

The fortress of the Raukar was in chaos. Word had spread rapidly about Hrothgar's fall. Men and women alike wept openly. There was talk of the British invaders and of the captives who were taken. Thorne and Guthrum led a procession up the winding avenue that led to Hrothgar's Hall. Torchbearers surrounded the stretcher upon which Hrothgar's remains lay. Six men on either side bore their fallen leader to his home.

"What has befallen me?" Lady Fleur cried out. "Where is my husband?"

"He is here!" Thorne exclaimed. "We have borne him to his great hall in honor."

Lady Fleur did not run down the stone stairs, but there was a quiver in her gait as she descended and went to her husband.

"I urge caution, Lady of the Raukar," Guthrum said. "He was badly burned."

The stench hit her like a wall, but she waived Guthrum off dismissively and looked beneath the great red banner that covered Hrothgar. After only a moment, she lowered the banner and looked up abruptly as if catching her breath. "Tell me," she said, "how comes he thus?"

"By unhappy chance, my lady," said Guthrum. "He—"

"He led the Raukar valiantly," Thorne interrupted. "Västervik is razed to the earth as you desired. But in the battle, Hrothgar fell."

"Who slew him?" Lady Fleur asked.

"No man slew him," Thorne lied. "For no man could. One of the gods deemed it time to bring Hrothgar's heroic soul to Valhalla. He had confronted Ulf the betrayer when a burning building fell upon him."

A single cold tear ran down Lady Fleur's cheek, but she did not weep aloud. And she wore a proud smile, for surely it had been the gods who had taken Hrothgar. It was just and honorable to die in battle. "What of my traitorous brother?" she asked suddenly. "Did he burn as well?"

"Ulf did not deserve to share Hrothgar's fire," said Thorne. He slid the bleeding stick out of its holster and held it aloft. "I slew him. His blood remains even now on my weapon."

"HRAH!!" the whole assembly cheered.

When the ruckus died down, Lady Fleur turned to her people and exclaimed, "Raukar, Hrothgar lived courageously and died all the better!"

"HRAH!!" they answered.

"Tonight, we will lay Hrothgar in the bosom of an able ship," she said, a tremble in her strong voice. "We will fill it with such things as he will need as he does battle until Ragnarok, the final battle of all our gods and heroes. Then we will let the ship depart, and we will weep no more."

Lady Fleur gave commands for Hrothgar's remains to be made ready. Then she led Thorne and Guthrum to a chamber behind the throne.

"You have done well, Thorne," she said. "I am in your debt."

Thorne nodded. "He was a fearless man."

"As are you," she replied. "When you first came to us, I thought you haughty, arrogant . . . or foolish. Now, I know differently."

"You are kind," Thorne said.

"Kind," echoed Lady Fleur. "That has never been a word associated with me. Think rather that I am precise."

Thorne accepted the rebuke without comment. He waited to see what the Lady of the Raukar would say next.

"We have much to discuss, Thorne. My grieving will wait until tonight. Guthrum tells me that there were flaws in our attack, flaws we do not wish to repeat against the British."

Thorne found himself tongue-tied. "Then," he stammered, "the Raukar will—"

"Still sail?" Lady Fleur asked. "Of course. The Raukar may have lain dormant for centuries, but now that we have been awakened, nothing, not even death, will stop us from seeking our right to the seas." She motioned for the Raukar door warden to step forward.

Guthrum spread a large chart on the table. "As I see it," Guthrum said, "we must strike the heart of the Britains. When London burns, the country will fall."

"I agree," said Thorne. "We must sail up the Thames right into the Port of London. It is certainly vulnerable to attack—so close to the water, easily within reach of the eldregn. But we must send our fire much farther into the city. Firing too short was the most serious of our mistakes at Västervik. England's standing army will be much more formidable."

"What of the British navy?" Lady Fleur asked.

"Ah," said Thorne rubbing his hands together. "You are precise. The British fleet is our biggest obstacle, for it is by this weapon that they control the Atlantic and the Spanish Main. At any given time, a scant third of the fleet occupies the Port of London. Others are scattered between Liverpool, Manchester, Essex, and the like. But the bulk of the fleet patrols the trade routes of the Atlantic and guards the settlements of the Caribbean. We may destroy London and leave the fleet headless, but—"

"But the rest of the fleet will still be unconquered." Lady Fleur pursed her lips and asked, "How many ships would the British still have to bring against us?"

"More than twice the Raukar fleet," said Thorne. "Given our weapons and our will, we could hunt them all down and defeat them, but . . . I suggest another course." Thorne waited, allowing the suspense to build. "What if we could have the majority of the fleet together at one time?"

"That would be an opportunity indeed," she replied.

"But such a force," objected Guthrum, "would be beyond us."

"I am afraid Guthrum is correct," admitted Thorne. "The entire British fleet might overcome the Raukar out of sheer number. But . . . not if we could be assured that most of the ships maintained only a skeleton crew."

"Speak plainly, Thorne," said Lady Fleur. "Will there be such a time?"

"Saint Alfred's Day." Thorne crossed his arms and then explained. "Every May twenty-first the British celebrate Saint Alfred's Day . . . commemorating their great Saxon warlord's defeat of the Danes in eight-seventy-eight."

"I know the occasion well," said Guthrum. "My namesake,

Guthrum the Old, led the Danes in that battle. The Saxon king was victorious only because the Danish army was decimated by injury and sickness."

"Nonetheless," Thorne continued, "the British celebrate this battle as one of the greatest military campaigns in their history. The majority of their fleet will gather in the Port of London to take part in the festivities. And here is where we gain our biggest advantage. The might of the British navy will be so preoccupied with making merry that they will turn a blind eye to the sea. The Raukar fleet will come upon them like a fiery storm. We will cripple the British fleet, its government, and its commerce. King George, if he's even in the palace, will be left with few choices."

"To destroy the British while they celebrate a victory over our Viking kindred . . . that would be a glorious day indeed," said Lady Fleur.

"Night," Thorne corrected. "We will come at night at the height of their celebration. We will use black sails and hood every lantern . . . until it is too late. There is, however, one problem."

Lady Fleur's eyes narrowed to slits. "And that is?"

"The British may already know of our plans."

"How could they?" Lady Fleur demanded.

"The British ship in Sigvard Bay," said Thorne. "I must know who sailed it and how they came here."

"They came in the morning . . . just before the sun," said Lady Fleur. "They fired a few cannon shots but surrendered when they realized that twelve Raukar ships had them hemmed in. It was sailed by a British commodore named Blake." Thorne cringed. If Blake was still in command, then Wetherby failed in his mission.

"As to how they came here," Lady Fleur continued, "you may ask them yourself."

"They still live?"

"For now," said Lady Fleur. "I will leave their fate in your hands."

"I need a chamber," said Thorne. "There must be only one way in. It must be private. And it must be a place that can get . . . wet."

"We have such a place," said Guthrum. "Plåga hus, we call it."

Thorne nodded. "It sounds ideal. Have four trustworthy warriors bring the British commodore—and his quartermaster if you can find him—to me in this plåga hus. I will find out everything we need to know."

"Oh, there is one other thing," said Lady Fleur. "One of the captives claims to be your friend, says he's working for you."

"Nigel," Thorne whispered.

"You know him then?"

"Regrettably," Thorne answered. "Have the guards bring him as well."

The guards arrived with Commodore Blake, his quartermaster Mr. Jordan, and Nigel Wetherby—all shackled at the ankles and hands bound behind them. Wetherby's eyes brightened the moment he saw Thorne.

"Captain Thorne," exclaimed Wetherby. "At last you've come. Tell these brutes to unshackle me."

Thorne nodded to the guards, and they freed him. The moment he was released, Wetherby threw a vicious punch into Commodore Blake's jaw. Blake swayed, but his knees did not buckle. He spat and glared up at Wetherby. Mr. Jordan struggled against his captors, but the Raukar guards held him fast.

"Did you enjoy that, Nigel?" asked Thorne.

"Very . . . very much," Wetherby replied. He grinned up at Thorne.

Thorne motioned to him. "Come, my friend, sit with me a moment."

Wetherby did as he was told, sitting in the chair across from Thorne. "Tell me, Nigel, did you complete your mission?"

"Yes, of course," said Wetherby, crafting his answer carefully. "As you requested, King George disbanded the pirate-hunting fleet and spurned the monks. Blake was relieved of his command."

Thorne smiled but scratched his sideburns. "I was told that Blake commanded the *Oxford* when it arrived here. How did that happen?"

Wetherby was silent, but Blake spoke up. "My crew mutinied on him, that's what happened. They know a real commander from a traitorous—"

"That will be all from you," said Thorne sharply, and his rebuke was so abrupt and full of rancor that Blake felt as if his breath had been stolen away. Thorne stared at Blake for several long seconds. Then he cast his stare back to Wetherby. "Is this true, Nigel?"

"Yes . . . ," Wetherby answered, feeling suddenly uncomfortable.

"Sir Nigel . . . why wouldn't you have Blake's loyal crew replaced or even hire a new one of your own?" Wetherby had no answer. "And, if Blake took command, how did he manage to find his way to Gotland?"

"He told us," Mr. Jordan blurted out.

"No!" exclaimed Wetherby, holding up his hands as if to keep Thorne away. "No, I didn't tell them. They found my sea charts. I would never betray you."

"Nigel." Thorne sighed and shook his head.

Wetherby saw the pistol a mere second before it went off. The shot hit him with deadly accuracy, sending his lifeless body crashing to the floor. Thorne motioned to the guards, and they brought

Blake over. One of the guards picked up the toppled chair and put it upright. "Sit," Thorne commanded.

Blake looked at the chair. It was spattered with blood. Blake said defiantly, "I think I'd rather stand."

One of the guards drew a long sword, and Thorne said, "If it will help, I can have the Raukar remove your legs."

Blake sat immediately.

"Commodore," said Thorne, "it was very foolish of you to sail here with just one ship. What did you think you were going to do?"

"Surrender," said Blake. He never once broke eye contact with Thorne.

Thorne's face betrayed no emotion. "Explain," Thorne commanded.

"They put me on trial, ridiculed me," Blake argued. "King George stripped me of my command . . . made me an outlaw in the country I worked so hard to defend. When my crew and I stole command of the *Oxford*, our lives in England became forfeit." Blake stole a glance at his quartermaster and said, "I thought . . . I thought I might be able to make a deal with you."

"So you've become a pirate?" Thorne laughed. "Of course, I don't believe you, but tell me the terms of your offer anyway."

Blake's cheeks reddened. "I don't know what you are planning to do in England," he said. "And honestly, I no longer care. My wife and I have said our good-byes to England. But spare New Providence. It is my home now. The island's been through enough already. Leave the island alone and prohibit others from attacking it."

"In exchange for?"

"British battle tactics," Blake replied. "I know most of the other commodores and captains. I know their strategies. I know where they are weak. I'll even show you our trade route coverage."

"Ah, Commodore Blake, you are a horrible liar," said Thorne. "British battle tactics? You'd lead me right into their teeth. But as transparent as you are, I must be sure of what you know." Thorne stood and took the sword from the guard. He leveled it at Blake's throat. "Now, tell me again, how did you know you would find me on Gotland Island?"

"Wetherby told my men," Blake said.

"Yes, and what else did he tell you?"

"Nothing else."

"I see," said Thorne. The tip of the sword touched Blake's neck. "And who else knows I am here?"

Blake jerked his head away from the blade, but it followed him. "No one but my men . . . we took command from Wetherby at Ipswich. We made no other stops."

"Did you send a courier from Ipswich?"

"No, Thorne! No one else knows you're here."

Thorne raised his sword. "I think you are lying to me, Commodore Blake." He made as if to swing the sword. Blake closed his eyes. But the blow never fell. "You don't care," said Thorne. "You'll die with your secret, won't you? Guard, take him." The Raukar warriors took Blake from the chair. "I wonder what your quartermaster's life is worth to you."

Thorne grabbed Jordan by the elbow and slammed him into the chair. "Blast it, Thorne!" yelled Jordan. "Brandon's telling the truth!"

"No, I won't be asking you any questions," Thorne said. He rammed the pommel of the sword into Jordan's temple. His head rocked back and forth. Blake gasped, then sighed with relief as Jordan shook his head and opened his eyes. "The questions are all for you, Blake. And it will go poorly for Jordan here if you lie."

Thorne paused and then asked again, "How did you know I would be on Gotland Island?"

"Wetherby told us," Blake said, glancing from Thorne to Jordan and back.

"And what did Nigel tell you about my activities?"

"Nothing else . . . just that you would be here."

Without a moment's hesitation, Thorne thrust the sword two inches into Jordan's right shoulder. Jordan screamed and struggled in his chair.

"THORNE!" Blake yelled, straining against the guards. "Wetherby didn't tell us anything else . . . nothing . . . I swear to you."

"I believe you," said Thorne, his voice thickening and hoarse. He did not remove the tip of the sword from Jordan's wound. "Now, did you send word to London telling them where I could be found?"

"No," answered Blake, now drenched in sweat. "They wouldn't have believed me if I did. I told you they stripped my commission."

Thorne slowly began to turn the sword blade, widening the wound. Jordan winced and then groaned.

"How easy it is for you to harm a helpless man!" Blake growled. "You weak, conniving—"

"Be silent," said Thorne. He removed the sword, and blood poured down Jordan's arm. "I am a reasonable man. Just one more question. Did you or anyone on your ship send word of my location to anyone who is not on the *Oxford*?" Thorne watched Blake and Jordan, looking for just a hint of betrayal. He saw it: just a flicker of the eyes between the two . . . a questioning and an answering.

When Blake answered, "No, we sent no word at Ipswich," Thorne had already drawn back the sword. He rammed it into

Jordan's upper thigh and pulled up. Jordan howled in agony, grow-ing louder and more frantic as Thorne lifted the blade. "You're lying," was all he said.

Blake's lips disappeared and his eyes bulged. He struggled vio-lently with the Raukar guards. Jordan's screams filled the chamber, and Thorne continued to pull at the flesh on the quartermaster's leg. "Tell me!" Thorne growled.

"Don't you say a blasted thing!" Jordan cried out, but Thorne twisted the blade.

"ROSS!!" Brandon Blake bellowed. "I left word in Edinburgh . . . for Ross . . ."

"What did you tell him?"

"I told him you're on Gotland Island . . . that's all. I didn't know anything else. I still don't!"

"Did he get the message?"

"No," seethed Blake. "No one in Edinburgh had seen Ross for months, and . . . he didn't show up while we were there."

"Thank you, Commodore Blake," said Thorne. "That will be all for now."

"Wait!" Blake exclaimed, as the guard dragged him bodily from the chamber and out into the sunlight. He heard Jordan cry out again—a wretched, guttural cry. "Thorne, wait! NOOOO!" And then there was silence.

Thorne had all of his belongings taken aboard the *Raven's Revenge*. Since the fire long ago, he never liked to put down roots on land. Thorne stared at the portrait and wondered if Heather would respond to his news.

Declan Ross? she said in his mind. *Those are ill tidings.*

"Likely he won't be coming to Scotland any time soon," Thorne countered. "Last I heard, he was skirting around my old haunts in the Caribbean."

Still, he must not be underestimated.

"No, I won't make that mistake again." Thorne picked at something in his teeth. "Ross knows nothing of our plans. If he comes here, he'll be taken just like Blake. In any case, I'll lead the Raukar fleet by the most southerly route. If Ross sails from Edinburgh, he'll miss us entirely by a hundred miles."

"Sir?" Teach's voice came through the door.

"What is it?" Thorne growled.

The door cracked open just enough to let Teach's head appear. "Lady Fleur wants to know what we'll do with the *Oxford*."

"Do?" Thorne replied. "We're going to use it to destroy London. That's what we'll do with it. Few ships have that kind of gunnery."

"And what about the prisoners . . . Commodore Blake and his wife?"

"There was a woman on the *Oxford*?"

"Yeah, a real fine lady . . ." Teach stopped suddenly, staring up on the cabin wall.

"What is it, Edward?"

"Well, sir," he replied, swallowing. "If you'll beg me pardon. She looks a fair bit like the lady in your paintin' there."

A chill scratched across Thorne's scarred hand. He found himself oddly short of breath, but he wasn't sure why. "Bring Commodore Blake," he said at last. "Bring his wife here as well, and imprison them below. Tell Lady Fleur she can do whatever she wants with the rest of the *Oxford*'s crew."

Bright blue eyes gleamed from the *Oxford*'s crow's-nest. They'd missed him somehow. Then again, he knew every place to hide on the ship. But they took everyone else . . . rowed away to shore. Hopper prayed they weren't killed. He waited silently up in the crow's-nest. He waited and watched, hoping there might be something he could do to help.

25
CLUES AND COLD TRAILS

Well, let Thorne take England!" said Cutlass Jack as he and Declan Ross stomped up a long pier toward their ships. They had just returned from a maddening discussion at the palace in London. "What did I tell ye, Declan? The Brits have cut us off."

"I'll see to it that you and your crew get taken care of," said Ross, glowering.

"I'll thank ye fer that," he replied. "But ye can't be payin' the whole Wolf fleet! With the king cuttin' 'em off like this, men'll be twice the enemy of England!"

"And what's more," said Ross, "they've stripped Blake of his command. He was the one man in the British navy I could trust."

The two captains stopped on the pier directly between their two ships. "What now?" asked Jack.

"There's no sign of Thorne," said Ross, rubbing the bridge of his nose with his thumb and forefinger. "No sign of Blake . . . ah! I need time to think this through."

"Not here, though," said Jack.

"No," said Ross. "Our welcome is worn quite thin."

"Well, I'm part a' yer plan, whatever it be," said Jack, slapping Ross on the shoulder. "But I pray yer not plannin' to head back t' the islands . . . are ye? I mean the lads are half-mad from sailin' non-stop like we did."

"No, you're right," said Ross, his eyes brightening. "We do need a break. We sail for Edinburgh."

"O'Lordan's?" Jack asked.

Ross grinned. "Is there any other place?"

"Ah . . . ," said Jack. "I can taste the meat pies now."

Anne had the wheel of the *Constantine*. She looked over her shoulder at the island of New Providence, now disappearing in the ship's wake. "I don't understand what has happened," said Anne.

Father Brun stood at her side. "I want to know why Commodore Blake was so abruptly called away to England."

"The servants certainly seemed concerned," said Anne.

"As am I." Father Brun's tone was unusually hard. "And just what does King George think he's doing reneging on our deal? He can spend or not spend England's wealth as he sees fit. But to stop payment to the pirate-hunting fleet and claim the Brethren's share of the treasure for England . . . we'll just see about that."

Wind suddenly snapped the sails taut. Anne looked off the starboard bow where an angry thatch of dark clouds swirled. "Glad we're not sailing through that," said Anne.

"Hurricane?"

"Hard to tell," Anne replied, shaking her head. "I've only seen a hurricane at sea twice, and one was when I was too little to remember."

She watched a white thread of lightning reach down from the distant clouds to the sea. "Bad enough. But the wind out here on its fringe will give us a bit more speed."

Father Brun also watched the storm. "Good. The faster we get to England . . . the better."

Hopper saw the cutter come to the big ship next to the *Oxford* and then go. And now it returned once more with the same man at the bow. But this time, seated in the stern between huge, armored guards were Commodore Blake and Lady Dolphin. Hopper looked at the mooring lines between the *Oxford* and the other ship. *The lines will get me to it, but it's not going to be much fun!* he thought. *And no mistake.* Still, he'd have to try. It wouldn't be the first time.

"You arrogant wretch," snapped Blake, standing before Bartholomew Thorne's desk in the captain's quarters. "You think I'll tell you anything after you murdered my quartermaster . . . my friend?"

"An intelligent man might have learned something from that," said Thorne, scraping flakes of blood from his bleeding stick with a dagger. "Your wife is waiting in a cell below. I see—"

Blake broke away from the Raukar guards and dove for Thorne's desk, but Edward Teach was there. He grabbed Blake by the shoulders and flung him back to the guards. "Commodore Blake," rasped Thorne, "you try anything like that again, and I'll peel the skin from your wife's body one inch at a time. Teach, go and get her. Then we'll see how cooperative Commodore Blake can be."

While Teach was gone, Blake glared at Thorne and said very quietly, "If you hurt her . . ."

"You'll what?" asked Thorne, taunting his captive. "Hang your-self in your own chains? You are in a position of weak—" Thorne never finished his thought. The door opened, and Teach led a woman into the room. And for Thorne, it was as if time had slowed. The room . . . the world had all gone to an ashen gray. For Heather had come alive once more, but not a voice . . . real . . . and in the room with him now. She was just as he remembered her: tall, slen-der but strong . . . the same pale skin that made her deep green eyes so mysterious . . . the fiery red hair. And yet there were some differ-ences. The line of her jaw was more squared . . . her brow more prominent. And she looked so young. Still, the resemblance was so striking that Thorne could think of nothing else.

"Sir?" asked Teach.

Thorne wheeled around, his face slack and eyes unfocused. "Seat her in the chair," said Thorne blankly. Teach did so, looking from Dolphin to the portrait and back.

Then for the first time, Blake noticed the portrait and gasped. The likeness was unmistakable. Then something Declan Ross had told him two years earlier came to mind. Blake bowed his head and moved it side to side as if searching the floor for answers. He thought, *It can-not be . . .*

Thorne lost all thought of torturing this woman. "How old are you?" he asked her.

Dolphin looked over her shoulder at her husband. He nodded. "Four and twenty," she replied, more than a little bitterness etching her features. "Why do you stare like that?"

Thorne did not answer. He remembered Heather had been nine and twenty when she died. He shook his head. It was unimaginable, but he asked, "Where were you born?"

"Just outside of London," she muttered. "Kingston it is called."

"And who are your parents?"

"Why do you bring me here?" Dolphin cried angrily. "Why—"

"WHO ARE YOUR PARENTS?" Thorne rose up with his hands pressed flat on the desk. His voice became low and viscous.

"Emma and Richard Kinlan," she whispered at first, but then grew fierce. "My mother died of malaria, and YOU killed my father!"

"Did I?" The name sounded vaguely familiar, but Thorne couldn't make a connection. He looked to the painting once more and back at Dolphin. The years were right. "Mister Teach," he said suddenly, "take Commodore Blake and his wife back to their cells. See to it that they have something decent to eat."

Teach looked at his captain and wondered about the sudden change. "Yes, sir," he replied.

Before they left the room, Thorne said, "In three days, sixty ships of war, including your *Oxford*, will sail for England." Thorne smiled, but it was a ghastly, skullish grin. "You will both live that long . . . for I want you to watch London burn."

After they were gone, Thorne unrolled a sea chart and tried to plan his attack. But his mind went back to a different fire . . . one that had burned four and twenty years earlier.

"Do ye have any idea how long it's been since I've been here?" Cutlass Jack asked as he and Declan Ross led a troupe of sailors from both ships up the always misty cobblestone streets of Edinburgh, Scotland. They'd sailed all afternoon, all night, and just arrived as the sun rose—and yet, compared to their recent crossing of the Atlantic, this little voyage seemed like a blink.

"Too long, I imagine," said Ross. He could see the familiar O'Lordan's sign just up the hill.

"Oooh, I'm gettin' me two meat pies," said Jack, rubbing his stomach.

"A skillet full of bacon and fried potatoes for me," Jules said, and as if on cue, his stomach rumbled.

"O'Lordan's has the best bangers and mash," offered Slash.

"Haggis or a pan of colcannon?" asked Red Eye. "I cannot decide."

St. Pierre snorted. "You English . . . you have no taste. To you a piece of clay topped with sawdust is succulent. Ah, I long for Paris."

Hack laughed and said, "Anything's better than Nubby's cook—"

"Watch yer mouth," said Nubby, pinching Hack's ear. "Or you might find something a wee bit unsavory in your soup next time."

"Besides, Hack old boy," Slash retorted, "by the look of you, you've enjoyed Nubby's cooking quite well." Hack feigned offense and made to draw his sword. The group laughed the rest of the way to the tavern. But Ross found it difficult to make merry.

Once inside, the two crews virtually took over O'Lordan's. Tavern keeps and serving maids shuttled tankards and platters back and forth. The kitchen nearly caught fire with so many meals cooking at the same time. Ross's mug was empty, and the serving maids were quite busy, so he went to get a refill himself. He'd half-filled his mug when the kitchen door flung open and a very familiar face stuck out. "Tell them we've no more bangers and mash!"—the curly-headed man said—"I've got meat pies and haggis to spare, and that'll have to do."

Ross couldn't believe his eyes. "MacCready?" he said.

"Aye," said the man. His moustache and beard were wavy and curled. Even his eyebrows were dark and unruly. He looked up and saw Ross. "Declan? Declan Ross, is that you?"

The two old friends clasped arms. "Musketoon MacCready," said Ross. "Last I heard you'd gone gold hunting in South America. What are you doing here?"

"Cookin', don't ye see?" MacCready answered. "And lovin' it."

"Tell me you didn't get rid of your guns," said Ross.

MacCready frowned. "Are ye daft? Of course, I haven't gotten rid of me babies."

But then MacCready grew serious. He spoke as if he were talking to himself. "I suppose he knew you were comin'."

"What?"

"The Brit," said MacCready. "Commodore somethin'."

Ross put down his tankard with a thud. "Blake was it?" he asked excitedly.

"Yeah, that's right. He left ye somethin' too." MacCready disappeared into the kitchen. Ross heard pots and pans clanking around, a tremendous crash, and a series of grunts. MacCready returned with a letter folded and stuck closed by a wax seal.

Ross glanced over his shoulder at his men whose revelry seemed to know no bounds. Then he broke the seal, opened the letter, and began to read.

A moment later, Ross looked up and asked, "How long ago was this?"

"A fortnight," MacCready answered. "Maybe more."

"He's not been back since?"

"Nay, Declan," MacCready replied. "What's the matter? Ye look a might worried."

Ross glanced at Blake's letter and asked, "MacCready, can you still fight?"

"Aye," he replied, puffing up his chest. "Ye want me to show ye?"

"Do you have a ship?"

"An old galleon," MacCready said. "Not much to speak of, but she'll sail. Declan, what's goin' on?"

Ross swallowed. He turned, caught Jack's eye, and motioned for him to join them. "It's Thorne." Ross saw MacCready's surprise. "No, he isn't dead. And he's planning something huge for England. I don't know what, but knowing that Blake's gone after him and hasn't returned . . . makes me nervous."

"Thorne, eh?" MacCready looked like he'd just eaten some bad haggis. "I owe him somethin', I do. Declan, say the word, and I'll get me boat."

"I'm saying the word, Mac," said Ross.

"Thorne's holed up on Gotland Island," said Jack.

"Sweden?" MacCready raised his eyebrows. "That's new."

"Yes, and I don't like it," said Ross. "Cutlass Jack, you, and I will sail after Bartholomew Thorne. But, Mac, Thorne has slipped out of my nets far too often. Not this time . . . this time his escape will mean a lot of blood. I can feel it."

MacCready nodded grimly. He thought for a moment and then said, "Declan, why don't ye visit the clans? There's good men— fightin' men—and sailors besides. I daresay there'd be more than a few willin' to cross blades with the likes a' Thorne."

"Ah, Mac, bless your curly head!" Ross grabbed MacCready's head and kissed him on the crown. "That's brilliant, but we need to go fast. Round up as many able men as will come and any ships you can find. Schooners, sloops—I don't care as long as they're seaworthy."

"When do we sail?"

"By sundown," said Ross. He breathed out a heavy sigh. "Can we do this, Mac?"

"Aye," he said. "That we can."

MacCready threw his apron in the kitchen, muttered a few words of apology, and ran out the door. Then Ross turned to his crew. The moment the men saw Ross's face, the merriment ended. "Where we b' going now?" Stede asked.

"Gotland Island," Ross replied. He told them of Commodore Blake's message and of his plan. There wasn't a word of complaint. Each man took a last bite or a last sip. Mr. Hack put a few fried potatoes, three pieces of bacon, and a couple of biscuits in a handkerchief for later. The procession back down that cobblestone hill was far less cheery than the one up it earlier that day. Hearing from Bellamy that Thorne was still alive had been one thing. That devilish man's claims could be discounted . . . even disbelieved. But Commodore Blake was a man of his word. If he said Thorne lived, then it was so. And with Bartholomew Thorne still alive, the blood tide would soon begin to rise.

26
SHADOWS

Vexing day! Bartholomew Thorne could scarce believe his misfortune. In just a few short hours, the Raukar fleet was due to sail for England. He'd decided to take the *Raven's Revenge* out to sea . . . just a short venture to put the ship through its paces one last time and to consider the unanswered questions that still plagued his mind.

And not twenty miles out to sea . . . the wind died. It had not diminished to a light breeze. No, that would have been manageable if not disappointing. But the air had gone completely still. This was not uncommon in the doldrums closer to the equator, but this far north, and at this time of the year, it was virtually unheard of. Worsening an already horrible situation, a strange chill had fallen over the area. A dense vapor cloud rose up from the water and crippled the visibility. Through the haze, the sun hung overhead, just an angry red ball seemingly stripped of its warmth.

A young ship's mate from the *Talon* hesitantly crossed the deck.

He was scarred from one corner of his mouth to his ear and spoke with a noticeable slur. "Sir?"

"What is it, Mister Jay?" Thorne rasped.

Jay knew the others were watching from several half-open hatches along the deck, but he'd come this far. He'd have to go through with it or face never-ending jeers. *Not that a sorry one of them have the courage to ask*, he thought. Then he said, "Well, sir, the wind hasn't stirred a whisper. And me and some of the others were thinkin' we might take the lull and sample some of that mead the Gotlanders gave us."

"Thought you might sample the mead?" Thorne echoed, his face impossible to read. To Jay's surprise, he said, "Go ahead, Mister Jay. Since we are evidently not going anywhere soon, you and the lads take that drink."

Astounded by the captain's generosity, Jay began to walk back to the hatch. Thorne wheeled around so fast, Jay didn't see it coming. An iron grip clutched Mr. Jay's throat, and he felt his body lifted clear off the deck. Thorne slammed Jay hard against the port rail and pushed his head over and down as if he might let him fall over the side. "You take that drink, Mister Jay, and it'll be the last thing to wet your tongue in this life . . . except for blood, that is. You and the rest of the crew will stay at your stations—and stay alert—until we make port back in Sigvard Bay. Do you understand me, Mister Jay?"

Jay couldn't speak. Hollow gagging noises escaped from his half-strangled throat. Thorne released him at last, and Mr. Jay slumped to the deck. Guthrum and Brandir cast disdainful looks and laughed. Thorne watched as the impudent deck hand crawled slowly away and slunk into a hatch.

"Captain Thorne!" a voice called from high on the mast.

"What is it, Mister Wren?"

"Something there, sir," Wren, the lookout, called back. "A shadow on the water . . . aft. I . . . I think it's a ship."

"Ready the port cannons!" Thorne rasped. "Brandir, ready the dragon necks." He gave the wheel to Mr. Teach. "Bring the ship about."

"But, sir, there's no wind," Teach replied.

Thorne ignored his quartermaster and clambered up onto the poop deck to stare out over the still waters. "Mister Tarber, are you sure? I don't see anything."

"Yes, sir!" he called back. "It was there in the mist. Then it—wait! There she is. But I don't think we need worry 'bout the cannons. It's just a skiff."

The mist parted and a dark, single-sailed craft emerged. It was twenty-feet long with a small block cabin and a narrow sail rigged like the blade of a knife on a thin mast. Though Thorne saw that the vessel approaching posed no immediate threat, he felt a strange gravity in the pit of his stomach. He did not belay the order to ready the cannons.

Thorne squinted. Was there someone aboard? Shadows moved out of the cabin onto its small deck. The thinning mist confirmed two hooded figures standing by the mast as the craft came closer. No one seemed to be rowing the small ship. Thorne looked up into the sails of the *Raven's Revenge*. They remained lifeless and still. *How then, does he sail?*

"Hold!" yelled a black-bearded deck hand named Davies. He and several of the Raukar leaned over the starboard rail and aimed muskets toward the water. "State your business or be dead where you stand."

A voice came up from the water. "It is for business that I have come," it said. Muskets wavered, and men stepped backward from the rail a pace as if they'd suddenly lost their balance. Thorne heard the voice even from where he stood, and it seemed to him that the chill in the air sharpened.

But Davies stood fast. He pulled back the hammer on his musket. "Advance no further!"

"Won't you cast aside your weapon and seek a rope ladder?" came the voice again. "The chill is no good for an old man. My associate and I have important matters to discuss with Captain Thorne."

"Sir?" Davies said. He stepped aside as Thorne came to the rail.

Bartholomew Thorne looked down. A hood hid the man's face in the small craft below. "I am Bartholomew Thorne. What business have you with me?"

"Much." The man said lowering his hood to reveal a sallow scalp with shrouds of wispy white hair. But in spite of the obvious signs of age, the man bore a powerful, penetrating visage. His brow was low and prominent. It overshadowed dark, depthless eyes that reminded Thorne of staring down well shafts. His nose was misshapen and pointed on the end. He grinned up at Thorne and revealed a mouth more full of cankers than teeth.

"What's the matter with you?" Thorne asked. "If you have the plague, you'd best—"

"Unwholesome eating habits . . . nothing more," he replied, and he began to chew on a brown root.

Thorne began to recognize the voice, and it must have shown on his face.

"Do you know me at last? . . . Then, Captain Thorne, have your man lower the ladder."

Thorne nodded to Davies, who hurled a rope ladder over the rail. And with surprising agility, the old man climbed aboard. The second man climbed up as well but did not remove his hood.

The Merchant stood before Thorne and inclined his head slightly. "I told you we'd meet again soon," he said.

"How did you find me?" Thorne asked.

"Eyes in many places," he replied.

"But . . . your ship?"

"Oh no . . . that skiff?" He laughed quietly. "We sailed to meet you in my fastest barque, the *Perdition's Gate*. But in this dense fog, I did not want to risk sending us both to the depths. My ship and crew wait for me to the west."

Thorne regarded him strangely. He looked over the Merchant's shoulder out into the murky white. No sign nor shadow of another ship. And how did it sail? The wind couldn't be any stronger a few hundred yards away—no sooner had the thought entered his mind than a stiff wind kicked up.

"What marvelous fortune," said the Merchant. "Now, Captain Thorne, we shall go below and discuss our . . . business."

The ship was unlike any Hopper had ever experienced. Still it had its storage space, its stacks of crates, and its nooks. Earlier that morning he'd gotten the gumption to traverse the mooring lines . . . and just in time as the *Raven's Revenge* left port not fifteen minutes later. He'd stayed hidden in the darkness behind a stack of crates containing . . . cabbage, by the smell of them. Ignoring the stench, Hopper chewed on a piece of jerk beef he'd brought with him and thought about his plan. He knew Commodore Blake and Lady Dolphin had been brought aboard as prisoners, not guests. It was likely they'd be kept in the cellblock. *Right*, Hopper told himself. *And just where is that?*

Probably the lowest deck, Hopper figured. *Down with the rats and bilge water.*

Hopper decided that was where he would look. But, of course, he'd have to navigate three decks down from where he was—all without being seen. Fortunately, there was a hatch only a few feet away. Hopper found it clear, but rather than climbing down the ladder, he swung from the nearest rafter into a corner behind a barrel. What was that sound of squeaks and groans? Then, when he peeked around the barrel, he understood. He'd descended to a gun deck, but one of the ones where crewmen slept when they were off. Hopper figured there had to be more than a hundred hammocks slung from the ceiling. They swayed back and forth—a few of them occupied—and made the terrible ruckus he'd heard.

Looking for the hatch, Hopper darted in and out of portside cannon bays. Finally, with about four more bays to go, he spotted a hatch . . . but it was on the starboard side of the deck. He couldn't walk between the dozens of crewmen sleeping the way the hammocks were swinging. To get across, he'd have to crawl beneath them and hope there was enough room.

Hopper went on all fours, crawling like a bug beneath the ever-swaying hammocks. A couple of the hammocks were slung so low that Hopper had to lie flat on his stomach to get across. He made it under that one and was almost to the hatch when he heard a burst of short snorts above, followed by mumbles, followed by snorting laughter. Hopper looked up and saw an upside-down bearded face hanging over the edge of a hammock. The eyes blinked open suddenly and fixed on Hopper. The man yelled. Hopper shrieked, scurried to the hatch, and disappeared.

The sun cast long shadows from the masts of twenty-one ships leaving Edinburgh, Scotland. Declan Ross's man-of-war, Cutlass

Then Thorne's eyes fixed on some part of the text and narrowed. He stopped breathing and clutched the edges of the parchment. He looked up at the Merchant and asked, "Is this a joke?"

The Merchant waved his hand dismissively. "I assure you I am serious."

"Why me?"

"Because I know you can do what few men can." The Merchant's dark expression grew eager. "These are the terms, Bartholomew Thorne. All that is left is to sign." The Merchant reached into his wide sleeve and pulled out his long dagger. He dragged it slowly across his palm and let the blood dribble onto Thorne's desk. Then he handed the dagger to Thorne.

Thorne cut across his palm, next to five previous scars. He opened his desk drawer and removed two quill pens. He gave one to the Merchant. Each man dipped his pen into the pool of his own blood. Then each man signed the parchment.

"Done and done," said the Merchant as he whisked the contract from the table. He examined the signatures for a moment. "Now that we've completed our agreement, I will show you what I've brought to sweeten the deal."

The Merchant stood, stepped near to the hooded man, and slowly revealed his identity. Thorne stood, nearly knocking over his chair. The young man standing next to the Merchant was Griffin Thorne, Bartholomew Thorne's son. The Merchant removed Cat's hood and said, "Go on, boy . . . say hello to your father."

Cat said nothing. A hundred images flooded his mind: whips, chains, blood, Dominica, the Isle of Swords. Cat wanted to run from the room, but he stood his ground.

"He was working with the Brethren," said the Merchant, "trying to find me. I thought you might like a chance to reform him."

Jack's xebec, and Musketoon MacCready's old g
way, followed by a hodgepodge of sloops, schoone
ketch or two. More than a dozen of Scotland's cla
sented in this new fleet. Declan looked back on his
pride. "They've no special love for England," he
"But still they left their fishing nets, their plowsha
lies, and their land."

"There comes a time to fight, mon," Stede rep
thunder gun in the holster at his side.

"You've come to specify your terms," said Thorne s
and staring across the vast tabletop to the Mercha
hooded man behind him. The ship's hull muted th
of the sea birds that had appeared when the haze
Raven's Revenge rolled ponderously on increasing

"You have your fleet," said the Merchant at la
days away from the victory you've longed for. Now
Merchant reached beneath his black cloak and remo
The parchment was watermarked, frayed at the e
with a blob of blood-red wax. He handed the scro
said, "Read it, but not aloud."

Thorne raised an eyebrow, received the scroll,
ously at the man who stood behind the Merchan
the seal and unraveled the parchment. As Thorne
room grew increasingly quiet. Nearly halfway t
Thorne's breathing became audible, raspy, and thi
sum," Thorne muttered. He continued reading
didn't know they were there . . . hmmm . . . I
charge." He laughed quietly at that.

Thorne spat. "I should have just drowned him the day he was born. He's of no use to me."

"Come now," said the Merchant, playing his hand carefully. "Young Griffin is a clever lad . . . and a gifted swordsman. Surely, with the proper motivation, he could be led to see things your way."

"He's worthless," said Thorne, his voice deep and raspy. He was getting upset, just as the Merchant had hoped. And from the look on Cat's face, his father's words were having just the impact the Merchant was looking to find.

Cat held no love for this man, but somehow, hearing these words now cut into him like long jagged blades. The anger he had struggled with so often kindled into a flash fire. Cat saw the Merchant's dagger, its tip already bloody, lying within reach on the desk. "I think," said the Merchant, picking up the dagger, "this should be put away for now."

Thorne stood up. "I want him dead before we leave for England."

"It shall be done as you command," said the Merchant, smiling, for his gambit had paid off. He put the gag back in Cat's mouth and tightened it. "You will never see Griffin Thorne again."

***

Dolphin sat in the darkest corner of her cell and wept. Her husband was two cells away and looked on helplessly. "The way he questioned me," she cried. "That painting . . . NO! It cannot be true." She looked through the bars and shadows to her husband. Her eyes were huge and pleading. "Tell me, Brand, tell me it cannot be true."

His silence was thunderous. "You knew then?" she said, her words heavy with accusation.

"I did not know until we stood in Thorne's presence," he said. "But I began to suspect from your father's journals."

"Why didn't I see it?"

"You couldn't have," he replied gently. "I once spoke to Declan Ross about Thorne. I wanted to know what drove the man . . . to better understand him so that I could capture him. Ross told me how Thorne's wife had been killed in a fire. But Ross never knew there was a child. I don't think even Thorne knew that the child had survived."

"Why do you say that?"

"I saw the way he looked at you," said Blake. "There was most definitely recognition. But even with all those questions about your age . . . your parents, I daresay he still doesn't know for sure."

"It were a shadow wid eyes!" Skinner cried. A small group of deck hands—Thorne's and Raukar—stood around him in a circle.

"A big rat, like as not," said Barnabas, who went back to swabbing the deck.

"Were not!" argued Skinner. "Lessun ye've seen rats wid arms and legs like a great big toad!"

"It was a toad now?" asked one of the Raukar.

Skinner growled. "I know what I saw."

"Don't be so stupid," said Hangman Pete, the ranking officer on the deck. "You just hadn't woke up yet. But seein's you are now, why don't you help Barnabas get this deck clean."

Two decks below, Hopper continued his search. Just as he found the hatch to the lowest deck, the ship started to move again.

27
St. Alfred's Day

The morning of May 21 dawned bright and warm in London. The port was already jammed with military vessels and merchants alike. Miles of the Thames River were near clogged with boat traffic. No one wanted to miss the celebration of St. Alfred's Day. As unpopular as King George was for his governing of England, he had managed to earn a reputation for throwing unforgettable parties. In fact, preparations for this year's event had begun the day after last year's party.

The bulk of the British navy had already moored. Brigantines like the *Liverpool*, the *Bristol*, and the *Valiant*, as well as first-rate ships of the line like the *Gallant*, the *Union Jack*, and the *Robert Elliott* were the latest naval vessels to anchor. Under the king's orders, merchant ships positively heaped with casks and barrels delivered their payloads to each of the navy ships. Commodores, captains, mates, and crews—especially those who had been out to sea for extended periods of time—were thrilled by the prospects of making merry and of spending time at home.

By late in the afternoon, a special barge was towed out into the center of the harbor. After dark, fireworks purchased from the Far East and from around the globe would be launched from this vast platform. All of London waited to celebrate one of England's most noble and effective warriors. But none of the revelers knew that the city would have dire need of men like St. Alfred that night.

Anne was at the helm as the *Constantine* drifted into Sigvard Bay. They'd searched most of Gotland's ports and small harbors for the *Perdition's Gate*, but with no success. When Anne saw what was waiting for them in Sigvard Bay, she said, "Uh-oh."

"Turn the ship around!" urged Father Brun. "Turn around!"

"It's too late," said Anne. "They've seen us."

And she was right. Three tall ships broke off from the small fleet gathered in the bay and approached the *Constantine*. But they did not fire.

"Are any of those the Merchant's barque?" asked Father Brun.

Anne squinted. "No," she replied, her voice detached and dreamy. "But I think I know one of those ships!" Then she leaped in the air. "It's my da's ship! And there he is!"

Moments later Declan Ross came aboard the *Constantine*, and Anne melted into his arms. "Oh, Da!" she cried, and tears drenched his shoulder. "Cat . . . Cat's gone. The Merchant drowned him— Da, Cat died to save my life."

Ross felt his own eyes burn, and he hugged his daughter. "Good lad," he whispered. In many ways, Declan Ross felt he'd just lost a son.

After exchanging stories of grief and victory, as well as news of how they each came to be there, it became clear that decisions had to be made.

"The Merchant and Bartholomew Thorne together?" muttered Father Brun. "I cannot imagine worse news."

"It gets much worse," said Ross. "We captured a young woman fishing on the shore here at Sigvard Bay."

"You captured a woman for fishing?" asked Anne.

"No," said Stede. "We didn't mind that her b' fishing. It was when she up and tried to put a spear in us that we nabbed her."

"She was very resistant at first," said Hack. "Wouldn't tell us anything."

"That is, until we invited Red Eye to assist us," said Ross. "She took one look at him and told us everything we needed to know."

"Red Eye," Anne said, feigning accusation, "what did you do?"

"Not to worry, Anne, I just cleaned my teeth," Red Eye said, shrugging, ". . . with my dagger."

"We learned that these Norsemen, the Raukar she called them, have built a fleet of some sixty ships," Ross said. They have now sailed with Thorne and the Merchant to Britain. And, Anne, she was not some 'poor' woman. When we finished questioning her, she spat on my feet, looked scornfully at our fleet, and told us we were all going to burn. I'm not sure what she meant, but I know England needs us."

"His terms were quite extraordinary," said Thorne. He stood by his quartermaster as the *Raven's Revenge* drifted on steady winds down the English Channel.

"I'll bet he asked for thirty percent of the new trade profits, didn't he?" asked Mr. Teach.

"Forty," said Thorne.

"Forty?! What's a blighter like him need with so much?"

"There was more," said Thorne. "After the British are defeated, he wants us to sail to Saba. Apparently the Brethren have their stronghold there."

"He wants us to finish off the monks too, eh?" Teach laughed. "Well, that ought not to be too hard."

"No, not with the dragon necks," said Thorne. "And now that we know where the Brethren are, I'm only too happy to carry out the Merchant's wishes. But his third term is something of a mystery. He wants me to kill him."

"What?!"

"The Merchant clearly stipulated that he wants me to kill him, as soon as he's had time to train an apprentice to his vocation."

"Are you goin' to do it?" Teach asked.

Thorne crossed the quarterdeck in three long strides. As he descended to the main deck, he said, "The contract is agreed upon in blood. I have no choice."

"Where are you going, sir?" asked Teach. "We'll hit the mouth of the Thames in an hour."

"I am going down below," Thorne replied. "There is someone I want to talk to in the cellblock."

His long fingernails scraped across the cell bars. "Awaken, young Griffin," said the Merchant. "Your destiny calls for you."

Cat lay on a cot at the far end of the cell. "Leave me be!" he yelled.

"No . . . ," said the Merchant. "If I did what you ask, you'd be dead already. Your father is quite set on your fate, I'm afraid. But I believe that Bartholomew, in his willfulness, lacks vision. He looks at you and sees nothing worth saving. I look at you and see history in the making. Think on that, Cat . . . history!"

"History in blood," Cat snapped back.

"Ever it has been," replied the Merchant. "Every king, every queen—even Scotland's beloved Robert the Bruce—had to splash a little blood to remake the world. The British, the French, the Spanish together have waged war upon war, spilling enough blood to fill the river upon which we sail."

"That's different," said Cat, his anger building. He got up and went near to the bars. "That's war."

"Is it?" The Merchant laughed. "And why do these nations fight? Over thrones, over tariffs, over plots of land? They merely want to stake a claim in this world. And that, lad . . . is precisely what we are doing. Tonight, Cat, in just a few hours, the world will change again. There'll be a new ship to sail, and I'm offering you the wheel."

Cat's arms shot through the bars, and before he knew it, Cat had one hand grasping the Merchant's cloak, the other hand clutching the Merchant's throat. Cat felt a sharp prick at his stomach and realized the Merchant's dagger was poised to stab him in the gut. Cat slowly released his grip. "You see," said the Merchant, "you were born a man of passion, born a man of action. Violence is a means to an end, that's all. And you are a master of violence."

The Merchant went to leave the cell deck, but hesitated a moment at the first step. "We will talk again soon . . . after London burns. But the choice is simple: rule the world as you see fit . . . or die knowing what might have been. Either way . . . much blood will be shed."

The fireworks display had humble beginnings. Three shots left the barge in the middle of the harbor—*Whump, whump, whump!*—and raced into the night sky. Hundreds of feet above the Thames and the hundred-plus ships anchored there, the shells burst into sparkling tendrils of blue, red, and white. A collective roar of approval came from the people gathered on the docks, on shore, and on the ships.

Having removed their hats and unbuttoned their vests, commodores and captains sat down on the decks to watch the show with the men they commanded. Each had a mug or tankard in hand and a barrel not too far away, for this night was made for celebration, not circumstance. Even King George watched the display. He reclined in a chair atop the gatehouse of St. James Palace while a platoon of servants brought him assorted beverages and delicacies. King George wanted to be sure the fireworks display had been worth the gold he'd spent.

And it truly was. Soon the sky over the Port of London was ablaze with sparkling majesty. Rockets streaked into the night, exploded with deafening thunder, and rained blinking flashes of color. Huge blossoms of purple and gold bloomed overhead, and whistling white comets raced this way and that.

Closest to the fireworks barge, Commodore James Hawthorne stood on the deck of the one hundred-gun ship *Gallant* and raised his tankard in salute of an especially fine series of rockets. Sunbursts of orange, red, and yellow fanned out in all directions, some seeming to come right toward his ship.

Hawthorne lowered his tankard and started to yell, but it was too late. The deck of the *Gallant* flashed red as something burst overhead. Fire rained down from above, igniting the masts and bundled sails. Hawthorne and a dozen of his men were killed instantly from the incinerating heat. Others were bathed in liquid fire and dove overboard only to die horribly as the water could not immediately quench the flames.

Something had gone dreadfully wrong with the fireworks display, most thought, as fiery shells exploded again and again right above the ships. Already ten vessels were ablaze, their crews leaping overboard or burned alive. Shrieks of terror went up from ship and shore, and all looked to the fireworks barge and wondered when the barrage might end. Yet the rockets from the barge continued to go up, continued to burst like flashes of lightning high in the sky. And in those flickers of light, the people of London finally saw . . . finally understood. For in those intermittent white flashes, sails appeared in the distance. Hundreds of sails. The mouth of the harbor teemed with rows of attacking ships—ominous, shadowy vessels erupting with cannon fire.

Fiery projectiles ignited the ships trapped in the river creating a floating inferno. And soon, the enemy's projectiles began to burst above the shore, raining fire on multitudes of screaming, fleeing people. As the invading ships grew nearer, they fired their cannon shots deeper into the city. Wooden buildings were engulfed in seconds. Fire trickled down stone turrets and columns and danced on brick battlements. Mantled by the blackest clouds of smoke and mirrored in the now-turbulent waters of the Thames, brilliant white flames flared and turned angry red as they reached a hundred feet into the air.

Not since the great fire of 1666 had the city endured such a conflagration. But the Great Fire of London that claimed 80 percent of the city in 1666 was not nearly as deadly as this one. Then people had warning and fled into the highlands or in boats into the Thames. This attack, there was no warning, and the river offered no escape.

The British ships that were not abandoned opened fire, as did the cannon batteries on shore. But their shots were rushed and poorly aimed. Few found their mark.

"Hit them again!" Thorne ordered, his voice thick and raspy. "Brandir, signal the fleet."

"But, sir," said Brandir, "we must save some for the monks."

"Monks?" Guthrum harrumphed. "Christians? They will fall easier than Västervik!"

"Still," said Thorne, thoughtfully rubbing the scar on his hand. "I will not underestimate them . . . especially since I do not know their defenses. Brandir, signal one more volley with the dragon necks. But keep our other cannons firing. Blast their vaunted navy to splinters!"

Brandir left his post at the starboard rail and raced to the poop deck. There, he unhooded three lanterns: a yellow, a white, and a red. First, he held up the white and waited for the next ship in line to signal likewise. Then he held up the red lantern once, followed by three quick bobs with the yellow lantern. The signal went from ship to ship around the fleet, and Thorne's commands were followed.

"Mister Teach, go down below decks!" Thorne commanded. "I want our guests to see their city burn."

"Aye, sir!"

"Guthrum, ready the Berserkers," Thorne commanded. "I want you to lead them into the city. Take the palace, and bring me the king's head."

The massive Raukar warrior's eyes gleamed. He drew his cold blade and exclaimed, "HRAH!"

Finally, Hopper had a chance. All but two of the guards had left the cell deck to watch the action unfolding topside. Hopper had hidden himself between stacks of crates close to the ladder up to the next deck. He'd been waiting for one of the remaining two guards to move close enough. And at last, one did. Hopper had never done anything like this before. Even during his occupation of the English fort at New Providence, Hopper had never harmed anyone to get what he needed. But this was different. Hopper couldn't fight them, and he needed their keys. So Hopper clutched the small plank he'd found in a scrap pile on the third deck. He aimed for the back of the soldier's head and prayed he had enough strength to knock the man out.

WHACK! Hopper hit the guard as hard as he'd ever hit anything in his life. The man groaned and fell in a heap by the crates. The second he struck, Hopper ducked back in the shadows. The other guard came running and bent over his fallen comrade. Swinging the board like he used to swing an axe to split wood, Hopper unleashed another powerful blow—this time on the crown of the surprised guard's head. The man fell without a sound—right on top of the other guard.

Hopper was out of his crevice like a shot. He didn't know if more guards were just outside of the room and on their way. Hopper grabbed the guard's keys and ran to the cell where Lady Dolphin stood at the bars. "Hopper!" she exclaimed.

From two cells down, Commodore Blake said, "Of all the unlooked-for . . . Hopper, we thought you'd been killed."

"Nay, Guv'nor," said Hopper. "I'm a slippery one."

"You are at that," said Dolphin, embracing him as soon as her cell was open. They worked the keys in Blake's cell door, and soon he was free as well.

"C'mon, Guv'nor, my lady," urged Hopper. "There's a balcony window in the captain's quarters, and he ain't there."

"Hopper," Blake said with admiration. "You've been in Thorne's quarters?"

"Yeah," he replied, enjoying their respect. "I've been all over the ship looking for you two. Now, c'mon. They'll be coming for us, and that no mistake."

"A moment." Blake took the swords from the two fallen guards and handed one to Dolphin. "I have a feeling we might be needing these."

The first thing Edward Teach saw when he entered the cell deck was a blur of motion at the other end of the deck. Then he saw the two guards out cold. Last, he saw the empty cells. Teach had no idea how the two captives had managed their escape, but he had the certain feeling that it would be his own head rolling if he didn't get them back.

Teach thought frantically. *Where would they go? To the cutters? No, not with fifty crewmen on deck. That would be suicide.* He thought they might try to duck out of a cannon bay, but again . . . so many guards. Teach's mouth dropped open. There was one place they could escape from. *Yes,* Teach thought. *That has to be where they've gone.*

Ascending the decks without being seen had not been easy. Twice, Blake and Dolphin had to use their swords along the way, but at last they made it to Thorne's quarters. The three fugitives charged into the room and closed the door behind them.

Hopper and Blake ran past a huge wardrobe, around Thorne's desk, and cranked open the gallery window. Dolphin stopped in the middle of the room and stared at the portrait of Heather Thorne. "I really do look just like her," she said.

"This is no time for a family reunion," Blake said, stepping up to the window sill. "Dolphin, get—"

The gunshot was so sudden and loud that Hopper screamed. None of them had seen Edward Teach step out of the wardrobe. The shot hit the commodore and, in spite of Hopper's efforts to grab him, Blake fell from the window, smacking the water hard, several stories below.

Sword raised, Dolphin started toward Teach—but he had a second pistol, and he pointed it at her head. "Drop your weapon!" he commanded. Dolphin pulled up short. Her eyes darted frantically. She couldn't speak. Trembling, she still hesitated to drop her sword.

Teach cocked the hammer back on the pistol. "Drop your weapon now!"

Hopper looked out of the gallery window, down into the water. He saw Blake's body floating there, a red stain spreading into the water near his shoulder. Hopper looked back at Dolphin, still holding the sword. He didn't know what to do. Either way, he'd most likely fail.

Then Teach noticed Hopper at the window. "Don't you move!" Teach yelled. But Hopper knew he would not take the gun off Dolphin. Hopper's eyes met Lady Dolphin's for a heartbeat, and then he jumped.

Just hours before dawn, Guthrum returned from the raiding party. He and the Berserkers came aboard the *Raven's Revenge* and found Thorne in a perilous mood. "What is your report?" Thorne rasped.

Guthrum explained, "The Port of London belongs to us. Much

of the city fled into Stratford and Hampstead. We chose not to follow. The British flag has been torn down from the palace, but we did not find King George."

"Arrgh-ah!" Thorne marched up to Guthrum and stared him in the eye. "I told you to bring me his head!"

But Guthrum did not shy away from Thorne. "I suspect King George has long planned a secret escape should he need a hasty exit from Britain. He is most likely on his way to Germany now. Do you now want us to invade Hanover?"

Thorne's face reddened, and, for a moment, he considered killing Guthrum where he stood. But, no, the rest of the Raukar might quail at that. "Very well," said Thorne, his voice a biting whisper. "Now get back on board the cutter. You will be responsible for maintaining control of the Port of London. I will take the rest of our forces to Saba and deal with the monks. You'll have twenty ships. You can hold on to the port until I return, can't you?"

Guthrum's eyes blazed. "Yes, Captain Thorne, I can."

28
LIBERATION DAY

London burned. From the docks to the depths of the city, every building had been scorched or utterly incinerated. Thick black smoke bubbled up from the wreckage and was sheered toward the west by the strong winds that had kicked up. The harbor was a smoking graveyard of ships. Hulls and burned-out skeletons of all manner of sailing vessels protruded from the murky, discolored water. They'd seen the smoke from ten miles up the Thames River, and that had led them to fear the worst for London. But nothing could have prepared Declan Ross, his crew, and his fleet for the smoldering carnage they would behold when they arrived in the port. As they surveyed the damage, they noticed several ships still afloat and seemingly unscathed from the battle. These were strange ships, long and thin, with rows of round shields hanging on their rails.

Ross knew they weren't British. He didn't say a word. He simply looked grimly at Stede and nodded. Then Ross went to the rail of the quarterdeck and saw Hack and Slash by the mainmast. Ross pointed to the sky. Hack and Slash went right to work pulling away at a long rope wound in a halyard. The black flag of the Sea Wolf rose high in the sky.

St. Pierre saw the flag go up, drew a long saber, and yelled, "All cannons, FIRE!!" Cutlass Jack's xebec and Musketoon MacCready's galleon opened fire as well. Even the small Scottish sloops and schooners—none of which had more than ten cannons—unleashed their fury as well. The Wolf fleet's first volley sent more than two hundred cannonballs careening toward the Raukar ships before even one of the Norse ships fired back.

One Raukar warship was struck three times in the same center section of the hull. It split in half and began to sink. Another ship caught an eighteen-pounder straight into its fore keel. The cannonball blasted in directly under the bowsprit and struck the mast below decks, cracking its base. The mast fell and tore up half the deck in the process. But the most devastating damage came from the cannonballs that fell on the main decks where the dragon necks and ammunition were kept. And that was the greatest flaw in the Raukar's eldregn weapon. In battle, the weapon had to be kept on the upper deck. When the Wolf fleet's cannonballs struck a stockpile of eldregn canisters, it resulted in absolute ruin.

One Raukar ship disappeared in a huge reddish fireball. The very air where the ship had been seemed to burn, and the water in a large circle was layered with liquid fire. Ross watched with fascination as the wind carried the fireball into the mast of another Raukar ship. The sails kindled immediately, and before the hapless sailors could leap from their decks, tendrils of fire found their own stockpiles of eldregn, and that ship exploded as well.

The hunters had suddenly become the hunted. But Guthrum was a skilled seaman, and he led a counterattack. He'd seen the wind shift.

And he'd seen what it had done with the eldregn. So, as his ship sailed behind the burning wreckage, he ordered his men to take the eldregn canisters to the lowest deck. Then he fired a salvo through the smoke at the Wolf fleet. Guthrum sank two of the Scottish sloops before Kalik spotted him from the crow's-nest on the *Bruce*.

"He be behind the frigit sheep!" Kalik screamed down excitedly.

"What?" yelled Red Eye.

Hack squinted. "I think he said there's a frigid sheep."

"Nonsense," countered Slash. "He's simply complaining that his behind is cold from sitting up in the crow's-nest."

"I said he be hiding behind the frigate ship!" Kalik glared down at Red Eye and the others. He tried once more to explain. "The burning ship over there. That's where he be!?"

Red Eye at last understood. He ran across the deck, leaped down the hatch, and ran to a cannon. "Loaded?" he asked a team of gunnery men.

They nodded. Red Eye aimed the cannon himself. Then he lit the fuse and watched. His shot sailed straight into the billowing smoke. He had no idea if he'd struck home, but the shot had gone exactly where he'd meant it to go. "Keep firing in just that spot!" he told the crew. And then he went from cannon bay to cannon bay, aiming for the same spot.

Hopper pulled with all his might but couldn't drag Commodore Blake any farther behind the bulkhead on shore. They were both spent from the arduous, maddeningly slow swim. If the enemy found them, Hopper knew they'd have no strength to resist or flee. Sudden cannon blasts sounded out on the water. The last volley had fired over an hour before, so Hopper looked up over the edge of the bulkhead. "Look, Commodore," said Hopper. "Someone's firing on the enemy!"

Blake sat up weakly. "It's Ross . . . thank God." Then he lay back down behind the bulkhead wall. Hopper clapped as the Raukar took a beating from the Wolf fleet.

A cannonball crushed the helm, leaving Guthrum holding the detached ship's wheel in his hands. And suddenly, it seemed to rain cannonballs. One struck the mainmast, which toppled off into the river. Another obliterated the forecastle and bowsprit. Then, just as one of the Raukar deck hands was about to ask his commander for orders, Guthrum was blown away by a direct hit. The only evidence he'd been there at all was the ship's wheel spinning on the deck.

The Raukar's London fleet was decimated by the fierce onslaught, but it was not their custom to surrender. For the Raukar, dying in battle was the quickest and surest way to gain Valhalla. But they were now outgunned—and in a poor defensive position. Some of the Raukar captains began throwing their eldregn canisters overboard to eliminate the explosive threat. One by one, the Raukar ships exploded or sank. The last vessel to remain was the commandeered *Oxford*, and the Wolf fleet had it surrounded.

Ross turned to Red Eye. "We'll keep them busy with cannon fire," he said. "I want you to take a cutter. Bring Jules, Saint Pierre, and . . ." Ross scanned the deck. "Take Hack and Slash too. Take the *Oxford* . . . intact if you can. And see if they've taken Blake as prisoner."

After the cutter launched, Stede took Ross's arm and said, "This can't b' the whole fleet, mon."

"I was thinking the same thing," said Ross. "And they don't fight like Thorne's in command here. Only twenty ships . . . and no Thorne. Where are they?"

On board the *Perdition's Gate*, already sailing with all speed across the Atlantic, Cat had fallen from his cot to the cell floor. The ship rolled on heavy swells, and the wind had made the passage rougher than usual. But Cat had not woken up. He merely stirred in his sleep as he dreamed. He was back in Dominica, and Thorne was leading him down that familiar, dreadful set of stairs below ground. Cat watched again as his father unscrewed the spiked head of his bleeding stick, transforming it into a flail weapon even more fierce and destructive than a cat-o'-nine-tails. Cat watched with revulsion as Thorne approached the prisoners chained to the ceiling and floor. This time Cat heard the blows each time his father swung. He heard the screams, the moaning agonies, and then the silence.

Then Thorne handed the weapon to Cat and gestured toward the next prisoner. This captive was still very alert, and he looked up at Cat and formed the word *no* with his mouth. Cat looked at the head of the flail weapon, saw the blood glistening. Then he looked at his own hands and saw the smeared blood from the handle. He heard his father's thick, scraping voice: *"Get on with it! Hit him! DO IT!!"*

Cat felt himself lift his arm. He could feel the weight of the weapon's head dangling behind his shoulder. And then he swung the bleeding stick. He swung it with all his might and struck his target with deadly accuracy. The weapon's head stuck hard into the oaken beam that ran along the ceiling. Cat turned to his father and said, *"I am not you!"*

Bartholomew Thorne's face contorted. He said, *"You are not worthy of my name.*" Then he drew back his fist and sent a crushing blow into Cat's jaw.

Cat suddenly woke. His nose had been bleeding from the fall, and his blood left a puddle on the cell floor. He stood up, wiping his nose with the back of his arm. He looked down at that puddle of blood and was reminded suddenly of the nails from the Isle of Swords, the Nails of Christ. And he remembered something Father Brun had told him. *"You know, the Holy Scriptures say, 'Old things are passed away; behold, all things are become new.'"*

What was it that the Brethren said to pray? Cat couldn't remember. *Something in Latin*, he thought. *But I don't know Latin!* They kneeled, that was it. But sometimes they stood. Other times they linked arms and looked toward the sky. Cat shook his head and decided it didn't matter. He'd just do it. And for the first time in his life, Cat tried speaking to God. Right there in his cell in the bottom of a ship full of enemies sailing on a violent sea . . . but none of that mattered anymore. And when he was finished, Cat knew just what he needed to do.

It hadn't taken long to liberate the *Oxford*. It was a small crew consisting of several Raukar warriors and only a few of Thorne's men from the crew of the *Talon*. When the others had fallen, Jules picked up a man named Tarber by the neck with one hand, held him at eye level, and said, "CHOOSE." Tarber promptly surrendered.

Back on board the *Bruce*, Ross had a few questions for Mr. Tarber. "Where is Commodore Blake? How many of your men are still on shore in London? Where has the rest of your fleet gone? Where are Captain Thorne and the Merchant?" Tarber did not answer, so Ross said, "Apparently, Mister Tarber is doing his best imitation of a clam. Red Eye?"

"Aye, sir?"

"Feel like cleaning your teeth again?"

"That I do, sir," said Red Eye as he slid a dagger from his boot. He grabbed Tarber by the shoulder and said, "Come with me."

Red Eye's skillful interrogation techniques had answered all but one of Ross's questions. There were close to three hundred warriors still on the shore. Thorne and the Merchant had taken more than half of the Raukar fleet to the Caribbean to conquer the Brethren on their island stronghold at Saba. But Tarber wasn't sure what became of Commodore Blake. The last he knew, Blake and his wife were still prisoners on the *Raven's Revenge*.

"Declan!" called Stede from the prow. "Yer not going to b' believing this, but there b' a little bald fellow in a rowboat over here. And he b' asking for ya by name." Stede looked back over the rail. "There b' another man with him . . . I think it's the commodore."

The crew raced over and worked together to carefully haul the rowboat up. Blake had been shot in the shoulder, and there was a lot of bleeding. He was not conscious, but he was breathing normally. Jules carried him below decks to the infirmary where Nubby would look after him.

Back on the deck, Hopper pleaded, "Please save him, sirs. He's a good man, he is."

"Commodore Blake is in the best hands—er, hand—possible with Nubby, our ship's doctor." Ross realized suddenly that Hopper was very young. "What is your name?" Ross asked. "And how did you come to be in the care of the commodore?"

Hopper told his tale, and during it, a hush fell over the crew. They could not believe a boy of maybe ten years had done so much.

"And, sir," said Hopper, "they still have Lady Dolphin. I had to decide. Lord, please, I don't want anything to happen to her. Please go after them, won't you?"

"We can't leave the Londoners with all these Raukar soldiers milling about," said Ross.

"Let MacCready and a few of the Scottish lads stay here," suggested Red Eye.

"Yes," said Ross. "They're more than capable." Ross thought for a minute. "We'll need to cobble together a crew for the *Oxford*. We can't leave that kind of firepower behind. Perhaps Mister Hack would care to command."

"I think he just might," said Red Eye.

"Good." Ross nodded. "Thorne and his fleet are nearly a day ahead of us. But we will pursue. Get word to Cutlass Jack and Anne. We've a long journey ahead."

29

SIEGE OF THE CITADEL

Thorne had been forced to change course due to a massive storm front that was building to his south. He'd already lost three of the lighter Raukar ships just on the fringes of it. He feared it might be a hurricane and might disrupt his attack on the Brethren. But the storm had been churning in his mind. He had gone to see Lady Dolphin almost every one of their ten-day journey across the Atlantic. He had tried every approach he could imagine. He'd brought her good food. He'd threatened her. But no matter what he tried, she still would not speak.

But the more he looked upon her, the more certain he became that she was his own daughter. Heather had been near the end of her pregnancy when the fire took her away, but Thorne had always assumed that the child had died. Dolphin looked so much like Heather it pained Thorne to look upon her. And yet he couldn't stay away from Dolphin. Making matters worse, Thorne found that he could barely stand to be in his own quarters. He felt oppressive guilt whenever he looked at the portrait of his dead wife. *She is dead*, he told himself. *No matter the voices. Heather is dead.* Still he felt as if she stared at him, accusing. All these matters had left Thorne with no sleep for days on end.

Thorne checked his instruments. They were just a few hours from Saba. Then he went back to pacing the deck of his ship.

Even with nightfall looming, Brother DiMarco could see the storm building in the east. He had rung the Citadel's heavy bell, and all the Brethren stirred like ants in the courtyards and in the fields. Terrible storms were not uncommon for the island of Saba, so the Brethren had gone to great lengths to make their fortress as sturdy as possible. But still, when a tempest arose, there was much to do to prepare.

And that is why Father Henry and Father Hoyt, who usually manned the Citadel's two battlement towers, did not at first see the approach of the dark ships.

"FIRE!!" Thorne yelled, and Brandir unleashed the first salvo of eldregn canisters. The Raukar fleet did the same. But to their dismay, the wind took the canisters and pushed them all hard to the west. Only a third of the initial volley exploded over the Citadel's walls or beyond. Still, that was destructive enough for such a small target. The front gatehouse went up in a wall of flame. The eldregn did not consume the stone, but anything not made of stone ignited and burned.

When the Brethren heard the explosions and saw the fire spring up, it did not take long for them to man their defenses. Brother DiMarco rang the church bell urgently, and Father Henry and Father Hoyt gathered their men at the Citadel's walls. In spite of the fire pouring down from the skies, the monks made their way to their posts.

Most visitors to the Citadel thought the square openings throughout the Citadel's walls, as well as those in its towers, were windows. They were not—they were cannon bays. And not just any cannons: Father Henry and Father Hoyt had nicknamed their heavy cannons "The Wrath of God" because each one fired twenty-five-pound cannonballs. They didn't have much range, but if anyone dared to get too close . . . it would be over before it started. When Father Henry and Father Hoyt gave the order, cannon muzzles appeared in those windows, and the Wrath of God was unleashed.

A twenty-five-pound cannonball slammed into a Raukar warship as it was setting up to launch a round of eldregn. The cannonball collapsed the ship's upper deck, and the eldregn canisters rolled into the gaping chasm. An explosion followed, sending a fountain of water laced with liquid fire spreading high into the air. The fiery flood came down on another ship that had been trailing near the first. It, too, went up in a fireball.

Thorne was livid. He took the wheel from his quartermaster. "Mister Teach, you're done here," he growled. "Go to the cell deck and make sure Dolphin is safe."

Edward Teach had just about had enough of being kicked around by Thorne. Still, he obediently went below.

"Brandir!" Thorne yelled. "Target the towers—those cannons have the greatest range!"

"Yes, Captain!" Brandir adjusted his dragon necks for the wind and fired.

Father Henry never saw the shot. There was a bright flash, followed instantaneously by a roaring explosion. And then an inferno poured into the tower.

Father Hoyt saw his friend's tower engulfed in flame and thought he saw the ship that had fired. He and three Brethren monks adjusted the heavy cannon and lit the fuse. The twenty-five-pound cannonball arced into the sky, heading straight for the hull of the *Raven's Revenge*. If it had had twenty more yards of range, it would have smashed out a section of the starboard bow. The *Raven's Revenge* would have sunk right there. But the range was just shy, and the cannonball fell just short. Father Hoyt had already begun reloading, but it was too late. He, too, saw a flash of orange light.

Ross stood on the quarterdeck next to the helm and had much on his mind. On the ten-day voyage, Nubby had managed to remove the bullet from Commodore Blake's arm. Blake had recovered enough to resume command of the *Oxford*. Hack was disappointed, but he honorably relinquished the ship to its proper commander. But before Blake left the *Bruce*, he'd told Ross about Dolphin. *Amazing*, he thought. *All this time and she never knew.*

"Her b' one terrible tempest!" Stede exclaimed, snapping Ross out of his thoughts.

"Can we get around it?" Ross asked, his voice high and desperate.

"Yes, mon," his quartermaster replied. "I'll get ya round it, but we b' getting to Saba right before the storm hits. I b' thinking that."

Ross looked over his shoulder. Only Anne, Cutlass Jack, and Blake were keeping pace with him. The Scottish schooners and sloops had all fallen way behind at sea. They just didn't have the sails to match the *Bruce*'s speed. In a way, Ross was glad. *Perhaps, they'll have the good sense to stay away from this hurricane.* He stared off the port rail at the curving black storm wall. *It's going to be a bad one.*

"They have abandoned the walls," said Brandir.

"Good," said Thorne. He looked at the burning walls, but the main buildings, the keep far beyond, were still unscathed. "Why aren't we hitting their fortress?"

"Wind and distance," said Brandir. "The monks were smart to build their keep so far from the shore. The storm robs us of even more range still. Our cannons will not reach them from here."

"Then," said Thorne, "we'll have to take the battle to land. Brandir, see to it that the Berserkers are ready. I will signal the rest of the fleet."

The main gate of the Citadel still burned and was uncontested. But when the Berserkers and other invaders came through it to the other side, they found more than they had bargained for. The monks had dug dozens of trenches, and the moment the invaders charged into the courtyard, the Brethren emerged and fired crossbows. The volley of arrows slammed into the attackers. Many fell. The Berserkers, numbed by their maddening elixir, took several darts each but still approached. They fought on, not caring or not realizing that they were already mortally wounded.

Ross saw the flames and smoke and feared that again they were too late. But as he looked through his spyglass, he saw that the Citadel's keep looked to be unharmed. The Raukar ships, including Thorne's, drifted ominously just off shore. But they had stopped firing, apparently content to let their ground forces finish the fight. But from the look of things, the monks of the Brethren were holding their own on shore.

Still, he thought, *there are so many ships.*

"We won't survive a fight with them," said Stede.

"I know," said Ross. "But we've got to try."

Red Eye appeared by the captain's side. "Sir, if I may?"

"Of course, Red Eye, what is it?"

"I've been talking to that Hopper lad, and he has an idea how we can get Lady Dolphin back."

"I'm listening," said Ross. When Red Eye told the plan, Ross looked up sharply. "You can't be serious. In these seas?"

Red Eye nodded. "Jules can row through that."

Suddenly, Hopper was right behind Red Eye. Ross looked at the brave young lad and shook his head. "I cannot allow this. You could be killed."

"If you'll pardon my sayin' so, Guv'nor," Hopper said, "we've all got to die some time. Might as well be tryin' to help someone as needs it. And I'm the only one who knows that ship. I know it top to bottom, sir."

Ross couldn't argue that. "Go ahead," said Ross. "But, Red Eye, don't—"

"I know," Red Eye interrupted. "Don't kill unless I have to."

"That's not at all what I was going to say," Ross said. He stared at Red Eye and felt they had reached an understanding.

As soon as the cutter bearing Jules, Red Eye, and Hopper was gone, Ross gave the order. Jacques St. Pierre commenced firing. Cutlass Jack and Commodore Blake opened up as well. Ross hoped the diversion would work. He wondered if Thorne would notice that not one shot was aimed to hit the *Raven's Revenge*.

30

THROUGH THE SPYGLASS

You made the right decision, Cat," said the Merchant. He stood by the helm of his ship, the *Perdition's Gate*. Cat was steering the ship through the rough seas two hundred yards from the Brethren's shore. "But I assure you, I am not very trusting." He pointed to two very strong sailors who stood three paces from each of Cat's shoulders. "This is Mister Guinness," said the Merchant. "And this is Mister Lambec. They will watch your every move. Should you do anything . . . out of character, you'll wish I'd killed you with my dagger."

"Don't worry," said Cat. "I know what I'm doing behind the wheel."

"Very well then," said the Merchant. "I propose a test." He pointed out to sea, just beyond the *Raven's Revenge*, at the silhouette of another ship. "I believe that is the *Robert Bruce*. Take us in close, Cat. I want to send Declan Ross to the bottom."

"Storm's comin' on now," Edward Teach said to Dolphin. "You can hear the wind a'howlin', can't you?"

Dolphin lay in the corner. She did not answer. "Aww, you're no fun." Teach threw a wood chip into an empty cell. He looked at his surroundings. "No fun at all," he went on. "I can't stand it. 'Teach, do this. Teach, do that,' Thorne says. I've a mind to slip a knife into his kidneys."

"Why don't you?" came a voice from behind. Two men of very different heights stood in the shadows. The shorter man came forward while the giant remained silhouetted. The smaller man was nonetheless fierce. He had a scar that ruined one side of his face and an eye that was blood red. This man lifted a pistol and pointed it at Teach.

"You know," said Teach, "I've had just about enough of this job. Here!" He threw a set of keys at Red Eye's feet. When Red Eye looked down to pick them up, Teach kicked the gun out of his hand. But Teach did not stay to fight. Instead, he ran the other way out of the cell deck.

"That was easy," muttered Red Eye. He picked up the keys and the pistol and said, "Hopper, you can come out now." Jules came forward, and like a puppy emerging from behind his master, Hopper came out from behind Jules. He trotted over to Dolphin's cell.

"My lady, get up," Hopper cried out. "It's time to go."

Bartholomew Thorne gripped the spyglass so hard it nearly cracked. He could not believe his eyes. Declan Ross had somehow found him after all this time. "But how?" Thorne asked aloud. "How did you know?" The *Robert Bruce* kept its distance but was firing madly.

Three other ships sailed near Ross and fired at the Raukar forces. Two of them Thorne did not recognize. But the other . . . the other was the *Oxford*. The blood drained from Thorne's face. "Blake . . . it cannot be!" Teach had assured him that Commodore Blake was dead. "MISTER TEACH!!" Thorne turned to look for Edward Teach but then remembered he'd sent his quartermaster down below to watch over Dolphin. "Brandir, come here, quickly!"

The Raukar warrior ran to his side. "Take the wheel," Thorne said. "Keep us clear of those three ships. Let the Merchant and the others take them on."

"Yes, sir," said Brandir, liking the feel of the wheel. "But, ah?"

"I've got to go below for a moment," Thorne warned him. "But I will be right back."

Lightning crackled overhead, but the thunder was lost in the blasts of a multitude of cannons. Just before leaving the quarterdeck, Thorne gazed at the dark, undulating sky. The hurricane and its winds seemed to have shifted somewhat to the north. Perhaps the storm would not strike the island with its full force after all. Thorne dropped down from the quarterdeck and ran to the hatch that led below. He had a few questions for Edward Teach.

"I see them," said Stede, looking through the spyglass, through the spray and chop. "They've got Dolphin! They've got her."

Ross grabbed the spyglass. He saw the little boat bobbing up and down between tall waves. "I just hope they can make it back."

"We're not quite in range," said the Merchant. "Closer, Cat!"

"I'm fighting the sea and the wind to stay on their stern!" Cat yelled back. "Ross's ship has teeth. Remember, if they are in our range, we are in their range."

"Anne!" yelled Father Brun from the deck of the *Constantine*. "The Merchant is maneuvering to the *Bruce*'s backside!"

"Two can play at that game," muttered Anne. She spun the wheel and a stiff wind slammed into her sails. The *Constantine* lurched forward and gained on the *Perdition's Gate*.

Thorne ran down the final flight of stairs to the cell deck. He turned the corner, ran into the chamber, and found Dolphin's cell . . . empty. Edward Teach was nowhere to be seen.

"NOOOO!!" Thorne bellowed, and he kicked the cell door shut. Thorne took his bleeding stick out of its holster and ran back up the stairs.

Edward Teach and two other men from the *Talon*'s crew found a cutter unguarded and slowly lowered it down from the stern. Then, like spiders hatching, they clambered down strands of rope to get to their escape vessel.

As they began to row, one of the men, a swarthy fellow named Bonds, asked, "Where are we going?"

Richard, the second man, laughed and said, "Nowhere but down in this gale!"

"Get us to Saba," said Teach. "We can ride out the storm there. After that, I don't know."

"I've heard Jamaica's nice," said Bonds.

Thorne appeared on deck and stormed toward the helm. He didn't see Dolphin. He didn't see Teach. They could be anywhere on the ship, but somehow, he knew they had gone. "Why?" he muttered. "Why would you take her?"

He put his bleeding stick away and grabbed his spyglass. He looked out on the water and scanned the waves. There! Off to the stern, he saw a cutter. There were three figures in it. He focused the spyglass. It was Teach! "You stealing maggot!" Thorne was about to take the ship's wheel from Brandir, but then he saw the other two people in Teach's cutter. They were men . . . crewmen from the *Talon*. Thorne was confused. *Then where is Dolphin?*

Thorne moved the spyglass back toward the *Robert Bruce*. "No!" Throne cried out. He saw another small ship—another cutter. It had almost reached the *Bruce*. It was too far away to see clearly, but in the briefest instant, Thorne thought he caught a glimpse of Dolphin's red hair.

31

DESPERATE MEASURES

Out of the corner of his eye, Cat saw the mast of the *Constantine*. It was just a fleeting glimpse—the tip of the mast, the rigging, a bit of sail—but it was enough. Cat's thoughts reeled. *There was no one on the* Constantine *who could fight the wind and still knife in on his flank like that, no one except . . . Anne! Anne was alive!* Cat was sure of it. The Merchant and his two goons, however, were not so observant. The Merchant was too intent on getting his own prey to see the threat to the *Perdition's Gate*.

Lightning flashed. The mast again. The *Constantine* was gaining, but Cat didn't turn his head, didn't want to alert the others. No, Cat wanted to let Anne pin them down. He wanted Anne to sink the *Perdition's Gate*. And he needed her to do it before the Merchant's ship got the *Bruce* in its sights. Another flash and the immediate thunder made Cat jump.

Cat didn't want to die, but if he had to lose his life to rid the world of a malignant rogue like the Merchant, then . . . that was what he would do. The mast came into view once more, again just a flicker in his peripheral vision—that's when a new plan began to form in Cat's mind. If Anne stayed after him, he might be able to . . . It would be a one-in-a-million chance, but he decided to try it. In this wind, who knew if it would even be possible to steer with such precision. The thunder continued to roll.

"Captain Ross!" yelled Jacques. "Dolphin, Red Eye, Jules, and Hopper are safely aboard."

"Yes!" Ross slapped Stede on the back.

Stede did not join in the merriment. "Declan," he said, "we b' having a bit of a problem, mon. Thorne must know what we done. He and the whole Raukar fleet b' after us now."

"The Merchant as well!" yelled Jacques. "That ship is moving up fast!"

In the flickering illumination of the lightning, Ross saw all the Raukar warships headed their way. Even with the wind kicking up, there was no chance they could outrun them all. *Wind*.

"I have an idea," Ross said.

"Ya worry me when ya say that, mon," said Stede. "I don't mind telling ya."

"Sail into the storm," Ross said.

"What?"

"Stede, I want you to sail into the hurricane."

Stede looked from Ross to St. Pierre, to Hack and Slash. "Declan, have ya gone mad? The tempest will tear the ship apart!"

"No, it won't," said Ross. "We sail into the outskirts of the storm . . . stay away from the eye."

St. Pierre's eyes suddenly opened wide. "Ah, magnifique!" he shouted. "It will work! Mon capitaine is crazy . . . crazy like a fox, or perhaps . . . like a wolf. Ha-ha! Let's do it!"

Cat saw the *Bruce*'s sudden turn, heading north into the storm, and all hope of trying his plan vanished like sea spray in a stiff wind. Sailing into any severe storm was taking a great risk, but attempting to endure a hurricane was nothing short of suicidal.

"The *Bruce* . . . they've seen us!" the Merchant yelled. "Go after him!"

"Into the storm?" Cat objected.

"My ship has endured worse," said the Merchant, a dangerous edge to his voice. He drew his dagger. "Follow him, or someone else can take the wheel."

"Since you put it that way," Cat said, turning the wheel. And suddenly, his plan came back to life. The *Constantine* was right behind them. He'd never have a better chance. He just hoped Anne would continue to close.

Cat turned the wheel sharply. The Merchant, Guinness, and Lambec stumbled sideways. Then, using the ship's wheel for leverage, Cat launched a sharp backward kick into Mr. Guinness's stomach. The big man doubled over. Cat dodged a lethal dagger swipe from the Merchant and ducked under Lambec's powerful slash. Then he grabbed Guinness's sword, stepped up on the man's prone back, and leaped to the rigging on the mainmast. He clambered quickly out of everyone's reach and raced to the horizontal spars. Then Cat slashed the ropes holding the main sail. The great white expanse of material flapped in the wind but no longer propelled the ship. The *Perdition's Gate* slowed markedly, but Cat wasn't finished. With several of the Merchant's men climbing after him on the rigging and pistol shots zinging past his ear, Cat continued up to the next horizontal spar. Then he slashed the topsails, and they, too, flapped uselessly in the wind. Deprived of two of its biggest sails, the *Perdition's Gate* lost its lead on the *Constantine*. In fact, the other ship was coming so hard and so fast that it was in danger of crashing into the Merchant's vessel.

That's what Cat was counting on. He continued to climb until he stood precariously on the highest spar and clutched the top of the mast. His foot slipped once, but he recovered. The fierce hurricane winds threatened to blow him off at any second, and the pelting rain made it so that he could barely see. "Come on, Anne!!" he yelled, but the wind carried his cry away.

"What is the Merchant doing?!" Anne cried out. She spun the wheel, but she saw the *Perdition's Gate* growing huge in front of them. It seemed to be turning right into their path and slowing rapidly all at the same time.

"Turn, Anne!" bellowed Father Brun. "TURN!!"

"I'm trying!" Anne saw the massive hull of the Merchant's ship. She saw the dark holes of the cannon muzzles. *If they fire*, she thought, and then she said, "If they fire . . . what am I thinking? FIRE STARBOARD CANNONS!!"

Brother Dmitri and the other gunners lit their fuses. The bow of the *Constantine* cleared the enemy ship by a few feet, and as they passed, seven cannons fired—all from the *Constantine*. At such close range, every cannonball burrowed destructively into the flesh of the *Perdition's Gate*. One even blasted out of the other side. The barque's stern was ruined and began to collapse in on itself. Still, the Merchant fired back, but it was too late. One shot connected. It smashed into a cannon bay, ruined a cannon, and scared the day-lights out of Brother Javier . . . but did very little damage.

"Anne, look!" Father Brun pointed high up to where the tops of the two ship's mainmasts passed to within thirty feet of each other. Anne saw it. Someone was high on the Merchant's mainmast. He suddenly leaped out and fell. His dark silhouette hung in front of the clouds for several breathless moments. He landed awkwardly in the weblike rigging of the *Constantine*, but could not grasp it. He rolled once, scrabbled for a handhold, rolled again toward the edge. With a last great effort, this man snagged the bottom of the rigging and held on.

Her attention divided between the Merchant's foundering ship and the man in the rigging, Anne steered the *Constantine* into bet-ter position. "Fire!" she yelled. And again, her cannons came to life. The damage this time was fatal. A gaping rent had opened on the stern of the *Perdition's Gate*, and it began to take on water. Then it began to sink.

Anne turned her attention to the acrobatic man in the rigging. He had made his way to one of the long ropes and now began to slide down it to the main deck. Brother Dmitri had his staff ready when the man landed. Anne gave the wheel to Brother Keegan. She drew her cutlass, leaped off the quarterdeck, and ran across the main deck.

The man hit the deck awkwardly and fell onto his back. "Well, I guess he's no threat to anyone," said Brother Dmitri.

But Anne dropped her sword and ran to him. "Cat!" she cried, taking him into her arms. His matted blond head fell against her shoulder. His eyelids flickered and closed. Anne couldn't tell if he was breathing.

"I hope you don't mind me dropping in," he whispered. Then she kissed him, and it was the first time anyone on board the *Constantine* had seen a captain kiss a quartermaster.

Brother Keegan called down from the quarterdeck. "One of you two want to come take the wheel? The *Bruce*, the *Raven's Revenge*, and the *Oxford* are all sailing deeper into the hurricane, and I don't really know what I'm doing."

"Can you stand?" Anne asked.

"Yes," Cat replied. She helped him to his feet, and they walked arm in arm to the quarterdeck ladder. Suddenly, the sky lit up with orange light. They looked out to sea and saw a gout of flame rise up from the water where the Merchant's ship had gone under. They also saw at least a dozen Raukar warships right behind the *Constantine* and closing fast.

"I'll take the wheel!" Cat and Anne said simultaneously.

"Tell you what," said Cat. "You take the wheel, and I'll just yell at you a lot."

"Deal," said Anne.

"Them b' coming, Declan!" bellowed Stede.

"Good," said Ross. "That's just what I wanted."

"Ya want to b' sailing into some treacherous storm, all the while we b' chased by a fleet of angry Viking warriors and a murderous madman who want nothing better than to skin ya alive?"

"Yeah," said Ross. "That about sums it up."

The *Robert Bruce*, the *Oxford*, and the *Constantine* had now passed under the outer canopy of the hurricane, and it was like entering a different world. The wind shrieked and snapped at the sails. The rain felt like pellets of rock, and lightning flashed incessantly overhead. But most perilous of all were the mounting swells that rose up suddenly out of the sea and threatened to cap-size any ship whose captain was unskilled or unwary. Ross was neither.

"It's like being in the crosscurrents again!" yelled Ross, referring to the intensely rough sea barrier that surrounded the Isle of Swords. "JULES!! Get down to the swinging bowsprit—Hack and Slash will need your muscle!"

"Aye, sir!" The massive sailor slip-slided his way to the front of the ship. Ross was glad to have a man with such brute strength.

St. Pierre suddenly appeared at Ross's elbow. "Mon capitaine, may I show you something?"

"Jacques, now isn't the time," he replied. "We're in the midst of chaos with dozens of ships right behind us!"

"Those pesky ships are why I have come. Ha-ha!" St. Pierre cackled. "Allow me to introduce my newest invention!" Jacques stepped out of the way, revealing a square crate resting on a small raft of planks. A very long string slithered out of a crack in the top of the crate and coiled on the deck next to it.

Ross squinted. "What does it do?"

"It explodes, of course!" Jacques laughed maniacally. "The fuse is waterproof, you see. This little bomb will float along and hope-fully go BOOM just as an enemy ship goes by. Do I have your per-mission to launch them?"

"How many have you made?" Ross asked.

"Not enough, I am guessing," replied the Frenchman. "Fifty, maybe."

Ross scratched absently at his sideburns. St. Pierre's weapons would work better at close quarters. In the open sea, even fifty such weapons could miss entirely. Still, it was better than nothing. "Fire away!" he said. As soon as Jacques was gone, Ross turned to Stede and said, "I know we'll lose some of our distance, but sail east a bit . . . allow Saint Pierre to spread his floating bombs."

"Aye, Declan," Stede replied.

St. Pierre, Red Eye, and a host of deck hands lit fuses and threw their floating weapons into the sea.

As the others watched below, Declan scanned the seas from the quarterdeck. Suddenly, the floating bombs began to go off. One after the other, they exploded, sending founts of sea spray up into the wind. But all missed. The *Raven's Revenge* and the other Raukar vessels continued to pursue. Jacques yelled and hopped around on the deck. "All that work for noth—"

One of the Raukar warships disappeared in a massive orange fireball. The floating bomb had gone off on the ship's port bow, exploding the eldregn stores and vaporizing the ship. It was a success, but not what anyone had hoped. Ross turned back to the seas.

"Declan!" Stede yelled above the wind. "The winds b' increasing! We b' getting too close to the eye. We b' about to tear the sails off the mast!"

Ross heard the ominous groans of his masts and prayed that they'd hold. "A little farther, a little farther," said Ross. "And then be ready to turn and fight."

"What about Anne?" Stede asked. "What about Blake and Cutlass Jack?"

Ross grimaced. "Let's hope they follow our lead."

32

THE VALLEY OF
THE SHADOW OF DEATH

Commodore Blake!!" a new deck hand named Craig cried out.
"Our masts are coming apart!"

Blake had heard the wood groan in duress, but the recent cracks
terrified him. He looked up and saw that the sails held, but the spars
that supported them were twisting in the wind. If the wind speed
increased by so much as a knot, he knew his ship would be destroyed, left to the mercy of the waves and then the Raukar. But
Dolphin was aboard the *Bruce* and was sailing with Ross deeper into
the storm. He had to do something, but every choice meant sepa-
ration from his beloved wife . . . perhaps permanently.

Commodore Brandon Blake had made thousands of difficult
decisions in his time as a ship's captain. But none were more personally devastating than this one. He called his makeshift crew up
on deck, even as he turned the wheel to bring the ship about.

"We goin' back, sir?" asked a young man named Timmons.

"Got to," said Craig. "Ship can't take no more'n this wind."

"As I see it, we have one option," Blake said. "Turn and fight. If we must go down, let's take as many of them with us as we can!"

"AYE, SIR!!" the crew yelled. There certainly weren't enough men to man the *Oxford* properly, Blake thought. But these men had more than enough heart.

It did not take long for the *Raven's Revenge* and the other Raukar warships to catch up to the *Oxford*. But Thorne did not stop to contend with Blake. He sailed past without firing a shot. Several Raukar vessels swung well out of range, and they, too, went by. But a pair of long, well-armed warships appeared to be heading straight for the *Oxford*.

"Mister Craig?" Blake called.

"Sir?"

"I want you to get everyone off the main deck . . . and every one of you man the cannons below."

"But, sir, the sails . . . the rigging . . . you ne—"

"I need you all on the cannons, but do not fire until my signal."

"What will that be, sir?" Craig asked. "Down below, we won't hear you over the wind."

Blake drew a pistol from his side holster. "When you hear this gun, I want every cannon on both sides of the ship to fire."

Craig turned and saw the two oncoming warships. "Sir, they're too close together. How will we—"

"I mean to split them."

"NOW, JULES!!" Ross yelled from the quarterdeck. Jules, Hack, and Slash operated the swinging bowsprit while Stede turned the ship's wheel. The *Robert Bruce* banked and came about faster than Thorne or the Raukar could have imagined. "FIRE!!" Ross yelled.

The *Bruce*'s cannons sent a wall of cannon shot toward the approaching enemy vessels. Anne and Cutlass Jack did the same. Ross scanned the sea. *Where is Blake?*

The first salvo took out three Raukar warships but fifteen, including Thorne's ship, remained. That didn't even the odds enough. Ross ordered his crew to fire again. He wanted to provoke them, bully them into using their fire weapon. And at last, they did.

Five of the closest Raukar vessels launched eldregn canisters at the *Bruce* and the others. Stede watched one sail high overhead, and he feared for the *Bruce*. But the canister seemed to hang in the air. When it exploded, a deluge of fiery rain blew back onto the ship that had launched it, as well as two others. Fire danced frenetically on the three Raukar warships as the storm's winds fought with the flames. But soon, all three ships exploded.

Bartholomew Thorne was not so ignorant. He refused to fire the eldregn, but unleashed his arsenal of conventional cannons instead. His first barrage slammed into Cutlass Jack's *Banshee* like a woodsman's axe, tearing up the port hull and sending deadly splinters of wood into the crew. The *Banshee* did not return fire.

"Uncle Jack!" Anne cried. They'd been helpless to stop the attack, but watched in horror as the *Raven's Revenge* devastated their friend.

"Anne, I don't think that ship's going to stay afloat," said Cat. "And Thorne's closing on him."

"They're not even firing back," whispered Anne. She turned the wheel. "We've got to help him."

Thorne was not content to disable the *Banshee*. He wanted to watch it die. He brought the *Raven's Revenge* within one hundred yards of the wounded ship and gave the order: "Fire port cannons!" The heavy sixteen- and eighteen-pound cannonballs crashed into the smaller ship's hull, collapsed the quarterdeck, and blew the rudder off the back of the ship. The stress of the now-twisting hull snapped the ship's keel, and the ship fell awkwardly on its side. Fires burned and hissed in the sea spray, and the turbulent water began to claim the ship.

"Dear God, he's killed Jack," whispered Ross. "Stede, he's killed Jack! Get us over there!"

"I b' trying Declan!" yelled the quartermaster. "But we b' fighting the very wind! I tell ya, we b' nearing the eye of this storm!"

The *Constantine* arrived too late to help the *Banshee*. Cutlass Jack's xebec had become a bonfire of debris. Through the wavering flames and smoke, Anne and Cat could see the *Raven's Revenge* moving slowly on the other side. It was as if Thorne were looking to make sure no one survived.

Anne's tears burned down her cheeks, but she did not weep on Cat's shoulder. She turned the wheel. "What are you doing?" Cat asked.

"We can't match the firepower of that ship," Anne said bitterly. "But we will stop him!"

Cat realized at once what she planned to do. "I'll get Father Brun and the rest of the Brethren," he said. "We'll be ready to board when the time comes."

Convinced that Cutlass Jack and his crew were dead, Thorne looked about for the *Robert Bruce* and saw it knifing in to starboard. "Coming right for me?" Thorne was surprised. "Ready the starboard cannons!" he yelled. In the seconds before the command to fire, Thorne imagined sending a volley right into the *Bruce*'s keel, breaking its spine . . .

Something hit the *Raven's Revenge* so hard that Thorne lurched forward and slammed into the ship's wheel. He fell to one knee . . . feeling disoriented and strange. When he stood at last, he saw that another ship had rammed them on the portside. Where had the ship come from? Who was it? He leaned over the rail of the quarterdeck and saw that the damage to the *Raven's Revenge* was extensive . . . but not fatal. Then he realized with dreadful certainty that the other ship's captain had made a grave error.

"Fire port cannons!" Thorne yelled.

Only a handful of the ship's port cannons opened up, but it was enough. Cannonballs tore into the *Constantine* and dislodged it from the *Raven's Revenge* . . . but not before dozens of intruders had come aboard. Thorne saw men climbing up the side of his ship. These men wore brown robes.

"The Brethren," Thorne hissed. "Raukar! To the deck!"

The *Bruce* was finally in range. "Fire!!" Ross yelled.

"NO, DECLAN!!" Stede grabbed his friend and pointed. "Look!"

"Belay that order to fire!" Ross screamed. He saw what Anne

had done and realized an errant shot could hit the *Constantine*. "Anne, what are you doing?"

"Nothing ya wouldn't have done, mon!" Stede answered.

Ross laughed. "You're right, Stede. Give me as much speed as you can!"

"Ohhh, Declan, ya not going to b' doing what I b' thinking?"

"I can't just leave her there!" Ross knew Stede understood his order, so he raced off the quarterdeck and warned his men to get away from the front of the *Bruce*. Then he went below and ordered Red Eye to round up everyone in sight for a boarding party.

"What ship are we boarding?" Red Eye asked.

"The *Raven's Revenge*."

"I was hoping you'd say that, sir," Red Eye said, and then he was off.

It was as if the *Constantine* had been blown right out from under them. Father Brun, Cat, Anne, and a dozen other monks had just leaped into the rigging of the *Raven's Revenge* when the cannons blasted the *Constantine*. Cat looked back over his shoulder and saw that the ship was already sinking. "No going back now," said Cat.

"There never was," Father Brun replied.

Thorne remained on the quarterdeck. He had a crew of two hundred Raukar warriors, at least a dozen Berserkers, and a handful of men from the *Talon*. The invaders stood little chance. Suddenly, the *Raven's Revenge* was rocked a second time, and Thorne flew into the portside rail. Standing and shrugging off the blow, Thorne saw the *Robert Bruce* smashed into his starboard bow.

Thorne couldn't believe Ross had the nerve, but it didn't matter. He'd do to the *Bruce* what he'd done to the first ship. "Fire starboard cannons!"

Thorne waited, but no cannons fired. "FIRE THE STARBOARD CANNONS!!" Thorne shrieked. But no cannons fired. Thorne realized that his men were up on deck, fighting the invaders. And somehow, the fight had just become a lot more even. Men poured over the *Bruce*'s rail, swung across on ropes, and even leaped from the masts into the rigging on the *Raven's Revenge*. Thorne's main deck quickly filled with combatants. Their silhouettes danced strangely in front of the myriad of fires that burned on the deck.

"Now it comes to it, Declan!" Thorne yelled. He drew a sword in one hand and the bleeding stick in the other.

Declan Ross put a hand on Stede's shoulder and said, "I'm going after Thorne."

"I b'right behind you, mon." Lightning flashed overhead. Thunder boomed. "The storm won't b' the only thunder." Stede took his huge gun from its holster.

The *Raven's Revenge* became a battlefield, and Red Eye led the charge. A huge Raukar warrior rose up in front of him. The Norse man hacked at Red Eye's legs, but Red Eye leaped, whirled in the air, and slashed his cutlass across his enemy's face.

Jules found a Berseker, or rather the Berserker found Jules. The crazed Raukar crashed into Jules, actually picked him up, and slammed him to the deck, crushing a burning barrel. Jules patted out a few licks of fire on his breeches, stood up, and cracked his knuckles. "You'll have to do better than that," he said. Then Jules drove a heavy punch into the Berserker's midsection and then hooked an uppercut beneath the man's chin. Teeth flew out of the Berserker's mouth and blood flowed, but the Berserker came back. He swung clumsily for Jules, but missed. Jules slammed his ham-sized fists into the Berserker's chest and then wailed away at his face. Still the Berserker would not fall.

St. Pierre appeared behind the Berserker and dropped something into a nearby Raukar's leather armor. "Jules," St. Pierre said, "I suggest you get out of the way!"

Jules and Jacques dove behind some crates on the deck just as the grenade went off. The Berserkers were no longer a problem.

Hack and Slash fought back to back, engaging four men at a time. Their system worked well . . . until it became fighting six men at a time. But with the aid of two Brethren monks, they survived to fight on.

Anne and Father Brun found themselves separated from Cat in the fighting with a sea of combatants between them. Several Raukar warriors drew swords and approached Anne and the monk.

"Are you ready?" Father Brun asked, pulling two fighting sticks from the sleeve of his robe.

Anne smiled and said, "Yea, though I walk through the valley of the shadow of death . . ."

33

THE HURRICANE'S EYE

The storm worsened. The wind blew so hard that men doing battle were blown off the sides of the ship. Fires still burned, and the wind whipped the flames wildly. What was left of the *Constantine* had drifted and sunk. The *Bruce*, its bowsprit still impaling the *Raven's Revenge*, groaned and creaked with every gust. Still, the fighting raged on.

Bartholomew Thorne slammed his bleeding stick into the lower back of Brother Keegan. The monk toppled to the deck. He tried to get up, but found that he couldn't move. Thorne approached, lifted his cutlass sword, and as he was about to let it fall—

"Nooo!" Cat yelled. He leaped out of the rigging and faced his father near the mainmast.

"My prodigal son returns . . . again!" Thorne shook with anger. "The Merchant didn't kill you. Seems I can't trust anyone these days!"

Cat didn't waste time with words. He lunged at his father. Thorne deflected the blow with his own sword and brought the bleeding stick around. But Cat was too quick. Ducking his father's strike, he dropped to his knees and slashed his cutlass across his father's thigh. Blood poured from the wound. Thorne stumbled backward and fell into a Raukar warrior. Thorne got back to his feet. The crowds parted as Cat pressed in on his wounded father, driving him across the deck. Thorne ducked around the foremast and charged up the ladder to the forecastle.

Cat followed quickly, but not quickly enough. As Cat reached the top rungs of the ladder, Thorne slammed a heavy boot into Cat's jaw. Then Thorne reached down, grabbed Cat by the neck, and flung him headlong into the starboard rail. Cat's sword clattered to the deck. Cat fell in a lump at the feet of another man.

Ross quickly stepped between Cat and Bartholomew Thorne. Ross's gray eyes blazed. The wind whipped his corona of coppery hair around his face. He raised his cutlass and said, "What kind of a man tries to murder his own son . . . his own flesh and blood?"

Thorne did not answer, but with a raging howl, he ran forward. Ross charged as well, his sword moving in a blur. Their clash was so fierce that others near the forecastle stopped fighting to watch. But at that moment, the wind and rain stopped. An eerie silence fell upon the two locked ships. Ross and Thorne parted for a moment and looked around. The clouds overhead swirled darkly forming a curving wall. As the storm drifted slowly over, Ross saw that the wall was actually the edge of a vast tunnel through the massive clouds. And to his astonishment, he could see stars in the night sky. *The eye,* he thought. *We've reached the eye.* Others had drawn the same conclusion, but the battle resumed.

When Ross's and Thorne's swords met again, the sound was incredibly loud and distinct in the absence of the wind. Ross tried to angle in on Thorne's sword arm and keep the bleeding stick out of range. Ross struck for Thorne's upper arm, hoping to disable it and force Thorne to one weapon. Declan's attack cut across Thorne's shoulder, but not deep enough. Thorne stepped away from Ross's blade and toward the bow. Then Thorne slammed the butt of his bleeding stick into Ross's midsection. Ross doubled over, and Thorne drove a knee to the side of Ross's head. Ross dropped his sword and fell to the deck.

Anne saw Cat fall and then her father, but there were too many enemies around her. She couldn't fight her way through. She was forced to watch from a distance while fending off attacks. "Cat!" she screamed. "Da!"

Dolphin stood on the main deck of the *Bruce* and saw Ross fall. She watched as Thorne cut a leather strap from his boot and lashed Ross's arms to the rail. Then he unscrewed his bleeding stick so it became a flail weapon. Dolphin cried out, but no one heard. She had no weapon. There was nothing she could do. Then, suddenly, it came to her. But she needed to get closer.

Thorne let the perilous head of his bleeding stick dangle and swing. Then he retreated a few steps and let the weapon fly at Ross's back, opening a huge bloody gash. He raised the weapon again and—

"Bartholomew, STOP!!" came a voice from behind.

Thorne knew that voice, and his next swing went errant. The head of the weapon embedded itself on the rail.

"How could you let the British get to me, Bartholomew?"

"Heather?" He dropped the handle of his weapon and turned slowly.

Lady Dolphin stood at the bow rail of the *Bruce*. Her eyes seemed vacant. Her crimson hair was matted from the rain, and thin red locks curled down her forehead and cheeks like blood trails from small wounds. Dolphin lifted her hand and pointed accusingly at Thorne. "You let me burn!"

"No!" Thorne lifted his hands.

Just at that moment, Ross revived. He took in the scene, saw Thorne distracted, and knew he had to act. The leather strap that bound his arms to the rail was not tight. Ross freed one arm and then the other.

Dolphin's voice rose to an agonizing shriek. "You let the fire take me . . . and our child!"

Thorne's mouth opened and closed, voicelessly mouthing "no . . . no . . . no."

Ross rose behind Thorne. Quick as lightning, he grabbed Thorne at the shoulder and waist and rammed his head into the rail. Disoriented a moment, Thorne fell to one knee. But he managed to draw his cutlass and began to rise.

Without a weapon himself, Ross grabbed the handle of the bleeding stick and slung a loop of its chain around Thorne's neck. He shoved the handle inside the loop, pulled it down, and tightened it like a noose. Thorne gagged and dropped his sword. He flailed, pulling at the handle for several seconds, and then slumped to the deck.

Streaks of rain and blood ran down Ross's face, but he wiped them away. He could only stare at the nearby still form of the man who had murdered his Abigail, had killed so many, caused so much agony . . . now dead at last. Ross backed away a few steps and then turned to look for Cat.

"Declan!" Stede appeared at the top of the forecastle ladder. Ross's old friend ran to embrace him but then he saw Cat lying in a heap near the starboard rail. Neither Ross nor Stede saw Bartholomew Thorne as he slowly clambered to his feet. The flail weapon's chain was still knotted around his neck, but Thorne drew a pistol and leveled it at Ross's back.

Dolphin saw the scene unfold from the *Bruce*. "Captain Ross!!" she cried.

A powerful gunshot blast thundered. Ross's eyes went wide and he swayed.

Thorne dropped his pistol and staggered backward. Blood spread from a dozen new wounds on his chest and stomach, and his mouth fell open. One raspy breath escaped before he slammed into the rail and fell overboard. The chain of Thorne's bleeding stick held, the noose tightened, and Thorne hung from the bow of his own ship.

Ross, still wide-eyed, stared at the smoking muzzle of Stede's thunder gun. "But just after we boarded, I heard you fire . . ."

Stede grinned. "I reloaded, mon."

Ross grabbed Stede by the cheeks and kissed his forehead. "That's another lifetime of friendship I owe you."

"I b'thinkin' that's seven now." Stede laughed. But the levity was short-lived. The *Raven's Revenge* pitched suddenly and began to shudder. Ross and Stede ran to Cat's side even as the ship began to list. Ross looked up and saw that the ships were shifting, separating from each other. Ross ran to the edge of the forecastle and bellowed, "Crew of the *Robert Bruce* . . . return to the ship!"

Ross and Stede managed to hand Cat up to Jules, who leaned over the rail of the *Bruce*, and then they went to work on the ship's wheel. Stede blasted the hub with his thunder gun, and he and Ross kicked at it until the wheel cracked and fell free. Then they tossed the wheel of the *Raven's Revenge* into the sea.

Just as the ships pulled apart, Ross and Stede went to the rigging and climbed for their lives. They dove from one ship to the other. Ross found Anne and Father Brun waiting on the quarterdeck. "Did we all make it?" Ross asked.

Father Brun looked up grimly. "All who were still living are back on the ship." They turned and watched the *Raven's Revenge* plunge back into the storm. They could still see Thorne's feet dangling as the wind swallowed up the ship.

Stede looked up at the approaching wall of clouds and said, "The *Bruce* b' not surviving another bout with the storm. B' no chance at all."

"I know," said Ross, glancing at Anne and the others assembled there. "At least we're all here together."

"It ain't so bad here, is it, my lady?" Hopper smiled at Dolphin, and then looked up through the hurricane's eye at the stars and said, "I like it here."

Anne said, "I like it here too."

Cat gave Anne's hand an affectionate squeeze. He looked up at Captain Ross and smiled.

34

OUT OF THE GRAY

Commodore Brandon Blake grabbed another armful of palm fronds and debris and carried it to a massive pile fifty yards from the Citadel's gatehouse. He was one of many moving silently from the fire and storm-ravaged walls to various mounds and heaps of wreckage. But even among the monks of the Brethren, Commodore Blake felt like the loneliest person on the face of the earth. He'd made a decision to let his beloved Dolphin sail out of his sight. She and the others had disappeared into the hurricane and had not returned. In fact, no one who sailed into that storm had returned.

The storm had indeed turned north, so it spared the island of Saba its most intense winds and rain. And even as the Brethren defeated the last of the Berserkers and Raukar invaders, the rain put out the last of their fires. The damage to the walls was considerable, but not permanent. The main keep was barely touched at all. But the Brethren had lost many of its faithful including Father Henry and Father Hoyt. Brandon Blake had lost everyone.

The mid-afternoon sky was still leaden and overcast. The winds still swirled and spat moisture, but the storm was gone. A merchant who arrived earlier in the morning reported that the storm weakened a great deal before dissipating over the Turks. Blake dropped off another armful of debris and stared out to the horizon. All the while, staring out to the gray, he walked to the shore, took off his boots, and let the water run over his feet.

The *Oxford*, what was left of it, was moored just offshore and floated ponderously on the light surf. Blake looked at the tattered sails and thought about the last several years of his life. He'd witnessed some of the vilest atrocities ever committed by a man. He'd also seen men change, seen them do good when they had every reason to do evil. And Blake wondered about that.

Something caught Blake's eye, and his heart jumped. There was something on the horizon—a ship. But as it came closer, he saw that it had only one square sail. *Just another merchant or fisherman.* Gulls cried overhead, and Blake watched them drift on the breeze. He turned back and looked again at the sail. *It is a tall ship for just one sail*, he thought. In fact, Blake didn't know of any ships of that size with one mast and one sail.

The bell in the Citadel's keep tower began to ring. Members of the Brethren streamed out of the keep and joined Blake at the shore. They pointed to the sea and whispered. The ship drew nearer still. Commodore Brandon Blake dropped to his knees. For even with its swinging bowsprit broken clean off, Blake knew the ship was the *Robert Bruce*. And standing at the bow rail was a woman with scarlet hair blowing in the wind.

"Three cheers for Hopper!" St. Pierre shouted, raising his goblet high.

When the cheers quieted, Declan Ross said, "Things would have gone very ill had it not been for your courage . . . and your cleverness."

Father Brun patted the young lad on the shoulder and said, "How very like the Almighty to use the weak to confound the strong."

Blake leaned over and whispered to his wife, "Was it Hopper's idea to stay in the hurricane's eye until the storm died out?"

"No," Dolphin replied. "Cat thought of that. But Hopper was the one who got Cat thinking about it."

"Our son is quite brilliant, wouldn't you say?" Blake asked with a wink.

"Son?" Dolphin embraced her husband. "So you've decided then?"

"I have." Blake looked at his wife and took in her beauty. "We'll make it official as soon as we get back to London."

Ross took Father Brun aside and led him to a small table next to Hack and Slash, who were busy playing chess. "It will take some time to rebuild London," said Ross. "And the British Royal Navy."

"There is much to be done here as well," said Father Brun. "But, ah . . . with the Merchant and Thorne gone for good, it may be that the Brethren can help. There are other treasures in our possession besides that which we retrieved from the Isle of Swords."

"You mean more gold and jewels?"

"You and I define treasure very differently, Declan Ross."

"You know, someone else told me the same thing," said Ross. "And at last, I think I know what it means."

"Do you?" Father Brun smiled. "I am glad to hear that."

35

NO REGRETS

He admired his reflection in the mirror in his little room above the Jamaican tavern. "Ha! Never grow a beard, he said! Now look at me." Edward Teach pulled at the thick black locks that grew down from his sideburns and finished with long, ragged braids below his chin. "I look positively terrifyin'!"

Teach picked up a dark tricorn hat and placed it on his head. He checked his bandolier. All six pistols were loaded and in their proper place. A dagger in each boot, one on his hip, and of course, a very nasty cutlass. He looked once more at his image in the mirror. *Terrifying*, he thought again.

"I need a name, though," Teach muttered. "Every good pirate needs a name. Hmmm . . . but what?"

Just then, Portis, the tavern keeper, cracked open the door. "Hey, you . . . blackbeard, your guests have arrived."

Teach waved the man off, but he did not follow directly. He stroked his beard once more and thoughtfully stared at his reflection.

Cat knocked on Captain Ross's door. "Come in," said Ross. Then he saw who it was and said, "Cat, you know you don't need to knock. You and Stede . . . and Anne, but everyone else has to knock!"

They shared a laugh. Then Ross said, "Have a seat, lad. What's on your mind?"

"Well, sir, do you remember when we were at the Citadel before?"

"You mean before everything," said Ross. "Yes, of course."

Cat's lips curled in a slight smile as he spoke. "Well, you re-member, I came to your chamber to ask you if you'd let Anne sail with me."

"I do," said Ross. "I remember it well."

"Do you regret your decision . . . to let her go?"

Ross thought hard for a moment. "My first thought was to say, yes, I regret it. Anne nearly lost her life. But now, no, I don't regret that decision. You kept her safe . . . well . . . you and the Almighty. Why do you bring this up now?"

"Because, Captain Ross, I have another question to ask you."

Acknowledgments

Thank you, Mary Lu, for enduring so many hours sailing our family ship solo while I sat, sequestered at the library or Panera, pounding the keyboard. 1C13. To my faithful crew Kayla, Tommy, Bryce, and Rachel: No captain's had finer lads and lasses. I love you!

Brian, Jeff, and Leslie: Thank you for filling my sails with love, encouragement, and imagination. Mom and Dad: Please remember that, in a very real sense, every word on every page that I write belongs to you as well. To the Dovel family: Thank you for being the best extended family a guy could ever ask for.

To my friends Bill and Lisa Russell, Dave and Heather Peters, Doug and Chris Smith, Danny Sutton, Warren Cramutola, Chris and Alaina Haerbig, Dan and Courtney Cwiek, Janet Berbes, Chris and Dawn Harvey, Don and Valerie Counts, Mat and Serrina Davis, and Jeff and Leslie Leggett: I look forward to sailing with you into many uncharted waters. Todd Wahlne, a great friend: Special thanks for the Swedish translations. Anne Marie, Pascal, and Juliette LaChance for providing French language assistance! Michelle Black: You continue to be a special encouragement in my writing.

The brilliant students of Folly Quarter Middle School: Thank you always for igniting my imagination and encouraging me to write on. Dr. Carl Perkins and Mrs. Julie Rout: Thank you for the time to share my books with others. To the sixth-grade team: Thank you for being such great friends and for your inspirational teaching.

Gregg Wooding: Thank you for bearing so many burdens and wearing so many hats on my behalf. All my friends at Thomas Nelson: Thank you for the opportunity to follow Cat into this new adventure. Thanks to Laura, Troy, and Jackie for your tireless efforts to bring my stories to the world. To Patti and the art team at TN: You produce the greatest covers in the world! And to Beverly and June for helping me make *Isle of Fire* worthy of being published.

To my writer friends Bryan Davis, Sharon Hinck, Christopher Hopper, Donita K. Paul, Jonathan Rogers, James Somers, and L. B. Graham: Thanks for sharpening my iron with your own phenomenal stories. And finally, to my readers, the most extraordinary horde of crazy, wonderful, enthusiastic pirates the world has ever known: Draw your sword and raise your mug with mine. There are stormy but wonderful seas to conquer.